The Palern

"DEAR READER,

THANK YOU FOR OPENING THE PAGES OF 'THE PALERMO AFFAIR'. THIS STORY, BORN FROM THE DEPTHS OF MY IMAGINATION, IS A JOURNEY I AM THRILLED TO SHARE WITH YOU. IT IS A TAPESTRY OF INTRIGUE AND HUMAN EMOTION, WOVEN WITH THE THREADS OF ROMANCE AND SUSPENSE. AS YOU TURN EACH PAGE, I HOPE YOU FIND YOURSELF AS CAPTIVATED BY THE WORLD OF VALENTINA AND ALEX AS I WAS IN CREATING IT. MAY THEIR STORY RESONATE WITH YOU, IN ALL ITS SHADES OF LIGHT AND DARK.

HAPPY READING!"

SCOTT THOMPSON

Chapter 1: Serendipity and Shadows

Valentina found herself unexpectedly captivated amidst the cool, gray streets of London. It was within the confines of a historic café, nestled between towering structures on a cobbled lane, that a familiar aroma whisked her away to the streets of Palermo. With hazel eyes sparkling, she gazed through the glass pane, mesmerized by a cannoli on display that bore a striking resemblance to her nonna's creations.

Her musings were Interrupted by a "oice' causing her to turn and face a tall, rugged man. With tousled brown hair, a mischievous smile, and eyes as clear and blue as the Mediterranean Sea, he seemed out of place amidst the hustle and bustle of London.

Curious, he asked, "Do you know if these taste as good as they look?"

Valentina, tilting her head, replied with her unmistakable Italian accent, "I wouldn't know for certain, but they seem reminiscent of the ones back home."

"Home?" Alex raised an eyebrow, intrigued.

"Palermo, Sicily," she elaborated.

"Ah, a beautiful place," he remarked. "I'm Alex, originally from Manchester, but living here in London."

Valentina offered a warm smile, introducing herself and extending her hand.

In that moment, as their hands touched, a faint current passed between them, an inexplicable sensation. Both chuckled awkwardly, withdrawing their hands.

Seizing the opportunity, Valentina took a leap of faith. "Would you like to join me in trying the cannoli?"

Alex smirked, "Only if you promise to tell me if they live up to the real deal."

Together, they settled into a cozy corner table. Amidst shared pastries and cups of cappuccino, their conversation blossomed.

Valentina discovered Alex's quick wit, his life in London, and his unwavering love for travel. Alex, in turn, was enchanted by Valentina's tales of Sicily, her aspirations of becoming a doctor, and her imminent return to Palermo to embark on a new role at a local hospital.

As their dialogue flowed, Valentina's phone buzzed, catching her attention. She glanced at it, her complexion slightly paling. "I have to go," she said abruptly, a hint of urgency in her voice.

Perceiving that something was amiss, Alex frowned and asked, "Is everything alright?"

She hesitated for a moment, then mustered a smile, albeit somewhat forced. "Just a reminder. I have a scheduled tour at the Tower of London. Can't afford to miss it."

Alex nodded, though his intuition told him there was more to her departure. "It was a pleasure meeting you, Valentina. Perhaps, if fate permits, our paths will cross again."

Valentina smiled, her eyes momentarily clouded with a hint of mystery. "Perhaps."

As Valentina departed from the café, Alex watched her for a fleeting moment, a curious expression adorning his face. He then retrieved his phone and sent a brief message to an encrypted number.

Unbeknownst to the unsuspecting tourists and locals navigating the streets of London, a romance intertwined with secrets, danger, and destiny had just taken center stage.

--

The soft glow of dim lights embraced the patrons of a riverside bar, casting a warm amber hue upon them. Tucked away from the usual tourist hotspots, this place was a cherished secret among the locals, offering a glimpse of the Thames without the bustling crowd. In the background, soft jazz melodies lazily drifted through the air. Although Alex had a mission at hand, he understood the importance of blending in, even if only for a fleeting moment of relaxation.

As he savored his drink, his gaze wandered across the room and settled upon a familiar face. Valentina. The lights gracefully accentuated her silhouette, her form framed by the gentle reflections of the Thames outside. Engrossed in conversation with a group, peals of laughter echoed around her. Enchanting and radiant, her hazel eyes shimmered with mirth.

Sensing his stare, Valentina's eyes shifted and met his gaze. Time seemed to stand still. The background noise faded into a distant hum, leaving behind only the intensified connection they had established earlier that day. A mischievous smile danced across her lips, and Alex reciprocated with equal warmth.

As the night unfolded, their paths intertwined amidst mingling and separation, guided by the hand of fate. Whether it was ordering drinks at the bar or swaying on the dance floor, they found themselves continuously drawn to one another.

When the opportune moment arrived, Alex approached her. "Seems like destiny is determined to bring us closer," he remarked, a playful grin playing on his lips.

Valentina chuckled. "Or perhaps this is just an exceptionally popular bar."

Their conversation flowed effortlessly once more, delving into their favorite London haunts. As the night neared its end, Alex took a deep breath. "There's a hidden gem I know, nestled by the water. Would you care to join me there tomorrow evening?"

Valentina pondered for a moment, her eyes gleaming mischievously, before replying, "Only if it surpasses this 'hidden gem'."

Alex laughed. "Consider it a date, then."

--

The following evening, Valentina found herself trailing down a labyrinth of winding lanes, guided by Alex, until they arrived at a charming restaurant nestled alongside a tranquil canal. The ambiance exuded serenity, with enchanting fairy lights adorning the surroundings, and the gentle lapping of water against the banks added to the romantic atmosphere.

They indulged in exquisite seafood, accompanied by fine wine, and their conversation effortlessly continued as before. They shared stories, dreams, and laughter, blissfully unaware of the world fading away around them.

As the night progressed, the two strolled along the canal, the city lights shimmering upon the water's surface, creating a mesmerizing spectacle. Alex reached out and gently clasped Valentina's hand, reigniting the electric connection they had felt during their initial encounter.

Both recognized the budding of something special between them, a connection they hadn't anticipated but were reluctant to relinquish. Little did Valentina know of the depths of secrets Alex held, and as for Alex, he was about to be drawn into a world as captivating as it was perilous.

--

Valentina sat on her hotel bed, gazing up at the ceiling. The soft hum of the city outside was a distant murmur, but her thoughts reverberated louder, echoing the memories of the previous night. The shimmering fairy lights reflecting on the canal, the warmth of Alex's hand in hers, the melodic rhythm of his laughter – it all played in her mind like a captivating film, urging her to ponder the possibilities.

She had found herself in similar situations before – fleeting romances, promises made and broken – but this time felt different. There was a profoundness, an intensity, a connection she couldn't ignore. Yet, she stood on the precipice of a new beginning in Sicily, a path she had tirelessly pursued. She had dreams to chase, a career to build, and a personal commitment to stay unwavering on her course.

Taking a deep breath, she reached for her phone and began to compose a message. Each word was chosen with care, each sentence meticulously crafted.

"Alex,

> Last night was truly unforgettable. I have ventured to many places, encountered countless individuals, but our evening by the canal will forever hold a cherished place in my heart. However, as I stand at the threshold of a new erter in my life, I must prioritize my dreams and aspirations.
>
> I hope you understand that it's not about us or what might have been, but about the promises I made to myself. Thank you for the beautiful memory, and I wish you nothing but the best.

Warm regards,

Valentina"

She hesitated for a moment before pressing send, a twinge of regret fluttering within her. Yet, she knew it was the right decision, at least for the present moment.

The following morning, as Valentina boarded her flight, she stole one last glance at the sprawling city of London. As the plane ascended and the landscape below dwindled, she leaned against the window, lost in contemplation. Alex's playful smile, the spark in his eyes, and the echoes of his laughter danced in her mind. She closed her eyes, allowing the memories to wash over her.

A new adventure awaited her In Sicily, and as eager as she was for her new job, a part of her couldn't help but wonder if her path would ever intersect with Alex's again. Only time held the key to that answer.

Chapter 2: When Worlds Collide

The emergency room of the hospital buzzed with frenetic activity. The symphony of voices, alarms, and hurried footsteps seemed endless. Valentina, amidst this chaos, exuded an aura of serenity and competence. She gracefully moved from one patient to another, providing aid, offering solace, and ensuring that the most critical cases received immediate attention.

Hours merged into a blur, and she lost count of the wounds she tended, the hands she held, and the reassurances she offered. After caring for a young boy with burn marks, her vision momentarily wavered, and the world tilted. Taking a deep breath, she regained her composure and completed her task.

However, fatigue was undeniable. Instead of heading home, she decided to seek respite in the on-call room. The room, though modest with a basic bed and subdued lighting, felt like a sanctuary to Valentina. She succumbed to a deep sleep almost instantly, the weight of the demanding shift finally catching up to her.

--

Meanwhile, as the sun set, a plane touched down at Palermo Airport. Among the passengers was Alex, his tall stature and confident stride setting him apart. He hailed a taxi, inhaling the familiar scent of the Mediterranean air.

Upon reaching the Grand Palm Hotel, he was escorted to his luxurious suite. The room exuded opulence, boasting a spacious balcony that offered a panoramic view of Palermo's rooftops and the shimmering sea in the distance. Stepping outside, Alex felt a wave of nostalgia and a deep connection to the land, but he remained focused on his mission.

He opened his laptop, its glow illuminating his face in the growing darkness. Several encrypted files captured his attention, but one stood out: *Operation Palermo Affair*. It meticulously detailed the key figures of the mafia operating in the region, their illicit activities, connections, and more. Although Valentina's name did not appear in the files, she held a pivotal role in Alex's personal plan. An old photograph revealed a young Valentina with someone Alex recognized from the operation's intricate details.

Closing the laptop, Alex leaned back, contemplating his next moves. Valentina was the missing piece he needed, but involving her would complicate matters after their brief romance. The boundaries between his personal sentiments and professional duty blurred. Alex understood the need for caution; both their lives hung in the balance.

--

The familiar sound of the coffee shop bell announced Valentina's arrival. The delightful aroma of freshly ground coffee beans surrounded her, providing a momentary respite from her busy morning. Dressed in her white coat, she swiftly placed her order and rummaged through her purse, retrieving some coins.

"Always in a rush, Dr. Valentina?" the barman, Marco, playfully teased with a wink.

She chuckled, "You know me too well, Marco. Emergency rooms don't wait."

The two exchanged a few more words, their lighthearted banter a testament to their long-standing friendship. Marco slid the cappuccino and croissant across the counter, a small note scribbled on the napkin underneath. Valentina caught it, smirking and shaking her head.

From his concealed position, Alex's piercing blue eyes observed the scene unfold. The newspaper provided excellent cover, but he had strategically positioned himself for a clear view of the entrance. The weight of his mission burdened him, yet witnessing Valentina in such a casual and genuine moment made him pause. Her laughter, her vibrant energy—it felt worlds away from the treacherous underbelly of Sicily he was here to investigate.

As Valentina left the coffee shop, the echoes of her laughter lingered in the air, tugging at Alex's guilt. He recalled their evening by the canal, the connection they shared. Involving her in this endeavor was risky, and his concerns extended beyond his operation. He worried for her well-being.

After waiting a few minutes, Alex folded his newspaper and departed, setting his course for Mondello. The drive led him along picturesque routes, where the beauty of Sicily unfolded before him. However, his destination was anything but ordinary.

The villa—or rather, the compound—in Mondello stood as a testament to power and influence. Nestled amidst lush greenery, it was encircled by towering walls and guarded gates, with security cameras strategically placed. Overlooking the Tyrrhenian Sea, it offered breathtaking views, but Alex knew that beneath its beauty lay dark secrets. This was the residence of Valentina's father, a name whispered in hushed tones, associated with rumors.

From a safe distance, Alex retrieved a pair of binoculars, observing the comings and goings. He took note of the guards, their routines, and the visitors. He needed to find a way to gather information without arousing suspicion. Valentina unintentionally became his link to this world, and he found himself torn between duty and the growing affection he held for her.

As the sun began its descent, casting elongated shadows across the landscape, Alex retreated to his vehicle. He couldn't help but wonder if he was about to cast a shadow over Valentina's life—one that could forever alter its course.

Chapter 3: Luciano Massotti: The King Behind the Shadows

Luciano Massotti was more than just a name; he represented an empire built on ruthlessness and cunning. At 60 years old, his salt-and-pepper hair, piercing dark eyes, and chiseled jawline bore the marks of a life lived on the edge. His tall, commanding figure was always impeccably dressed, whether in custom-made Italian suits or casual linen shirts at his seaside villa. Every detail, every gesture spoke of a man accustomed to having the world at his fingertips.

Only a select few knew Luciano well, and they spoke of his dual nature. To the outside world, he was ruthless—a man who eliminated threats without hesitation. However, within the private quarters of his expansive villa, he revealed a different side. He adored his wife, Isabella, a stunning beauty whom he had won over despite their different social standings. Their love story became legendary, testifying to Luciano's softer side.

His daughter, Valentina, was his pride and joy. Luciano ensured she received the best education, shielding her from the darker aspects of his life, and dreaming of her achieving greatness. Valentina embodied a combination of his fierce drive and Isabella's gentle soul.

And then there was Dante, Luciano's faithful Doberman. Trained as both protector and companion, Dante stood by Luciano's side as a silent sentinel.

Luciano's thirst for power was insatiable. In his world, power was the ultimate legacy. Manipulating deals, threats, and alliances, he orchestrated them all like a grandmaster on a chessboard.

As Alex examined the photo in the dossier—a candid shot of Luciano at a vineyard, a glass of red wine in hand, Dante by his side—he couldn't help but be captivated. The luxurious background hinted at opulence, but it was Luciano's expression that revealed the most—a mix of contemplation and determination.

As Alex delved deeper into the documents, he realized the enormity of his task. Infiltrating Luciano's inner circle seemed nearly impossible, given the man's notorious caution. Alex knew he needed an edge, something unexpected. But what?

Valentina emerged as the unexpected link, yet involving her presented moral and ethical dilemmas. Still, the more Alex immersed himself in Luciano's world, the more he understood that sometimes justice required venturing into gray areas.

Brainstorming a plan, Alex acknowledged that his first objective was to gain Luciano's trust—or at least get close enough to gather concrete evidence. Time was of the essence, and every move had to be calculated. The game was afoot.

Chapter 4: Serendipity in Sicily

The Vespa Bar hummed with lively conversation and laughter, drawing both locals and tourists. Its blend of rustic charm and modern aesthetics made it a beloved spot among Palermo's young crowd. Near the bar, a trio of vivacious young women laughed and chatted animatedly. Valentina, adorned in an elegant red dress that accentuated her silhouette, exuded a radiant glow that evening.

"Val," one of her friends, Isabella (affectionately known as Bella), remarked, "You're positively glowing. Has the ER not drained your energy yet?"

Valentina chuckled, "More like it's finally Friday, and I don't have to be summoned at an ungodly hour for once!"

Another friend, Francesca, chimed in, "And who knows, perhaps tonight you'll encounter someone intriguing."

Valentina playfully rolled her eyes, raising her glass to her lips for a sip. Just then, the soft buzz of her phone captured her attention. A message illuminated the screen: "Nice dress."

Her heart skipped a beat. Who could have sent it? Fueled by curiosity, she scanned the room, searching for a familiar face or someone giving her extra attention. And there, as her gaze settled on a secluded corner, she found him—Alex, holding a glass of whiskey, his piercing blue eyes fixed on hers. A wave of emotions washed over Valentina: surprise, elation, and a hint of trepidation.

As Alex rose, a subtle grin on his face revealing genuine delight, Valentina's friends observed the scene, their earlier conversation suddenly making sense.

"Talk about perfect timing," Francesca whispered to Bella, who nodded in agreement.

Valentina stood up as Alex approached their table. "Alex, what on earth brings you here?"

He chuckled, "Fate? Or perhaps just good fortune. I'm here for work, but I didn't want to intrude. I secretly hoped our paths would cross."

The group settled into effortless conversation. Alex's charm was undeniable, and it didn't take long for Bella and Francesca to warm up to him. Stories were shared, drinks were replenished, and laughter filled the air.

As the night progressed, Valentina and Alex stole moments for private conversation, reigniting the spark they had felt in London. Their connection was palpable, and by the time the Vespa Bar began to empty, a plan had taken shape.

"Tomorrow, then?" Alex confirmed, a glimmer of hope in his eyes.

"Tomorrow," Valentina replied with a smile.

Their paths had converged once again, but the enigma of what lay ahead was just beginning.

--

Sunlight streamed through the sheer curtains of Valentina's bedroom as she stood before her closet, contemplating her outfit for the day. The warm hues of the Sicilian morning bathed her room. After careful consideration, she chose a light, flowy sundress and comfortable sandals, perfect for leisurely walks around Palermo.

Taking a moment to apply a subtle touch of makeup, Valentina admired her reflection, her eyes brimming with excitement. Today wasn't just about showing Alex around; it was an opportunity to delve deeper into the enigmatic man she had met, to unravel more layers of his intriguing persona.

Their rendezvous point was *Bar Marinara,* a charming establishment by the port. The salty tang of the sea filled the air as Valentina approached. Spotting Alex leaning against a railing, lost in thought and gazing out at the boats, she couldn't help but feel a surge of happiness.

"Ciao Bello," she greeted him, a playful smirk gracing her lips.

Alex turned, his face breaking into a wide grin. "ma ciao bellissima."

She laughed. "Alright, charmer, ready for a tour of my town?"

As they embarked on their leisurely stroll, the narrow alleys of Palermo revealed stories of history and culture. From the grandeur of *Teatro Massimo* to the intricate beauty of the *Cattedrale di Palermo,* each location had its own tale. Valentina played the role of the perfect guide, interweaving personal anecdotes and lesser-known legends.

"You know," Alex remarked as they passed a bustling marketplace, "back in London, amidst the chaos, I never realized how much I missed places like these. Places with soul."

Valentina looked at him, her eyes softening. "I believe every place has a soul, Alex. Sometimes, you just have to dig a little deeper."

They paused for gelato at *Gelateria da Carlo,* where Valentina insisted that Alex try the pistachio flavor. Sitting on a bench, savoring their treats, they watched children play in a nearby fountain.

"You've lived quite a life, haven't you?" Valentina pondered, noticing the distant look in Alex's eyes.

He glanced at her, then back at his gelato. "I've seen many things, Val. Some beautiful, some… not so much."

She playfully nudged him. "Well, today, let's focus on the beautiful, shall we?"

As the day unfolded, their conversations grew more profound. They bared their dreams, fears, and aspirations. Despite their contrasting lives, they discovered shared threads of understanding, weaving a tapestry of intimacy.

By the time the sun began its descent, their hands had found each other's. The day had been a blend of flirtatious banter, heartfelt revelations, and moments of comfortable silence.

Standing by the port, gazing at the sun sinking into the horizon, Alex turned to Valentina. "Today was special, Val. Thank you."

She smiled, her eyes mirroring the golden hues of the sky. "Sometimes, the most unexpected encounters lead to the most beautiful memories."

Chapter 5: Shifting Sands and Silenced Stories

The hum of the jet ski echoed across the glistening expanse of the Tyrrhenian Sea as Alex skillfully steered closer to Luciano's sprawling compound. Through his research, he had learned about the concealed entrance beneath, strategically constructed for covert operations. Approaching the site, he retrieved his waterproof camera, swiftly capturing a few shots. The entrance proved more camouflaged than anticipated, hidden behind cascading rocks and overgrown foliage. However, the dark, gaping opening was unmistakable.

After securing the necessary images, Alex turned the jet ski around, putting a respectable distance between himself and the compound. The adrenaline rush from the mission subsided as he neared the shore. Cutting off the engine, he hauled the jet ski onto the beach, feeling the sand cling to his wet feet. This sensation grounded him, pulling him away from the depths of his undercover operation and back to the present reality of a sun-drenched beach in Palermo.

Shielding his eyes with sunglasses, he took a deep breath, savoring the simple pleasures of life—like the warmth of the sun on his skin. Lost in his thoughts, his eyes suddenly became covered by hands, accompanied by the scent of coconut sunscreen and a familiar voice playfully teasing, "Guess who?"

A smile crept across his face. "Do I get a clue?"

The hands fell away, and as he turned, he discovered Valentina's radiant face mere inches from his own. Beside her stood Bella, holding the leash of a handsome Doberman named Dante, who seemed more interested in digging a hole than in the meeting unfolding before him.

"Surprised to see me?" Valentina asked, her tone a blend of amusement and curiosity.

"Just a little," Alex replied, his gaze drifting to Valentina's figure adorned in a swimsuit. It was impossible not to notice her athletic physique, a testament to the demands of her profession and perhaps a few hobbies. She, in turn, observed his lean yet muscular frame, evidence of hisa man who works-out.

Their mutual admiration hung palpably in the air, but neither voiced it. Instead, as Valentina's eyes lingered a moment too long on a faded scar that traversed his side, unspoken questions flickered in her gaze. Questions she was not yet prepared to ask, and he was not ready to answer.

Breaking the silence, Bella interjected, "Well, aren't you two a sight for sore eyes? But, Val, we should keep moving. Dante seems eager to reach our usual spot."

Valentina nodded, offering Alex a wistful smile. "Duty calls. But let's catch up later?"

"Absolutely," he replied, a touch of regret coloring his tone.

As Valentina walked away with Bella, Alex watched her retreat, her hair tousled by the sea breeze. He knew he was navigating treacherous waters, not just with his mission but with the bond he was forming with Valentina. Still, as he gazed at the horizon, he couldn't help but wonder where the tides of destiny would guide them next.

--

The gala held at Villa Igiea stood out as one of Palermo's most highly anticipated events of the year. It brought together an elegant blend of esteemed investors, influential business magnates, and the occasional politician. Yet, for Alex, it held a deeper significance. It served as the grand stage for the next phase of his intricate plan.

As Valentina's executive car glided to a stop at the majestic entrance of the Villa, the rapid clicks of camera shutters filled the air. The press, always eager to capture glimpses of the city's glitterati, had flocked to the scene. And when Valentina emerged from the car, impeccably styled leg first, the flashbulbs erupted into a frenzy.

Valentina gracefully stepped out, her dress gracefully embracing the ambient light in a mesmerizing play of shadows. The black fabric, adorned with delicate embroidery, accentuated her figure flawlessly. Her tastefully chosen jewelry added an extra sparkle, but it was her genuine smile that truly stole the spotlight.

Standing by the entrance, Alex found himself momentarily breathless. Though he had seen Valentina in various settings, this was undeniably different. She exuded an aura reminiscent of classic Hollywood glamour, and he felt fortunate to be the man on her arm for the night.

With their arms interlocked, they made their way inside. The Villa bathed in golden light, its chandeliers casting a warm glow, while a live orchestra set the enchanting mood. Amidst the mingling crowd, Alex flawlessly played his role as a "consultant," engaging in investment discussions and skillfully acknowledging the right buzzwords. Yet, his gaze never strayed far from Valentina. They laughed, shared stories, and danced, as the world around them faded, lost in the rhythm of the waltz.

As the night drew to a close and the car carried Valentina back to her father's villa, she felt a mixture of exhilaration and apprehension. The grandeur of the Massotti estate unfolded as the mansion gates swung open. The car glided up the driveway, its path illuminated by the house's radiant lights. Before the car came to a full stop, Luciano emerged from the entrance, his authoritative presence commanding attention.

Valentina stepped out of the car, her heels echoing against the cobblestone. Her father's keen eyes scanned her, searching for any signs of the evening's events.

"Did you have a pleasant evening, polpetta?" Luciano's deep voice carried a deceptively gentle tone, the nickname he had given her since childhood a testament to their bond.

"Yes, daddy, it was truly wonderful," Valentina replied, her voice brimming with warmth.

Luciano's gaze shifted, as if attempting to peer past his daughter and catch a glimpse of the man who had captivated her attention. "I look forward to meeting this Englishman," he stated, an undercurrent lacing his words.

Valentina paused, sensing the hidden meaning behind her father's words. "In due time, daddy," she responded with a touch of playful ambiguity.

Inside, Luciano watched as the car departed, his thoughts swirling. Alex's calculated risk had undeniably paid off; he had been noticed.

--

The Massotti estate was bathed in a golden glow, courtesy of the sun. Against the backdrop of the traditional Sicilian villa, vibrant flowers in full bloom added splashes of color. The air was filled with rhythmic laughter and the clinking of glasses, complemented by the enticing aroma of grilled meat. It was a scene straight out of a postcard, the epitome of leisure in Sicily.

With a slightly racing heart, Valentina approached her father, accompanied by Alex. Luciano Massotti, his broad shoulders squared and attentive eyes missing nothing, was busy overseeing the preparations. By his side lounged Dante, the family's loyal dog, lazily enjoying the day.

"Daddy," Valentina began, her voice a blend of excitement and a hint of nervousness, "this is Alex."

Luciano looked up, his intense gaze assessing the Englishman. Alex, unperturbed, met the older man's eyes with calm confidence. "Mr. Massotti," he greeted, extending his hand. "It is an honor to be here."

Luciano accepted the handshake firmly. "Luciano," he corrected gently. "Welcome, Alex."

There was an initial tension, an unspoken test of character between the two men. However, as the afternoon progressed, they discovered common ground. Luciano, always cautious when it came to men around his beloved daughter, found himself disarmed by Alex's genuine charm and wit. Their conversation spanned various topics, from the beauty of Sicily to Luciano's passion for wine-making, and even the complexities of modern-day investments.

Valentina observed with a mixture of pride and relief. She had hoped for their accord, but to witness her father genuinely laughing with Alex surpassed her expectations.

As the sun began its descent, casting a warm, golden glow over the garden, Luciano turned to Alex with a playful glimmer in his eyes. "So, Alex, have you ever tried your hand at making pizza?"

Caught off guard, Alex chuckled. "I must admit, my attempts have been less than stellar."

"Well," Luciano replied with a smile, "it's time for a lesson. You can't court a Sicilian woman without mastering the art of pizza."

Father and suitor made their way towards the outdoor oven, while Valentina exchanged amused glances with her friends. The day, filled with the apprehension of introductions, was transforming into a joyous celebration of connection.

Embraced by the warmth of the Sicilian evening, as Dante chased after thrown balls and the aroma of pizza filled the air, it became evident that Alex had not only captured Valentina's heart but also found a place within the Massotti affections. At least for now.

--

As twilight descended, fairy lights adorned the garden, casting a romantic glow over the gathering. Guests mingled, enjoying their drinks, their conversations harmonizing with the soothing chirping of cicadas.

Seizing the moment, Alex turned to Valentina, speaking softly and intimately. "Would you be so kind as to give me a tour of your exquisite home? I'm eager to explore further."

Valentina hesitated briefly, her eyes lighting up. "Certainly. It would be my pleasure."

Their journey commenced in the grand foyer, featuring a sweeping staircase and intricate tilework. Valentina shared glimpses of her childhood, revealing her cherished hideouts and recounting tales of youthful mischief. Alex attentively absorbed every detail, noting the placement of doors, windows, the intricate layout, and even the watchful gaze of security cameras.

As they strolled, Valentina pointed out various rooms, narrating their historical significance. Yet, Alex's attention remained fixated on one room in particular: Luciano's study. He knew it held the secrets he sought.

While Valentina engrossed herself in describing a portrait of her ancestors, Alex spotted a sturdy oak door at the end of a corridor. A guard stood sentinel beside it, his vigilant eyes scanning their surroundings. His presence confirmed Alex's suspicions. Without a doubt, this was Luciano's private sanctuary.

Catching his gaze, Valentina followed his line of sight. "That is Papa's study," she whispered, a hint of pride in her voice. "It's strictly off-limits. Even I am not allowed inside without his permission."

Alex masked his curiosity with a light chuckle. "How mysterious. It must contain valuable treasures."

Valentina smiled, a playful sparkle in her eyes. "Perhaps. Or maybe it's simply an old man's way of preserving a semblance of privacy."

They continued their tour, with Alex etching every detail into his memory. Each room held a fragment of the Massotti legacy, from cherished heirlooms to rare works of art. Yet, Alex's thoughts remained fixated on the heavily guarded study. He had obtained what he came for: an understanding of the house's layout, the study's location, and crucially, knowledge of its security measures.

Their journey through the villa concluded on the balcony, offering a view of the enchanting gardens as the cool evening breeze caressed their skin. Alex, ever the charmer, drew Valentina closer. "Thank you for enlightening me with this captivating tour," he whispered, their faces inches apart.

As their lips met, conflicting emotions wrestled in Alex's mind. The stakes had never been higher.

From the balcony, they gazed at the magnificent view of the gardens, the distant sounds of the party fading into a gentle murmur. The warm Mediterranean breeze carried the delicate fragrances of lemon and jasmine as Valentina leaned against the balustrade, her eyes mirroring the starlit sky.

Beside her, Alex leaned casually, finally broaching the topic he had been subtly guiding towards all evening. "Your father has truly built an impressive empire," he began, his tone relaxed. "May I inquire about his line of work?"

Valentina's gaze shifted from the stars to the gardens below, her expression momentarily inscrutable. "He is in business," she replied simply, then added with a hint of amusement, "The kind of business that attracts both friends and foes, I suppose."

"Sounds rather intense," Alex prodded gently, sensing her evasion.

She chuckled, though it lacked a fullness in her eyes. "Isn't every business at that level? But my father... he keeps his work very private. Even from me." Her words carried a lightness, yet Alex detected an underlying distance in her tone.

He yearned to delve deeper, to uncover whether she suspected the true nature of her father's dealings, but he hesitated. As they stood there, the openness between them contrasting with the vulnerability she unknowingly displayed, a pang of guilt washed over him. He was there under false pretenses, similar to the life her father surely concealed from her.

Their eyes locked, and in that fleeting moment, an unspoken understanding passed between them. Alex's heart ached with the realization that their budding relationship was built upon a lie.

Caught in this silent understanding, the balcony doors swung open. Valentina's mother, a graceful woman exuding elegance, emerged. "Darling, the guests are leaving," she whispered softly.

The enchantment was broken. Valentina offered Alex a small, apologetic smile. "Duty calls," she said as she brushed past him, her hand briefly grazing his arm in a fleeting caress.

Alex nodded, burdened by the weight of his deceit. "I should depart as well," he murmured, more to himself than to her.

Descending the stairs and bidding farewell to the remaining guests with a smile that failed to reach his eyes, Alex felt the piercing gaze of Luciano upon him. He wondered if the man sensed a rival, not for his daughter's affection, but for the power he wielded.

The evening air grew colder as Alex made his way to where his car was parked, his mind consumed by a storm of strategy and emotion. He had a mission to fulfill, but at what cost to Valentina and his own conscience? The question lingered unanswered in the night.

Chapter 6: Intricate Deceptions

In the serene, sterilized break room of the Palermo hospital, Valentina's laughter filled the cozy space, creating a soft melody. Across the cluttered table, her colleague Martina leaned forward, resting her elbows on the surface.

"So, he just appeared out of nowhere at your father's barbecue?" Martina's voice was a mix of excitement and disbelief.

Valentina nodded, her eyes gleaming as she recounted the story. "Yes, and you should have seen the look on my dad's face. But Alex... he effortlessly charmed everyone, even Dante, the most suspicious Doberman you'll ever meet."

"And he's only here for 'business'?" Martina asked, smirking as she air-quoted.

"That's what he claims. Investment consultancy or something of the sort," Valentina replied absentmindedly, stirring her coffee.

"It sounds mysterious... Almost too good to be true," Martina teased, her gaze sharp.

Valentina's smile faded slightly. "Perhaps, but when I'm with him, everything feels right."

Simultaneously, in a high-security briefing room at Interpol's regional office in Lyon, Alex's new commanding officer, Jameson, sat in front of the video call. The room was sparse, the air heavy with the weight of their conversation.

"So, you've ingratiated yourself with Massotti. What's your next move?" Jameson's voice cut through the silence, sharp and direct.

"I've earned myself some trust, but I haven't yet identified the link to the London syndicates," Alex replied, maintaining unwavering eye contact.

Jameson tapped a file on the table. "We need concrete evidence connecting Massotti to the London groups. Your romantic involvement, is it a liability?"

Alex's jaw tightened. "Valentina is not involved in Luciano's business. She's an innocent civilian."

"A civilian with potential ties to our targets. Emotions can be leveraged, don't underestimate that," Jameson warned. "Keep your relationship professional. Your purpose is to gather evidence, not play house."

"The relationship grants me access. Massotti is cautious. He won't slip up in front of someone he doesn't trust," Alex argued, his voice steady despite the internal conflict.

Leaning in, Jameson emphasized his point. "Your access has an expiration date before suspicion arises. Use it wisely. Find that connection, or we'll have to extract you and take a more direct approach."

Alex nodded, silently acknowledging the order. "Understood. I will find the evidence we need."

As nightfall settled over Palermo, the warm lights of 'Graziano al Mare' painted the waterfront in golden hues. The restaurant, with its soft ambiance and the gentle sound of waves, provided the perfect setting for an intimate evening.

Valentina, adorned in a delicate white dress that made her appear ethereal against the backdrop of the Mediterranean, engaged in animated conversation with her mother. Across from them, Luciano, always observant, observed as Alex perused the wine list.

Alex cleared his throat, "I've heard this place is renowned for its Brunello di Montalcino. Shall we give it a try?"

Luciano, an appreciator of fine wine, nodded. "Very well."

As the wine was poured and pleasantries were exchanged, Alex subtly steered the conversation towards business. "Luciano," he began, effortlessly rolling the name off his tongue, "I've recently come across an exciting investment opportunity in London, something that may capture the interest of someone of your... stature."

Luciano raised an eyebrow, his curiosity piqued. "Go on."

Leaning in slightly, Alex kept his voice low and conspiratorial. "It's an emerging tech firm specializing in advanced cybersecurity. Their projections are astronomical, but they're seeking private investors before going public. With the right support, they could dominate the European market."

Luciano took a sip of his wine, his gaze fixed on Alex's face. "And why present this to me?"

Alex paused for a moment, carefully choosing his words. "Because I believe in mutually beneficial partnerships. The potential returns on this venture are substantial, and you immediately came to mind."

A half-smile formed on Luciano's lips. "You're a shrewd individual, Alex. I will consider it."

The evening continued with laughter, anecdotes, and a genuine camaraderie that seemed unlikely given the underlying motives at play. Valentina emanated radiance, and for fleeting moments, Alex could almost forget the impending storm on the horizon.

However, as he escorted Valentina home later that night, the weight of his duplicity bore heavily upon him. Watching the moonlight dance in her eyes, Alex keenly felt the heartache he was about to inflict. Every second with her felt both like a stolen treasure and a ticking time bomb.

He pulled her close, the salty sea air mingling with her perfume. "Valentina," he whispered, his voice thick with emotion, "No matter what happens, always cherish the beautiful moments we've shared."

She looked up at him, perplexed by his sudden seriousness. "Certo. Of course, I will."

Alex kissed her forehead and sighed. The next phase of his plan was about to unfold, and he desperately hoped to shield Valentina from the impending chaos.

Chapter 7: Shadows and Whispers

Moonlight draped a silver sheen over the sprawling grounds of the Massotti estate. Among the blooming roses, marble statues stood sentinel, their faces kissed by pale light. Fountains softly murmured in the distance, their waters shimmering and rippling. Even in the dead of night, the opulence of the Massotti family was showcased in all its glory.

Alex's footsteps treaded silently on the expertly manicured lawns. Each stride measured, each breath controlled. He had trained for moments like this, but carelessness was a luxury he couldn't afford. The estate sprawled far and wide, its security measures concealed from prying eyes.

Cloaked in darkness, Alex moved like a shadow, darting between sculptures, topiaries, and ornate benches. The villa itself stood as an imposing structure, merging old-world charm with modern luxury through elegant arches and balconies.

Approaching the building, a chilling sensation prickled at the back of Alex's neck. Swiftly turning, he found himself face to face with Dante, the sleek and formidable Doberman guarding the premises. Yet, instead of hostility, the dog tilted his head, as if recognizing a familiar presence. The rapport they had built during the barbecue now proved to be Alex's salvation. Dante, though cautious, allowed him to pass without a sound.

With Dante's silent approval, Alex pressed forward. The side entrance of the villa led him into the grand hallway, where rich tapestries and portraits of stern ancestors adorned the walls. Moving swiftly, Alex avoided the central staircase, opting for a discreet route. A narrow servant's passage guided him directly to the heart of the mansion: Luciano's study.

The room felt cavernous, its tall ceilings swallowed by shadows. A colossal chandelier hung overhead, its crystals casting a myriad of reflections. The mahogany desk stood meticulously organized, aside from a solitary laptop that symbolized Luciano's blend of tradition and modernity.

Aware that time was slipping away, Alex worked with precision. He discreetly planted the listening device beneath the desk, ensuring its concealed position. However, just as he prepared to retreat, a distant conversation grew louder, reaching his ears. The guards were drawing near!

Panicked, Alex scanned the room for an alternative exit. An open balcony offered a swift escape route. Swiftly swinging over the balustrade, he descended using a trellis smothered in vines.

Yet, as he neared the boundary of the estate, a guard's flashlight sliced through the darkness, briefly illuminating Alex's figure. Alerted voices reverberated, "Intruder! Intruder!"

Pushing himself harder, Alex sprinted towards his hidden getaway vehicle, his heart pounding. Every passing second seemed like an eternity until the bike roared to life, and he vanished into the night.

Back at the estate, Luciano stood in his study, trying to piece together the events of the evening. A swarm of guards buzzed around, reporting their findings. "The cameras show nothing," one exclaimed.

Luciano's gaze, however, fixated on Dante, who now lounged on the patio, seemingly unperturbed. "He didn't bark," Luciano whispered to himself. This was more than a mere break-in; it was a message. Someone had infiltrated his sanctuary, and the game of cat and mouse had just begun.

In the twilight, Palermo's Teatro Massimo stood proudly, its neoclassical I radiating a golden glow. Excited patrons filled the theater, their chatter filling the evening air. Amidst the bustling crowd, one reunion held more significance than all the rest.

Dressed in a tailored suit, Alex anxiously waited near the entrance. His thoughts were interrupted when Valentina emerged from a sleek black Mercedes. She appeared ethereal in a flowing dress that mirrored the elegance of the theater. However, what caught his attention was not just her beauty, but the imposing figure that followed her – her bodyguard.

Approaching with caution, Valentina greeted Alex with a hesitant smile. "Alex," she said, her voice tinged with strain.

"You look absolutely stunning, Valentina," he complimented, trying to ease the tension.

She nodded, a faint blush gracing her cheeks. "This is Rocco," she introduced, gesturing towards the protective bodyguard.

Rocco nodded, his eyes scanning the surroundings before settling on Alex with a touch of suspicion. "Signor," he acknowledged.

Together, the trio entered the theater, with Rocco trailing just a step behind. The grandeur of the Teatro's interior never failed to amaze visitors, and on this night, it shimmered with opulence. Crystal chandeliers, intricate gold leaf details, and plush velvet seats set the stage for an evening of exquisite artistry.

As they settled into their seats, Alex attempted to strike up a casual conversation. "I thought 'Madama Butterfly' would provide the perfect escape for both of us. A tragic love story set in a world far removed from our own."

Valentina offered a faint smile. "I do adore Puccini. But, Alex, things have changed. My father... he's become more protective than ever."

Leaning in, Alex lowered his voice. "I've noticed. Rocco, right? He seems capable."

She sighed. "It's not just Rocco. It's the entire atmosphere at home. The break-in, the heightened security... it's all overwhelming."

The opera began, capturing their attention as the tale of love, betrayal, and sacrifice unfolded. The haunting notes of Puccini's score filled the theater, seemingly dissipating the palpable tension between them.

During the intermission, they stepped out onto the balcony, seeking a moment of respite in the cool night air. Alex gently took Valentina's hand. "I'm sorry for everything that's happening. I wish I could make it easier for you."

Her eyes searched his, filled with questions. "There's so much I want to ask, but I'm afraid of what the answers might be."

Alex sighed, burdened by the weight of his secrets. "Give it time, Valentina."

The second act commenced, and as Butterfly's tragic tale unfolded, Alex couldn't help but draw parallels to their own story. Was their relationship also destined for tragedy, or could they find a way to rewrite their ending?

As the curtain fell and the audience erupted in applause, the duo quietly made their exit, both lost in their thoughts, the divide between them growing wider with every step.

Chapter 8: Echoes of Suspicion

Mondello beach's shimmering sands, usually a serene escape, now set the stage for Alex's mission. The sun's rays danced on the waves, casting a golden glow over everything, providing a picturesque backdrop to Luciano's sprawling villa in the distance.

Sporting dark sunglasses, Alex lounged in a beachside chair, a drink at hand. Despite his relaxed appearance, his observant eyes discreetly scanned the property. He mentally cataloged the guards' sporadic movements, the pattern of their patrols, and the sections of the estate that seemed particularly well-guarded.

The rhythmic sounds of the lapping waves and distant chatter were interrupted by the familiar, joyful bark of Dante. The handsome Doberman energetically trotted towards Alex, his tail wagging with abandon. Following closely was Rocco, Valentina's vigilant bodyguard, though his pace was more measured. His sharp gaze locked onto Alex.

"Signor," Rocco began, nodding at Alex, his face reflecting a mix of recognition and suspicion. "Dante seems unusually fond of you."

Alex chuckled, extending a hand for Dante to sniff and giving the dog a friendly pat. "I suppose we made quite an impression on each other. Just here to soak up the sun. Mondello's irresistible."

Rocco continued to scrutinize him. "This beach offers many spots, yet you seem drawn to this particular one. Close to the villa."

Alex met his gaze, maintaining his casual demeanor. "Can't blame a man for wanting a good view, can you? The villa's architecture is truly captivating."

Rocco's eyes narrowed slightly, as if attempting to decipher an underlying message. "Just remember, that's private property. We wouldn't want any... misunderstandings."

"Understood," Alex replied, raising his drink in a half-toast.

With one last warning look, Rocco whistled for Dante and began to walk away. As the distance between them grew, Alex released a quiet sigh of relief. He realized his visit had attracted attention and that he would need to be more discreet.

As evening settled, Alex found himself back in the comforting embrace of his hotel room, reflecting on the day. Each encounter, each potential lead, brought him closer to the culmination of his mission. However, with every step, the lines between his duty and his feelings for Valentina blurred further.

His reverie was interrupted by the soft chime of his phone. Valentina's name flashed on the screen. Taking a deep breath to compose himself, he answered.

"Alex," Valentina's voice, typically warm and joyful, sounded strained. "Rocco mentioned seeing you at the beach today. Near our property. Papa is growing more suspicious. I trust you, but why didnt you tell me you were at the beach."

"I'm sorry," he replied, genuine regret permeating his words. "I genuinely love Mondello. I had no idea I was drawing attention."

There was a pause, pregnant with unspoken words and emotions.

"Listen," Alex began, choosing his words carefully. "Valentina, we need to talk. There's so much I want to share with you. Can we have dinner tomorrow? At my hotel?"

Another, longer pause ensued.

"Alright, Alex. Tomorrow night. But promise me... no more surprise beach visits?"

Alex let out a soft chuckle. "I promise."

As the call ended, the weight of the situation settled heavily upon him. The intertwining of his mission and his growing affection for Valentina made every decision crucial, every move precarious.

The restaurant exuded an ambiance of elegance and refinement. Through large windows, the breathtaking view of the coastal city unfolded, showcasing baroque churches and historic palaces illuminated against the evening sky. Soft melodies played by a pianist, candlelit tables, and the hushed murmur of intimate conversations enveloped Alex and Valentina in a serene bubble.

Seated at a secluded corner table, they found themselves surrounded by an exquisite array of sushi dishes, each one a work of culinary art. The warm glow of overhead chandeliers complemented the radiant beauty of Valentina's visage, casting a golden hue throughout the atmosphere.

Alex watched Valentina with genuine affection as she delicately picked up a piece of sushi. It wasn't just her external allure that captivated him, but also the strength and intelligence that shone through her expressive eyes.

"Valentina," he began, his voice tinged with a hint of tremor, revealing the weight of the words he was about to utter. "I'll be leaving Palermo in a week."

Her face, previously illuminated with joy, suddenly turned somber. "Why?"

He sighed, "My work... it's coming to an end. But that doesn't mean I want to leave everything behind. Especially not... us."

Their eyes locked, both searching for assurance and understanding. After a pause that stretched like an eternity, Valentina spoke, her voice filled with emotion, "I don't want this to be the end either, Alex."

Silence settled once again, the only sound being the soft melodies emanating from the piano. Alex took a deep breath. "You know, we could spend more time together before I leave. Truly savor each moment. Maybe even tonight."

She looked up, her eyes glistening, reflecting the soft light. "What are you suggesting?"

He leaned in, lowering his voice. "Stay with me tonight, in my suite. Let's not let time dictate our moments."

A mixture of anticipation and uncertainty fluttered within her. But as she gazed into his earnest eyes, she nodded gently, her heart guiding her decision.

The walk to his suite felt like a journey through time, every step resonating with the depth of their blossoming connection. As the door closed behind them, the outside world blurred, leaving only the two of them in sharp focus.

He approached her, his hands tenderly cradling her face. Their lips met in a slow, profound kiss, a dance of passion and longing. The energy between them was palpable as they explored each other, surrendering to the moment and shedding their inhibitions.

Their clothes became mere obstacles, discarded as they sought a closer union. The cool sheets of the bed contrasted with the warmth of their entwined bodies. Their lovemaking was a harmonious blend of passion and tenderness, each movement a testament to their genuine affection for one another.

Hours melted into minutes, and as dawn approached, they found themselves on the terrace of his suite. The soft glow of the rising sun bathed the rooftops of Palermo in a golden hue, while the distant sea shimmered under its early light.

Naked, they stood intertwined, embraced by the cool morning breeze caressing their skin. Against the backdrop of the city's skyline, their bodies formed a silhouette, their love a testament to the profound connection they shared. In that moment, the world seemed distant and inconsequential compared to the depth of their intimacy.

Alex whispered into Valentina's ear, his voice filled with raw emotion, "I wish this moment could last forever."

She turned to face him, her eyes teary but bright. "Every second with you feels like an eternity, and yet, time seems to fly."

They stood like that for what felt like hours, holding each other close, drawing strength and comfort from their shared intimacy.

As the sun rose higher, heralding the beginning of a new day, Alex and Valentina saw it as the dawn of an uncertain future, one they would face together, no matter the odds.

--

The morning after was serene, with the soft sunlight peeking through the delicate drapes of the hotel suite. Outside, the world was slowly awakening, but inside, time seemed to stand still for Valentina and Alex, wrapped in a tender embrace. Their night together had been the culmination of stolen moments, lingering gazes, and unspoken words that now found their voice in the silence.

It was Alex who suggested leaving the city. "Let's escape somewhere far away from all of this," he whispered, his hand tracing gentle patterns on her back. Valentina, her head resting against his chest, could hear the steady rhythm of his heartbeat as she agreed, a soft murmur of anticipation for the day ahead.

Their journey out of Palermo was a tapestry of sensations - the cool breeze caressing their faces through the open car windows, the distant hum of the city giving way to the idyllic Sicilian countryside. Ancient olive trees stood like silent sentinels on the rolling hills, alongside vineyards and fields of wildflowers swaying in harmony with the wind. The scent of the sea grew stronger as they approached their destination.

Castellammare del Golfo emerged before them like a scene from an Italian painting. Nestled between rugged cliffs and the tranquil sea, the town burst with vibrant colors. Hand in hand, they meandered through its streets, Valentina pointing out hidden nooks, tiny chapels, and the little shop where she had scraped her knee as a child.

Lunch was a leisurely affair at Marina Blue, a cozy eatery overlooking the harbor. They chose a table on the terrace, with the boundless sea stretching out before them. Conversations flowed freely, ranging from the delicate flavors of the local cuisine to the fishermen mending their nets and the sun-kissed tourists lounging under the Mediterranean sun.

As they savored a symphony of flavors, Alex found himself entangled in a whirlwind of emotions. With each of Valentina's laughter, every touch, and the sharing of secrets, he felt himself being pulled deeper into the enigma of their love. Valentina, seemingly unaware of his inner turmoil, animatedly recounted mischievous adventures, her laughter a melody he wished to embrace forever.

An unexpected invitation emerged amidst a discussion of Valentina's favorite sea shanties - to join her and her father on their yacht. Hope sparkled in her eyes as she extended the offer. Alex's heart raced at the opportunity, even as he concealed his excitement behind a smile and a simple, "I'd love to."

As the day transitioned into evening, the sky became a canvas of colors, painting the perfect backdrop to their unfolding story. They stumbled upon a secluded bar tucked away from the bustling streets. The gentle waves lapped against the shore, the clinking of glasses and murmurs of other patrons creating a symphony of background noise as they sipped chilled Prosecco.

--

In that tranquil space between day and night, Valentina's words emerged, tentative yet filled with emotion. "Alex, in such a short time, you've become a part of me. A part that I didn't even know was missing. I think I'm falling in love with you," she whispered, her voice carrying the weight of her realization.

The confession hung in the air, a testament to their undeniable connection. Alex held her gaze, seeing the vulnerability and truth reflected in her eyes. He pulled her closer, the sea breeze mingling with the scent of her hair, and whispered in return, "Valentina, you have bewitched me in ways I never thought possible."

They sat there, embraced under the burgeoning stars, a symbol of new beginnings and unspoken promises. As the moon ascended, a shimmering witness to their bond, they held each other tighter.

--

Approaching the villa, Alex was mesmerized by the glimmering sunlight dancing on the tranquil waters, accentuating the magnificence of Luciano's yacht. Gracefully anchored, it seemed poised to conquer the open sea. Alex had encountered many vessels during his assignments, but this one possessed an unparalleled allure.

Valentina greeted him with an affectionate kiss, accompanied by her effortlessly elegant mother, Isabella, who wore a delightful summer dress. "You're just in time! Papa is already preparing everything," Valentina exclaimed cheerfully.

Luciano, visible from the shore, commanded the crew with his characteristic white linen shirt, emanating authority with a mere gesture or glance.

Isabella playfully nudged Alex, a mischievous smile on her face. "Don't let him overpower you today. This may be his kingdom," she gestured towards the yacht, "but we won't let him forget that he's outnumbered."

Alex chuckled. "I'll do my best to remember."

The trio stepped onto the yacht, feeling the gentle sway of the boat beneath their feet. Valentina and her mother settled comfortably on the sun deck, their laughter floating through the air as they arranged their towels and applied sunscreen.

Approaching them, Luciano extended his hand to Alex. "Glad you could join us, Mr. Englishman."

"Wouldn't miss it for the world," Alex replied, shaking Luciano's firm grip.

As the yacht glided through the azure waters, Luciano led Alex to the seating area. Between them sat a meticulously crafted wooden chessboard, its pieces arranged in perfect order, ready for a game.

"Do you play?" Luciano inquired, raising an eyebrow.

"I've been known to make a move or two," Alex said, a mischievous sparkle in his eyes.

Luciano chuckled. "Ah, excellent! They say you can assess a man by his skill in chess."

"Is that so? Then let's see what we're both capable of."

The game commenced, a silent ballet of strategy between two seasoned players. Luciano's moves mirrored his assertive nature, while Alex employed a combination of defense and meticulous planning. As the sun shifted above them, casting alternating shadows and light on the board, the game progressed.

Valentina and Isabella observed from a distance, captivated by the silent duel. "Who's winning?" Valentina whispered to her mother.

Isabella squinted at the board. "It's too early to tell. But look at them, like two gladiators in an arena."

After what felt like hours, both men deeply engrossed, Alex executed a decisive move, checkmating Luciano. Leaning back, a satisfied grin adorned his face. "Well played."

Luciano studied the board for a moment before bursting into laughter, extending his hand. "You're quite the player, Alex. I admire that."

The tension of the game dissipated, replaced by camaraderie and mutual respect. The yacht excursion proved to be more than a simple getaway; it became a bridge that strengthened bonds. As the sun began its descent, painting the sky with golden and crimson hues, the group gathered, their laughter and stories resonating into the evening, sealing the memories of a day well spent.

The yacht's engine hummed gently as it approached the private jetty of the villa. The twilight sky had transformed into a mesmerizing shade of lavender, mirroring the tranquility of the still waters below. Luciano, filled with contentment from the day's events, turned to Alex.

"Care for a drink?" he offered, displaying a bottle of aged whisky, its golden liquid shimmering.

"I would be honored," Alex replied, accepting the unspoken invitation to prolong the evening.

Stepping onto the dock, the warm glow of the villa's lights welcomed them. They entered the grand hall, where Luciano guided Alex to his study, a room that had piqued Alex's curiosity earlier. Heavy wooden doors swung open, revealing a space adorned with bookshelves filled with timeless classics, family photographs, and an array of precious antiques. A majestic mahogany desk stood at the center, flanked by two plush leather chairs.

Luciano poured the whisky into crystal glasses and motioned for Alex to sit. The amber liquid radiated under the soft illumination of the room as Luciano savored a deep sip, relishing its flavor. He paused, allowing silence to hang in the air, before finally broaching the topic that had occupied his thoughts.

"Alex," he began, his voice low and measured, "I have lived long enough to recognize genuine emotions. I have observed the way you gaze at Valentina, and the way she in turn gazes at you. But I must know... what are your intentions with her?"

Alex, slightly taken aback by the directness of the question, took a moment to compose his response. "Luciano, meeting someone like Valentina was beyond my expectations. She is truly remarkable. My intentions are sincere, as I deeply care for her."

Luciano's penetrating gaze searched Alex's face for any trace of deceit. "You must understand, she is my world. I have seen many come and go, with promises and fleeting emotions. But Valentina deserves more than transient sentiments."

Alex nodded earnestly. "I comprehend, and I promise you, my feelings for Valentina are genuine. I am not here for a fleeting romance. I genuinely desire to know her, to be a part of her life."

Luciano took another sip of his whisky, the weight of their conversation reflected in his eyes. "And what about your own life, Alex? Can you provide for her? Can you keep her safe?"

Sensing the underlying layers of the question, Alex replied with conviction, "I have a stable job and a clear sense of direction in life. I can provide for her, and I pledge to protect her with all that I possess."

The two men locked eyes, an unspoken understanding passing between them. Finally, Luciano's lips curved into a faint smile. "You are a good man, Alex. I see that. Just... take care of her. She is precious."

Feeling a burden lift from his shoulders, Alex nodded appreciatively. "I will, Luciano. You have my word."

As the evening progressed, the two men continued their conversation, gradually transitioning from weighty topics to shared anecdotes and laughter. The barriers between them dissipated, replaced by mutual respect and comprehension. With the passage of time, Luciano's study transformed from a room of enigma to a space of camaraderie.

--

Valentina and her mother, Isabella, stood on the yacht's deck, serenaded by the rhythmic lapping of waves against the hull. The twilight sky painted soft hues, casting a gentle glow upon their faces.

Lost in her thoughts, Valentina gazed towards the horizon, absentmindedly toying with the rim of her wine glass. Sensing her daughter's distance, Isabella, the perceptive mother, broke the silence. "You seem preoccupied tonight, my dear. What troubles your mind?"

Valentina sighed, her eyes shimmering with a blend of hope and uncertainty. "It's Alex, Mama. I... I believe I may be in love with him."

Taken aback by this sudden confession, Isabella studied her daughter's face for a moment. "Love, my dear, is a profound emotion. Are you absolutely certain of your feelings, or could it be the thrill of a new romance?"

Valentina hesitated, searching for the right words. "It's different with Alex, Mama. I have never experienced such emotions before. There's a deep connection, as if our souls recognize one another. I feel safe and understood in his presence. It's as if he completes a part of me that I never knew was missing."

Maternal instincts tingling, Isabella took a moment to process her daughter's heartfelt words. "Valentina, love is a beautiful thing, but it also brings vulnerability and challenges. You have always been my brave and independent girl. Just... do not lose yourself in this."

Valentina nodded, appreciating her mother's wisdom. "I understand, Mama. But with Alex, I feel like I am discovering more of myself, not losing it. I only wish Papa could see him the way I do."

Isabella smiled gently, her fingers delicately tucking a stray hair behind Valentina's ear. "Your father only wants what is best for you. He is protective because he loves you. But remember, he too was once a young man in love, trying to win over a father's heart."

Valentina chuckled, imagining a young Luciano wooing her mother. "Were you ever as confused as I am, Mama?"

Isabella laughed softly, memories of her youth flooding back. "Oh, my dear, if only you knew the half of it. Love is never straightforward, but it is the journey that makes it worthwhile. Trust your heart, but trust your instincts as well. And remember, no matter what, you will always have me."

The two women shared a heartfelt embrace, the weight of their conversation lingering in the air. The evening breeze carried the promise of new beginnings and challenges.

--

As Alex stepped out of the grand villa's gates, the tranquil ambiance of Mondello embraced him. The soft rustling of palm leaves in the midnight breeze and the rhythmic lapping of the sea against the shore orchestrated a harmonious symphony. It was late, and the resort town had settled into a serene stillness, occasionally broken by the distant hum of a passing car or the murmurs of late-night beachgoers.

Though he could have hailed a taxi to return to his hotel, an inner voice urged him to walk, to process the whirlwind of emotions that had stirred within him throughout the evening.

With each step on the paved beachside walkway, his internal conflict seemed mirrored. The moonlight's shimmering reflection on the tranquil waters captivated him, yet his mind raced with the evening's events. Luciano's villa, with its breathtaking view of the beach, symbolized a life filled with contradictions.

In the distance, the soft glow emanating from beachside cafes painted a tranquil scene. Yet, the silhouette of the occasional lone fisherman preparing for a late-night catch reminded him of the simple, honest lives led by many in this town. Lives that stood in stark contrast to the enigmatic world Luciano inhabited.

Valentina's genuine laughter, Isabella's motherly warmth, Luciano's unexpected moments of vulnerability — all seemed at odds with the dossier he had studied. The man described in those pages was ruthless, a kingpin drenched in blood. And yet, the family man he had encountered tonight appeared worlds apart from that image.

Could Luciano, despite his power and alleged crimes, also be a man who loves and is loved in return? he pondered.

His thoughts then turned to Valentina. Her smile, her touch, the way she gazed at him — it was intoxicating. Her confession of burgeoning feelings tugged at his heart, intensifying the anguish caused by his deception. How could he reconcile the genuine affection he felt for her with the duty that bound him?

Lost in contemplation, he scarcely noticed when a taxi slowly approached, its headlights briefly casting a shadow on his path. The driver rolled down the window, offering him a ride. After a moment's hesitation, he decided to continue walking, needing more time alone with his thoughts.

As Mondello gradually transformed into the outskirts of Palermo, the urban landscape began to dominate, and the soothing sounds of the sea faded into the distance. It was then that he resolved to hail the next taxi he encountered, signaling the end of his introspective journey.

Seated comfortably in the taxi, he realized that the days ahead would challenge him in unforeseen ways. He walked a treacherous path between duty and emotion, and as the city lights blurred by, he understood that he must prepare for the inevitable storm that brewed on the horizon.

Chapter 9: The Revelation

Alex's heart raced as he recognized Luciano's unmistakable voice. The introspection and internal conflict of the previous day momentarily took a back seat as he refocused on his mission. The soft static of the bug's transmission filled the room, along with the weighty anticipation of potentially uncovering something significant.

"Yes, I understand. Transfer five million to the London account discreetly," Luciano's voice remained calm yet assertive.

Alex listened intently, jotting down notes. He knew that covertly moving large sums of money often signaled illegal activities.

"And the other amount?" A second voice inquired. The voice was unfamiliar to Alex but carried an air of professionalism.

"Three million to the Cayman account. Ensure it cannot be traced back to us," Luciano responded.

Alex's hands trembled slightly as he documented every detail. This was the evidence he had been hoping for. If he could connect these transactions to any illicit operations in London, it would be a significant breakthrough.

"I have implemented the necessary diversions, Mr. Luciano. As always, they will appear as legitimate business transactions," the accountant reassured.

"Good. And remember, discretion is paramount. If any information were to leak, it could jeopardize everything we have built."

The call abruptly ended, leaving Alex with a pulsating silence and a recording that could alter the course of his mission. However, having the conversation alone was not sufficient; he needed to uncover the destination of this money in London and its purpose.

Taking a deep breath, Alex began drafting a coded message to his contacts back at the agency. The game was intensifying, and with each move, the stakes grew higher. His relationship with Valentina, the bond forming with her family, and now this – it all became an intricate dance of deception and genuine emotion.

Sitting back on his bed, Alex gazed out of the hotel window. The morning sun cast a golden hue on the ancient city of Palermo, painting a beautiful scene that sharply contrasted with the complexity of his situation. He contemplated the choices he would have to make and the consequences they would entail. For now, he must focus on tracing the money and unraveling Luciano's web of operations in London.

--

Valentina's eyes widened in surprise as she spotted Alex leaning against the reception desk, cradling a bouquet of roses in his arms. A warmth spread through her, unable to contain her delight. He always found ways to astonish her.

"Hey," she greeted, her voice resonating softly in the vast hospital corridor.

"Hey yourself," Alex replied with a grin. "Thought I'd surprise my favorite doctor with lunch. Are you too busy to take a short break?"

Valentina shook her head. "I believe I can manage a brief respite. What's the occasion?"

"Do I need one?" He winked, handing her the roses. "Let's just say it's for making my time here unforgettable."

She beamed, inhaling the sweet fragrance of the roses. "Thank you, Alex. They're exquisite." Pausing, she added, "But I'm afraid I'll be working late tonight."

"That's alright," he replied quickly, a tad too quickly, concealing his relief. "I actually have a business meeting tonight. Something unexpected came up."

She arched an eyebrow, playfully remarking, "You and your enigmatic affairs. Sometimes, I feel there's so much about you I have yet to discover."

Alex's heart skipped a beat. Her every word echoed the intricate layers of deception he was managing. "In time, Val," he murmured, gently tucking a stray hair behind her ear, "There's much to unravel."

Lunch became a whirlwind of conversation, touching on everything and nothing. They laughed, flirted, and Alex savored the simplicity of these moments. As they spoke, Valentina occasionally glanced at her phone, her fingers brushing over a notification she wasn't ready to share with him. A flight confirmation. But this wasn't a romantic getaway; it was a business trip, an assignment that tied her even closer to her father's empire than Alex could imagine.

As they bid farewell, Alex held her close. "I'll see you soon, alright? Tomorrow?"

She nodded, her voice tinged with gravity, aware that the secrets they both held might soon come to light.

--

Later, in the quietness of his hotel room, Alex sat, enveloped by the gentle hum of the air conditioner. A slender lead lay before him, a mere Italian name, as common as "John" or "Michael" in the English-speaking world. Without a surname, it felt akin to searching for a needle in a haystack.

Determined, he replayed the recorded conversation, hoping to catch any elusive clue—perhaps a nickname or a meeting place—from Luciano's carefully chosen words. However, Luciano proved to be too cautious, a veteran in the game, never letting slip more than he intended.

Alex pondered the bug he had planted. Could it yield more valuable information? Yet, he knew better than to rely solely on that. He needed to take a proactive approach.

His fingers danced across the keyboard of his laptop, summoning a private and secure browser. Accessing Interpol databases, he meticulously sifted through financial transactions connected to Luciano and his associates. He sought patterns, substantial payments, or consistent transactions that could lead him to the enigmatic accountant.

Hours slipped away, straining Alex's eyes. Just as frustration threatened to consume him, a pattern emerged. A sequence of payments made to a shell company in Milan, unvarying in amount. Delving deeper, he discovered that the company was linked to financial consultancy services.

Could this be the breakthrough he sought?

Alex delved further into the company's records, unearthing its owner, a man named Giuseppe—sharing the same first name. However, countless individuals bore the name Giuseppe. What set this one apart? It was the frequency of contact with Luciano and the nature of the shell company that made him a prime suspect.

With newfound determination, Alex gathered everything he could find on this Giuseppe: photographs, addresses, and known associates. A surge of adrenaline coursed through him; he knew he was inching closer.

Yet, caution prevailed. Directly approaching Giuseppe, if he indeed was Luciano's accountant, could raise suspicions in both of them. Alex decided to keep this lead close, concealed within his pocket. Milan would be his next destination after leaving Palermo, but for now, he would keep this discovery to himself.

Chapter 10: One Last Dance

As the sun began to set, Piazza Pretoria shone in warm hues, illuminating its majestic fountain and sprawling statues. The ancient structures surrounding it cast long shadows across the cobblestone. Alex deliberately chose this location, aware of its romantic ambiance, making it the perfect setting for their final evening together.

After waiting for a few minutes, a black Mercedes pulled up. Valentina stepped out, exuding Italian beauty with her hair flowing freely and dressed in a chic, yet simple dress. Their eyes met, and even from a distance, their connection was undeniable.

Walking towards her, Alex extended his hand and said, "Val, you look absolutely stunning."

She smiled and took his hand. "You look pretty dashing yourself"

They chuckled and began walking hand in hand, their spirits light and playful, trying to momentarily forget the looming reality.

After a short walk, they arrived at 'La Note Blu,' a hidden jazz club known only to locals and the occasional fortunate tourist. The low vaulted ceiling, stone walls, and dim golden lighting created an intimate atmosphere. Soft jazz tunes filled the air, providing a soothing backdrop to their evening.

They found a cozy corner booth and placed their orders. Over a meal of bruschetta, risotto, and fine wine, they engaged in conversations about everything and nothing, completely engrossed in each other's company. The live band started playing, the sultry tones of the saxophone blending seamlessly with the melodious voice of the singer.

"Would you care to dance?" Alex asked, extending his hand.

Valentina smiled and replied, "I thought you'd never ask."

They moved to the dance floor, their bodies swaying in perfect rhythm. The rest of the world faded away, leaving just the two of them in that magical moment.

After their dance and a few more songs, Alex suggested, "How about a walk? The seafront must be breathtaking at this time."

Leaving the jazz club, they were greeted by a gentle breeze as they walked towards the nearby seafront. The sound of waves crashing softly and the city lights reflecting on the water created a serene ambiance. Their conversation deepened as they spoke of dreams, hopes, and the uncertain future.

As midnight approached, Alex said, "I have some wine back at my hotel. Would you like to join me?"

Valentina looked into his eyes, sensing the significance of the evening, and nodded.

At the hotel, they shared a bottle of wine on his terrace, gazing at the Palermo skyline stretching out before them. Words became scarce as they sat, sipping their wine, cherishing the moment.

Eventually, the night led them to his room, where they surrendered to their emotions, culminating in a passionate embrace. The weight of their impending goodbye only deepened their connection.

Later, wrapped in each other's arms on the terrace, they watched as the first light of dawn slowly spread across the city. Both silently vowed to treasure the memories of that night, regardless of what the future held.

--

Golden rays of morning sunlight poured into the hotel room, casting a warm glow upon the pristine white sheets that enveloped them. The distant sounds of Palermo awakening seeped through the windows. Alex and Valentina lay entwined, their breaths harmonizing, lost in the embrace of the room's warmth and the lingering euphoria of the night before.

When the growls of their stomachs became impossible to ignore, Alex ordered a sumptuous breakfast. Trays adorned with fresh pastries, fruits, cheeses, and fragrant Italian coffee arrived, and they indulged in bed, laughter and playful banter filling the air. Their fingers brushed against each other, and tender touches prolonged the intimacy they had shared the night before.

After breakfast, Valentina glanced at the clock. "I must be on my way," she sighed, running her fingers through her tousled hair.

Alex drew her closer, savoring one more lingering kiss. "I'll see you tomorrow at the airport, an early breakfast perhaps?"

She nodded, a hint of longing in her eyes. "After my shift. I wish I could stay, but..."

He silenced her with a gentle touch on her lips. "I understand. Duty beckons."

With one final embrace, she departed. Watching her fade into the distance, a pang of guilt pierced through Alex's heart, mingling with the fading warmth of their shared morning. As much as he treasured their time together, he had a mission to fulfill.

Without delay, Alex immersed himself in his tasks. He reached out to his handler, receiving updates and plans regarding the accountant's whereabouts in Milan. A coded message also arrived, revealing Valentina's deeper involvement in her father's operations. The revelation hit him like a sucker punch, leaving him grappling with conflicting emotions, struggling to reconcile the woman he had grown to care for with this newfound information.

His afternoon became a whirlwind of activity: meetings with contacts, procuring surveillance equipment, and ensuring his movements remained concealed. He meticulously prepared for a clandestine departure, determined to slip away undetected by those closely monitoring him.

As twilight blanketed Palermo, Alex found himself at a familiar spot – the beach bar near Luciano's villa. Sitting there, drink in hand, he gazed at the rhythmic crash of waves upon the shore. He contemplated the intricate web of deception and intrigue in which he was entangled, and pondered Valentina's role within it. Was she genuinely involved or an unwitting pawn?

As night deepened, Alex returned to his hotel room, reviewing his plans for Milan. The following morning would be marked by farewells and new beginnings. The dichotomy of his life – love and duty – had never been more profound.

Chapter 11: Close Encounters in Milan

The bustling coffee shop at Palermo's Falcone-Borsellino Airport was infused with the scent of freshly brewed coffee and warm baked goods. Alex and Valentina sat facing each other, their hands entwined on the petite table. Their half-eaten breakfast seemed insignificant compared to the impending departure that loomed over them.

"I'll be back in a few weeks," Alex assured, gazing deeply into Valentina's eyes. "This isn't farewell, it's merely 'until we meet again'."

Valentina's eyes shimmered, revealing her emotions. "Promise me you'll call when you arrive in London."

Alex hesitated for a brief moment before nodding. "Of course, every step of the way."

Their breakfast was interrupted by prolonged silences and tender gestures. When the announcement for Alex's flight reverberated through the terminal, they both stood up. The space between them was heavy with the strain of farewell. They clung to each other, sharing one last intense kiss.

"Take care of yourself," Valentina whispered into his ear, her voice cracking.

"I will. And you too. I'll see you soon," he whispered back, gently caressing her face.

With one final lingering gaze, Alex turned and made his way to the boarding gate. He could feel her eyes on him until he vanished from sight.

The flight to Milan was brief, but Alex's mind was a whirlwind of thoughts. As the plane touched down and he navigated through the bustling Milan Malpensa Airport, he mentally shifted gears, focusing on the mission ahead.

After retrieving his small bag, Alex hailed a taxi and provided the driver with the address of his Airbnb. During the drive, he took in the cosmopolitan city's blend of contemporary skyscrapers and historic architecture.

His Airbnb was a modern loft apartment tucked away in an unassuming building. Its primary allure, for Alex's purposes, was the unobstructed view it offered of the accountant's office across the street. Upon entering the apartment, he swiftly familiarized himself with its layout. The expansive windows in the living area provided an ideal vantage point.

Changing into athletic attire, donning a baseball cap, glasses, and even affixing a fake beard for added measure, Alex inspected himself in the mirror, content that even someone who knew him well would struggle to recognize him.

He positioned his high-resolution camera with a zoom lens on a tripod, ensuring a clear view of the accountant's office. Adjacent to it, he placed a listening device, ready to be discreetly planted inside the office should an opportunity arise.

The hours melded into a stakeout as he observed, eagerly waiting for any sign of the accountant or any clue that would propel his mission forward. Occasionally, he would jot down notes, capturing details and timing, constructing a profile of routines.

As twilight descended upon Milan, Alex contemplated the dichotomy of his existence. Just this morning, he shared an intimate breakfast with Valentina in Palermo, and now he found himself immersed in deception in Milan. The contrast was stark.

Settling into the night, he prepared himself for the lengthy surveillance that lay ahead, hopeful that the next day would yield the breakthrough he desperately sought.

The distinct clatter of a tram's wheels against the rails stirred Alex from his sleep. Rubbing his eyes and stretching, he peered out of the window, checking the building across the street. The early morning light bathed the Milanese streets as the city began to awaken.

Feeling the pangs of hunger, he descended the stairs to the quaint bar attached to his building. The aroma of fresh coffee and baked goods wafted through the air, almost as captivating as Valentina's perfume. Taking a seat by the window, he had a clear view of the entrance to the accountant's office.

As he relished the rich flavor of his cappuccino, dipping a freshly baked croissant into the velvety foam (a breakfast routine he had come to adore in Palermo), a familiar face caught his attention. It was him – the accountant.

The man walked briskly, a leather satchel draped over his shoulder, engrossed in a phone call. Without hesitation, Alex abandoned his breakfast, pushed away from the table, and hastily crossed the street. His pulse quickened; this was the opportunity he had been waiting for.

Entering the opulent lobby of the building, with its marble floors and shimmering chandeliers, a striking contrast to his more modest Airbnb, he spotted the accountant once again. The man stood by the elevator, still deep in conversation.

Alex reached into his pocket, his fingers brushing against the small listening device he had prepared earlier. Timing was crucial. Approaching the accountant, he feigned clumsiness, lightly bumping into him. "Mi dispiace," Alex muttered an apology, ensuring that in that fleeting moment, the bug found its way into the inner pocket of the accountant's finely tailored jacket.

With that accomplished, he swiftly retreated, unwilling to linger and arouse suspicion. Returning to his apartment, he set up the receiving end of the bug. The speaker crackled to life, and soon, the sounds of the accountant's office filled the room. The distant murmur of conversations, the tapping of computer keyboards, and the accountant's voice discussing figures and transactions echoed throughout the cozy loft space.

Alex felt a surge of adrenaline. Now, with both visual and audio access, he was perfectly positioned to gather the evidence he needed. Every conversation, every transaction, every piece of the puzzle was within his grasp.

Chapter 12: London Calling

Valentina's plane smoothly touched down at Gatwick Airport, and the familiar buzz of the city immediately embraced her. London had always been a striking contrast to the chaotic streets of Palermo, with its rapid pace and gleaming skyscrapers. However, today Valentina wasn't here to soak in the sights or indulge in leisure; she had a mission.

Clad in a sharp business suit, a far cry from her usual relaxed Palermo style, she moved with purpose. The Hilton Hotel became her first destination. After swiftly checking in, she wasted no time and made a call. The voice on the other end was curt and businesslike. They discussed timings, confirming plans that were already set in motion. The meeting at the O2 Arena stood as her primary objective.

The arena, with its iconic dome structure, would soon host a medical conference with a special focus on Dr. Enzo Bellini's groundbreaking treatment for addiction. Bellini's findings had sent shockwaves through the medical community, and tomorrow he would present his research to his peers and potential investors.

However, Valentina's interest lay not in the research itself, but beneath the very stage where Dr. Bellini would stand. Her objective: to discreetly plant a device there before the event commenced.

After scouting the venue, she realized she had a narrow window in the early morning when the stage setup would take place. It would be her best opportunity to slip in unnoticed and place the device.

That evening, Valentina dined quietly in her hotel room, meticulously going over the plan in her mind. Balancing her family's delicate matters with her personal life had always been her forte. The next morning, she knew, would put her resolve to the ultimate test.

As dawn broke, she arrived at the O2. With the confidence of someone who belonged there, she swiftly made her way backstage. The hustle and bustle of the crew setting up provided the perfect cover. She identified the spot, planted the device, and just as swiftly, made her exit.

By the time the conference attendees began to fill the arena, Valentina had seamlessly blended in. Sporting her medical ID from the Palermo hospital prominently displayed, she took a seat at the back of the hall. Her credentials as a doctor were not merely for show. Addiction posed one of the most significant challenges her hospital faced. She listened intently to the speakers, absorbing the information and analyzing how it might impact her hospital's approach to treating addiction.

But beneath her genuine interest in the subject, lay a dark truth. Addiction was also a substantial source of her father's wealth. While she genuinely cared about her patients and wanted the best for them, she couldn't ignore her family's deep entanglement in the very crisis they were discussing. The duality of her life was evident as she sat there, torn between her dedication to medicine and her loyalty to her family.

--

The gentle hum of Milan's midday traffic filtered through the apartment's window. Alex sat hunched over the desk, his eyes fixed on the screen displaying the feed from the listening device. Hours passed, and apart from mundane calls and transaction confirmations, there was no significant information.

However, as afternoon turned into early evening, Giuseppe received a call that heightened Alex's senses. The voice on the other end was undoubtedly Luciano's.

"Giuseppe, it's imperative we move the money by tomorrow," Luciano's voice came through, carrying a sense of urgency.

"I understand, Luciano," Giuseppe cautiously replied, "but the sum is substantial. It will draw attention."

There was a brief silence before Luciano responded, "I'm well aware. But there are certain urgencies. We need to divert it into the London account. Our operations can't come to a halt."

Giuseppe let out a sigh, "Alright. I'll make the necessary arrangements. But we must tread carefully. Our moves are being watched."

The call ended, and Alex's mind raced. This was the evidence he had been seeking. Luciano was taking steps to move his assets, and Alex was on the verge of uncovering more than he had hoped for.

As night began to fall, Giuseppe left his office. Alex, making sure not to draw attention, followed at a distance. The streets of Milan, illuminated by the warm glow of street lamps, bustled with evening activity. Finally, Giuseppe stopped at an upscale restaurant and made his way inside.

Alex took a moment to contemplate, then decided to follow. He would delve deeper into the enigma of the Sicilian mafia's operations in Milan, still blissfully unaware that Valentina was on an entirely different mission in London.

As the Milanese twilight dissolved, the allure of neon signs and the gentle hum of evening activity took over. Alex's camera, his silent accomplice, documented the clandestine movements of a man who concealed his true life behind a public facade.

The mistress was striking - a young woman whose beauty emanated not only from her symmetrical features but also from her vibrant energy. She possessed the kind of allure that turned heads and paused conversations in mid-sentence. With cascading dark hair and a figure that exuded both youth and maturity, she tastefully accentuated her form with her attire. Her dress clung to her like a whispered secret, bold yet elegant.

In stark contrast, Giuseppe embodied middle-aged complacency and indulgence. Deep wrinkles creased the corners of his eyes, telling stories of years gone by - years that had transformed him from an ambitious youth into a man bound by the life he had built. A life now marked by hidden indiscretions. While an accountant on paper, Alex had discovered from the Interpol files that Giuseppe's reality was far more intricate and shaded. He lived a double life.

Their intimacy felt incongruous, amplified by the disparity in their ages. Amidst the backdrop of fine dining and the clinking of expensive cutlery, their laughter echoed. Leaving the restaurant, Giuseppe's arm wrapped around the young woman, their different strides underscored the contrast - his steady and calculated, hers sprightly and carefree.

Alex observed and waited, capturing images that silently testified to Giuseppe's secret life. Eventually, the couple disappeared into the accountant's office, a space meant for balance sheets and ledgers but now transformed into a private stage for forbidden acts.

From across the street, concealed in shadows, Alex's lens captured images that would shatter Giuseppe's facade of fidelity. These photographs held more than mere evidence; they held power.

As dawn approached, Giuseppe emerged from the apartment building, bidding farewell to the woman he had promised to spend his life with - a promise now fractured by his actions. The morning kiss he shared with his wife, captured relentlessly by Alex's camera, became a tragic pantomime of the commitment he had forsaken.

In this game of shadows and deception, these images possessed a potent currency in Alex's hands - a currency of influence. Yet with every snapshot, he felt a twinge of conflict, knowing that each revelation of Giuseppe's infidelity brought him closer to completing his mission but further away from the possibility of a normal life with Valentina.

Chapter 13: A Precise Calamity

Within the O2 Arena, a specific hall witnessed the calculated devastation of an explosion, executed with clinical precision. Once a hub of intellectual discourse and medical promise, the room now lay in ruins, engulfed in calculated chaos.

The hall's elegant royal blue drapes, now blackened and tattered, hung mournfully, bearing witness to the tragedy. Scattered across the room were overturned chairs, some marked with the scorch of the explosion. The dais, where the keynote speaker had delivered their address, remained eerily untouched, save for the slight tilt of the microphone.

With coordinated efficiency, emergency response teams flooded into the hall, a stark contrast to the scene of disarray. While most attendees managed to escape serious harm, the shock and terror were etched on their faces. Some received oxygen, others sought solace, while many grappled with the abrupt shift from enlightening discourse to a nightmarish reality.

The sole casualty, the keynote speaker, lay motionless, covered near the podium. He was the intended target, a victim of a bomb meticulously packed despite its small size. Amidst the contained destruction, his lifeless form spoke of a deliberate act, not aimed at spreading panic, but at eliminating one man.

Minutes before the blast, Valentina discreetly slipped away, her exit unnoticed. She moved purposefully, each step betraying a foreknowledge of the impending catastrophe. There was no panic, no furtive glances over her shoulder, only a calm and methodical retreat.

In the sanctuary of her suite at the Hilton, Valentina sought to distance herself from the scene. She filled the bathtub, allowing the steaming water to envelop her, perhaps in an attempt to cleanse herself of the day's actions. Pouring a glass of deep red Nero D'avola, she tasted the familiar flavors of home, a stark contrast to the cold calculations that had marked her day.

Her well-planned and precisely executed actions weighed heavily on her conscience. The bath, the wine, and her attempts at respite offered only temporary escape from a reality growing increasingly complex and dark. The repercussions of the day's events would inevitably extend to unforeseen shores. Valentina, ensnared in her self-made web, could only wonder about the consequences that lay ahead.

--

As sunlight streamed through the delicate curtains of Valentina's hotel room, a new day dawned, in stark contrast to the preceding evening's events. She stretched languidly in the embrace of luxurious sheets, the weight of yesterday replaced by the buoyancy of today's plans. Her thoughts turned to Alex, to rekindling the moments of romance and surprise they had shared. Memories of their time in Palermo flickered through her mind like a cherished film reel.

Reaching for her phone, she dialed his number, her heart fluttering with anticipation.

The ringtone echoed, awaiting the familiar sound of his voice. And then, "Hello?"

"Hey there, it's Valentina," her voice carried a playful, teasing tone. "Can you guess where I am?"

After a momentary pause, Alex responded in surprise, "Val? This is unexpected! Where are you?"

With a giggle, Valentina revealed, "I'm in London! I wanted to surprise you. Maybe we could grab a coffee or have lunch? Or perhaps something more," she added, her voice taking a sultry tone.

There was a longer pause this time. Alex, now entangled in his own web of deceit, struggled for words. He was actually in Milan, not London. "Um... Valentina, that sounds amazing, but..."

"But what?" she asked, sensing that something was amiss.

"I... I had an emergency meeting. It came up last minute," he hesitated, carefully choosing his words, "I'm in Manchester for the day."

Valentina's brow furrowed. This was not what she had expected. "Manchester? When will you be back?"

"Late tonight, maybe early tomorrow. I'm truly sorry, Val. If only I had known, I would have rescheduled," Alex's voice filled with apology, tinged with a hint of panic.

A sigh escaped Valentina's lips as her dreamy day suddenly faded away. "It's alright, Alex. We can always catch up later. I understand the demands of business." She tried to sound cheerful, but her disappointment was evident.

"We'll make it up, I promise. How about tomorrow? Lunch? Anything you desire," he said, hoping to lighten the mood.

She let out a small laugh, "Alright, Mr. Busy. Tomorrow it is. Just don't leave me hanging."

"I wouldn't dare. I'm already counting down the hours."

--

The sun hung low in the Milanese sky as Alex hurriedly packed his belongings. The captivating turn of events had altered his plans. With Valentina in London, he needed to return swiftly. Given the urgency, a commercial flight wouldn't suffice. Dialing a number he had saved for critical situations, he arranged for a private plane to whisk him directly from Milan's Linate Airport to London City Airport.

The plane exuded sleekness, resembling a silver bullet against the backdrop of the azure sky. Inside, the muted colors of the cabin contrasted with the vibrant landscape racing beneath. During the short flight, he contemplated the intricacies of his life—the secrets, the passions, and the responsibilities.

Upon landing, the bustling hum of London embraced him. The city was an orchestra of sounds, sights, and emotions, and amidst it all stood The Shard, piercing the sky with its 95 stories of glass and steel.

His apartment on one of the upper floors of this iconic building epitomized modern luxury. The interiors exuded a minimalist charm, dominated by blacks, whites, and greys, occasionally punctuated by splashes of color in the form of artwork or decorative pieces. The furniture was sleek, more functional than ornate, perfectly befitting a bachelor pad. Yet, there was an undeniable warmth, a personal touch. Whether it was the well-stocked bar boasting select labels of scotch and bourbon or the state-of-the-art entertainment system, it was evident that a man of taste resided here.

However, the pièce de résistance was undoubtedly the view. Floor-to-ceiling windows offered a panoramic vista of London, stretching from the meandering Thames to iconic landmarks such as the Tower Bridge and St. Paul's Cathedral, and beyond. In the daytime, it resembled a sprawling urban jungle, and at night, it transformed into a galaxy of lights—a city that truly never slept.

Yet, amidst all its grandeur, Alex barely had time to appreciate it now. Swiftly dropping off his bags, he took a moment to freshen up, applying a dash of his signature aftershave, before heading for the elevator. The descent felt unusually long, as anticipation caused every second to stretch.

When the elevator doors slid open at the lobby, there she was. Valentina, her eyes sparkling with mischief and joy, donning a simple yet elegant dress that accentuated her natural beauty. Turning towards the elevator, her gaze met Alex's, and in that fleeting moment, all the complexities, deceptions, and dangers of their worlds faded away, leaving only the two of them and the magic they created together.

The dining area at The Shard was a masterclass In elegance and exclusivity. Towering windows framed the sprawling city, with the fading evening light painting the skyline in hues of orange and purple. The gentle notes of a piano in the background intertwined with the low murmurs of other diners, creating a cozy cocoon amidst the vast expanse of the city.

Alex and Valentina were escorted to a prime spot, a table right next to the window. As they settled into their plush chairs, an opulent chandelier overhead bathed them in a golden glow. The view was nothing short of spectacular—the meandering Thames, the iconic landmarks, and the city lights beginning to twinkle. Yet, despite its beauty, an initial awkwardness lingered between them.

Valentina, her lips curling into a slight smile, ventured, "The view is truly breathtaking."

"Indeed," Alex agreed, momentarily gazing out before turning his attention back to her. "Although I must confess, Palermo's sunset holds a certain charm at this very moment."

She chuckled softly. "Are you implying that you miss Sicily?"

He leaned in, his voice filled with playfulness. "Perhaps. Or maybe I'm just biased because of the company I had there."

The ice began to melt as they reminisced about their shared moments in Sicily, weaving a tapestry of cherished memories and laughter. Valentina couldn't help but burst into laughter as she recalled a particularly clumsy dance move Alex had attempted at a beachside bar. "You nearly sent that poor waiter flying with his tray!"

Alex groaned theatrically. "I had hoped you had forgotten about that. But, in my defense, I may have had one too many Aperols."

As they delved deeper into their memories, the waiter discreetly approached, placing menus before them. They exchanged recommendations and playfully teased each other's culinary preferences. "You and your peculiar fondness for chili chocolate," Alex remarked.

"It's an acquired taste," Valentina defended with a smirk, "much like your preference for... what was it again? Ah yes, octopus salad."

They seamlessly transitioned from one memory to the next – the exhilarating motorcycle rides, the hidden beaches they had stumbled upon, the misadventures, and the serendipitous moments. The evening was punctuated with hearty laughter, good-natured banter, and occasional touches – hands overlapping, fingers entwined.

By the time the main course gave way to desserts – her tiramisu oozing with the essence of coffee and his indulgent chocolate mousse – the weight of their hidden truths had begun to dissipate. Within the confines of their shared memories, the complexities of their present faded, if only for a while.

As they exited the restaurant, making their way towards the elevators, Alex looked at Valentina, his voice tender. "Tonight was... perfect. Thank you."

She smiled warmly. "No, thank you. For the memories we've created and the many more that lie ahead."

The familiar chime of the elevator marked their arrival at Alex's apartment. As the doors slid open, Valentina was greeted with a breathtaking sight. Floor-to-ceiling windows offered an uninterrupted panoramic view of the sprawling city below. The skyline came alive with shimmering lights, pulsating with energy. The apartment itself exemplified refined minimalism, adorned with muted grays, plush white carpets, and strategically placed modern art.

A gentle touch on her arm redirected Valentina's attention to Alex. His eyes held a mix of anticipation and vulnerability. Without a word, he led her deeper into the living space, past a sleek kitchen and a cozy sitting area, until they reached a door that opened into his bedroom.

Like the rest of the apartment, the bedroom embodied a fusion of modern elegance and simplicity. The centerpiece was a large bed draped in silvery silk sheets that seemed to glisten under the ambient lighting. However, it was the view that truly stole the show. The bed was strategically positioned to create the illusion of floating amidst the London skyline.

Valentina's fingers delicately traced patterns over the smooth silk as Alex approached from behind, wrapping his arms around her waist and pulling her close. Their combined warmth dispelled the chill from the expansive windows. "The view is mesmerizing," she whispered, her breath causing a tingle on his bare neck.

"Just like you," he murmured in response, turning her around to face him.

What followed was a dance as timeless as the ages. Their lips met, hands gently explored, and they gave and took in a way that felt simultaneously familiar and thrillingly new. The world outside faded away as they lost themselves in each other, with the vibrant city lights serving as a backdrop to their passion.

As the hours melded into one another, their frenzied urgency gave way to tender caresses and whispered words amidst the sheets. With dawn approaching, they lay entwined in each other's arms, the silk sheets cradling them as they gazed out at the awakening city.

Valentina rested her head on Alex's chest, listening to the rhythmic beating of his heart. Her fingers lazily traced patterns on his skin as they both drifted into a peaceful slumber, the warmth of their embrace contrasting with the cool beauty of the London sky.

The sharp ringtone of Alex's phone shattered the gentle morning haze. Startled awake, he glanced at the screen to see the name *Jameson* flashing. He answered immediately.

Valentina watched through sleepy eyes as he responded with short, affirmative sentences, his expression growing increasingly serious. "I'm on my way," he finally said before ending the call.

He looked at Valentina, his eyes filled with apology. "I'm sorry, Val. Something urgent has come up at work. I need to go to the office."

Valentina, though groggy, tried to sound understanding. "Of course, Alex. Do what you need to do."

With a lingering kiss and promises of his swift return, Alex hastily dressed and left the apartment. Valentina heard the faint sound of the elevator doors closing in the distance.

Basking in the lingering glow of their passionate night, Valentina's innate curiosity was piqued. She quietly embarked on a tour of Alex's apartment, finding the main living space meticulously organized, reflecting a sense of precision and order. Each book, gadget, and piece of furniture had its designated place.

Yet, it was an inconspicuous safe tucked beneath Alex's desk that captivated her attention. Its small and sleek design hinted at its high-end nature. Valentina couldn't help but wonder about its contents. What could someone involved in investments want to conceal? A flicker of jealousy momentarily consumed her. Could it hold remnants of past relationships or confidential work documents?

Valentina hesitated, torn between respecting Alex's privacy and her burning desire for answers. She shook her head, realizing it was not her place to pry. Taking a deep breath, she made her way back to the bedroom to get dressed.

However, just as she was about to leave the desk behind, her eyes fell upon a picture frame, facing downwards. Gently picking it up, she discovered a photograph of a younger Alex standing beside a woman she presumed to be his mother. Their shared smile and the warmth emanating from the image tugged at her heartstrings.

Carefully returning the photograph to its place and adjusting it with precision, Valentina retreated to the bedroom. The safe and its potential secrets lingered in her mind, but she pushed those thoughts aside, acknowledging that some things were better left unexplored, at least for now.

--

The conference room, situated on one of the highest floors of the MI6 building, basked in the soft glow of London's early afternoon sun. Through the expansive glass windows on one side, the city's skyline unfolded, with the Thames meandering through it. Inside the room, adorned with a rich mahogany table, plush leather chairs, and state-of-the-art video conferencing system, an air of authority and seriousness prevailed.

Seated at the head of the table was Jameson, Alex's boss, exuding his usual sharpness. A tall man in his late fifties, with meticulously groomed steel-gray hair and piercing blue eyes that revealed nothing, he seemed to absorb every detail. Despite his age, he radiated an undeniable vigor. His charcoal-gray suit fit him flawlessly, and the dark tie he wore served as a deliberate reminder of the gravity of their mission.

To Jameson's right sat Agent Thompson, a woman of African descent in her mid-thirties. With a stylish afro and keen hazel eyes that observed her surroundings with precision, she was renowned for her analytical skills and composure under pressure. Dressed in a smart navy blue blazer over a crisp white shirt, her discreetly glinting earpiece added to her air of professionalism.

Beside her was Agent Mitchel, a distinct Liverpudlian in his early forties. He possessed the refined Merseyside accent associated with the city's more affluent suburbs. Tall, with sandy hair and sharp features, Mitchel's background in psychological operations made him particularly skilled at extracting information. Today, he exuded elegance in a well-tailored beige suit.

Alex took his seat, appreciating the collective experience and expertise assembled in the room. The screen behind Jameson displayed various details pertaining to their mission, including photographs of the accountant, Giuseppe, and snippets of the intelligence Alex had gathered.

"Very well," Jameson commenced, "We're all aware of the significance of obtaining those account numbers, and leveraging Giuseppe presents our best opportunity. Thompson, Mitchel, please elaborate on the approach."

Agent Thompson leaned forward, "Utilizing the photos Alex acquired, we have a distinct advantage. Our aim is to subtly corner Giuseppe in a location where he feels secure. The vulnerability he exhibits with his young mistress in those images is unmistakable."

Mitchel continued, his refined Liverpool accent permeating his words, "Once we have Giuseppe in a compromised state, we will emphasize the potential consequences. A scandal, a shattered family, professional disgrace. These are stakes he will want to avoid. Given the age difference and the provocative nature of the photographs, he will be more than willing to cooperate. We need only hint at the possibility of these images reaching his family or professional circle."

Jameson nodded, "It is crucial that we handle this situation with finesse. Giuseppe serves as our link to Luciano."

--

The Shard stood tall as a sentinel, overlooking London. From Alex's apartment, the sprawling city unfolded beneath, offering a mesmerizing view. As he stepped into his modern dwelling, the gentle lighting softened the edges of its minimalist design. Whites and chromes dominated the space, punctuated by abstract art on the walls, adding splashes of color. The living area, bathed in the warm orange hue of the setting sun, was illuminated by the signature floor-to-ceiling windows.

Valentina reclined on the plush white leather couch, engrossed in a book. As Alex entered, her striking eyes met his, a blend of curiosity and warmth shining through. Her relaxed attire—a loose-fitting tee and jeans—contrasted with the tension he had seen in her for days.

"Hey," Alex greeted, his voice betraying a hint of weariness, yet his eyes sparkled with hidden excitement.

Valentina sat up, setting her book aside. "You seem to be in a good mood. What happened?"

He grinned, removing his jacket and draping it over a chair. "Some clients I was supposed to meet today postponed our meeting, so I have a few days free. How about I join you in Palermo? Apparently, there are some 'investors' I need to touch base with there."

Surprise danced in Valentina's widened eyes. "Really? That's unexpected, but... a pleasant surprise." A cautious smile played on her lips. "Does this mean we get to spend more time together here in London?"

He nodded, closing the distance between them and enveloping her in a gentle embrace. "Absolutely. We can explore the city, have dinners, or simply unwind." Pausing, his voice turned more serious. "Val, when I said I wanted to spend time with you, I meant it. Despite the complexities of our lives."

Valentina gazed up at him, her expression softening. "I want that too, Alex. These past few days have been a whirlwind, but when I'm with you, everything feels... simpler."

They remained in each other's arms, oblivious to the world beyond. The glow of the setting sun enveloped them, casting a golden hue over the room, and for a fleeting moment, perfection seemed within reach.

Alex pulled back slightly, locking eyes with Valentina. "Since we have some time today, how about we go somewhere special?"

An intrigued eyebrow arched on Valentina's face. "Oh? And where would that be?"

He grinned mischievously, the playful glint returning to his eyes. "Borough Market. Have you ever been?"

She shook her head. "No, but I've heard of it. Isn't it one of the oldest and most renowned food markets in London?"

"Exactly," he responded. "It's a paradise for those who appreciate fine cuisine. And I have a few favorite spots there that we could explore. Fresh cheeses, artisanal bread, and exotic spices from around the world. Furthermore, I thought we could gather some ingredients."

Valentina gazed at him with a curious smile. "Ingredients for what?"

He leaned closer, whispering in a conspiratorial tone, "I was considering cooking for you tonight. A special dinner. How does that sound?"

She laughed, wrapping her arms around his neck. "Sounds like an offer I can't refuse. Handsome and a chef? Is there anything you can't do?"

Alex chuckled, giving her a playful wink. "Well, I do have a few tricks up my sleeve. But first, let's head to Borough Market. Are you ready?"

She nodded, excitement gleaming in her eyes. "Absolutely. Let's embark on this culinary adventure."

--

The vibrant energy of Borough Market enveloped Alex and Valentina as they entered the bustling space. Stalls adorned with a kaleidoscope of fresh produce, artisanal cheeses, and sizzling street food stretched as far as the eye could see. The air buzzed with animated conversations, the cries of vendors, and the enticing aroma of diverse cuisines melding together.

They made their way to a cheese stall, where Valentina selected a wedge of aged cheddar, taking a small bite and emitting a contented "Mmm."

"This is heavenly, Alex," she exclaimed, handing him a piece. "So rich and tangy!"

He grinned, savoring the cheese. "That's one of the things I adore about this market. Everything is so fresh and bursting with flavors."

She nodded in agreement, her gaze drawn to a nearby stall showcasing an assortment of vibrant tomatoes. "Look at those. You can almost taste the sun in them."

They approached the stall, Alex carefully choosing the ripest tomatoes. "You know, Val, there's something enchanting about cooking with fresh ingredients. It's like bringing nature's palette to your plate."

Valentina smiled, her hand brushing against a bundle of fresh basil. "I can see the passion in your eyes. Cooking is clearly more than just a hobby for you."

"It is," he confessed. "There's an art to it, an alchemy. Taking raw ingredients and transforming them into something extraordinary."

Their shopping spree continued, with each stall offering something delightful. At a fishmonger's, Alex selected a piece of fresh salmon, while Valentina convinced him to purchase some jumbo prawns, their shells shimmering. At a greengrocer's, they gathered zucchini, asparagus, and fragrant garlic.

Finally, they came across a charming wine stall, where they discovered a bottle of Nero D'Avola, a homage to their time in Sicily. With a smile, Valentina remarked, "It's our wine," reminiscing about their shared memories.

As they continued strolling through the market, Alex's eyes caught sight of an old English pub tucked away in a quaint side alley. "Shall we take a brief respite before heading back?" he suggested.

Valentina's expression lit up as she gazed upon the pub's timbered I. "It looks so inviting! Let's go."

Upon entering, they were welcomed by the pub's softly lit interior, exuding a cozy ambiance. Settling into a secluded corner table, they ordered pints of ale. With each clink of their glasses and every shared story, their connection growing stronger with every laugh and whispered confidence.

As they bid farewell to the pub, the sun began its descent, casting a warm golden glow upon the streets of London. Armed with bags of fresh ingredients and a spring in their steps, they made their way back to Alex's apartment, anticipation building for an unforgettable evening ahead.

The sleek kitchen was bathed in the soft glow of pendant lights, creating a warm ambiance. The windows offered a breathtaking panorama of the London skyline, painted in a magical hue by the golden hour.

Valentina occupied a seat at the dining table, adorned with a pristine white tablecloth. The perfectly placed cutlery flanked each immaculate plate. The air carried the tantalizing aroma of a freshly cooked meal, a testament to Alex's culinary prowess.

Approaching the table, Alex carried a large serving dish brimming with a perfectly seared salmon, resting on a bed of garlic-sautéed asparagus and zucchini. The golden and crisp giant prawns sat invitingly atop the salmon. The enticing scent alone was enough to make one's mouth water.

Setting the dish down, he looked at Valentina and grinned. "Mangia," he said playfully, recalling their shared moment in Palermo.

Valentina laughed, noting the Italian vibe he had embraced. "You really got into this Italian spirit, didn't you?"

He nodded, pouring them each a glass of wine. However, as he settled into his chair, his playful demeanor shifted. His usually lively eyes now carried a weight.

Immediately noticing the change, Valentina's concern filled her gaze. "What is it, Alex?"

Taking a deep breath, he hesitated for a moment. "Valentina," he began, his voice soft but firm, "I haven't been completely honest with you about something. There have been whispers and rumors, and I've received information about... your father."

Her frown deepened, her pulse quickening. "My father? What about him?"

Alex met her gaze squarely. "I've been informed that he might be involved in some shady business. Now, I want to hear it from you. Can you tell me everything you know about your father's operations?"

Valentina's eyes widened, clearly taken aback by his statement. She tightened her grip on the wine glass, her fingers turning white. "Alex, my father's business... well, it's family business. I've always been kept out of the details."

Leaning forward, Alex's intense gaze remained unwavering. "Valentina, if we are to have a future together, I need to know that I'm not walking into something dangerous. Secrets can be barriers, even dangers. I need to understand what we're dealing with."

She took a deep breath, her chest rising and falling noticeably. "Alex, I understand why you'd be concerned. My family's reputation in Palermo isn't the cleanest. But I promise you, I've always kept my distance. I've chosen medicine, healing people, not getting involved in the other... aspects."

Alex sighed, rubbing the back of his neck.

Hurt and betrayal flashed across Valentina's expression. "So, you've been investigating my family?"

"No!" Alex quickly interjected, genuine panic in his eyes. "Val, it's not like that. I... I've been meaning to tell you something too. Something about my own work. But every time I try, I can't find the right words."

Valentina stared at him, her eyes searching his for answers. "Alex, if we're being open and honest, then let's lay everything on the table. Now."

He took a trembling breath, grappling with his internal conflict. "Valentina, I don't work in investments, well I do, but. My role... it's more intricate than that. I'm involved in intelligence, and at times, my work intersects with individuals engaged in activities that are, let's say, not entirely legal. But I promise you, meeting you, loving you, was never part of any assignment. It was genuine."

She blinked, processing his words. The gravity of the situation hung heavily between them. Valentina leaned back, taking a moment to gather her thoughts, her fingers toying with the rim of her glass. The view from the Shard was breathtaking, but the atmosphere in the room had turned somber.

"You've been forthcoming about wanting to know more, so allow me to shed some light. My father," she began with a slightly cautious tone, "isn't just any businessman. He is the money man, the business figure of the mafia. When they require their money to be laundered, he's the person they turn to. When they seek ways to safeguard and expand their operations, he's the mind behind it."

Alex's face remained impassive, yet he could feel his heart rate quicken as he processed her words.

Valentina continued, her voice resolute yet tinged with melancholy, "You may think it's all about power and privilege, but that comes with an ever-present shadow. He is committed, and sometimes, it's nearly an addiction to him. However, there's a side that many never see. He yearns for legitimacy, to step away from the criminal world and establish a genuine reputation."

She sighed, her gaze drifting momentarily. "But that's the dilemma of being so deeply entrenched in this world. It's not easy to simply walk away. My father's identity is intertwined with it. On one hand, he is the loving man who raised me, who shared laughter at my silly jokes, who comforted me during difficult times. But on the other hand, he is someone I know can be... ruthless."

Leaning forward, she locked eyes with Alex. "Now, you've been honest about certain things, and while I appreciate it, I can't help but wonder, what are you keeping from me?"

Alex swallowed, taken aback by her directness. "Val, it's not that simple. I—"

She gently interrupted him, "No, Alex. If we're going to do this, lay it all bare, then it must be complete transparency. No half-truths."

He nodded, taking a deep breath, preparing himself for the forthcoming conversation. Valentina, absorbing the weight of her own revelations, now found herself faced with another set of disclosures. Alex's expression was serious, his eyes reflecting a blend of concern, determination, and hesitation. The room, illuminated by the city's glow, transformed into a stage for a delicate dance of truth.

"I am indeed involved in investments, Valentina. That's true. But it's not in the way you imagine," Alex began slowly, carefully choosing his words. "It's not about managing funds or advising affluent clients. It's about investigating those investments that conceal darker realities."

Valentina furrowed her brow slightly, her forehead wrinkling as she tried to grasp the implications of his statement.

Alex continued, "I gather intelligence, insights, and evidence on illicit deals and transactions that exploit and harm others. Unfortunately, these deals impact numerous innocent people."

A shiver ran down Valentina's spine. She couldn't discern if it was from his words or the way he delivered them. His confession was methodical, layering each brick carefully, ensuring he didn't ensnare her with his words but instead paved a path for her to follow.

"When we first met, when all of this started... I had no knowledge of your father or his operations. I swear," he emphasized, hoping she could sense the sincerity in his voice. "Only recently did certain things come to light, connecting his name to the type of cases I handle. That's why I've been distant lately. It's not about us; it's about the conflict between my work and our relationship."

There was a moment of silence. The city's hum outside seemed more pronounced. They stood at the edge of trust, both aware that the next words spoken could make or break their bond.

Valentina's voice was gentle yet resolute when she finally spoke, "So, where does that leave us, Alex? What does it mean for... this?" She motioned vaguely between them, underscoring the intangible connection they shared.

Valentina's eyes, which had previously reflected a mix of hurt and confusion, now assumed an expression of profound contemplation. Alex tightened his grip around her hand, his intense emotions unmistakable.

"I love you, Valentina," he began, his voice infused with a passionate sincerity. "Please believe that what I'm about to ask is solely because I need to protect you, and perhaps, safeguard our future."

Her heart raced. Despite the gravity of their conversation, the mere declaration of his love evoked a surge of emotions within her. Yet, she suppressed them, focusing solely on his words.

"Val, have you ever been directly involved in your father's affairs?" he asked gently, searching her face for any trace of deceit.

Meeting his gaze, her eyes remained clear and resolute. "No, Alex. I am aware of his dealings, but he has always shielded me from direct involvement. Although I am his daughter, he has endeavored to keep me safe, away from his world."

Alex nodded slowly, absorbing her words. "Valentina, I urge you to exercise extreme caution. Based on the information that has come across my desk, your father is treading a perilous path. And sometimes, those close to the primary target can become collateral damage."

A weighty silence descended upon them. Valentina's mind raced, attempting to piece together the implications. Finally, she whispered, "What can we do, Alex? How can we navigate through this treacherous terrain?"

"We will find a way," he replied with unwavering determination, pulling her closer. "Together."

--

In Alex's luxurious penthouse, the softly lit room was filled with the tantalizing scent of expertly seasoned dishes. Despite the slight disruption caused by their previous conversation, the ambiance began to mend as Alex endeavored to steer the evening back into familiar territory. The mesmerizing city view, the gentle flicker of candlelight, and the meticulously set table once again captured their undivided attention.

With a half-smile, Alex began, attempting to lighten the atmosphere, "You know, I did slave away in the kitchen for this. We might as well savor it while it's still warm."

Valentina responded with a soft laugh, a genuine smile illuminating her eyes. "Alright, Mr. Chef, let's dig in."

As they indulged in the shared meal, the tension gradually dissolved, the couple striving to momentarily forget the profound revelations that had just unfolded.

--

Meanwhile, in the operations room of the MI6 building, an air of urgency permeated the atmosphere. Expansive screens displayed live feeds, intricate data streams, and complex mapping. Diligently, agents and intelligence officers worked to assemble the puzzle surrounding the O2 bombing.

Agent Jameson, exuding a commanding presence and seasoned demeanor, meticulously scrutinized every detail. While reviewing a list of event attendees, a particular entry caught his attention. He motioned for an analyst nearby. "Retrieve the payment details for this ticket," he demanded, pointing at Valentina Massotti's name.

A few minutes later, a young analyst named Lisa returned with the requested information. "Sir, this ticket was paid for using an account linked to Luciano Massotti."

Jameson's features hardened. "I knew that name sounded familiar." A disquieting realization settled in as he connected the dots. "This isn't just any name; it's Valentina Massotti, connected to our own Agent Alex. He's involved with her."

Lisa's eyes widened in surprise. "Do you believe there's a connection between the two investigations?"

Jameson let out a deep sigh. "It's too early to tell. However, it's a lead we cannot overlook. Monitor all communications from that account. And discreetly keep an eye on Alex. We need to comprehend the magnitude of what we're dealing with."

Lisa nodded in agreement. "Understood, sir."

The stakes had escalated, and Jameson was acutely aware of the delicate equilibrium they now had to uphold.

Chapter 14: The Subtle Approach

Under the noon sun of Milan, the city shimmered with a golden elegance, epitomizing its status as Italy's fashion capital. A pair of figures emerged from the private jet terminal, exuding confidence as they strode forward, their sophistication perfectly aligned with the ambiance of Milan.

Mitchel, a tall man dressed in a meticulously tailored navy-blue suit, exuded an air of distinction. His accent blended regional intonation with refined articulation. With each confident step, his polished leather shoes softly echoed on the cobblestone.

Beside him, Thompson carried herself with equal poise. Her rich dark skin provided a striking contrast against her sharp white blouse, and her stylish short afro crowned her head, exuding regal sophistication. Her keen hazel eyes constantly scanned the environment, reflecting a mind that was always at work. A smart navy blue blazer completed her outfit, complementing her poised demeanor.

Though seamlessly blending into Milan's upscale backdrop, their presence in the city was anything but casual. Armed with a cover story, they aimed to gain entry into an inconspicuous office building not far from their current position. A modest two-story structure that belied the significance of the individuals it housed.

As they settled into the plush backseat of a waiting black Range Rover, Thompson leaned over and whispered, "Remember, Mitchel, for now, we are just potential clients. But if things go according to plan and we win him over, this ruse becomes our shield for future encounters."

Mitchel responded with a wry smile, "Just follow my lead, Thompson. We've got this."

Mitchel would assume the identity of Daniel Harper, a businessman eager for Italian expansion, while Thompson would become his financial consultant, Clara Richardson. This guise was designed to pique the interest of a discreet Italian accountant. However, beneath this facade, they held a more urgent agenda: leveraging the accountant with the photos Alex had entrusted to them.

Their journey offered a brief tour through Milan's historic streets, adorned with boutique shops and cafes. Finally, they reached the entrance of the office building, mentally preparing themselves for the challenges that awaited within. Unbeknownst to the accountant, who awaited his next appointment behind a wooden door on the second floor, a storm was about to unfold.

--

As Mitchel and Thompson stepped into the marble-floored lobby, the cool air welcomed them, providing a refreshing escape from the warm Milanese midday sun. A modern chandelier hung overhead, casting a soft glow on the intricate Italian designs that adorned the walls. The overall ambiance of the office building stood in stark contrast to its exterior.

Behind a gleaming mahogany desk sat a neatly dressed receptionist with raven-black hair, exuding a slightly nervous demeanor. Looking up, she greeted them with a practiced smile, revealing impeccably white teeth. "Buongiorno, how may I assist you today?"

"Good morning," began Mitchel, adopting his best English businessman tone. "We have an appointment with Mr. Giuseppe Romano. I'm Daniel Harper and this is Clara Richardson."

After a quick glance at her schedule, the receptionist picked up the phone, her voice lowering to a whisper as she spoke in rapid Italian. Within moments, she hung up and gestured towards the waiting elevator. "Mr. Romano is expecting you. Please proceed to the second floor."

As the elevator doors slid open, they were met by a tall woman with a sleek bun, sharp features, and an impeccably tailored suit. Her badge identified her as 'Lia, Personal Assistant'. She extended her hand and said, "Mr. Harper, Ms. Richardson, welcome. Giuseppe is ready for you."

Thompson and Mitchel followed Lia through a well-lit corridor adorned with tasteful artwork. Finally, they arrived at a door elegantly engraved with 'Giuseppe Romano, CPA'.

Upon entering the spacious office, Thompson's keen eyes immediately noticed something that piqued her professional instincts. Amidst a pile of documents and ledgers on the oak desk stood a polished silver photo frame. It contained a family portrait: Giuseppe, a slightly younger-looking woman who appeared to be his wife, and two children. Adjacent to it was another frame displaying a photo of the very mistress they possessed compromising photos of. Unaware of the trap being set for him, Giuseppe stood up from behind the desk to greet his visitors.

Mitchel discreetly glanced at Thompson, a hint of a smirk on his face. The game had begun.

Mitchel leaned forward, radiating confidence and affability. "Mr. Romano, in our line of work, discretion and trust are of utmost importance. While we have collaborated with numerous consultants, we always ensure they meet our high standards. Could you enlighten us about some of the clients you have served? Of course, without compromising their confidentiality."

Giuseppe reclined in his chair, interlocking his fingers thoughtfully. "Certainly. Over the years, I have had the privilege of working with various prominent individuals. Without divulging names, I have managed financial portfolios for renowned film directors, award-winning musicians, and even a few international sports icons. Their trust in me speaks to my discretion and expertise."

Thompson beamed warmly, her hazel eyes keenly observing Giuseppe. "Impressive, Mr. Romano. It is evident that personal connections and values hold great significance in your profession." Her gaze settled on the family photograph on his desk, and her voice softened. "Speaking of personal connections, you have a beautiful family. They must bring you immense pride and joy."

Giuseppe's face lit up, clearly moved by the compliment. "Thank you. Yes, that is Bonnie, my wife, and our children, Marco and Sofia. They mean the world to me."

Thompson leaned in, her tone intimate. "It is evident, Mr. Romano. Shared values and trust form the bedrock of any successful partnership. It warms my heart to see that you prioritize family so highly."

Her gaze subtly shifted to the adjacent photograph, her voice carrying a note of playful curiosity. "And this captivating young lady? A relative, perhaps?"

Caught off guard, Giuseppe hesitated, his eyes darting to the picture. "Ah, that is... my niece, Gabriella. She is pursuing a career in fashion in Milan."

Thompson leaned back, feigning casual interest. "Your niece? She is truly stunning. I assume you share a close bond?"

Giuseppe cleared his throat, discomfort evident in his eyes. "We were... close, once upon a time. But with her busy life, we have grown apart."

Smiling enigmatically, Thompson slid a manila envelope towards him. "Family and connections are truly fascinating, Mr. Romano. Perhaps these will pique your interest."

His fingers, trembling and pale, opened the flap. The compromising photographs spilled out, and the atmosphere grew heavy with unspoken implications.

Giuseppe found himself in a tense standoff, his plush office serving as the backdrop. Adorned with mahogany furniture and polished silver trinkets, it exuded an air of grandeur. As the weight of the situation pressed down on him, the accountant's eyes darted anxiously from the incriminating photographs to the two agents. Rising from his seat, a surge of fury and indignation emanated from every fiber of his being. "Who on earth are you two?" he bellowed, his Italian accent growing more pronounced with each passing moment.

Across the room, Mitchel, the stoic Liverpudlian, remained unfazed. He calmly raised a hand, palm facing Giuseppe, a gesture that exuded control and dominance. It silently conveyed the message: Sit down. Calm down. The absence of an immediate response, the quiet assertion of authority, proved more menacing than a barrage of words ever could.

Thompson, ever graceful, reclined in her chair, her gaze fixed on Giuseppe. With a tone that dripped with a mix of condescension and genuine concern, she began, "Mr. Romano, this situation can either be very simple or exceedingly complex. Believe it or not, the choice is yours."

Following suit, Mitchel leaned forward slightly, his hands clasped together. "You see, we find ourselves in a position where we possess considerable knowledge about you. Not just the prominent celebrities and politicians who entrust you with their finances, but also your... personal exploits." He allowed his words to hang in the air, leaving Giuseppe's mind racing.

Thompson picked up the photograph of Giuseppe and his mistress, mockingly examining it. "Such a charming niece you have," she sneered sarcastically. "I must ask, do family gatherings ever become awkward?"

The room was filled with the tense atmosphere, punctuated by Giuseppe's heavy breaths as he desperately searched for an escape plan. "What is it that you want from me? Money? Is this some form of blackmail?"

Mitchel shook his head, his expression grave. "Not money, Mr. Romano. We seek something far more valuable. Information."

Thompson's voice turned chillingly soft as she added, "And as you contemplate our proposition, consider the scandal that would ensue. Not just for you, but for your esteemed clientele. Let us not even delve into how your wife might react."

--

In the dimly lit study, a soft amber glow bathed Alex as he concluded his call with Jameson. The weight of the newfound information pressed upon his chest, almost tangible in its force. The name "Valentina Massotti" had echoed like a thunderclap, reverberating through the ensuing silence. The mundane sound of the computer shutting down seemed out of place, failing to acknowledge the gravity of their conversation.

As he departed from the study, a whirlwind of thoughts consumed his mind. Doubts began to cloud the trust he had painstakingly built with Valentina. Could it all have been a façade? But he couldn't allow his trepidation to show; he needed to hear her side of the story. She deserved that much.

In the living room, Valentina stood, her silhouette outlined by the sprawling London skyline beyond. Despite his growing doubts, he couldn't ignore the serene beauty she emanated. The city lights danced in her hair, creating an enchanting spectacle that starkly contrasted with the turmoil brewing within him.

Taking a deep breath, he approached her, each step laden with a heavy burden. "My love," he began, his voice a controlled calm that concealed the storm raging inside. "You didn't inform me that you were at the medical conference where the bomb detonated?"

Valentina turned, her expression momentarily unreadable, only to gradually soften into mild confusion. "The conference? I don't understand. I was here, with you," she replied evenly, her eyes searching his for the meaning behind his question.

"But your name was on the guest list," Alex persisted, scrutinizing her every move. "a collegue informed me."

A fleeting emotion flickered in Valentina's eyes—was it fear? Annoyance? It vanished before he could discern it. "It's a mistake," she finally asserted, rising to face him directly. "I can assure you, I had no intentions of attending any conference."

Her denial was resolute, yet Alex sensed the delicate balance of their relationship teetering. "I want to believe you, Val," he murmured softly, "I truly do. However, this... this is a grave accusation. Your name has been linked to a crime scene."

Valentina's unwavering gaze met his; her voice remained steady as she spoke. "Then, we must unravel the truth, mustn't we?" Her hand reached out, her fingers gently brushing against his. "Together."

Alex felt the warmth of her touch, but he remained vigilant. The game they found themselves entangled in, willingly or not, carried high stakes and concealed shadows. Trust was a luxury that neither of them could afford to leave unchecked.

Alex maintained a calm facade, but internally, a whirlwind of thoughts and emotions raged. He paused, trying to steady himself, feeling his heart rate quicken as he grappled with the possibilities.

Could she have been involved in the bombing? The mere thought was gut-wrenching. Attending the conference would make sense for her; after all, she was a doctor. It was only natural for her to be in such places, sharing knowledge and collaborating with peers.

But why would she lie about it? Alex pondered, attempting to piece together a plausible explanation. Every instinct as an intelligence officer urged him to dig deeper, to be cautious. However, his feelings for her clouded his judgment.

God, could Valentina truly have played a part in this?

This woman, a healer, bound by an oath to save lives, not destroy them. Alex felt a pang in his chest, the weight of doubt bearing down on him. He had witnessed the worst in people throughout his career, the lengths individuals would go for power, revenge, or ideology. But Valentina? It seemed inconceivable.

The room was tense, each breath heavier than the last. Alex mustered a smile, concealing the weight of his suspicions from Valentina. "I just remembered," he casually began, "I need to grab some papers from the office before we head off to Sicily. It won't take long."

Valentina nodded, her face a mixture of concern and confusion. "Alright," she murmured. "I'll finish packing and wait for you."

As the door to his apartment clicked shut behind him, Alex's expression immediately shifted. The pleasant facade was replaced with a resolute determination as he made his way to MI6 headquarters.

Inside the ops room, the glow from multiple screens bathed the room in a faint, cool light. Agents hurriedly moved about, some intensely focused on their tasks, while others conferred in hushed tones. The recent bombing had shaken everyone to the core, and the urgency to find answers was palpable.

"Alex," a familiar voice called out. It was Agent Daniels, a colleague and friend from Alex's training years. Daniels' face displayed signs of exhaustion, but his eyes remained sharp. "You seem troubled. What brings you here?"

"Personal matters," Alex responded curtly, not yet willing to delve into the details. "I need to review the footage from the O2 bombing."

Daniels raised an eyebrow but refrained from probing further. He gestured towards a terminal. "It's queued up over there. But I must warn you, it's not easy viewing."

Alex nodded his appreciation and approached the terminal. With each passing moment, as he meticulously went through the footage, the heaviness on his chest grew. The scenes were chaotic, people running, screaming. The unmistakable panic of an unforeseen tragedy.

Then, like a piercing blow to the heart, he spotted her. Valentina. She was leaving the conference hall, a sense of urgency etched on her face. The timestamp revealed it was mere moments before the explosion. Walking briskly, her coat billowing behind her, she glanced back once before vanishing from the frame.

A cold sweat formed on Alex's brow. His worst fears were materializing right before his eyes. Every fiber of his being wanted to deny it, to find an explanation, a justification. But the evidence was there, in high definition.

Daniels noticed Alex's reaction. "You found something?"

Alex's voice barely rose above a whisper, choked with emotion. "Yes... something I had hoped I wouldn't."

--

The ops room was suffocating, the intensity palpable. Alex's heart raced as he hurriedly left. Each step felt burdensome, every sound reverberating in his ears as he replayed the revelations in his mind. Avoiding eye contact, he couldn't shake off the uncertainty and anger that gnawed at him. He needed to find solace, to think.

MI6's location by the River Thames always offered a serene view from the windows, and now, more than ever, Alex sought that tranquility. He made his way down to the concealed jetty beneath the building, a place rarely visited by agents, reserved for covert departures or arrivals. There, a few kayaks lined up, used for training or occasional escapes like this.

Without hesitation, Alex seized one, barely feeling its weight in his heightened state. Urgently, he launched it into the water, disregarding any need for a life jacket. As the paddle sliced through the water, a rush of cold air brushed against his face, momentarily bringing clarity.

With each stroke of the oar, he tried to push away the trepidation, the confusion. The glistening water seemed to absorb some of his frustration, providing a temporary escape from the chaotic reality.

The rhythmic splash of the oar echoed Alex's heartbeat, each pulse reflecting the dichotomy within him. The water's cold touch, contrasting with the warmth of Valentina's embrace, triggered a deluge of thoughts.

Can I truly immerse myself in her world if we return to Sicily? Could I bear the weight of suspicion? Every touch, every glance would be tainted. I'd remain on edge, constantly vigilant, analyzing every word.

Navigating the River Thames, London's towering structures cast elongated shadows, mirroring the doubts clouding his mind. Alex paused his rowing, allowing the gentle current to guide him forward, seeking wisdom from the river.

But if I stay here, investigating her from a distance, won't the torment be even worse? The perpetual wondering, sleepless nights, unsure if she's in danger or if she poses a threat.

He tightened his grip on the oar, feeling the coolness seep into his palms, grounding him. The city's ambient sounds – distant murmurs of cars, occasional foghorns – deepened his sense of solitude amidst the chaos.

What if there's more to her involvement? What if she's trapped, manipulated, or threatened? She's a doctor, for God's sake. They take an oath to save lives. How could she be entangled in something so sinister? Yet, everyone has their secrets, their hidden facets. Have I been naive, blinded by love?

Alex took a deep breath, inhaling the damp, earthy scent of the river. He felt a kinship with it, a river with its own stories and secrets, flowing resolutely despite the obstacles. The Thames had witnessed love, betrayal, wars, and rebirth. Today, it bore witness to a man's soul-searching.

His gaze fixed on the horizon, where the sun began its descent, enveloping the city in an ethereal glow. Alex knew one thing for certain: the choice he made now would alter his life forever.

--

As Alex's kayak cut through the river, leaving the MI6 building behind, it symbolized the path he had chosen. He wasn't forsaking his duty but merging it with his deepest calling. Sicily beckoned, with its enchanting coastline, tantalizing cuisine, and hidden secrets nestled within golden sands and verdant vineyards.

Arriving at the jetty, his mind was focused and resolute. He securely moored the kayak and returned to the MI6 building to gather essential supplies for the journey. His office, typically a haven of organized chaos, now appeared different. The photos from previous missions, the notes on ongoing cases, and a picture of Valentina captured during one of their early dates — her smile reaching her eyes.

Swiftly assembling a bag with crucial tools of the trade — encrypted communication devices, a compact drone, forged identification documents, and other necessities, Alex also included something more personal: a locket that had belonged to his mother. It had always been a source of strength, a constant reminder of her words, "Love and duty often go hand in hand. Never forget that."

During the car ride back to his apartment, thoughts of Valentina consumed him. Surely, she had her reasons. Perhaps she was in danger or being blackmailed. Her dedication to saving lives clashed with the possibility of her involvement in ending them. If so, there must be an explanation; there always was.

As the bright lights of London flickered past his window, Alex formulated his plan. He needed to remain close to Valentina, earning her trust further and coaxing her to confide in him. He would observe, listen, and, above all, protect. Discreetly, he would utilize his resources to uncover more about the bombing and her connection to it.

Arriving home, he discovered Valentina packing for their trip. The sight of her, humming softly to a tune, folding clothes, occasionally pausing for a sip of wine, disarmed him. Pausing at the doorway, he watched her, appreciating the simplicity of the scene — a stark contrast to the complexity of their circumstances.

"Hey," he greeted, his voice tender, reflecting the emotion of their recent conversation.

She looked up, a smile gracing her face, though it failed to reach her eyes completely. "Almost finished here," she replied. "Excited for our trip?"

"Absolutely," Alex replied with genuine enthusiasm. He approached her, wrapping his arms around her waist from behind. "and to be with you."

She leaned back into his embrace. "Me too," she whispered.

As they stood there, holding each other, the unspoken weight hung heavily between them. Yet beneath it all, an undeniable love thrived.

--

Under the scorching sun at Palermo Airport, Alex and Valentina headed towards their rental car. Racing along the coastal roads of Mondello, the enchanting landscapes of Sicily surrounded them — a turquoise sea on one side and rugged, verdant cliffs on the other. Soon, they caught sight of the grand villa, its majestic presence standing in stark contrast against the rugged cliff backdrop.

As they drove up the gravel driveway, the intricately designed iron gates closed silently behind them, creating a haven of privacy. Valentina's parents awaited them at the entrance. Isabella, a graceful woman with expressive eyes, opened her arms wide, and Valentina melted into her embrace. Luciano, slightly graying at the temples but with a strong physique, eagerly awaited his turn. As he enveloped his daughter in a protective hug, his gaze met Alex's.

With Valentina still in his arms, Luciano extended a hand towards Alex. Their handshake was firm, the grip of a man who knew his own strength, yet there was warmth in it, acknowledging Alex not just as Valentina's companion, but as a potential member of the family.

"Benvenuto, Alex," Luciano said, his genuine smile accompanied by an enriching Italian accent.

"Thank you, Signor Massotti," Alex replied, taking in the surroundings, the heartfelt family reunion juxtaposed with the weight of his recent revelations in London.

As they entered the villa, Valentina's steps faltered, her face slightly pale. "I need to freshen up," she murmured, veering towards the nearest restroom. The rhythmic sound of retching briefly echoed before the door closed.

Isabella, full of concern, excused herself and followed her daughter. In the opulent surroundings of the villa's restroom, the marble counters reflected the soft ambient light.

"Valentina, cara mia," Isabella began, her hands gently caressing Valentina's face as she splashed water onto it. "You've never been sick from traveling before. Are you feeling alright?"

Valentina hesitated, meeting her mother's gaze in the mirror. "I don't know, mamma. It just hit me suddenly on the plane."

Isabella's brows furrowed with worry, her maternal instincts on high alert. "You should see a doctor. This isn't like you."

Valentina sighed, offering a weak smile. "Maybe I just ate something that didn't agree with me. Don't worry, I'll be fine."

The pathway leading to the villa was flanked by meticulously maintained gardens, bursting with vibrant flowers and towering palms. Though the enchanting beauty of the surroundings captivated Alex, his trained eyes discreetly surveyed each corner, noting the presence of the security detail. One guard stood tall by the main entrance, concealing his gaze behind dark shades. Another patrolled the grounds, periodically checking the state-of-the-art surveillance system. A third guard lingered near the cliff-side exit, where the gaping mouth of the sea cave enticed with promises of hidden treasures and swift escapes.

Upon entering the villa, a fourth figure caught Alex's attention. Standing silently by a grand archway was Rocco. Unlike the others, his attire exuded refinement – a crisply tailored suit that accentuated his muscular frame. With a curt nod, Rocco acknowledged Alex, his eyes betraying no emotion. Rocco had a reputation; he was not merely a bodyguard, but Luciano's confidante, right-hand man, and, in many illicit dealings, his enforcer.

The interior of the villa matched the breathtaking splendor of its exterior. High vaulted ceilings adorned with frescoes depicting scenes from Roman mythology, and French windows that opened up to the vast expanse of the Mediterranean Sea. Luciano guided Alex to a terrace overlooking the azure abyss below. The crashing waves and the scent of salt in the air created an almost serene atmosphere.

Luciano reached into a nearby ice bucket, retrieving two chilled bottles of beer. As he handed one to Alex, the clinking of glasses echoed in the brief moment of silence. With a swift motion, Luciano opened his bottle and took a deep gulp.

"To new friendships," Luciano toasted, raising his beer. Despite the warmth in his voice, there lingered an undercurrent of scrutiny, as if Luciano was attempting to decipher Alex's true intentions.

"To shared memories," Alex replied, nodding in agreement. His mind raced, attempting to piece together the intricate puzzle that was the Massotti family.

They both took sips of their drinks and stood in silence for a moment, gazing at the horizon.

Valentina glided into the room with grace, sunlight dancing on her hair, illuminating it. Her mother, Isabella, exuded a similar elegance, though age had replaced youthful energy with dignified poise. The two shared a laughter that was infectious and delightful.

"Ah! The stars of our family," Luciano announced, rising from his seat to pull out a chair for his wife.

Isabella smiled and playfully swatted his arm. "You say that every time, Luciano," she chuckled.

Valentina took a seat next to Alex, giving his knee a reassuring squeeze. "You won't believe what happened in London," she began, mischief sparkling in her eyes.

Luciano raised an eyebrow. "What did you two get up to this time?"

She laughed, "We went to that new café in Covent Garden, the one everyone's raving about. I ordered an espresso, and Alex, trying to blend in, asked for a 'Full English Tea'."

Isabella chuckled. "And?"
Valentina giggled, "They brought out this enormous tray! A tea pot, scones, clotted cream, jams, sandwiches, and even a mini trifle."

Alex playfully rolled his eyes. "I thought it was just going to be tea! It was more food than I've ever seen for one person. Val dared me to finish it all."

Luciano burst into laughter. "And did you?"

"Well, I gave it my best shot," Alex grinned, "I managed to finish the sandwiches and one scone before admitting defeat. But Val helped a bit too."

Valentina chimed in, "Just a bit! Mostly, I was laughing too hard."

Isabella laughed, reminiscing, "Ah, to be young and in love in London. It reminds me of our time there, Luciano."

Luciano nodded, a hint of nostalgia in his eyes. "Yes, when our biggest worry was ordering too much at a café."

Chapter 15: Silent Infiltration

Onboard a nondescript fishing vessel anchored off the coast of Mondello, an elite MI6 assault team gathered in the dimly lit cabin. Maps and diagrams of the Massotti villa and its surroundings lay scattered on the central table. Overhead views from infrared cameras mounted on drones and underwater sonar mapping of the sea cave leading to the villa's private jetty provided valuable intel.

Jasmine Thompson, now dressed in a tactical black outfit, commanded the team with her trademark authority. Her hazel eyes gleamed with determination. "Listen up, everyone. We have one shot at this."

Mitchel, also dressed in black, stood by her side, ready to provide specific details. He used a laser pointer to indicate the villa's main entrance, the positions of the guards, and the path to the sea cave.

"Our primary entry point will be the sea cave," Jasmine began. "Thanks to Agent Alex's intel, we know the cave leads directly beneath the villa with a private jetty. We'll utilize the new ESE-Stealth boats. They are silent, swift, and efficient."

One of the agents raised a hand. "Should we expect resistance inside the cave?"

Mitchel answered, "According to the intel, the cave is primarily used for private getaways and is not regularly guarded. However, we should be prepared for any scenario."

Another agent asked, "What about once we're inside?"

Jasmine nodded. "Our first priority is to secure the guards- the family is in the dining room Mitchel and I lead, we take them all at once. Remember, Alex is undercover, keep it that way."

A tall agent with a scar across his cheek questioned, "Once we have control of the villa, what's the extraction plan?"

Jasmine replied, "That's when we call in the Carabinieri. They will arrive to make the formal arrests and secure the perimeter. You'll exit the same way we entered, through the sea cave, and rendezvous with our vessel."

Mitchel chimed in, "Remember, our primary objective is to secure evidence linking Massotti to London."

Jasmine concluded the briefing with a firm tone. "Time is of the essence. At dusk, we move. Gear up and ensure your comms are functioning. We enter silently but prepared for anything."

The agents nodded, the weight of the mission evident in their eyes. They began checking their equipment, ensuring everything was in order for the operation that lay ahead.

The lounge of the Massotti villa exuded opulence. Expansive French windows stretched from floor to ceiling, welcoming the fiery hues of the setting sun. Golden rays bathed the room, casting a luminous glow on the exquisite decor: majestic portraits of ancestors, intricate tapestries, and treasures gathered from Luciano's travels.

Leading the way, Valentina's silk dress whispered against the marble floors. "Isn't the view divine?" she remarked, her eyes mirroring the orange and crimson sky.

"It's breathtaking," Alex replied, pausing to admire the vast expanse of the Tyrrhenian Sea merging seamlessly with the horizon. Tranquil waves gently crashed against the cliffs below, creating a melodic rhythm that enhanced the villa's charm.

Luciano, followed closely by his wife Isabella, gestured toward the dining area. An elegant table draped in a white tablecloth awaited them. The silverware glistened in the waning sunlight, and delicate porcelain plates held the first course: a fresh Caprese salad with buffalo mozzarella, vibrant tomatoes, basil, and a drizzle of the finest Sicilian olive oil.

A maid, dressed in a pristine white uniform, moved gracefully amongst them, pouring a ruby-red wine into their glasses, presumably from the Massotti vineyards.

Raising his glass, Luciano initiated the toast. "To family and the joys of life," he declared, his voice brimming with warmth.

Valentina added, "And to new beginnings and cherished memories." Her gaze lingered affectionately on Alex, conveying more than her words.

Isabella joined in, her eyes gleaming playfully. "And to finally having Alex here with us. It's about time!" Laughter filled the room, creating an atmosphere of genuine merriment.

The evening air carried the tantalizing scent of the delectable dishes that awaited them. As they indulged, laughter, reminiscences, and optimistic plans for the future filled the room.

Outside, the world faded into twilight, but within the villa, there was only radiance, warmth, and the promise of an enchanting evening.

--

The sky transformed into a deep indigo hue, adorned only by the sparkling stars and the crescent moon casting a faint silver glow. Tension hung heavy in the air as the assault team approached the entrance of the cave, their synchronized movements echoing the silence of the night itself.

Jasmine Thompson, her sharp hazel eyes scanning the surroundings, swiftly decided to abort the initial entry plan upon spotting the lone guard inside the cave entrance. Time was of the essence, leaving no room for lengthy discussions.

The black boat, nearly invisible against the night, gently bobbed against the rocks as the team disembarked. Thompson signaled, and they made their way towards the cliff face outside the cave. The jagged and uneven limestone provided some grip for their ascent. Clad in black gloves to ensure a firm hold, and equipped with soft-soled shoes for quiet and efficient movement, they pressed forward.

Above them, the sprawling villa stood with its majestic glass facade, a silent sentinel. It appeared serene, but the team understood the deceptive nature of appearances. Each step they took carried calculated risks, knowing that a misstep or an alert guard could jeopardize the mission.

Right behind Thompson, Mitchel retrieved a compact device from his pocket—a miniature drone, no larger than his palm. Launching it into the air, the drone's tiny rotors hummed silently. Its live feed was transmitted to his wrist-mounted screen, granting the team a bird's-eye view of the villa's garden, mapping out the positions of guards and potential entry points.

"They have patrols," Thompson whispered, observing the moving blips on Mitchel's screen. "Two in the garden, and another one near the pool."

Reaching the top of the embankment, their silhouettes concealed by the shadows of dense foliage, Thompson signaled for them to split into three pairs. Their objective was to neutralize the guards discreetly and locate a safe entry point into the villa.

Every rustle of a leaf, every distant conversation from the villa, and every chirp of a nocturnal insect heightened their senses. The luxurious garden, adorned with exotic plants and intricate statues, transformed into a tactical battleground.

As they advanced, the soft glow emanating from the villa painted a surreal scene: inside, life appeared normal and relaxed, as a family enjoyed their dinner. Outside, the game of cat and mouse had begun.

-

Mitchel and Rodriguez stealthily approached the first guard from different angles. Engrossed in his phone, the guard remained oblivious to Mitchel's soft footsteps on the grass. Rodriguez discreetly retrieved a small cloth doused in a quick-acting sedative from his pocket. As Mitchel created a diversion with a subtle rustling sound, Rodriguez swiftly covered the guard's mouth and nose with the cloth. Within seconds, the guard slumped, unconscious. They carefully moved his body out of sight behind some elaborate shrubbery.

Agents Carter and Bennett positioned themselves near the main entrance of the elegant villa, observing the third guard. This guard, slightly older with a salt-and-pepper beard, appeared to be the most experienced and diligent of the trio. No discernible patterns or obvious distractions were evident.

Carter collected a few pebbles from the ground and signaled their plan to Bennett. With a nod of agreement, Carter tossed a stone in the opposite direction of their hiding spot, creating a soft noise. The guard's attention immediately shifted towards the sound. Seizing the opportunity, Bennett approached the guard from behind. With swift precision, Bennett locked his arm around the guard's neck in a chokehold. The guard's struggle was brief; Carter aided the process with a quick jab to a pressure point. Within moments, the guard succumbed to unconsciousness.

Thompson, overseeing the seamless takedowns, felt a surge of satisfaction. Maintaining this momentum was crucial. She signaled for the team to advance, whispering into her earpiece, "Perimeter clear. Proceeding to the villa."

The villa's architectural elegance, combined with the tranquil evening, crafted an almost ethereal atmosphere.

Inside, the sounds of laughter and clinking glasses sharply contrasted with the tension outside. Rocco stood with his back against the expansive glass doors, his vigilant gaze scanning the room for any potential threats to the Massotti family. Despite his sharp suit, Rocco's muscular physique hinted at years of rigorous training, possibly in the military or private security.

Mitchel recognized that Rocco was no ordinary bodyguard. He had earned a reputation within private security circles for his impeccable reflexes and unwavering protective instincts. Mitchel knew he had to exercise extreme caution.

Removing his shoes to minimize any noise, Mitchel discreetly concealed them in the shadows of a large potted plant near the door. He patiently awaited a lull in the conversation inside — a brief distraction, any opportunity that would grant him an advantage.

That moment arrived when Luciano rose from his chair to retrieve another bottle of wine from a nearby cabinet, momentarily capturing Rocco's attention. Seizing the opportunity, Mitchel cautiously slid open the door just enough to slip through. Moving as silently as a phantom, he approached Rocco from behind.

Mitchel's small syringe filled with a fast-acting sedative. With his free hand, he swiftly grasped Rocco's head, tilting it to expose his neck. With precision, he plunged the syringe into a vulnerable spot.

Rocco's eyes widened in shock, his hand instinctively reaching for the injection site, but it was too late. The sedative took effect almost instantly. Before he could react or put up a fight, Rocco's knees buckled, and he began to crumple to the floor.

Mitchel's training kicked in. He gently lowered Rocco's unconscious body, ensuring minimal noise. With Rocco neutralized, Mitchel discreetly signaled the team outside "GO GO"

The warmth and intimacy of the Massotti family dinner shattered in an instant. The glass doors burst open, accompanied by a gust of cool evening air. Six figures in tactical gear stormed into the room, their faces concealed by balaclavas, and their weapons aimed at the family. The soft orange glow of the setting sun outside was replaced by the cold blue gleam of tactical lights mounted on their weapons.

Luciano's immediate reaction was to rise and protect his family. His chair scraped harshly against the marble floor as he stood, his hands raised, his eyes filled with defiance. However, he was swiftly met with the barrel of a gun inches from his forehead, halting him in his tracks.

"Remain calm, and no one will be harmed!" Jasmine's voice was authoritative and clear, cutting through the tense silence in the room. The family, including Alex, obediently raised their hands, their expressions ranging from shock to terror. Valentina's eyes darted from one face to another, her confusion palpable. Beside her, her mother tightly held her hand, visibly trembling.

Despite his vulnerable position, Luciano never took his eyes off the intruders. "Who are you? What do you want?" His voice carried a restrained fury, his loyalty to his family evident in his protective stance.

"We only need some information, and if you cooperate, this will be resolved quickly," Thompson replied, her voice slightly softer yet determined.

Amidst the chaos, Alex's heart raced. He had to maintain his cover, even if it meant staying silent while his loved ones were in danger. He quietly breathed a sigh of relief when one of the agents, unaware of his true role, pointed a gun at him, fitting perfectly into the narrative that he was just another family member. Keeping his expression neutral, he briefly locked eyes with Luciano, hoping to silently convey a message of reassurance.

-

In the opulent study, walls adorned with mahogany bookshelves showcased an impressive collection of leather-bound books. Casting a warm glow, a grand fireplace provided a stark contrast to the chilly atmosphere brought in by the agents. Above the mantle, a family portrait loomed, capturing a younger Luciano alongside his parents and siblings. This room served as a testament to Luciano's accomplishments and lineage, with meticulously displayed awards and certificates from esteemed business associations.

Mitchel closed the door behind them, stealing a quick glance at Luciano before nodding to Thompson. Having meticulously planned this moment, both understood the gravity of extracting information from Luciano efficiently and without causing harm.

Forced into a high-backed leather chair, Luciano stared defiantly at the agents, his hands resting on the polished oak table, each finger tapping a rhythmic beat. Though he appeared calm, the tightly clenched jaw and the hard glint in his eyes betrayed the storm brewing within him.

Thompson took a seat opposite him, her posture rigid, while Mitchel stood to the side, maintaining a watchful eye. The room was thick with tension, only interrupted by the crackling of the fire.

Finally, Thompson broke the silence. "Mr. Massotti, our intentions are not to harm you or your family. We simply seek information. By cooperating, we can bring an end to this without any further theatrics."

Luciano scoffed. "You invade my home, threaten my family, and now you expect me to cooperate?" Leaning forward, his eyes locked with Thompson's. "What is it that you want?"

Thompson slid a photograph across the table. It displayed a still from a CCTV feed, capturing Valentina at the O2 Arena. "We need to understand why Valentina was there."

Luciano's gaze darted to the picture, and for a fleeting moment, his stoic composure wavered, revealing a flicker of genuine concern. He looked back up, carefully choosing his words. "My daughter is a doctor. Why wouldn't she attend a medical conference?"

From the sidelines, Mitchel observed Luciano's slight hesitation. "It's not her presence that concerns us," he interjected, "but rather her absence during the bombing."

Luciano swallowed, beads of sweat forming on his forehead. "I don't know what you're insinuating," he replied, his voice hoarse, "but my daughter had no involvement in that tragedy."

Thompson leaned in, her voice low yet resolute. "Then help us understand, Mr. Massotti. Help us protect her. Because if we discover her involvement, the consequences will be severe, for both her and you."

Luciano's face turned pale as Mitchel and Thompson relentlessly questioned him about Valentina. Each inquiry pierced him, reminding him of the danger he had exposed his daughter to.

"Luciano," Thompson began, her voice soft but firm, "we have information that Valentina was present at the conference. We know she had contact with certain individuals just before the bombing. Explain why."

Luciano's eyes narrowed, and he shifted uncomfortably in his seat. Every fiber of his being yearned to defend his precious daughter. However, he also recognized the seriousness of these agents. "You're chasing the wrong lead," he growled. "Valentina is innocent."

Mitchel leaned in, his face mere inches from Luciano's. "We are not so convinced. Evidence places her at the scene. And considering her… unique background, she fits the profile of someone capable of orchestrating this."

Luciano's heart raced. Valentina had always been his secret weapon – a phantom lurking in the shadows. She could assimilate anywhere, become anyone. The perfect tool for his criminal empire. But he never envisioned her getting caught or her actions haunting him.

"Why would she bomb a conference?" Thompson pressed. "Was it a message? A diversion for something grander?"

Luciano's eyes darted around the room, calculating his next move. He sensed the walls closing in. He had to safeguard Valentina, but he also needed to protect himself. If they discovered her, it was only a matter of time before they connected the dots to him. But had they already unraveled the truth?

"Valentina is… passionate," he finally admitted, choosing his words cautiously. "She believes in causes, in making a statement. But I find it hard to believe she would resort to this."

Mitchel smirked. "Oh, we suspect she is more than just 'passionate.' We believe she is the mastermind behind the entire operation. And if she is, we need to identify who she is working for."

Luciano clenched his fists, struggling to maintain his composure. They were on Valentina's trail, but not his… not yet. "I will speak to her," he offered, desperation creeping into his voice.

Thompson leaned back, studying Luciano intently. "We were hoping you would say that." She paused for effect. "But remember, Luciano, if she is involved, she will face the consequences. And if we discover you had any part in it… you will face them alongside her."

Luciano gulped, the weight of the situation bearing down on him. The rules of the game had changed.

--

The serene villa was now a scene of controlled chaos. Agents moved with precision, securing every corner of the majestic mansion. The opulent furnishings, exquisite china, and luxurious fabrics juxtaposed the austere nature of the situation. Luciano's family, once the epitome of authority in the villa, were now being escorted out like common criminals.

Luciano's proud demeanor gave way to a defeated stance, a stark contrast to the commanding figure he had been just moments ago. As Mitchel and a Carabinieri officer guided him towards the awaiting black SUV, Luciano attempted to steal one last glimpse of his family, his empire, and the world he had constructed.

Beside another vehicle, Jasmine firmly held Valentina's arm, directing her with unwavering strength. Valentina's face displayed a flurry of emotions — defiance, fear, and disbelief. She stole a glance at Alex, searching his eyes for any reassurance or support.

In return, Alex was equally bewildered and stunned. Led away in restraints to a separate car, he locked eyes with Valentina. Their once loving and trusting relationship now felt entangled in a complex web of secrets and betrayal. Would they ever find their way back to each other amidst this intricate situation?

Isabella, Valentina's mother, was accompanied by two Carabinieri officers. Tears welled in her eyes as her family was torn apart, and her cherished home transformed into a crime scene. She held onto hope that somehow, they would navigate their way out of this turmoil.

As the engines roared to life and the vehicles began to depart, the once-majestic villa stood motionless, illuminated by the Sicilian Moon. Perhaps, it marked the end of an era, while the gentle crash of waves below remained indifferent to the drama that had just unfolded above.

Chapter 16: Echoes of Secrets

The once-luxurious villa, previously filled with frenetic energy, now rested eerily quiet. As the car carrying Alex stopped outside the grand entrance, he took a moment to gather his thoughts. The massive wooden door loomed ahead, a testament to the grandeur and the secrets concealed within.

Stepping out of the vehicle, the gravel beneath Alex's boots echoed through the evening silence. The house, now dimly lit, cast foreboding shadows that danced along the walls, adding a slightly menacing aura to the opulent abode.

Having spent considerable time in the villa, Alex was familiar with its layout. Yet today, he would explore it with a different purpose. Accompanied by two agents, they approached the door, held open by a nodding Carabinieri officer.

Entering the expansive living room, memories of family dinners, laughter, and shared moments flooded Alex's mind. But now, the room felt devoid of warmth. The moonlit sea framed by the large glass windows cast ethereal reflections on the marble floor. Alex gestured for one agent to search upstairs and the other to explore the basement.

He himself headed towards Luciano's study, knowing it to be the heart of the house's enigmas. Luciano's desk, a magnificent mahogany piece, displayed an organized array of papers, pens, and a few personal mementos. As Alex began rummaging through the drawers, he stumbled upon an encrypted USB drive. 'This could be something'.

Continuing his search, he ventured towards the bookshelves adorning the walls. Drawing books at random, he eventually stumbled upon a concealed switch lurking behind a leather-bound edition of Machiavelli's "The Prince." A section of the shelf shifted, unveiling a hidden safe. However, cracking it would have to wait for another time. He mentally noted the discovery and captured it in a photograph.

Moving through the house, Alex's keen eyes scoured for anything peculiar or out of place. In Valentina's room, a delicate scent lingered in the air, while photographs depicting various stages of her life adorned the dressing table. Within a drawer, Alex stumbled upon a collection of passports, each featuring her picture but bearing different names and nationalities. It became increasingly evident how she had maintained her composure; she was no stranger to such matters.

--

The sleek black car gracefully maneuvered through the winding Sicilian roads, its engine's rhythmic hum muffled by the tranquil night. Jasmine, entirely focused, occasionally glanced at Valentina through the rear-view mirror. The seemingly docile woman stared out the window, her face devoid of expression, yet Jasmine sensed an underlying tension.

Amidst the dim light illuminating the car's interior, the Carabinieri officer, a stocky man with graying hair, discreetly reached into his pocket and retrieved a small vial. Unnoticed by Jasmine, he surreptitiously passed it to Valentina, their hands briefly making contact. Valentina reciprocated with a nearly imperceptible nod.

Approaching a narrow bridge, Valentina swiftly uncapped the vial and spilled its contents onto a cloth. Seizing the opportunity when Jasmine momentarily shifted her attention to navigate the tight curve, Valentina lunged forward, pressing the cloth against Jasmine's face. The agent momentarily struggled, but the potent fumes quickly took effect, causing her to slump unconscious behind the wheel.

The car veered perilously, but the Carabinieri officer, displaying surprising agility, extended his arm to seize the steering wheel, guiding it safely to a stop just inches away from the bridge's edge.

Valentina, a mixture of relief and urgency, swiftly exited the vehicle. The officer followed suit, speaking rapidly in hushed tones, "The safe house lies two kilometers from here. Head east through the olive groves. They won't find you there."

She nodded, pulling the hood of her jacket over her head. "Grazie," she whispered, her voice laden with emotion.

And with that, she vanished into the obscurity of the night, her figure blending seamlessly with the shadows. The officer took a deep breath, aware of the risks he had undertaken and the potential consequences that awaited. But within the intricate web of loyalties and betrayals, he had chosen his side.

--

The phone vibrated, its sound echoing through the silence of the villa. The caller ID read "Jasmine." Alex, taken aback, swiftly answered the call.

"Alex! She's gone," Jasmine's voice was a mix of anger and frustration.

"What? Who's gone?" Alex replied, trying to conceal the panic that was creeping into his voice.

"Valentina," she split. "She and that Carabinieri officer took me out. I should have seen it coming. Did you have any part in this?!"

Alex, momentarily shocked, managed to respond, "Jasmine, I'm still inside the villa. I had no idea she would escape. Why would I compromise the mission?"

There was a short pause. "I don't know, Alex. Emotions can complicate things," she replied with a hint of accusation.

"You think I would risk everything for her? Look, she may hold some significance to me, but not at the expense of the mission. We need to find her," Alex insisted.

Jasmine sighed, "I should have been more alert. Damn it. We need to regroup and determine our next move."

"Agreed. Head back to the villa. We can't waste any more time. She couldn't have gone far," Alex said, his mind racing with possibilities.

"Alright, I'm on my way. And Alex? When we find her, I need to know whose side you're truly on."

The call ended, leaving Alex in a deeper quandary than before. The walls of the villa seemed to close in on him as he contemplated his next move and the implications of Valentina's escape.

The weight of Jasmine's words hung heavily in the air even after the call ended. Alex's mind raced like a hurricane of thoughts and emotions.

Valentina escaped? The shock of it sent waves through his system. *How could this have happened? How did we let our guard down?*

His heart throbbed painfully in his chest, a mix of fear and concern. *Is she alright? Where could she have gone? Would she even want to see me after all this?*

The mention of the Carabinieri officer's involvement was another blow. *Should I have seen that coming?*

Jasmine's doubt stung him. He always prided himself on being an agent above reproach, above suspicion. But Valentina had introduced an uncertainty into his life, a depth of feeling he hadn't anticipated. *Does Jasmine have a point? Is my judgment clouded?*

The walls of the villa seemed to press in on him, the opulence suddenly feeling claustrophobic. *Valentina was a master of disguise. Even now, after everything, she managed to elude us.*

A bitter taste settled in his mouth. *We had them. We had all of them. And in a split second, it's unraveling.*

I need to find her. Not just for the mission, but for himself. He needed answers. *Can love and duty coexist?* He was about to find out.

The plush carpeting muffled Alex's footsteps as he carefully navigated Valentina's room, pausing to appreciate the ambiance. It was a tapestry of her life, infused with the opulence the Massottis flaunted. Her room was grand, boasting an intricate mosaic of colors, designs, and personal touches. Crystal chandeliers cascaded from the ceiling, refracting the soft golden glow of the room's lights.

He approached the dresser, a finely crafted piece made from what appeared to be mahogany. The drawers slid open with a gentle tug, revealing a world of her personal belongings. There were neatly folded clothes, meticulously arranged in a gradient of colors. Beside them, a collection of perfume bottles, each emanating its own unique and delicate fragrance. Their scents mingled, telling stories of her travels, her choices, her memories.

Concealed beneath a stack of handkerchiefs was a small jewelry box. He gingerly opened it, unveiling a collection of photographs and old letters. It offered a more intimate glimpse into her life. There was a candid photo of her laughing on a beach, the sun setting behind her. Another captured a family portrait from years ago, showcasing a younger Valentina, innocent and unburdened. The letters, some sealed, others worn from frequent reading, whispered secrets of a life Alex was only partially privy to.

Drawn towards the ensuite, he yearned for more substantial clues. Pushing the door open completely, he revealed a spacious bathroom with white marble floors reflecting the ornate ceiling. Golden faucets, a claw-foot tub, and a shower space that resembled a luxurious spa.

However, it was the sleek black bin that captured his attention. Positioned beside the sink, it seemed out of place in such an extravagant room. Driven by instinct, he bent down and lifted the lid.

There, amidst discarded cotton balls and face wipes, lay the unmistakable pregnancy test. The result window displayed two distinct lines. Positive. As his fingers grasped the small plastic device, its weight seemed to bear the weightier news it carried.

Emotions overwhelmed him—a blend of joy, shock, panic, and a surge of protective instinct. His heart raced, its rhythm echoing in his ears. Is it mine? Why would she keep such news from me?

Lost in a whirlwind of thoughts, he momentarily forgot the covert nature of his mission. The realization that their circumstances had dramatically evolved, that Valentina was not just a lover or a suspect but potentially the mother of his child, grounded him in a new reality. It was no longer solely about the mission; it had become personal, intimate, and infinitely more complex.

Chapter 17: Confrontation and Revelation

The interrogation room at the Carabinieri station presented a striking contrast to the opulence of Luciano's villa. The cold, fluorescent lights overhead emphasized the dreariness of the gray walls and the simple metal table that separated the three men.

Despite being shackled, Luciano exuded an aura of authority. He sat with impeccable posture, unwavering in his demeanor. His deep eyes surveyed the two men before him, revealing no fear, only a hint of annoyance. To his left, Mitchel appeared resolute. As a seasoned Interpol agent, he had encountered numerous criminals, but this was a capture unlike any other. Across from Luciano, Commander Alberto Russo, a high-ranking officer of the Carabinieri, shifted uncomfortably in his seat. Known for his incorruptibility, interrogating a man of Luciano Massotti's caliber was no ordinary task.

"You know," Luciano began, his voice gravelly yet composed, "this won't end well for you, Agent Mitchel. You're in my territory now."

Leaning forward, Mitchel maintained his stern expression. "This is not about territory, Mr. Massotti. This is about justice. And regardless of our location, justice will always win eventually."

Commander Russo cleared his throat. "Mr. Massotti, you are being held on charges of organized crime, money laundering, and now, the O2 bombing. Cooperation would be in your best interest."

Luciano smirked confidently. "You have no proof. I am a legitimate businessman."

Before Mitchel could respond, the door swung open abruptly. A sharply dressed man entered, radiating confidence. His polished patent leather shoes echoed on the tiled floor, and his suit was impeccably tailored. He pushed his designer glasses up the bridge of his nose.

"That's enough!" he declared, placing a briefcase on the table. "This interrogation is over. You do not have permission to question my client without his legal representation present."

Mitchel's eyes darted to the newcomer. "And who might you be?"

"Antonio Bellini," he replied with a smirk, "Luciano's attorney."

Commander Russo stood, attempting to regain control. "Mr. Bellini, you will wait outside until we are ready for you."

Bellini chuckled. "No, Commander. You will wait for me. My client has rights, and if you violate them, the consequences will be severe."

Luciano leaned back, a satisfied smirk playing on his lips. "Ah, Antonio. Always punctual."

Mitchel's jaw clenched. This situation was turning out to be far more complex than he had anticipated.

--

Commander Russo took a deep breath, straightening himself and shuffling a stack of papers before him. "Luciano Massotti," he began, his voice assuming a formal tone, "You are under arrest on multiple charges, including money laundering, racketeering, illegal narcotics distribution, involvement in organized crime, and most gravely, acts of terrorism and multiple counts of murder in connection with the recent bombing."

Luciano's smirk faded slightly, but he managed to maintain his composed I. He glanced at his lawyer, who subtly nodded.

Mitchel interjected, "These are grave charges, Massotti. Your criminal empire is finally collapsing around you."

Bellini raised a hand, attempting to defuse the confrontation. "Hold on, Agent Mitchel. Let's not get ahead of ourselves. Allegations are not evidence. You may have apprehended my client dramatically, but you will need solid proof to support these charges."

Luciano nodded in agreement, "Precisely. You may think you have me, but this," he gestured around the room, "is just a temporary inconvenience."

Commander Russo leaned forward, "Every aspect of your empire will be scrutinized, Massotti. We will uncover the evidence. And if your daughter is implicated, as the evidence suggests, she will face the same consequences."

Luciano's calm I momentarily cracked. The mention of Valentina, his beloved daughter, being involved struck a nerve. He took a deep breath and locked eyes with Russo, "My daughter has nothing to do with my business. She's innocent."

Mitchel seized the opportunity, "Then why was she present at the bombing site? And why did she flee?"

Bellini sharply interjected, "Enough of this! Until you provide solid evidence, these are mere accusations. We are willing to cooperate, but within the confines of the law."

The tension in the room was palpable. Each man assessed the other, fully aware that this was just the beginning of a complex, high-stakes dance.

Chapter 18: Unveiling Secrets

The sun dipped below the horizon, casting long, inky shadows across the lavishly adorned interior of the villa. Alex, burdened with responsibility, cautiously treaded through the dimly lit rooms, his ears alert for any telltale sounds. It had been a while since the police vehicles departed, leaving the villa eerily silent, save for the faint echo of the sea outside.

Advancing towards Luciano's study, anticipation quickened Alex's heartbeat. He recalled their earlier conversation, during which the mafia boss subtly alluded to a personal safe where he safeguarded his most prized possessions. Each step Alex took was measured, replaying that discussion and searching for hints.

Finally reaching the wall behind Luciano's majestic mahogany desk, he ran his fingers along the smooth surface, searching. As he pressed down on an intricately designed switch that seemed out of place, a panel slid open, unveiling a sturdy, old-fashioned iron safe. Its imposing presence was almost theatrical, eliciting a smirk from Alex — Luciano always had a flair for the dramatic.

Equipped and prepared, having practiced on similar safes, Alex wore a stethoscope around his neck, which he carefully placed against the safe's door. Each turn of the dial, each muted click, was a symphony of opportunity. After a few tense minutes that felt like hours, the lock relented with a soft yet gratifying 'click.'

Inside, amidst stacks of cash and other documents, lay an exquisite leather-bound diary. Its craftsmanship was unparalleled. Alex gingerly retrieved it, feeling the weight of its significance. This was no ordinary diary; its elaborate design and placement within the safe hinted at its importance.

Flipping it open, Alex skimmed the pages. Entries filled with coded references, names, and dates — a written account of Luciano's operations and dealings. Alex's eyes widened at the meticulous records of money laundering activities, connections within the police force, and even notes on Valentina's involvements.

Yet, it was the most recent entries that seized his attention. They hinted at an imminent operation, something even more colossal than the O2 bombing. With the diary in his possession, Alex knew he held the key to dismantling the entire operation. However, his priority was to safely transport it back to headquarters.

Securing the diary within his jacket, Alex silently departed from the villa. Every second now held significance.

As the police station loomed into view, a nondescript building bathed in the harsh glare of fluorescent lights, Alex reached for the diary once more, cradling its weight in his hands. The worn leather felt cold and foreign, a stark contrast to the secrets concealed within its pages.

His thumb glided over the coarse pages, settling on the entry that detailed Valentina's involvement in the mafia operations. It meticulously chronicled missions, names, and dates. Rereading it, his heart constricted, the gravity of Valentina's actions becoming even more palpable. But emotions had to be set aside for now; he had to take action.

With deliberate movements, Alex carefully tore out the pages that exposed Valentina's involvement. He neatly folded them and concealed them deep within his jacket pocket. It was a risk, but a calculated one. The diary would serve as the most substantial evidence against Luciano, but Valentina's role would remain a secret, at least for the time being.

As his car came to a stop in front of the police station, a flurry of thoughts raced through his mind. The potential impact of using the diary's contents to persuade Luciano, to transform him into an informant, loomed large. It would be a monumental victory for Interpol. Luciano's insider knowledge held immeasurable value, an absolute treasure trove of information. And if Luciano agreed to cooperate, there was a glimmer of hope for Valentina. Perhaps a deal could be struck, offering leniency in exchange for vital information.

However, it was crucial for Alex to maintain the illusion that he was an outsider, an unwitting participant caught in the midst of this tempestuous storm. That responsibility would fall squarely on Mitchel's shoulders.

Stepping out of the car, clutching the diary tight, Alex made his way into the police station. He would hand it over to Mitchel, an observer at the center of this intricate drama. The weight on his shoulders was burdensome, yet he clung to the hope that a path would emerge to rescue Valentina and dismantle the criminal empire that ensnared them all.

Chapter 19: Escape to Ustica

Under the scorching sun, the Tyrrhenian Sea glistened, its waves shimmering like precious gemstones. Valentina stood against the speedboat's railing, her hair dancing in the wind, trying to process the recent events. As Palermo's distant silhouette grew smaller, she could almost envision the chaos unfolding back at her family's villa.

Ustica called out, offering a sanctuary from the turmoil. She loved its crystal-clear waters and captivating marine life, Ustica held a special place in Valentina's heart. Her family owned a secluded estate there, a haven of memories and solace. It was a refuge where she could disappear, if only for a while.

As the boat's powerful engines hummed, she felt the salty mist on her face and inhaled the familiar scent of the sea. It was a scent of freedom, a fleeting sensation she desperately clung to. But beneath it all, an unsettling feeling lingered. She was on the run, and the weight of that realization weighed heavily on her.

Thoughts of Alex consumed her. Was it truly a betrayal? She grappled with the whirlwind of emotions swirling within her. She loved him, she trusted him, and yet, she couldn't shake the nagging feeling that he harbored secrets.

The boat captain, a trusted associate of Luciano's, glanced back at her, offering a reassuring nod. No words were exchanged. He understood their destination. Everyone in her father's circle knew that Ustica served as their sanctuary in times of crisis.

As the island came into view, she admired its rugged coastline and the whitewashed walls of their villa peeking through the lush vegetation. For generations, her family had called this place home away from home, a haven shielded from prying eyes. But as the boat docked and she stepped onto the island, Valentina couldn't help but sense an ominous presence.

For now, Ustica would be her refuge.

Chapter 20: The Bargaining Chip

Tension hung thick in Jameson's temporary on op office, the air itself seeming to bear down on them. Every element in the room, whispered of hidden secrets and covert operations. The diary, now resting amidst the chaos of Jameson's cluttered desk, appeared to shout them out.

"Alex, this diary," Jameson began, shaking his head in disbelief, "It's incriminating. We possess enough evidence here to imprison Massotti for the remainder of his days. Every transaction, every deal, every...secret."

"But is that what we truly want?" Alex leaned forward, his gaze brimming with intensity. "What if we could exploit this to our advantage? We have him, yes, but what if we could offer him something he values more than his freedom?"

Jameson arched an eyebrow, his skepticism apparent. "You're proposing we convert him into an informant? After all he's done?"

Alex nodded resolutely. "Precisely. Think about it, sir. The information contained within this diary is invaluable, but the knowledge and access Massotti could provide as an active informant would be unparalleled. We could dismantle the Mafia from within."

"And you believe he would agree to such an arrangement?" Jameson inquired, his doubt lingering.

"We possess leverage," Alex asserted firmly. "Valentina. He adores his daughter. With her involvement, which remains mostly concealed, we hold a card to play. We could offer her an escape, protection. He would do anything for her."

Jameson paused, mulling over the proposition. "It's a daring move, Alex. If we extend an offer to him and he accepts, we are essentially reintroducing a known criminal into the world, back into a life of power."

"But under our vigilant watch," Alex countered. "With the constant threat of exposing this diary should he ever betray us. It is indeed a gamble, I understand, but the potential rewards could be monumental."

Jameson sighed, rubbing his temples wearily. "You realize, should we proceed and it goes awry, our lives will be on the line."

Alex took a deep breath. "I firmly believe the risk is worth it, sir. For the potential good we can accomplish and for Valentina."

Jameson gazed at the diary for a prolonged moment, the weight of the decision evident in his eyes. Finally, he met Alex's gaze and nodded. "Very well, let us set the plan in motion. But we proceed cautiously, every step of the way."

Chapter 21: The Proposition

The interrogation room presented a stark contrast to Jameson's office. It emanated a cold, grey, and sterile ambiance, intentionally designed to peel away facades and expose the raw truth. The faint hum of overhead fluorescent lights only heightened the prevailing sense of unease. One wall was dominated by a two-way mirror, concealing observers who could clandestinely witness the proceedings. In the center of the table sat a discreet recording device, its red light serving as a silent testament to its ability to capture every uttered word in the room.

Seated on one side of the metal table was Luciano Massotti, the feared and revered head of the Mafia. His demeanor remained inscrutable, despite the gravity of the situation. Impeccably attired in a tailored black suit, crisp white shirt, and silk tie, he betrayed only a subtle clenching of his jaw and a flicker of intensity in his eyes.

Jameson occupied the seat opposite Massotti, strategically placing the diary between them as a tangible symbol of the power dynamics at play. "Mr. Massotti," Jameson began, leaning back in his chair, "You find yourself in quite a precarious predicament."

Luciano's dark gaze locked onto Jameson's, his voice laced with impatience. "Cut the small talk. Why am I here without my lawyer?"

"We both know your lawyer is deeply entwined in the Mafia's webs, just as you are. No, Luciano, this conversation is solely between you and me," Jameson replied evenly.

A sardonic smirk tugged at Luciano's lips, though his eyes betrayed no trace of amusement. "So, what is it that you want?"

Jameson tapped the diary, deliberately drawing attention to it. "We have you, Luciano. Everything. And with this, we possess the means to ensure you spend the remainder of your life rotting away in prison."

Massotti's eyes flickered with a mix of defiance and restraint, but he remained silent.

"But," Jameson continued, leaning forward, "There exists an alternative. A way out for you. But it comes at a cost."

The Mafia boss arched an eyebrow, his curiosity piqued. "I'm listening."

Jameson took a deep breath, his voice softening slightly. "You become our informant. You provide us with every shred of information necessary to dismantle the Mafia from within. Names, locations, operations."

Luciano chuckled, devoid of any semblance of mirth. "You think I would betray my own? For what?"

"For Valentina," Jameson stated, his voice carrying a touch of compassion. "We are well aware of her involvement. We can offer her protection, a chance to escape. But only if you cooperate."

The mention of his daughter struck a nerve. Luciano's countenance darkened, and he leaned forward, his voice icy cold. "You dare to threaten my daughter?"

"No," Jameson replied calmly, asserting his stance, "I am offering her salvation. And you, an opportunity for redemption. The choice, Luciano, is yours."

Luciano's eyes darkened further, the weight of the decision pressing heavily on him. "Only twelve hours?" he exclaimed, disbelief lacing his tone. "You expect me to determine the fate of my life, my family, my empire, in such a short span of time?"

Jameson leaned back, his unwavering gaze fixed on Luciano. "Sometimes, Mr. Massotti, the most crucial decisions are made under pressure. They reveal our true nature."

Luciano's gaze shifted to the diary, then back to Jameson. "And if I refuse?"

"Then you will face the full force of the law," Jameson stated firmly. "Every transaction, every order, every crime documented in this diary will be used against you. We possess enough evidence to incarcerate you for multiple lifetimes."

Luciano clenched his jaw, attempting to suppress the rage brewing within him. "Do you think turning against me will be effortless? I have enemies, Jameson. Enemies who would not hesitate to obliterate me and everyone I hold dear if they discovered I was collaborating with you."

Jameson's demeanor softened slightly. "We are aware of the risks, Mr. Massotti. And we are prepared to provide protection, not only for Valentina but for you as well. All we require is your cooperation."

Luciano glanced at the two-way mirror, undoubtedly contemplating who else might be observing this confrontation. He then fixed his gaze back on Jameson, his voice low and brimming with menace. "You are playing a perilous game, Jameson."

"I could say the same about you, Luciano," Jameson calmly replied. "Remember, the clock is ticking. Twelve hours."

With a delicate touch, Valentina eased the throttle, igniting the engine's roar and propelling the vintage single-seater plane forward. The propeller sliced through the air, casting a gust over the lush foliage that surrounded the airstrip in Ustica. Even from the ground, the untamed beauty of the island was evident, with dense groves of trees jostling for space and the rocky terrain painting a rugged backdrop.

As the small plane gained momentum on the short runway, each rotation of the wheels faster than the last, the trees at the end of the airstrip drew closer. Just when it seemed as if they would engulf the aircraft, Valentina pulled on the stick, and the tiny plane took flight, leaving the land behind.

Beneath her, the Tyrrhenian Sea sparkled like a vast expanse of sapphires, the sun's rays dancing on its surface, transforming it into a shimmering tapestry of blues. The silhouette of Ustica diminished as Valentina headed northeast, the horizon stretching infinitely, beckoning.

In the cockpit, Valentina experienced a sense of liberation. The world outside reduced to just her and the boundless blue. It was an escape, a respite from the intricate web of family and duty that constantly sought to ensnare her. The wind rushed past the plane, its constant hum strangely comforting.

Approaching the Italian coast, the distinctive shape of Tuscany emerged. Rolling hills adorned with vineyards and cypress trees, ancient villas dotting the landscape, and further inland, the unmistakable peaks of the Apennines.

Valentina initiated her descent, aiming for a small airstrip nestled beyond the coastline. Secluded amidst a patch of trees, resembling the one in Ustica but slightly larger, she skillfully maneuvered the plane. Her hands steady on the controls, her eyes scanning for any obstacles. The wheels touched down softly, and she taxied to a halt, the engine's roar giving way to silence.

Shutting down the engine, Valentina took a deep breath, inhaling the fragrance of the Tuscan countryside.

Stepping out of the cockpit, her heels crunching on the gravel, Valentina made her way towards a tan colored BMW discreetly parked in the shade of the trees. Its presence was the only indication that this trip held a greater purpose.

Sliding into the plush leather seat, the faint scent of polish and leather enveloped her. She inserted the key, and the engine purred softly to life. Without wasting a moment, she drove out of the airstrip, merging onto a narrow, winding road.

Under the moon's watchful gaze, casting long shadows through the trees, Valentina skillfully navigated the twisting Tuscan roads. The golden fields of wheat, vibrant vineyards, and rows of olive trees were breathtaking, but her focus remained solely on her mission.

Approaching the outskirts of Lucca, the rural charm gradually gave way to urban features. The industrial zone lay to the east of the town, and Dr. Bellini's factory and research lab were nestled in its heart. Surrounding the compound was a high metal fence, security cameras positioned at every corner, and guards patrolling the grounds. It was evident that Dr. Bellini understood the significance and potential dangers associated with his research.

Valentina parked the car a distance away to survey the area. The factory sprawled across the landscape, its various buildings interconnected by walkways. She deduced that the central building was the main laboratory where groundbreaking research took place, while the peripheral structures likely served as storage and office spaces.

Peering through her binoculars, she meticulously counted the guards stationed around the premises: a total of four, evenly dispersed. Ideally, the cover of night would be the opportune moment to strike, but time was not on her side.

Inspecting the trunk, she discovered her equipment neatly organized: a set of stealthy black garments, a suppressed pistol, a compact crossbow equipped with tranquilizer darts, and carefully packaged explosives. Swiftly, she changed into her attire, concealed by the open doors of the car, securing the pistol at her waist and the crossbow on her back.

Taking a deep breath, she initiated her approach. Employing stealth, she maneuvered from one concealment to another, deftly evading surveillance cameras and guards, inching closer to the heart of the facility. Once inside, her primary objective was locating the server room, as it housed crucial digital records of the research that needed to be eradicated.

The laboratory exuded an eerie stillness, dim lights casting a somber glow over the immaculate corridors. Valentina effortlessly located the server room, her experienced fingers deftly configuring a device designed not only to erase the data but also to corrupt the backup systems.

Proceeding diligently, she strategically planted explosives throughout the facility to ensure its complete XXXollapse. Time was of the essence. The timer was set for 20 minutes, allowing her a narrow window to escape undetected.

As she made her way towards the exit, a sudden sound halted her in her tracks. It was a janitor, humming a tune while diligently cleaning a nearby hallway. Presented with two choices, Valentina deliberated whether to incapacitate him or patiently wait for him to depart. Opting for the latter, she concealed herself in the shadows, observing his every move. The minutes sluggishly ticked away, testing her patience.

Finally, with a mere five minutes remaining, the janitor strolled away, granting her the opportunity to flee. Darting out of the building, skillfully circumventing any remaining guards, she swiftly returned to her car and sped away, leaving behind a resounding explosion that consumed the laboratory in its fiery embrace.

Navigating through the enigmatic Tuscan night, Valentina couldn't help but contemplate the weight of her choices and the far-reaching consequences they entailed. However, for now, the mission was accomplished, and she needed to swiftly retreat and maintain a low profile. The reverberations of her actions would undoubtedly reverberate across time and space.

--

The rolling hills and vineyards of the Tuscan countryside gradually faded into the distant horizon as Valentina accelerated along the winding roads. Her destination was the makeshift airstrip where her plane patiently awaited her return. The sound of approaching sirens echoed in the background, but they were not meant for her; they were rushing towards the burning building she had left behind.

The aircraft, a single-seater that she knew intimately, stood ready, its engine idling for a swift departure. Valentina had chosen this particular plane for its compact size and agility, both essential qualities for a quick getaway. After swiftly conducting a pre-flight check, she gracefully climbed into the cockpit, finding solace in the familiar touch of the controls that settled her racing heart.

With one last glance at the land below, Valentina acknowledged that this might be her final farewell to Tuscany. She throttled up, unleashing the roaring power of the plane's engine, and raced down the improvised runway. Within moments, she was airborne, watching the Tuscan landscape shrink beneath her.

As the Mediterranean stretched out below her, its deep blue waters shimmering in the moonlight, Valentina felt a sense of relief. The vastness of the ocean both intimidated and comforted her, offering a temporary respite from the perils and intrigues of her life.

Her thoughts drifted towards the enigmatic higher-ups, the shadowy figures that cast a constant shadow over her existence. Even with the success of her mission, their ominous presence remained ever-present. Yet, for now, she had managed to buy herself some time. The cure for addiction threatened many, not just her own father, and she couldn't help but shudder at the thought of the fate that awaited her had she refused this mission.

Gradually, the small island of Ustica emerged on the horizon. It was a familiar sight, a sanctuary where she could disappear for a while. As Valentina approached, she commenced her descent, skillfully aiming for the narrow airstrip nestled amidst the trees. With a smooth landing, her expertise became evident.

Securing the plane within its hidden hangar, Valentina wasted no time. She navigated the secret pathways she knew so well, making her way towards the family house. Every step was taken with utmost caution, for even in this seemingly safe haven, danger could still lurk. However, tonight, the island remained serene and undisturbed.

As she stepped inside the familiar walls of her family home, Valentina was enveloped by a sense of comfort and security. The house stood silent, its walls blissfully unaware of her brief but perilous adventure. Silently, she moved through the corridors, finally reaching the sanctuary of her own room.

Exhausted, Valentina sighed with relief. The mission was accomplished, and for now, the threats that loomed over her were temporarily subdued. She sank into her bed, swiftly succumbing to sleep as the Mediterranean waves whispered promises of tomorrow. In this moment, she felt safe within the confines of her sanctuary.

Within the vivid hues of Valentina's dreamworld, a familiar backdrop painted itself before her. She found herself standing amidst a bustling street, surrounded by faceless figures. The cobblestone streets glistened as if kissed by a recent rainfall. The sounds of chatter and distant car engines reached her ears, but they were muted, as if heard from beneath the surface of a tranquil sea.

But the focal point of her dream was Alex.

He approached her with a solemn expression, his unwavering gaze locking onto hers. Dressed impeccably in official attire, she could almost imagine a faint smile playing upon his lips. However, as he drew closer, his countenance grew colder, devoid of any hint of warmth.

Valentina's heart raced as he reached out, grasping her arm with an unyielding grip. His voice sounded distorted, as if coming from a distance. "You're under arrest, Valentina." She tried to protest, but her voice failed her. Her surroundings blurred, the ground beneath her feet became unstable, and she descended into an abyss of darkness and panic.

With a sudden jolt, Valentina woke up. Her heart pounded in her chest as she sat up, sweat dampening her forehead. Morning sunlight filtered through the gaps in the curtains, casting dappled patterns across the room. For a moment, she struggled to distinguish between the dream and reality.

Taking deep breaths, Valentina tried to shake off the remnants of the disorienting dream. Memories of the last time she saw Alex flashed in her mind—the piercing siren, the screeching tires, the chaotic escape.

Reaching for the glass of water on her bedside table, Valentina tried to quench the sudden dryness in her throat. Since leaving Palermo, she had cut off contact with the outside world. Reaching out to anyone, even trusted allies, was a luxury she couldn't afford for fear of being discovered.

Yet, the dream about Alex stirred something inside her. Was he okay? Did he truly suspect her? The last time they spoke, there was a strange tension between them, unspoken words and feelings hanging in the air. But now, everything was different.

Valentina leaned back against her pillows, lost in thought. She reminisced about the early days of their relationship—the stolen glances, the shared secrets. Now, those memories felt like shards of glass, sharp and painful. She longed for some sign, some indication of where he stood now.

As the sun continued its ascent, casting golden hues into her room, Valentina knew she couldn't dwell on these thoughts for long. There were still tasks to complete, secrets to guard, and a life to rebuild. But for now, she allowed herself a brief moment of vulnerability, wondering about the paths their lives had taken and where they might intersect once more.

Valentina gracefully moved through the charming kitchen, the gentle patter of rain outside providing a soothing backdrop to her contemplations. The warm wooden cabinets and rustic tiles usually grounded her, evoking a sense of home. However, today, her surroundings seemed hazy and distant. With practiced precision, she measured out the rolled oats, combining them with milk in a pan. Placing it on the stove to simmer, this ritual was meant to bring her comfort. Yet, her mind was consumed by turmoil.

As the first bubbles emerged on the surface of the porridge, a wave of nausea threatened to overpower her. She knew this was more than just any sickness; it was morning sickness. Memories of the positive pregnancy test she had discovered at the villa flooded back, vivid and clear amidst the fog of her other thoughts.

Every emotion felt magnified. There was a blossoming joy, an unexplainable connection to the life growing within her. However, this warmth was regularly overshadowed by waves of anxiety. The world she inhabited was rife with treachery and danger, constantly forcing her to make choices that blurred the lines between right and wrong. How could she possibly bring an innocent life into such a tumultuous existence?

Her thoughts Invariably drifted to Alex. Their stolen moments, unspoken promises, and the palpable tension that hung in the air whenever their paths crossed. In a different world, they might have stood a chance. Did he know about the baby?

Absentmindedly, she stirred the porridge, the once comforting aroma now exacerbating her nausea. Turning off the stove, her appetite vanished, and she sank into a chair. Each breath she took felt like an attempt to ground herself, a desperate defense against the encroaching panic.

The child within her was both a beacon of hope and a source of profound vulnerability. Her past choices, often driven by necessity rather than desire, now reverberated with consequences that impacted not only her but also the future of her unborn child. A fierce, primal instinct arose within her, compelling her to protect and shield her child from the dark world she found herself in.

Yet, the undeniable reality of her current situation loomed large. The pervasive influence of the mafia cast long shadows, and while the island of Ustica provided a temporary sanctuary, she knew it would not last. Hiding was merely a temporary solution. She needed a strategy, a way to reclaim her autonomy and ensure her child's safety.

Summoning her resolve, Valentina understood that she could not afford the luxury of paralysis. Decisions had to be made, and allies had to be sought. The future remained uncertain, fraught with challenges yet unseen. However, one thing remained crystal clear: she would fight with every fiber of her being for the safety and happiness of her child.

Chapter 22: Ultimatum in Shadows

The dim light within the cell cast long shadows, accentuating Luciano's already worn appearance. His once pristine suit now lay rumpled, and a thin layer of perspiration adorned his forehead. However, his eyes still emanated a piercing sharpness. The four walls of his confinement reverberated with Jameson's ultimatum, eliciting a wry smile from Luciano.

"Mr. Jameson," Luciano began, his voice unwavering despite the gravity of the situation, "Throughout my life, I have danced perilously between the realms of heaven and hell. Do you believe that twelve hours within this cell will shatter me?"

Luciano's resolute gaze met Jameson's unwavering stare, both men unwilling to yield in this tense standoff. Jameson's response cut through the silence, his voice as steely as his resolve. "This isn't about breaking you. It's about presenting a choice. We possess the diary. We hold knowledge of your every move, every transaction, every clandestine tie. You can return home, continuing to reign over your empire, this time as our informant. Alternatively, you can languish within a cell so deep that the light of day becomes a distant memory."

Luciano's fingers drummed rhythmically upon the cold steel table in his cell. The discovery of the diary had shaken him to his core, a chronicle of his every step, every deal, and every hidden alliance. In the wrong hands, it spelled his demise. Yet, in the hands of Interpol, it transformed into a bargaining chip.

"You have a daughter, Luciano," Jameson continued, his voice softer yet laced with an implicit threat. "Valentina. We can offer her safety, ensuring she possesses a future untainted by her father's sins."

The mention of Valentina caused Luciano's posture to stiffen. It was a low blow, but Jameson understood the necessity. Luciano's love for his daughter constituted his sole vulnerability, and Jameson intended to exploit it.

A protracted silence ensued, punctuated solely by the distant hum of the police station beyond the cell. Finally, Luciano broke the silence. "What assurances do I possess? That once I provide you with what you seek, you won't betray me? Or my family?"

"We are not the mafia, Massotti," Jameson retorted. "We adhere to codes. Laws. Collaborate with us, and you and your family shall remain unscathed. But make no mistake, defy us, and there will be no corner of this earth in which you can seek refuge."

Luciano reclined in his chair, the weight of his decision bearing down upon him. "Allow me to consult with my attorney."

"You fail to comprehend," Jameson sneered, "Your attorney does not factor into this equation. It is solely you, me, and the future you choose."

Luciano's eyes, brimming with decades of guile and decisions forged within the shadows, met Jameson's unyielding gaze.

--

Leaning against the cold metallic wall of the cell, Luciano tried to maintain an indifferent facade. However, the slight twitch in his eyes betrayed his concern. The mere mention of Valentina always had that effect.

Drawing closer to the bars that separated them, Jameson's voice dripped with calculated menace as he spoke in a lowered tone, "Listen, Massotti. We have your empire in our grasp. We possess enough evidence to condemn you for lifetimes. But, I am willing to propose a deal. Your daughter's future in exchange for your cooperation."

Luciano's gaze hardened as he asked, "What are you implying?"

"It's quite simple," Jameson replied, pacing in front of the cell. "That boyfriend of Valentina's, Alex, isn't he? He's still under our custody. He hasn't disclosed much, but he doesn't need to. I can send him back to you, along with your wife, as if nothing ever happened. Light the fireplace, pour a glass of wine, and await your daughter's return. Maybe, just maybe, if you play your cards right, Valentina might escape the full consequences of Interpol. But only if you assist us."

Luciano's nostrils flared at the thought of his family being used as pawns. However, he also recognized an opportunity when he saw one. "And what exactly do you want from me?" he growled.

Jameson smirked, "For now, nothing. You may resume your life and your operations. But there will be a new addition to your entourage, someone we trust. They will be constantly by your side, your shadow. As long as they remain unharmed and you remain cooperative, your family will remain unharmed as well."

Luciano's eyes darted around, desperately seeking an escape or hidden angle, but he was cornered. He looked up at Jameson, feeling the weight of the situation heavy on his shoulders, "And if I refuse?"

Jameson's expression turned cold. "Then you, and everyone you hold dear, will discover the true extent of Interpol's reach. The choice is yours, Massotti."

Chapter 24: Pawns and Promises

In the sparsely lit office, Alex and Jameson sat facing each other, surrounded by the remnants of countless stakeouts and late nights. Pinned maps, scribbled notes, and half-empty coffee cups marked the room. The only sound breaking the tense silence was the hum of the air conditioner.

Finally, Jameson leaned back, stretching his legs. "Playing this game with Massotti is risky, Alex. Trusting him wasn't part of the plan when we signed up for this job."

Alex nodded in agreement. "I never expected it either, but it's our best chance. Using him to infiltrate the core operations of the mafia... it's a golden opportunity."

Jameson interlaced his fingers. "We'll free the wife and you, the boyfriend, as planned. And Valentina... we have to ensure she's kept out of this mess. Gaining Luciano's full trust is crucial, and her freedom will serve as a positive gesture."

"But she remains a threat, Jameson. We can't guarantee that she won't plot against us the moment she's free," Alex expressed, worry evident in his eyes.

Jameson sighed. "We're taking precautions. Surveillance, trackers... We need to know her whereabouts at all times. And as for you," he looked directly at Alex, "you'll be back under deep cover. Can you handle being so close to her again? Emotions in this line of work can be complicated."

Alex swallowed, his resolve unwavering. "I knew what I signed up for. And yes, it's... complicated with Valentina. But I can handle it. Besides, with Luciano under our surveillance, I'll have a closer look at what's happening."

"Good," Jameson replied, retrieving a file from his drawer. "We're moving Luciano tomorrow. He'll receive a briefing, be made comfortable, and the following day, he'll return to his world. But this time, we'll be monitoring his every move, listening to every whisper."

Alex nodded, determination radiating from him. "We have a real chance to dismantle the largest mafia operations. We can't afford to make any mistakes."

Jameson extended his hand across the table. "Agreed. Let's get this done." The two men shook hands, sealing the fate of their perilous undertaking.

--

The soft glow of moonlight filtered through the heavy drapes that adorned the windows of Valentina's home in Ustica. The room was tranquil, with only the rhythmic sound of her breathing creating a soothing melody. Antique furniture graced the space, a testament to the rich history of the old Sicilian villa. The shadows danced on the walls, as if whispering secrets from the past, imbuing the room with a sense of life.

At the center of the room stood a grand wooden bed with intricately carved posts, its sheets crumpled from a restless night's sleep. On the bedside table rested an old Nokia phone, a relic in a world of technological advancement, yet indispensable to Valentina's discreet existence. It served as her sole connection to her former life and the outside world, a tether that kept her grounded, although she questioned her desire to be part of that world.

Suddenly, the silence shattered as a soft chime announced an incoming message. Startled, Valentina stirred in her bed, her deep brown eyes opening in confusion. With a sleepy hand, she reached for the phone, rubbing her eyes with the other.

Blinking to focus on the tiny screen bathed in a soft blue light, she read the message: "charges dropped, you're in the clear, go home." The weight of those words quickened her heartbeat. The realization washed over her—the nightmare was finally over. The suffocating walls around her began to retreat.

She sat up, pushing back her tousled hair, attempting to comprehend the gravity of what she had just read. Could she truly return home? To the life she once knew? To the family that anchored her?

But the message also carried a deeper meaning—there were intricate games being played at higher levels, moves and counter-moves from which she was excluded. She knew she had to tread cautiously, but for now, hope blossomed within her. The prospect of reuniting with her family, of seeing Alex, even if uncertain about their relationship, tantalized her.

Taking a deep breath, Valentina made a decision. She would go home. But first, she needed to prepare.

--

The heavy wooden doors of the villa swung open, revealing the majestic interior that had once exuded warmth. The setting sun cast long shadows over the furniture, lending an air of unfamiliarity to everything. The walls, once vibrant, now appeared dull, with every scratch and scuff magnified in the evening light.

Isabella, Valentina's mother, entered with a heavy heart. Each step she took echoed through the vastness of the house, a constant reminder of the family's recent hardships. Her usually immaculately styled hair was now pulled back into a simple bun, her face devoid of its usual makeup. Her once commanding posture now exhibited exhaustion.

Alex followed closely behind, his sharp eyes scanning every corner. His training made him acutely aware of the changing energy within the house. It was no longer a private family residence, but a stage where every action and word would be scrutinized by unseen observers.

Isabella instinctively made her way to the kitchen, her hands trembling ever so slightly as she filled the kettle with water. A palpable silence enveloped the room, each person lost in their own thoughts, all playing their roles in this intricate dance of pretense.

Alex pulled out a chair and took a seat at the kitchen table, the cold metal sending a shiver down his spine. He maintained a neutral expression, his gaze fixed on a point on the table, careful not to betray any emotion.

The coffee machine hummed, momentarily breaking the silence, as Isabella busied herself by pouring two cups. She placed one in front of Alex and took the seat opposite him. The rich aroma of the coffee filled the air, providing a stark contrast to the tense atmosphere.

She reached for the remote and switched on the television, filling the room with the familiar sounds of a local news channel. The flickering images on the screen depicted scenes of daily life in Palermo, but neither of them truly paid attention.

Isabella took a sip from her cup, her gaze never leaving Alex's face. "You must be weary," she murmured, her voice barely audible.

Alex nodded, taking a slow sip from his cup. "It has been a long day."

Both of them were acutely aware that they were walking on thin ice, burdened by unspoken words and hidden secrets. But for now, they played their assigned roles, awaiting the next act in this unfolding drama.

--

Valentina stood on the ferry's deck, gazing out over the expansive Tyrrhenian Sea. The evening sun painted a golden hue, causing the waters to shimmer and dance with light. Her grip tightened on the railing as the cool wind whipped her strategically placed scarf, covering most of her face. With her hair bundled up and plain clothes, she aimed to blend seamlessly with the other passengers, concealing her identity. Yet, despite her efforts, she felt completely exposed.

Each rolling wave brought forth a whirlwind of thoughts. Was this an elaborate trap? The safety she once knew had shattered, and trust had become an unaffordable luxury. The message had seemed genuine, but in her world, appearances often deceived.

The salty breeze carried snippets of laughter and casual chatter from families and tourists aboard, but Valentina was adrift in her sea of doubt and trepidation. Every step of this journey danced with danger. The coastline of Palermo drew closer, accompanied by a relentless stream of questions that gnawed at her.

Would Alex be waiting there? The same Alex who had unexpectedly woven himself into her life. Memories of their stolen moments and whispered secrets flashed before her eyes. The image of Alex arresting her loomed large in her thoughts. Was he truly what he seemed? An agent or a lover? Perhaps both. The realization that he was the father of her unborn child added another layer of complexity to the already tangled web she found herself trapped in.

A churn in her stomach brought her back to the present—the baby. She gently placed a hand over her abdomen as if to shield her child from the storm of emotions brewing inside her. This innocent life knew nothing of the chaotic circumstances of its conception or the perilous world awaiting its arrival.

The ferry's horn blared, signaling their approach to the port of Palermo. Valentina caught sight of the bustling docks, the queue of cars waiting to depart, and the eager faces of those ready to disembark. She took a deep breath, attempting to steady herself. The next few hours would determine everything.

--

She descended the stairs, her feet touching the solid ground of Palermo once more. The familiarity of the place offered little comfort. Every shadow, every face became a potential threat. She had stepped back into the lion's den, and all she could do was hope that the received message was genuine.

As the crowds moved around her, Valentina cast one final glance at the sea, drawing strength from its vastness. She had made her move.

Valentina weaved through a sea of passengers, each absorbed in their own world, oblivious to the turmoil brewing within her. The bustling atmosphere of Palermo's port created a stark contrast to the serenity of Ustica. The sounds of vendors haggling, cars honking, and distant music formed a cacophony that was both familiar and unsettling.

She tightened her scarf, her eyes darting from one corner to another. Every step, every glance, she analyzed for potential danger. Was that man in the fedora following her? Did that woman whisper about her? Or was it just her imagination playing tricks?

Thoughts of her mother, the unwavering pillar of strength in her life, flooded her mind. The image of her mother sitting at the kitchen table, brewing coffee, seeking solace in mundane routines, filled Valentina with determination. She needed to return home.

And then there was Alex. The mysterious man who had both blessed and cursed her life. The mere possibility of seeing him again stirred a whirlwind of emotions. The tender moments they shared, entwined with the shocking revelation of his true identity, left her in a state of confusion. Could love truly blossom amidst deception? She contemplated the life growing inside her, a symbol of their union, yet a constant reminder of the intricate web that entrapped them both.

--

The road leading to her villa felt longer than she remembered. Each step sparked memories of happier times, when life was simpler and love uncomplicated. She yearned for that simplicity, a time when the boundaries between friend and foe were clear.

As she approached her home, the grand facade of the villa came into view. Its imposing structure, once a symbol of safety and luxury, now served as a haunting reminder of the life she had left behind. A faint glow from the kitchen window hinted at her mother's presence inside.

Taking a deep breath, she approached the main gate, prepared to embrace whatever awaited her. Whether it was a reunion with her family or a confrontation with the truths she had been evading, she was ready. The next chapter of her life was about to unfold.

--

Valentina paused at the threshold, her heart pounding in her chest. With a deep breath, she pushed open the door and was instantly enveloped in her mother's warm embrace.

"Valentina!" Her mother exclaimed, tears streaming down her cheeks. "Mia bella figlia, I was so worried!"

Valentina held her tightly, finding solace in her mother's familiar arms. "Mamma," she whispered, her voice choked with emotion, "mi dispiace. I'm so sorry for everything."

Her mother gently cupped Valentina's face, her eyes searching her daughter's. "Non importa ora. You're home, and that's all that matters."

Before Valentina could respond, she felt another presence in the room. She turned and locked eyes with Alex. The weight of unspoken words hung in the air between them.

Alex took a step forward, his eyes filled with a mixture of regret and relief. "Valentina..."

She interrupted him, not ready to hear his explanations just yet. "I know, Alex. I know."

For a moment, they simply gazed at each other, forgetting the outside world. Then, slowly, Alex reached out and pulled her into a tight embrace. The warmth of his body and the familiar scent of his cologne overwhelmed her.

Sensing the tension, her mother discreetly cleared her throat. "I think I'll go make some coffee," she said softly, "I'll leave you two to catch up."

As her mother left the room, Valentina and Alex remained locked in their embrace, unwilling to let go. They both knew there was much to discuss, but for now, the simple act of being close to each other was enough.

--

Valentina's gaze fell to the ground, absorbing Alex's words. The silence enveloped them, heavy with the weight of their shared history. Finally, she raised her eyes, searching his face for any trace of deception. To her surprise, she found only warmth, sincerity, and an unexpected emotion: joy.

"Alex... how did you...?" she began, alluding to her pregnancy.

He gently took her hand, guiding it to his chest where she could feel the rapid thud of his heart. "A little birdie told me," he replied with a playful grin. "But honestly, it doesn't matter how I found out. What matters is that we're in this together."

Tears welled up in Valentina's eyes. "I was so frightened," she whispered. "Afraid of what this entails, afraid of others' judgment, afraid for our baby..."

Alex tightened his grip, drawing her closer. "You don't have to be scared anymore, Val. I'm here. Whatever challenges come our way, we'll face them together."

She took a deep breath, exhaling slowly. "Even after everything? You still want this? Want me?"

He leaned in, his forehead touching hers. "Always," he murmured, his voice soft and filled with emotion. "No matter what happened in the past or what lies ahead in the future. It has always been you, Val. It will always be you and me."

In that moment, the weight of the world seemed to lift from Valentina's shoulders. A profound sense of relief washed over her. Amidst the chaos, she found solace in the love of a man whose life was just as entangled as hers. Together, they would navigate whatever came their way, united in their journey.

The grand hallway of the villa was dimly lit, with only the soft glow of moonlight to guide their steps. The gentle rustling of curtains and the fragrance of blooming jasmine from the garden created a serene ambiance, a striking contrast to the recent chaos.

As they approached Valentina's bedroom door, she hesitated, a hint of vulnerability flickering in her eyes. "It's a bit messy," she admitted, her cheeks blushing slightly.

Alex lightly touched her arm, a reassuring smile on his face. "Don't worry about it. After everything, a few misplaced items won't bother me."

Opening the door, they entered her sanctuary. The room was bathed in the gentle, silver luminescence of the moon, while a gentle breeze made the curtains dance.

Valentina paused for a moment, feeling the weight of the situation. But as Alex took her hands and drew her close, the world seemed to fade away. Their eyes locked, a whirlwind of emotions swirling between them: relief, passion, longing.

Without a word, Alex leaned down and captured her lips in a passionate kiss, their pent-up feelings unleashed. Time stood still as they lost themselves in each other, momentarily forgetting the anguish of the past few days.

When they finally broke apart, breathless, Valentina whispered, "Stay with me tonight."

Alex nodded, gently cupping her face. "Always," he murmured, sealing their promise with another kiss.

Guiding her towards the bed, they lay down side by side. The reality of their situation, the impending arrival of their child, and Luciano's return on the horizon weighed heavily on their minds. But for now, they sought solace and comfort in each other's arms, holding onto the hope that love would guide them through the storm ahead.

--

The warm rays of the sun began to embrace the terra-cotta tiles of the villa as a sleek black SUV rolled into the driveway. Coming to a halt, two men dressed in impeccably tailored suits emerged from the car. They scanned the surroundings with coordinated and precise movements, akin to predators ensuring no threats lurked nearby.

The back door of the SUV swung open, revealing Luciano Massotti. He appeared slightly weathered, with more pronounced lines etched on his face than Valentina remembered. However, his stormy gray eyes remained fierce, betraying nothing of his recent ordeal.

Valentina couldn't contain her emotions and rushed to him, tears welling up in her eyes. They embraced tightly, the weight of the past few days evident in the strength of their grip. Valentina's mother followed suit, enveloping her husband in her arms and letting out a quiet sob of relief.

Meanwhile, Alex stood a few paces away, observing the reunion. He felt like an outsider, intruding on this intimate moment. Yet, when Luciano's gaze finally met his, there was a silent acknowledgment, a wordless expression of gratitude for Alex's role in bringing him home.

"You're back," Valentina whispered into her father's ear.

"Always for my family," Luciano murmured in response, pulling away to gaze at his daughter's face. There was a pause, a moment of tension as he noticed the subtle changes in her – a newfound maturity, a weight that hadn't been there before.

Approaching, Alex extended his hand. "Mr. Massotti, I'm glad you're home."

Luciano took his hand, gripping it firmly. "Thank you, Alex."

The two undercover agents who had arrived with Luciano commenced coordinating with the others already strategically positioned around the house. Luciano noticed this and turned towards Valentina. "They will be accompanying us for a considerable duration," he explained, emphasizing the significance of their presence for their own safety.

Valentina nodded, comprehending that this was the necessary sacrifice they had to make in order to secure their freedom, albeit temporarily.

As they ventured inside, the once cold and desolate villa came alive with warmth and vitality. The aroma of freshly brewed coffee permeated the air, courtesy of Valentina's mother preparing a hearty breakfast.

Yet beneath the surface, a subtle unease lingered. Despite being physically reunited, the family found themselves treading uncharted territory, and the presence of the guards served as a stark reminder of the precariousness of their situation.

Luciano, sinking into his cherished armchair, surveyed the familiar room before turning his gaze upon his family. "We shall endure this together," he affirmed, speaking more to himself than to anyone else.

Chapter XXV

The MI6 building loomed impressively against the gray backdrop of the morning sky in London. Its modern architecture stood in stark contrast to the historic landmarks of the city, symbolizing the UK's relentless march forward in the realm of espionage and intelligence.

As Jameson entered the grandiose lobby, the sound of his polished black shoes clicking on the marble floor resonated. Security personnel greeted him with nods, showing reverence for the man known as one of MI6's top brass. The murmurs of analysts, the shuffle of papers, and the intermittent buzz of phones created a tapestry of sounds synonymous with the heart of British intelligence.

Meeting him halfway, Jameson's sharp-witted assistant, Elaine, wore a face of concern, breaking her usual composed demeanor. In her hand, she held a neatly tied stack of freshly printed briefings.

"Morning, sir," she greeted, her voice tinged with urgency.

"Elaine," he curtly responded, his mind already racing through the potential tasks ahead.

She handed him the stack, tapping the topmost file with her red-lacquered nail. "This one, sir. You need to see it right away."

Jameson raised an eyebrow but refrained from further questioning. Opening the folder, his eyes swiftly scanned the document. His pace slowed, and with each sentence, his brow furrowed deeper. The title blared glaringly at the top: **Explosion in Tuscany: Bellini Lab Destroyed.**

Accompanying images displayed a once-pristine building reduced to rubble, a haunting aftermath of a powerful explosion. Emergency responders were still working amidst the settling dust. The article chronicled the loss of decades of research, all the work of Dr. Enzo Bellini.

His heart thudded louder in his chest. This was no ordinary lab. It was the lab of the keynote speaker, the man who had invented a potential cure for addiction. Tragically, his life was cut short in an explosion allegedly orchestrated by Valentina Massotti.

The gravity of the situation sank in. If Valentina was indeed involved in this new explosion, the stakes had skyrocketed. It would not only endanger the deal with Luciano but also potentially expose Alex's cover.

Jameson looked up, meeting Elaine's anxious gaze. "Get me all the information on this and keep it discreet," he ordered in a hushed tone.

Elaine nodded, already heading off to coordinate with the analysts. Jameson took a moment, inhaling deeply, attempting to steady the whirlwind of thoughts swirling in his mind. The game had changed, and he needed to strategize his next move.

--

Leaning back in his leather chair, Jameson allowed the pages to sprawl before him. The details of Dr. Bellini's research proved captivating. The enzyme, known as "Inhibizone" in the files, emerged from years of genetic research and bioengineering.

The mechanism was ingeniously simple: Inhibizone, once consumed, would traverse the bloodstream and bind to specific receptors in the brain responsible for the 'craving' signals experienced by addicts. By binding to these receptors, Inhibizone rendered them inactive, effectively suppressing any feelings of addiction or craving.

The brilliance of Dr. Bellini's approach lay in the delivery method. Rather than pills or injections, the enzyme could be consumed in yogurt, facilitating mass distribution and consumption. It was a game-changer.

Jameson's mind raced with endless possibilities. He contemplated the countless lives that could be saved, the families kept whole.

"No more children growing up without parents lost to addiction, no more communities ravaged by the effects of drugs. Hospitals would no longer be overwhelmed by overdose cases. Economies could flourish without the weight of addiction-related issues holding them back."

However, as hope surged within him, a realization struck him. The global illicit drug trade was valued at hundreds of billions of dollars. A cure for addiction would decimate this market. And who stood to lose the most? The organized crime syndicates, including the infamous Mafia.---

A wave of understanding washed over him. If this enzyme were to become public knowledge, the demand for drugs would plummet. Cartels and mafias would witness their profits evaporate overnight. They would stop at nothing to prevent this breakthrough from coming to light.

In that moment, the gravity of Valentina's alleged actions at the convention and the destruction of Bellini's lab became clear to him. The Mafia's motives extended beyond territorial protection; they were fighting for their very survival.

The room seemed to shrink, the weight of the situation bearing down on Jameson. The battle against the Mafia had entered a whole new realm. The stakes were no longer confined to matters of crime and justice; they encompassed the destiny of humanity itself.

Jameson gazed out of the window, captivated by the sprawling city. "You know, Thompson, it's not just the Massotti family that would suffer from Bellini's discovery. We're talking on a much grander scale."---

Thompson furrowed her brow. "You mean..."

"Yes," he interjected, "the global mafia syndicates, cartels, and underground networks. The entire foundation of the illicit drug trade would crumble."

Leaning forward, she expressed her curiosity. "But it doesn't stop there, does it?"

Jameson shook his head, burdened by his thoughts. "No, it doesn't. Big pharmaceutical companies have been profiting from addiction treatments for decades. Methadone, Suboxone, Naltrexone – all billion-dollar industries. Bellini's breakthrough could bring them all down."

Thompson took a moment to process, her mind racing. "So, we might be facing more than just the Massotti family and their associates. It could be a global consortium determined to keep this enzyme hidden."

A deep sigh escaped Jameson's lips. "That's the magnitude of what we're dealing with. Taking on the mafia was already an enormous challenge, but this... this changes everything. If they're collaborating or pursuing a common objective..."

Thompson interrupted, "It means Valentina's actions, assuming she's responsible for the explosion, might not solely be driven by her family's orders. She could be entangled in something she doesn't fully comprehend."

Jameson nodded solemnly. "Exactly. We must proceed with caution. The very balance of power hangs in the balance. Our next moves will shape the outcome of this conflict."

..

Jameson's office was dimly lit, with London's overcast light barely penetrating the thick curtains. His desk was cluttered with files, a lamp, and a series of photographs showcasing the aftermath of the latest explosion site.

"Valentina, once again," Thompson began, gesturing towards the photos. "It seems she's connected to this. This is the second time."

Jameson let out a sigh, massaging his temples. "I thought she was our gateway to infiltrating the Massotti operations, not a wildcard trying to sabotage research facilities."

"Perhaps both," Thompson countered, taking a seat. "Regardless, we can't overlook this. Should we bring her in?"

Jameson paused, lost in thought. "What would that accomplish? Currently, Luciano Massotti represents our best chance of delving deeper into this network. If we apprehend Valentina now, he will either go silent or, worse, become unruly."

Jasmine leaned forward. "But if she continues these actions, we're risking more than just research data. Lives could be lost, Jameson."

The weight of the situation bore down on both of them. A moment of silence passed before Jameson spoke up, his eyes filled with contemplation. "I've been studying the European Open Science Cloud, the EOSC. It serves as the final backup for Bellini's research. If his work is as groundbreaking as we believe, it must not fall into the wrong hands."

Jasmine blinked, her curiosity piqued. "Do you think they would target it?"

"If I were them, I wouldn't hesitate," Jameson replied. "However, EOSC is not an ordinary facility. It's a cloud network. While the main server may be located in one place, backups and data distribution nodes are spread throughout Europe."

"We need to enhance the security around EOSC everywhere," Jasmine insisted. "If they realize its significance, it will become their next objective."

Jameson nodded. "Already taken care of. But physical protection alone won't suffice. We require cybersecurity experts to monitor every move, ensuring no breaches occur."

He leaned back, gazing at the ceiling tiles. "This goes beyond Valentina, beyond Massotti. If this 'cure' becomes public, it will disrupt not only the criminal organizations but entire industries. Caffeine, alcohol, hell even fast food.

Thompson took a deep breath, fully comprehending the magnitude of the situation. "So, what's our next step?"

"We utilize Luciano, keep a close eye on Valentina, and secure EOSC," Jameson declared, determination gleaming in his eyes. "We're standing at the precipice of either a groundbreaking achievement or a catastrophic disaster. Either way, the world is watching."

Thompson leaned in, lowering her voice. "And what about Alex? We can't ignore that he's entangled in all of this, and he has an emotional connection to Valentina."

Jameson ran a hand over his stubbled chin, his gaze distant. "I've been contemplating that. Given the circumstances, we must be cautious about the information we reveal. If he knows everything, there's a risk he might act impulsively. Presently, we need stability, not unpredictability."

Jasmine nodded slowly, concern etched in her eyes. "His bond with Valentina could make him vulnerable or, worse, a liability."

"We'll closely monitor the situation. For now, let's keep him in the dark. When the time is right, we'll bring him into the loop," Jameson decided.

Both agents rose from their seats, fully aware of the critical days ahead. Stepping out of the MI6 headquarters, they were greeted by a stark contrast to the dimness of Jameson's office. London buzzed with activity, its grey skies mirroring the uncertainty of their mission. Cars honked, red double-decker buses passed by, and pedestrians hurriedly traversed the streets, oblivious to the covert operations unfolding within the old brick walls.

Jameson took a deep breath, relishing the crisp air filling his lungs. The weight of responsibility was palpable, but there was a task at hand. Looking up, he caught a glimpse of the Union Jack fluttering atop the MI6 building, serving as a constant reminder of his duty to both nation and world.

Chapter XXVI

In the room, shadows cloaked every corner, with thick curtains blocking any hint of light. The scant illumination from a single lamp cast an interrogation-like glow over Giuseppe, the accountant, who sat rigidly at one end of the elongated mahogany table. His hands fidgeted nervously, betraying the tempest of anxiety brewing within him.

At the other end, where darkness lingered most persistently, sat a figure – a woman whose age and features were indiscernible, shrouded in the room's dimness. Her voice, however, sliced through the thick, still air with surgical precision.

"Mr. Giuseppe Romano," she began, her tone as cold as the darkness enveloping her, "your expertise lies in numbers, not loyalty. We seek reassurances."

Giuseppe swallowed hard, his voice barely a whisper against the gravity of the room. "My loyalty lies with the numbers... and those who control them."

"And yet, your recent... associations suggest otherwise. You've been in contact with certain agencies," the woman stated, her voice carrying a menacing edge tinged with curiosity.

Giuseppe's mind raced, carefully weighing each word before it left his lips. "Conversations are just that—mere talk. The numbers, however, do not lie. And they indicate that I am still here, serving the best interests of... our associates."

Leaning forward slightly, the woman's eyes glinted in the sparse light. "Our 'associates' demand more than mere service. They demand silence, discretion... obedience. Can we still expect that from you, or has your allegiance shifted?"

Giuseppe steadied his breath, summoning the cold confidence instilled by his profession. "My allegiance is dedicated to the longevity of our operations. Rest assured, it has not wavered."

Silence hung in the room, suffocating and heavy. After a tension-filled moment, the woman reclined back into the shadows.

"Very well," she declared, the decision seemingly made. "But remember, while numbers may not lie, accountants can. We are watching, Mr. Romano."

Giuseppe nodded, silently acknowledging the warning. The meeting had concluded, but the message was crystal clear: in this room, darkness reigned supreme, and it brooked no forgiveness.

--

The villa basked in the gentle warmth of the sun, causing the azure waters of the pool to shimmer with an irresistible invitation. Joyful melodies filled the air as birds chirped merrily from the surrounding trees, while a light breeze rustled through the leaves, creating a peaceful symphony. The scene unfolded like a tranquil family gathering, offering a stark contrast to the storm of recent events.

Valentina and Alex found solace in the cool embrace of the pool, seeking respite from the sweltering heat. Beneath the surface, their hands intertwined, engaging in a silent and intimate game of their own. Immersed in conversation, their voices carried softly through the air, muted by the distance.

"I never imagined we would experience a moment like this again," Alex remarked, gently brushing a strand of wet hair away from Valentina's face.

Valentina responded with a soft smile, her eyes shimmering with emotion. "We now have an opportunity, a fresh start. For us and for our little one."

Nearby, the outdoor kitchen wafted with the tantalizing aroma of fresh basil and ripe tomatoes. Donning an apron over his attire, Luciano skillfully chopped vegetables, occasionally sneaking a cherry tomato or two for himself. His wife, her hands immersed in a large salad bowl, playfully swatted his hand away each time he reached for a tomato.

"Luciano! Leave some for the salad," she chided, though her eyes sparkled with playful delight.

He feigned innocence, raising his hands in defense. "I'm merely ensuring their quality," he retorted, before leaning in to plant a tender kiss on her cheek.

Their interactions epitomized the ease and comfort of their enduring relationship. Years of shared memories, overcoming challenges together, and finding joy in the simple pleasures of daily life had solidified their bond.

With graceful movements, the maid moved between the kitchen and the veranda, meticulously setting the table. The clinking of cutlery and glasses, combined with the tantalizing aroma of the dishes being prepared, signaled that the time for pranzo, the midday meal, was drawing near.

Luciano, wiping his hands on his apron, turned to his wife. "Its a joy to all be together like this," he remarked, his voice filled with emotion.

She nodded, her gaze momentarily distant. "Yes, but now we are here, together, and that is what truly matters." Pausing, she looked towards Valentina and Alex. "Our family is growing, Luciano. We have so much to anticipate."

In that fleeting moment, the weight of recent events seemed to lift ever so slightly, replaced by a glimmer of hope and the promise of brighter days to come.

--

The aroma of freshly cooked food permeated the air, a testament to Palermo's rich culinary heritage. Crispy chickpea fritters, known as panelle, were perfectly deep-fried, accompanied by a tangy and sweet eggplant dish called caponata. Plump arancini balls gleamed under the sun, their golden hue indicating their irresistible crunchiness. A bowl of busiate pasta dressed in vibrant Trapanese pesto invited hungry gazes. This magnificent spread was a true celebration of Palermitan cuisine.

As they took their seats, Valentina sat beside Alex, subtly resting her hand on his. Her mother, wearing a contented smile, cherished the moment of having her family together. The clinking of glasses and the unfolding of napkins set a rhythm for the occasion.

Luciano raised his glass, prompting the others to follow suit. His deep voice resonated with emotion as he spoke, "To family, to love, and to the promise of a future where we stand united, always."

The glasses clinked together in agreement, their unified sound symbolizing the unity felt by the Massotti family.

As they began to indulge in the feast before them, Luciano's gaze turned introspective. On the surface, he savored the food, appreciating the flavors, but internally, a storm brewed.

Can I truly protect them? he pondered. *They hold onto hope for a brighter tomorrow, but what if darkness awaits us?*

Each bite reminded him of the legacy he was part of, the choices he had made. The vibrant colors of the dishes blurred as his thoughts took a darker turn.

Interpol watches my every move. The mafia will not release me easily. And now, with Bellini's discovery... it's a ticking time bomb.

Feeling a hand on his, Luciano looked up to see his wife, her eyes searching his, silently conveying unwavering support. With gratitude, he squeezed her hand, drawing strength from her touch.

Clearing his throat, he addressed everyone, although his gaze primarily focused on Valentina and Alex. "These are uncertain times for us. I implore each of you to remember that, no matter what lies ahead, you must remain united. Look out for one another. Our bond, our love, is the sole force that can guide us through."

Valentina's eyes welled up, but she nodded, gripping Alex's hand tighter. Luciano's message was clear - the road ahead was uncertain, but together, they could face anything.

Each person had a small glass of 'Amaro del Capo' before them, a deep amber digestif known for aiding digestion after a hearty meal. The bittersweet scent wafted up, contrasting sharply with the weight of Luciano's words.

Raising his glass, Luciano locked eyes with each individual present. When his gaze met Alex's, a hint of suspicion and an unspoken challenge flickered. "Difficult times lie ahead," he began, his voice low and grave. "I have absolute faith in each and every one of you." The emphasis on "faith" and the lingering look he gave Alex conveyed an unmistakable message.

Alex's throat tightened as he sensed the shift in Luciano's demeanor towards him. Valentina, too, picked up on the tension and offered Alex a comforting squeeze beneath the table.

Luciano continued, his gaze sweeping across the faces of his family. "In the coming months, each of us will play a vital role. Our family will endure. We all understand the high stakes." His words carried a weight, hinting at undisclosed dangers and challenges that lay ahead.

He paused, allowing the gravity of his words to sink in, before adding, "When I ask something of you, hesitation cannot exist. In times like these, I must be the head of our household, safeguarding our business, our home, and our lives."

--

The Massotti villa, immersed in the embrace of the night, presented a picturesque tableau of a family entrenched within their own fortress. Each member occupied a distinct space in the tapestry of their grand home.

Alex, sprawled on the plush couch, was illuminated by the azure glow of his laptop. Papers and digital documents were scattered across the screen, their details revealed by the dim light. The soft clicking of the keyboard punctuated the silence of the living room as he delved into the depths of a criminal world, all while outwardly appearing engrossed in the routine work of a diligent employee.

By the poolside, Valentina and her mother found solace in an idyllic escape. The serene water mirrored the tranquility of the night sky. Their conversation, like the wine they savored, was rich with history and undertones of worry for the future, yet held a bouquet of hope that lingered with every word. Occasional laughter slipped through, a testament to their resilience and defiance of the darkness that had sought to permeate their lives.

In stark contrast, Luciano's study exuded an aura of quiet intensity. Agent Mitchel stood with a stance that blended interrogation with the protection of a potential asset. Luciano, the master of his domain even in these challenging times, faced Mitchel with a stoic yet weary demeanor.

"You were present when Bellini's lab burned," Mitchel began, his voice unwavering. "So we know you're not directly involved. But what about Valentina? Where was she?"

"I have many flaws, Agent Mitchel, but I would never use my daughter as a pawn in my dealings," Luciano replied, his voice tinged with a father's protective edge. "Valentina has no part in this. She was away, seeking to regain some semblance of a normal life after what she's endured."

Mitchel paused, contemplating the patriarch's words. "We need a comprehensive understanding of the entire picture here, Luciano. If not you, then who stands to benefit from Bellini's silence?"

Luciano's gaze turned inward momentarily before he responded. "I am but a piece in a much larger game, one that I am still striving to comprehend. As I've mentioned before, this family, our business, it is merely a fraction of a far more intricate structure. Bellini's work threatened not only local players but the global stage as well."

Mitchel's eyes narrowed. "Are you suggesting an international conspiracy?"

With a resigned sigh, Luciano reclined in his chair. "All I know is that there are forces at play, entities I dare not even speak of. The destruction of the lab could serve as a message to anyone who dares disrupt the current order, extending far beyond the reach of the mafia. And if they are willing to go to such lengths to silence one man, imagine what they would do to safeguard their interests."

The conversation continued, a delicate dance of information and innuendo, as each man played his role in a game where the rules were as elusive as the shadows that cloaked the villa.

Chapter XXVII

Soft ambient lighting bathes the living room in muted hues. The rustic Italian design, adorned with artworks and plush furnishings, presents a stark contrast to the underlying tension in the room. The gentle hum of evening cicadas and distant sounds of the sea weave through the partially opened window.

Luciano, his weariness evident from his conversation with Mitchel, emerges from the study. He walks with an air of gravitas, each step a testament to the weight he carries, not only as the head of the family but as a linchpin in the impending crisis.

Observing Alex's swift screen change, Luciano raises an eyebrow but remains silent. He approaches the minibar, retrieving a crystal decanter filled with a deep amber liquid. Pausing for a moment, he lets the aroma waft.

Raising the decanter, he asks, "Alex, care to join me?"

Caught off guard, Alex nods slowly and replies, "Sure, thank you."

Luciano pours a second glass and hands it to Alex. As their glasses clink softly, a fleeting truce emerges amidst uncertainty. They both take a sip, the warmth of the whiskey and the cool evening breeze.

Breaking the silence, Luciano begins, "Alex, I am aware of our... differences. I cannot claim to fully know or trust you. However, at this moment, we are united. For the sake of my daughter, if nothing else."

Gazing into the depths of his glass, Alex responds, "I understand your reservations, Luciano. I have no intention of causing harm, especially to Valentina. You have my word."

Luciano, sporting a faint smile, remarks, "Words come easily, young man. It is our actions that define us. And right now, every move we make carries weight. A greater game is being played."."

Luciano smirks and declares, "For Valentina, and for the future." They raise their glasses once more, sealing their newfound alliance, at least for the time being.

Perched on the cliffside, the Massotti villa stood proudly against the backdrop of the starlit Mediterranean. Inside, the world seemed distant, as if time itself had momentarily paused, granting its inhabitants respite from the impending storm.

Valentina, draped in a flowing white nightgown, stood by the window, her silhouette framed by the ethereal moonlight. The gentle sea breeze played with tendrils of her hair. Despite her heavy heart, solace found her in the rhythmic sound of waves crashing below. Alex approached, his comforting hand resting on the small of her back, their fingers intertwining effortlessly.

"Isn't it a beautiful night?" Alex whispered, planting a tender kiss on her temple.

"It is," Valentina murmured softly, her voice barely audible. "But beauty can sometimes deceive."

He pulled her into an embrace, their hearts echoing each other's fears and hopes. "We will overcome this," he vowed, holding her tighter.

In another part of the villa, memories captured in old photographs lay scattered on a bed. Luciano picked up a picture of his younger self and his wife, a reminder of simpler times. His wife leaned into him, her fingers tracing patterns on his hand.

"We have weathered many storms, mio amore," she said, her voice tinged with melancholy. "But this one feels different."

Luciano kissed her forehead, masking the uncertainty in his own eyes. "Remember, every sunrise after a storm is brighter. We must endure until dawn breaks."

Outside the comforting walls of the villa, shadows loomed closer. The vastness of the beach was interrupted by six figures, moving in perfect synchronization. With each step, their forms became clearer against the sand, yet their faces remained hidden, revealed only by the eerie green glow of their night vision goggles.

The only sounds were the tranquil waves, the chirping of night crickets, and the soft padding of boots on the sand. Every step was purposeful, every movement calculated. The villa, brimming with warmth and cherished memories, was their target.

As the night deepened, the impending threat grew larger. Unaware of the storm about to descend, the Massotti family remained cocooned within the safety of their ancestral home.

The delicate balance between tranquility and turmoil, safety and danger, hung precariously in the air. And as the first light of dawn threatened to break, the dice of destiny were about to be cast.

---

to be continued.

Printed in Great Britain
by Amazon

VOLUME ONE

ALPHA'S DESIRE

AN MC SHIFTER ROMANCE

RENEE ROSE
LEE SAVINO

BURNING DESIRES

Copyright © March 2018 Alpha's Desire by Renee Rose and Lee Savino

All rights reserved. This copy is intended for the original purchaser of this e-book ONLY. No part of this e-book may be reproduced, scanned, or distributed in any printed or electronic form without prior written permission from the author. Please do not participate in or encourage piracy of copyrighted materials in violation of the author's rights. Purchase only authorized editions.

Published in the United States of America

Renee Rose Romance and Silverwood Press

Editor: MJ

This e-book is a work of fiction. While reference might be made to actual historical events or existing locations, the names, characters, places and incidents are either the product of the author's imaginations or are used fictitiously, and any resemblance to actual persons, living or dead, business establishments, events, or locales is entirely coincidental.

This book contains descriptions of many BDSM and sexual practices, but this is a work of fiction and, as such, should not be used in any way as a guide. The author and publisher will not be responsible for any loss, harm, injury, or death resulting from use of the information contained within. In other words, don't try this at home, folks!

ALPHA'S DESIRE

She's the one girl this player can't have. A human.

I'm dying to claim the redhead who lights up the club every Saturday night.

I want to pull her into the storeroom and make her scream, but it wouldn't be right.

She's too pure. Too fresh. Too passionate.

Too human.

When she learns my secret, my alpha orders me to wipe her memories.

But I won't do it.

Still, I'm not mate material—I can't mark her and bring her into the pack.

What in the hell am I going to do with her?

1
———

Jared

Three months I've been hard for this human.

I know, woe is me, right? Try telling that to my cock when she's up on that box in her miniscule shorts doing her little go-go dance for all the patrons of my Alpha's nightclub.

Angelina. The red-headed dynamo who single-handedly transformed Eclipse into *the* happening place in Tucson on Saturday nights.

And right now some asshole just put his hands on her thighs.

I shove my way through the nightclub, ready to pound skulls. Lucky for me—unlucky for the handsy asshole—that's my job.

Heat comes off the crowd in waves. The music thumps. The clubbers part to make room for my hulking frame. I carry two hundred and twenty pounds of solid, tattooed

muscle. Not many try to mess with me or any of the other bouncers at Eclipse.

We don't even have to pull out our shifter strength to show force.

Garrett doesn't appreciate his bouncers getting overly aggressive, but dialing it back is an impossibility for me when I see Angelina's annoyance at Handsy's unrelenting come-on.

I shove my body between him and Angelina's go-go box and fold my arms over my chest, mostly to keep me from closing my fist around his fragile human neck.

"Whoa, whoa!" He throws his offending palms up with an affronted air, like I'm overreacting.

"Hands off the dancers. You do it again, you're eighty-sixed."

"O-*kay*. Jeez. I was just saying hello."

"You want to argue with me?" I challenge. Of course I'm pretty much dying for him to say yes, because wiping that attitude off his face would almost be as satisfying as receiving the grateful look Angelina's sending my way.

Come on into the storeroom after closing and I'll let you thank me properly.

I wish. Not that she hasn't given me the signals. Not that I haven't fucked at least a hundred human girls in that storeroom since Eclipse opened.

But I'm a little too hot for her.

And humans are off-limits for relationships. At least they were before Garrett decided to mate one.

Besides, she's totally out of my league.

Fresh-faced and passionate, she's a dance major from the University. She couldn't be more clean-cut and innocent.

Meanwhile, I'm motorcycles and tattoos.

And a shifter.

Alpha's Desire

Definitely not the right guy for her. And if I fucked that hot little body? I'd ruin her for everyone else.

Not to sound conceited about my abilities, but I pay attention to what a girl likes. I'm over-the-top rough and dominant, but I never force, never harm. I just coax their surrender and show them the way of the wolf.

Trey calls it Jaredizing. Once a girl's had a taste, she keeps coming back for more. And then I have to end things, feelings get hurt. Something Angelina never deserves.

Handsy backs away, smarter than he acted at first. "No, man. I'm not arguing. Sheesh." He shakes his head as he turns and ducks away into the crowd.

I look up at Angelina. "You okay, baby?"

Fuck if she doesn't run her fingers over my closely cropped hair, her wide smile revealing one deep dimple. "Thank you," she shouts over the music. "You're my knight in shining armor!"

The music shifts to Lady Gaga's latest hit. Angelina jumps up and down, clearly thrilled with the DJ's choice. "Woohoo!"

I stay, grinning up at her like an idiot, because this girl draws me like a magnet.

I see the glint of excitement in her eyes right before she launches herself at me. Straddling one shoulder, she pumps her fist in the air.

Holy Mother of God. My hand snaps up to her back to hold her in place as she fucking rocks her pelvis, dancing on my shoulder.

At least I think she's dancing. My brain tells me that's what this activity is, but my cock is certain she's begging to be fucked. Especially considering her pussy is *inches* away from my face.

I sink my teeth into her inner thigh.

RENEE ROSE & LEE SAVINO

She screams and grips my head with both hands, which only makes my dick think she wants more.

Yeah, this isn't going to work. If I don't put her back down on that box now, my mouth is going to *go to town* on the little scrap of fabric standing between me and that sweet pussy of hers.

I duck down to lower my shoulder and reluctantly let her slide off, back to her perch. I can't resist slapping that irresistible ass of hers before I turn and walk away.

I don't look back—I *can't*—but I'm satisfied knowing I left a good handprint on that bare flesh she's been shaking for everyone tonight.

And seriously, I might have to tell her to come with her ass covered next week.

No. I can't. Because:

A) The short shorts that only cover half a girl's ass are in style. All the college girls are sporting them.

B) The go-go dancers and their delectable asses are part of why the club goes over-capacity every Saturday night. Garrett would not approve of me making changes to their costumes. Not that we have any artistic license over their act.

It's Angelina's show. Her brainchild, her proposal, her execution. She brought her crew of dancers and they make the place pop.

If only she didn't leave me so blue-balled every time they performed.

A*ngelina*

Oh, lordy.

Jared, the beefy bouncer with the tattoos and dark flirty manner has me all a-flutter. My butt stings where he smacked me and I don't have to look to know he left a big, red print for all to see.

I have a feeling that was his intention.

Damn my fair, red-headed complexion, because the flush creeping up my neck and spreading across my face is probably visible for all to see.

I watch him disappear into the crowd, disappointed he doesn't look back. The man is beautiful. A perfect specimen of raw masculinity. He's rough-mannered and tattooed, but damn, he has enough charm to take all the edges off what might otherwise be an intimidating presence.

And wow, that little show of force with the guy who was bugging me?

Total turn-on. I've always had a thing for heroes.

I turn my head to catch the eyes of the other two dancers on shift tonight and the three of us go into a pre-arranged combination, changing from freestyle to synchronized movement.

Talya and Remy are both a little bit drunk, but we all know this routine so well we could do it in our sleep. Plus, professional or semi-professional dancers like us, with the amount of training in our bodies, can make anything look purposeful and choreographed.

The song ends and our set is over. We get the last hour to play—drinks on the house. That was the deal I worked out with the owner, another huge and quite intimidating man named Garrett Green. Fifty bucks each and free drinks in exchange for go-go dancing every Saturday night. Most of

the girls on my makeshift dance team would do it just for the free cover and the attention they get up on those boxes.

Me? I don't know why I do it. Not for the drinks—I don't do well with alcohol. Just for the sheer joy of creation, I guess. It's fun to insert real dance into everyday life.

Yes, I'm the type who loves musicals, where people suddenly break into song in public places. I'm the girl who rides her cart down the aisle in the grocery store, resisting an arabesque, choreographing a performance piece in my head for the shoppers I pass.

Don't worry, I don't actually execute it. Not that I wouldn't, if I could talk other dancers into joining me.

I weave through the crowd, pretending I'm not looking for the sexy man-hunk, Jared. There. By the door to the back patio. I head to the bar because I don't want to be too obvious. I don't think he's actually interested. I mean, I've given him the signal for weeks and although he gives me smoldering looks, he never actually asks for my number or suggests I hang out after hours.

Total disappointment.

I saddle up at the bar and order a tonic water with lime. It's my stupid trick to make it appear I'm drinking a gin and tonic or vodka and soda, when really I'm just hydrating. My friends get their drinks and mingle and I pretend to play it cool. A guy comes over to me, but I'm not interested, so I give a polite smile and head to the bathroom.

When I get out, Jared stands there in the hallway.

"Come here, little girl." He crooks a finger at me. I follow him through the staff-only door, into the storeroom, packed high with boxes of alcohol.

Damn, if a fraternity ever wanted a place to rob, this would be the jackpot.

Alpha's Desire

My heart pounds, face heating even though I don't know what he wants.

I mean, I know what I *hope* he wants.

And I shouldn't hope for it.

From all accounts, Jared is a player. He hooks up with girls and never calls. That's what everyone says, including his best buddy, the other bouncer, Trey. I've been warned off this guy, but I still can't stop the thrills of excitement fluttering through my body.

Jared picks up one of my hands. Before I have any clue what he's doing, he spins me around to face a wall and slaps it there. Then he picks up my other wrist and stacks it with the first, pinning both with one powerful palm.

My breath clogs my throat as his hand crashes down on my backside. Like before, he catches the underside of my butt, the bare part below my short shorts.

I gasp, but don't protest, way too turned on to want it to stop.

He smacks the other cheek, just as hard. "That is for wearing shorts that make every guy in the building want to fuck this juicy ass."

I'm pretty sure I stop breathing. I've never been spoken to in such a rough and dirty manner, but I'm definitely not complaining. My lady parts squeeze and swell, planning a party for whatever else Jared has to offer.

He spins me back around to face him. My butt hits the wall and I lose my breath on an exhale. His hand goes right to the notch between my legs and he cups my mons.

"And the next time you put this pussy so close to my mouth—" He undulates his hand, pressing over my shorts in tandem from clit to anus. I gasp and rise up on my toes. "—you're going to find out just exactly what I'd like to do with it."

A shiver of epic proportions runs through me. More like a shudder, only that sounds bad. And what I'm feeling is really freakin' far from bad. My insides turn liquid, heat pours down my thighs, straight to the arches of my feet.

I now understand where the phrase *he curls my toes* comes from.

He slowly slides the firm contact of his fingers over the fabric just above my slit, which has completely dampened my panties. "Understand, beautiful?"

I swallow. "Yeah." My pussy clenches.

His fingers delve under the crotch of my shorts, into my panties and I mewl.

"Baby, you wear these shorts to Eclipse again, I'm gonna take you back here and spank this juicy ass so red every guy watching you dance will know you've been claimed."

He jerks his head back and shakes it, as if he's surprised by what he just said, but his fingers glide, glide, glide over my slit. I moan softly, my gaze staying at the level of his chest.

"Eyes on me, baby," he commands and I obey without thinking. Dancers are by nature obedient creatures. We've spent our lives molding our bodies and minds to do anything and everything a director or teacher asks of us. Any dancer who doesn't gets weeded out fast. There are always ten more waiting to take your spot if you're not willing to give five hundred percent.

He holds my gaze as he screws one finger into me.

I whimper, not out of pain, but out of need. I'm not a virgin but I've literally never been so turned on in my life. My nipples poke against the tight fabric of my shirt and my pussy is sopping.

I writhe against his hold on my wrists, grind down to take his finger deeper.

Alpha's Desire

He leans his head down by mine, so we're temple to temple. "You okay, angel?"

It's a little late to be double-checking for my permission, but I appreciate the ask. "Yeah," I breathe.

"Good." He shifts and wedges a second finger inside me.

I buck my hips, rising up on my toes.

"You're dancing for me now, aren't you, baby?"

"Oh God," I moan.

He's worked both fingers deep inside me and now he stops moving. Just stops!

"Wh-what at are you doing?"

His grin is all shades of sexy. "Just making sure you really want it."

I roll my hips. "I said I did."

He pumps slowly. Too slowly. "Say it nicely. Tell me who you're dancing for."

"You. I'm dancing for you," I cry, growing desperate for release.

"You want more of my fingers, angel?"

"Jared," I pant.

His eyelids droop.

One part of me gets pissed. Is he making a fool of me here?

He must sense my resistance because he says, "Nah, fuck it. I should be begging you. I can't wait to watch you go over the edge, beautiful." He pumps his fingers in and out until my shimmying legs are ready to give out. "Come for me, Angelina. Show me what you've got."

I have no idea what he means by that, but, again, my body follows his command. I give into his skilled torture. The moment my muscles start to squeeze his fingers, he shoves deep and waits, letting me tighten and ease in waves of pleasure and release.

"Aw, fuck, baby." He leans his forehead against mine as he eases his fingers out. "That was even better than I imagined."

I'm not sure what he means, since I'm the one who got off, but it still inspires a giddiness that revives me from the relaxation coursing through my muscles.

The doorknob rattles and Jared jerks away, releasing me and tugging down the hem of my shorts just before the door swings open.

One of the bartenders bustles in, then stops when he sees us, throwing us a curious look.

Jared steps in front of me, as if to shield me from scrutiny, and I appreciate the gesture, late though it may be.

"I'd better go find my friends," I murmur. It's not that I want to leave Jared. Wait—yes I do.

Embarrassment takes over, along with the realization that he's probably brought dozens of girls back here. That's why the bartender doesn't seem surprised.

I push past Jared toward the door.

"Wait, angel. Just *wait*." He catches me around the waist.

I go still but I don't look at him.

"I'm sorry," he murmurs, keeping his voice low so only I will hear. "I definitely didn't mean to make you feel used or cheap."

I'm not sure if that's how I was feeling, but now that he's named it, a sick feeling spreads through my belly.

"Hey, I really I have to go," I insist.

Jared releases me. I sense his reluctance, even though I refuse to meet his eye. I just want to get out of there.

I'm the only one of my friends who didn't drink tonight and I'm the one making the bad decisions.

"Just wait. Can you give me a second?"

I slip out of his reach. "That's okay," I mumble, without

Alpha's Desire

looking back. "We can talk later." I bolt from the storeroom before he can say anything else. I sense him behind me, but I don't look back, just beeline it for the bar to find my friends and get the hell out of here.

What was I thinking? Apparently all it takes is a couple slaps to my ass and I'll let a guy do anything to me.

Damn. I need to tell my friends never to let me be alone with Jared. Ever. Especially not when I'm ovulating.

Danger zone.

I find Talya and Remy just as the overhead fluorescents come on, signaling the club is closing. The crowd gives a collective groan and people scurry out like cockroaches caught in the sun.

"Come on," I urge my friends. "Let's get out of here. I've had enough."

J*ared*

I screwed up. Big time.

I *knew* I was supposed to keep my hands off Angelina. She's my female kryptonite. My self-control goes to shit around her.

Now I've gone and degraded her in the worst way.

It was almost worth it. *Almost.*

Fuck, I will be jacking off to the memory of her orgasm face every night for a week. It was even better than I pictured it would be.

I scan the crowd remaining, people who need encour-

agement to leave. Men and women trying to find or solidify their hookups before they go.

"Time's up," I call out. "Everybody out."

I get *fuck me* looks from a couple girls who hang back.

I'm not tempted. Not really. But part of me thinks maybe I should fuck one of them just to get that red-headed beauty out of my system. Out of my fantasies. Damn she's been the main feature of them ever since she showed up here at the beginning of the semester with her bold new idea for having go-go dancers.

Somehow, I'd even volunteered to make the boxes the dancers perch on.

A blonde, who'd been prettier in the low lighting than she is under the bright glare, toddles toward me on six inch heels.

I frown and give my head a short shake and she wheels about and teeters out the door instead. I shake my head again, more at myself than anyone else, and help get the rest of the crowd out. As I run the dust mop to pick up the litter of plastic cups, straws, and cocktail napkins, I try to think of something else—anything but the sweet curves of Angelina's ass when she was dancing up on that box. Or the slight curl of her lip when I penetrated her. The way her mouth opened and eyes rolled back when she came.

I'm still replaying it all after we lock up.

"What's with you, dude?" Trey asks as we walk to our parked motorcycles in the lot.

"Nothing." I sound surlier than I mean to.

"Did something happen between you and that dancer?"

"Shut up, asshole." Trey's my best friend, but sometimes he doesn't know how to leave well enough alone.

"Uh huh. I thought so. Damian said you were fucking her in the storeroom."

Alpha's Desire

I grab Trey's collar and fist it up tight, getting my face right into his grill. "I was *not* fucking her."

"Okay," he says quickly, holding up his palms. "Whatever you say, bud."

I know all I've done is dug my grave now, so I release him and jerk my chin toward his bike. "Go on. I'll see you at home later."

"Where are you going?" he asks suspiciously.

"For a ride."

Trey shrugs and takes off. I wait until he's gone before I straddle my bike, turning it on with a louder rev of the engine than is necessary.

I tear out of the parking lot. It's almost three in the morning and no cars are left on the road. At least that's what I tell myself. The truth is that I'm still back in that fucking storeroom, replaying the part that went south with Angelina.

That's why I pull out of the alley without looking.

I don't see the car coming. Not until I'm flying over it as glass shatters like a burst of confetti from a party balloon.

2

Angelina

I don't know if all the screams are mine. Someone whimpers in the back seat.

That would be Remy. Talya's in the front seat beside me. Yeah, she's screaming, too.

I clamp my lips shut to stop the terrible sound and force my brain to work. I hit something. Someone.

Oh God. I just hit a motorcycle.

I lurch out of the car and stumble around to the front. The impact crushed my front grill, crumpling the hood. One of my headlights is out—broken by the impact. The remaining one casts an eerie beam over the horrible scene. A huge motorcycle is on its side in front of the car, but the rider—

Please don't let him be under the car.

A pitiful whimper comes out of my throat. I drop to my knees to peer under the carriage, but I can't see anything.

Talya and Remy tumble out of the vehicle, too. They

were drunk when we left Eclipse. We'd be home by now, except Talya made me wait to drive home until the car stopped spinning for her.

"Wh-what's happening?" she croaks.

Remy stares at the bike. "Where's the driver?"

"I don't know," I wail, running around to the back of the car.

There.

A large crumpled form is lying on the alley pavement behind my car. I cover my mouth with my hand. Is he dead?

Please don't let him be dead.

No, he's moving, trying to sit up.

I run to him and squat beside him. "I-I don't think you're supposed to move."

He groans and pulls off his helmet. One arm wraps protectively around his ribs.

"Jared!" My heart rockets to my throat, choking me.

I've hurt Jared. I hit Jared. This is bad. Bad, bad, bad, bad.

"Jared, don't move. I'm going to call 911." I fumble in my back pocket for the phone, cursing myself for not calling the second it happened. Or maybe this still is the second it happened. I can't tell. Time seems very slow at the moment.

"No." Jared snatches the phone out of my hand, cracking the case in his powerful grip.

I gape at him.

"No ambulance." He staggers to his feet and shoves my phone in his pocket. Blood runs down his forehead, pouring into his eyes.

I'm trembling from head to toe, my legs barely holding me up. "Wh-what? No, you need an ambulance."

He limps toward my car.

"Jared."

He walks around to the front and picks up—yes *picks up*

Alpha's Desire

—his motorcycle. I don't mean from the ground, I mean, *into the air*. He carries it around behind a dumpster and stows it there.

"Jared, are you all right? I think you need medical attention, right away."

"Yeah, definitely." Shock reverberates in Remy's voice. I wonder if mine sounds the same.

He-man—the Hulk—Neanderthal Joe just keeps going, dragging himself to the driver's side of my car and getting in.

"What? You can't drive. What are you doing?" I know I sound like the stupid one here, but he's acting crazy. He can't get in and drive a car. He probably has broken bones and a concussion. Not to mention the fact that he needs stitches on his forehead.

"Get in." The order is deep and scratchy and it carries so much command behind it, the three of us scramble to obey, even though he's in no position to be taking charge of this situation.

I climb in the passenger seat and Remy and Talya jump in back.

Jared puts the car in drive and takes off down the alley. I reach around to the floor of the back seat where I keep my dance bag and fish out a pair of tights. "Uh, here." I hand it to him, pointing at his bleeding forehead.

Confusion flits across his expression at first, but he accepts the fabric and swipes at his face, mopping the blood up. "Thanks." He hands it back like he doesn't need to use it for compression. Like it was just a scratch.

"Are you driving to the hospital?"

He gives a quick shake of his head. "I'm driving you three home. You're too shook up to drive, and they're drunk."

He's so matter of fact—sounds so completely capable—I almost forget for a moment he's in no condition to drive.

"Tell me where to go."

"Um..." My brain won't work at all. He's right, I'm way too shaken up. I can't even function.

"Who do you drop off first?"

"Talya." The answer comes as a relief. "Campbell and Third."

He gives a nod and puts on his blinker, driving my bashed up car as if nothing happened.

"I-isn't this illegal? Leaving the scene of an accident?"

A smile tugs at his lips. "The other party is in the car with you."

"But don't we have to notify the cops? How will I file the insurance report? I wasn't drinking or anything. Were you afraid I'd get in trouble?" I know I'm babbling. I can't stop myself.

None of this makes any sense.

"Are you hurt?" he asks suddenly, glancing over at me. His forehead is creased, green eyes flash with alarm.

"Um." I rub the back of my neck, checking for whiplash.

"Any of you?" he barks, looking in the rearview mirror.

"No. I'm okay," Talya slurs.

"Me too," Remy says.

"Angelina?" He looks back at me. "Talk to me, baby."

"Jared, *you're* hurt," I manage to say.

He gives a dismissive shake of his head. "I'll be fine by morning. Just a few bumps and scrapes. But tell me you're okay, or I'm going to lose my shit here."

"I'm fine."

Jared's shoulders relax, but the crease remains between his brows.

"You're sure?"

Alpha's Desire

"Yeah, I think so. Just shaken up."

"Of course you are." He drops a hand on my knee like he's offering me comfort. This is more like the Jared I know. Neanderthal Jared is fading away.

"I'm sorry I hit you," I blurt, the tears that have been threatening since the impact falling now.

"Aw, no. It was my fault, baby. I didn't expect anyone to be coming down that alley at this time of night, but I should've looked first."

"Were *you* drinking?" I don't want to sound like a bitch, but I'm still trying to figure out why he wouldn't let me call for help.

"No, baby. I'm fine. That's why I'm driving." He moves his hand to my nape and squeezes, gently kneading my muscles.

We reach Third Avenue and I point out Talya's house. He pulls over and she climbs out. "Are you guys sure you're okay?" She leans back in the open door. Her breath reeks of alcohol.

"Yeah, yeah, we're fine," I say. "Goodnight."

"G'night." She gives a sloppy wave and slams the door shut.

Jared waits until she's safely in her house before he starts driving again. I direct him to Remy's house and then to my little casita. Jared stops the car there and gets out.

Is he coming in?

I should definitely ask him to stay, in case he goes into a coma or something during the night. But when he walks around to meet me, he's no longer limping. On closer inspection, I see the cut on his head isn't bleeding anymore, either. In fact, it no longer looks fresh. It has the appearance of skin that's already been stitched closed for a week. It must be a trick of the light.

25

"Come here." Jared wraps me in a bear hug.

I didn't know how badly I needed it until I'm in his strong arms, my face pressed against his massive chest.

A few more tears leak out as he burrows his fingers in my hair and massages my scalp. The shock and aftershock quickly morph into something different. Something dangerous and needy.

I pull away, remembering how awkward our parting had been at Eclipse. My hands flutter. "Um, do you want to come in? I mean, you should stay the night. Just to be sure you're all right. Not because I want you to spend the night—" Ugh. I'm making a mess of things.

Jared, as usual, takes the lead, taking my elbow and walking toward my door. "I'll stay on your couch, if you have one. To make sure you're all right."

To make sure *I'm* all right.

This guy is seriously out of touch with his own body.

Except he looks fine. He's not clutching his ribs anymore. His pupils are the same size. Where did the limp go?

What in the hell just happened?

We stop on the porch and he examines my keyring, correctly guessing which key opens my door. Inside, he looks around my tiny place and sets the ring on the stand in the entry.

"I'll just clean up." He peels his bloodied shirt off and heads to my bathroom.

My jaw might have dropped a bit seeing his bare shoulders and back. Tattoos curl around giant, telephone pole size arms. The muscles in his back would put the Hulk to shame.

Yum.

But no.

Alpha's Desire

I'm not going to fool around with Jared anymore because:

A) He's here to recuperate from the accident, and

B) He's a player. Except

C) I'm not sure I care.

I trail him to the bathroom, telling myself it's because I need to make sure he's all right. Check out his injuries for myself.

It's *not* because I want to gawk at his very fine chiseled body.

He splashes water over his face, washing off the blood and when he straightens, I gasp.

The cut is almost completely gone.

My brain tries to make it work, to fit it into a scenario that makes sense, but I can't. I *saw* that cut gushing blood, not more than thirty minutes ago.

He catches me looking and slaps his hand over his forehead, hiding the cut, which only makes this weirder. Like *Twilight Zone* crazy.

I stumble back, my breath caught in my throat. "Who... what... *are* you?"

J*ared*

F*uck fuck and double fuck.*

I drop my hand and reach for her. I can't stand the way her face has paled, the way she shrinks from me like I'm some kind of freak.

27

I grab her by the waist and pick her up, plopping her down on the bathroom counter. "It's okay, baby. You don't have to be afraid. Not of me."

She swallows. "You didn't answer my question," she whispers.

Dammit.

How am I going to get out of this one?

It's against shifter code to reveal ourselves to humans. I remember when Garrett, my boss and alpha, fell for the hot little lawyer who lived next door. Until he mated her and sealed her fate with ours, Trey and I were worried as fuck.

The oldest code says humans who know have to be put down. *Eliminated.*

I haven't heard of that happening in my lifetime, but I'm sure it still happens in some backwards packs.

A more common solution is to hire a memory wipe from a leech. But I would never do that to Angelina. She doesn't deserve having her brain tampered with by a fucking vampire.

I need to figure out something to say that won't reveal me or the pack.

"I'm... uh... special," I say.

Yeah. That's brilliant, J.

She stares up at me with those big blue eyes.

I lean my hands on the counter, caging her between my arms. "Not dangerous."

"Not dangerous," she repeats, her full lips looking so damn kissable, it's all I can do not to claim that pouty mouth.

"Right."

"Special how?"

"Uh..." I remember that I picked up my motorcycle in front of her—something I wouldn't have done if I hadn't just

Alpha's Desire

flipped over a car and landed on my head. "I'm just really strong. And I heal fast. Kinda like a superhero."

A superhero.

Wow. That's a great line. I don't know why I don't use that more often with the women.

She reaches her fingertips out and tentatively brushes my chest with them. A jolt of pleasure runs through me at the contact. "So you're... totally fine? Not hurt at all?"

Jesus, fuck, is that all she's worried about? Thank the fates.

"Totally fine, baby. Now, are you going to let me kiss you?"

Dammit, I didn't mean to come in and seduce her. It totally wasn't my plan. But I can't fucking resist my hot little dancer.

When her full lips part and her eyes drop to mine, I don't stop myself. I catch the back of her head to hold her captive for my kiss. My lips drag across hers, suck, nip. When her tongue darts between my lips, I lose all control. I palm her scantily covered ass, yanking her core right up against my straining cock as I go to town on her sexy mouth.

She opens to me, yields so willingly. Her legs wrap around my waist and tighten and *goddamn* her inner thighs are strong! That's the dance training, of course.

I pick her up and carry her to the bedroom. I want to fuck her brains out. To reward her for not freaking out about my unnatural healing abilities. Hell, to reward her for being her.

Because she is something magical and unique.

I drop her on the bed and go for the button on her shorts. The scent of her arousal fills the room. I rub the crotch seam over her slit with one knuckle as I work the button open.

She moans and wriggles, which makes it easy to strip her bottoms off. I leave the go-go boots on, because—yeah —they're hot.

Hands hooked under her knees, I spread her wide. For a moment I just stare, which makes my girl squirm.

A blush spreads up her neck and across her cheeks. "Wh-what are you doing?"

"Looking at the most perfect pussy on the face of the Earth." And it is. Dewy and plump, her pink heart open, begging to be licked. And yeah, the carpet matches the drapes, not that there was any question if she was a natural redhead.

"Jared." She tries to wriggle free of my grasp, but I hold her down and lower my head, laying a soft kiss right over her clit. The last moment of tenderness she's going to get before I bring it with everything I've got.

She shivers, her flat belly fluttering.

I part her lips with my tongue and trace along the insides, swirl my tongue around her clit.

She makes cute girl-sex sounds—adorable little *ung-ahs* that make my already throbbing dick harder than stone.

She's already had my fingers tonight, so I keep working her with my tongue. I'm going to work until she's screaming my name and tearing out my hair. She needs this release after the fright she had.

I suck and nip and lick until the pitch of her voice takes on a desperate keen, then I affix my lips to her clit and suck hard. I release it and flick it with my tongue. Then repeat. Because I'm a dirty guy and an ass man, I can't stop from pushing my thumb between her asscheeks, seeking her little back pucker.

The moment I hit it, she shrieks, squeezing her buns together and shoving her dripping pussy against my mouth.

Alpha's Desire

I keep torturing her with my tongue as I make slow circles with my thumb, massaging her anus.

She thrashes beneath me, babbling incoherently.

I apply a little more pressure with my thumb and she goes off, screaming, thrusting against my mouth, her hands pushing my face against her core as her muscles do their squeezy thing that signals her orgasm.

"That's it, beautiful," I say when she finishes. "I love the way you come."

She gives a shaky laugh that rings with disbelief.

"I do." I reach up and pinch her nipple through her thin t-shirt and bra. "Dancers must do it better."

She smiles and pushes her hair out of her face. "I'm sure we do."

I roll her over. "Let me look at this firm little ass of yours." I give it a slap. Her ass is all toned muscle, like her thighs. So spankable.

I prod her legs apart and rub her pussy with my fingers. I let my thumb quest again for her anus.

She squeezes her butt again.

"I know, baby. You're an anal virgin, aren't you?"

She doesn't answer, but I'm sure she is.

"I'd love to take this ass. I'll bet it's so fucking tight. But I'm not going to do it now. We'll save that for when you've been naughty and need another spanking."

Her bottom clenches again and I chuckle.

But I shouldn't have mentioned what happened back at the club, because it must remind her of how she felt after. I think I made her feel cheap and used—something I never wanted to do.

She rolls over and sits up, pulling the bedspread over her waist. "I, um... I don't know if this is a good idea." Her

eyes travel down to the bulge in my jeans and guilt flits across her face.

I adjust my cock. *Down, boy.* "No, you're right."

I can't be in a relationship with this girl, and she deserves so much more than a one night stand.

I back up. "I'll just, ah... You know, I should probably go. I'm gonna take your car to my friend Tank's shop. We'll get it all fixed for you at my expense, okay? The accident was my fault."

She stares at me with those guileless blue eyes, so wide and alert, it's all I can do not to go back to her and kiss her senseless.

"Can you Uber until I get it back to you? I promise I'll make it happen fast."

"Um, yeah. Okay. Thanks."

"It's the least I can do. What's your phone number?"

I enter her number into my phone and remember I still have her phone in my back pocket. I toss it to her. "Get some sleep. I'll text you with an update on the car." After I stow my phone, I shove my hands in my pockets to keep from reaching for her, settling instead for dropping a kiss on the top of her head.

"Goodnight, angel."

"'Night." Her voice is soft and sweet and that single syllable makes me want to go right back and worship between her legs again, but I force myself to leave.

Dammit. I fucked up again. I hope she doesn't hate me for this.

3

_____

Angelina

I wake up at noon and pad to the bathroom on auto-pilot. Then I see the huge black, blood-crusted t-shirt on my floor and it all comes flooding back.

Jared and his super strength. His super healing abilities.

What the hell? Was I on drugs? I accepted his explanation so easily last night, but in the light of day, it sounds insane.

Jared, the superhero.

Except he does have all the qualities of a superhero, doesn't he? Hero. Strong. Protective. Giving.

Oh boy did he give last night.

And I gave absolutely nothing in return.

Because I really don't want to be another notch on his bedpost, or whatever the dumb cliche is. Jared is a player, through and through.

But then again, I already went pretty far with him.

What's the difference between having sex and what we did, really? Would it have been so horrible for him to get off, too? Considering I did, twice. I could've at least blown him. I'll bet his cock is as impressive as that hard body of his...

Oh God, what am I even thinking?

I need to erase this man from my mind. He may be hot, charming and endowed with superhero powers, but—

No, really. Why am I trying to erase him? He's better than a movie hero. I carry his bloodstained shirt to my laundry closet and toss it in the washer. The least I can do is wash his clothes for him.

That brings up all kinds of lurid images of domestic servitude. Me, in a fifties housewife outfit (nothing but an apron and panties and a pair of red heels, of course) waiting for him with dinner when he gets home.

Me, naked except for a pair of pearls and a raincoat, surprising him at work...

Except he works at a bar. And that just fizzled my fantasy completely.

No, this guy isn't husband material. Or even boyfriend material. He's a hot finger-bang at a nightclub. A ride home after a car crash.

The guy who fixes your car for free.

Okay, that's beyond attractive to me.

Because, seriously, my dad would've shit when he found out about the crash. He would've lectured me on and on about insurance rates going up and about how irresponsible I am driving home at three in the morning from a nightclub.

Of course, I'll probably still have to tell him about the crash tonight. My parents live here in Tucson and insist on Sunday dinners. Sometimes I really wish the best dance program in the country wasn't at the university in my hometown.

Alpha's Desire

I smirk, imagining bringing someone like Jared over to meet my parents. His appearance alone would shock their Foothills sensibilities to the core.

They keep dropping hints about getting me to meet some local multi-millionaire software mogul.

Not. Interested.

And it's only because my dad wants the guy to acquire his small niche software company. Sure, Dad, pimp your daughter out for your own gain. These are definitely still medieval times. Grrr.

I start the washing machine and check my phone.

Jared's already texted. *Your car is in good hands. I'll have it back to you tomorrow, and you'll never know the difference.*

And my resistance melts a little more.

I text back, *Thank you. What about your motorcycle? Do you need me to pay for the repairs?*

Not that I have any money, but I should offer. I will figure it out, if I need to. Maybe I can pick up another teaching gig at a local dance studio.

He responds immediately, *I have it covered. Don't sweat it.*

I smile at my phone. It's really hard not to feel warm and fuzzy about Jared. And also itchy and needy to see him again.

But I put the kibosh on that. I don't want to be his booty call or hookup or whatever it is he does.

It was definitely the right decision.

So I should stop getting fluttery thinking about him bringing my car to me tomorrow. Or asking me out. Or pinning me against a wall and spanking me again.

Yeah.

J ared

If I didn't think he'd bust my ass, I wouldn't even tell my alpha what happened.

But a car accident in the alley outside his club constitutes a phone call. Especially when it involves a girl seeing my body spontaneously regenerate.

Dammit.

I'd rather keep Angelina completely out of this conversation, but I can't do that either. Not only can shifters pick up on dishonesty, lying to Garrett would be a banishable offense, even if he wasn't one of my closest friends.

But I put the call off as long as I can. It's Sunday and he has a new mate. He doesn't want me calling with a shit story first thing in the day.

I wait until late afternoon to dial him, telling myself it's better to get the car and motorcycle repairs going first.

I told Trey this morning. He told me I was a fucking idiot and if I thought Garrett was going to let it slide that Angelina saw my injuries heal, I'm even dumber than I look. But that's standard shit-talk between the two of us.

I stand outside Tank's auto shop and lean my ass against our packmate's truck.

Garrett answers on the second ring. "What's up?"

Right away I start walking, like staying in motion is going to make this go down easier. "Hey, I had a little incident last night."

"What kind of incident? At the club?"

"Yeah. I pulled into the alley without looking and Angelina, the little go-go dancer, hit me."

Alpha's Desire

Garrett curses. "Was she hurt?" Of course he wouldn't ask if I'm hurt, because—yeah—we're shifters.

"No. Neither were the other two dancers. I drove them home and took her car to Tank's."

There's a pause, and Garrett, who knows me too well, says, "What aren't you telling me?"

I crack the knuckles of my free hand. "She saw a cut regenerate."

Garrett curses again.

I hear his mate, Amber, murmur something in the background.

"It's all right. Just pack shit. Don't worry, baby," I hear him reply. To me, he says, "Wipe her."

I grind my teeth. I don't want to fucking wipe her.

"She's doesn't know," I insist, but my insistence sounds flimsy, even to my own ears.

"She knows you're a paranormal. You know the rules. She gets wiped."

"You didn't wipe Amber." I'm an asshole to point it out, and also operating from an artificial sense of security, because if we were in the same room, my alpha probably would've flattened me.

Garrett's warning growl crackles through the phone. "Amber's different. She's a paranormal, too."

Garrett's mate has psychic abilities that he used to find his sister when she was kidnapped by the harvesters last spring.

Yeah, well Angelina's a beautiful dancer with a bright future. Right. Not a strong argument. Good thing I left that one unspoken.

"Jared?" There's alpha command in his voice.

"Yes, sir."

"Don't make me fucking tell you twice."

"Consider it done," I mutter and end the call before I dig myself in any deeper.

Dammit.

I rub my forehead. I can't come up with any way around Garrett's order. I look up at the sky. Sun's still out. I'll have to wait until sundown to get help from a leech, which gives Angelina a few more hours to keep her memories intact.

And I have to meet with some shifters from San Diego about setting up a fight in Tucson.

Maybe I can do it tomorrow night. When I bring her car back to her.

Yeah, that should work. And when Garrett asks, I'll tell him it's going to happen, as soon as possible. And tomorrow is as soon as it's possible.

A*ngelina*

"D*riving* downtown after the bars have closed is paramount to suicide," my dad lectures as he neatly cuts his steak. I love the man, but he drives me nuts. As predicted, he's freaking over the car accident.

We're at their long formal dining room table for Sunday dinner and I've chosen to tune out the lecture while I eat the baby broccoli my mom steamed just for me. At least tonight she and dad are eating the same thing I am, though their vegetables are dressed with lemon butter, and mine are not.

While he goes on, my mind runs over the scenes with Jared. The last one, mostly. Where he showed me exactly

Alpha's Desire

how experienced and clever he is with his tongue and then let me off the hook the moment I got uncomfortable.

He really is a gentleman.

Funny how my gratitude to him for treating me with such honor and respect makes me want to run and jump his bones. My unwillingness to have sex with him has completely vanished.

But no. I'm the kind of girl who gets attached.

"How's school going, honey?" My mom pipes in, to change the subject.

"Fine. Good." My stomach knots up.

"How did auditions go for the spring concert?"

"Pretty good."

It's not a lie. I did my best, and I'll probably get into several pieces. But the truth is, I feel like a misfit in the dance program. Not because I'm not a good dancer—I'm decent. Lord knows my parents spent enough on my training since the day I turned three. It's just that I don't want to be an automaton anymore. I don't want to work hard to please my teachers and hope they give me a good part in their dances.

I want to choreograph my own dances. No, not just dances—shows. I want to direct my own company. Stage big daring productions. A modern version of The Firebird. A ballet choreographed to Lady GaGa.

The trouble is, the undergrad program isn't really geared toward that. I could stay and hope to get into the MFA program, but I am honestly tired of working hard to please everyone else.

My whole life has been spent making my parents proud. Being the picture perfect princess they both wanted me to be. It was my mom who put me in dance. I have no idea why.

Honestly, I think it was because some wealthy friend had her daughter at the studio, so it seemed like the thing to do.

Keeping up with the Joneses and all that.

"You're keeping your weight down?"

I set my fork down. "Yes, mom." I infuse my voice with total teen impatience. Because she reduces me to a surly teenager in the blink of an eye. I'm an independent, almost college grad, but five minutes in their house and I'm chafing against my childhood constraints again.

"Well, I know how you worry about those things."

"No, I'm not worried. I never should've told you about the fat letter. I'm sure it's a myth, anyway."

The rumor is, the faculty will send you a fat letter if they think you're getting too porky. Personally, I dare them to. It seems like a civil liberties case to me. But what do I know? I'm not a lawyer. I'm definitely not as rail-thin as some of the bun-heads in the program, but I'm not doughy either. And I definitely don't want to obsess over my weight like almost every dancer does. I've worked hard since my high school days of eating disorder tendencies to love my body and appreciate all the hard work it does for me.

I'm their only child, and my mom was a stay-at-home mom, so I became the object of a mountain of attention. Angelina ballerina, with straight A's, straight teeth, and sweet manners. A good girl.

God, I'm sick of it.

"I don't know why you keep that job at the nightclub anyway," my dad says, back on his soap box. "You're not making fine art and the pay isn't that great."

"The pay is perfect." My jaw gets tight. I'm even more defensive about my time at Eclipse than I am about my weight.

Alpha's Desire

It may be sad, but I feel the biggest thing I've accomplished since I started school was setting up the go-go dancing gig for me and my friends at Eclipse.

I guess it's because it was like one tiny baby step toward directing my own company.

But my parents don't support that angle, at all.

My dad made me double major in business because he thinks I should run a dance studio when I get out.

Which is fine. I like to teach. It's just... it would be nice to follow my own dreams for a change.

Instead of the neatly laid out plan my parents have set for me.

"I still don't understand why this Jared character took your car to be fixed. There's something fishy about it. How well do you know this guy?"

Oh God, please don't let me blush.

Sometimes I hate being a redhead.

"I know him pretty well, Dad. He's a bouncer at the club. Really nice guy. I told you, he said it was his fault he pulled out in front of me, and he has a friend with a repair shop, so he was going to take care of it."

"How do we know the repair shop is reputable? What if he does a shoddy job on it? How do you know he didn't just steal your car? You should have called the cops. Were you drinking?"

I roll my eyes. "*No*, Dad. I wasn't drinking. I'm sure the job will be professional, and you should be grateful I didn't call the cops and get the insurance involved, because my rates would've gone through the roof."

"Well, that's true."

You can always reason with my dad through his wallet.

"How's business, Dad?" I ask pointedly.

My father takes a sip of wine. "Good. I'm still working on the acquisition proposal for SeCure."

"Did you get a meeting with their CEO yet?"

Frustration flits across my father's face and for a minute, I pity him. For all his drive and dominant tendencies, he can't bend the entire world to his bidding. He has a vision for his retirement—going out with a bang, of course—but he hasn't been able to execute it yet.

"We're hosting a fundraiser for his favorite charity—Save the Catalina Mountains—and our event planner asked him to make an appearance to entice participation from other big donors. His secretary made it sound like he was considering it."

"That's great!" I'm honestly happy for him. Except I know what's coming next.

"We'd like you to be here, dear," my mom chirps. "It's a really important event for your dad."

"Of course," I say automatically. After a lifetime of being trotted out to society as the perfect daughter to complete the perfect family, I'm well-trained. I check my parents' plates, and seeing the neatly stacked silverware, stand up. "Well, I'd better get going. I have a lot of homework to do." I pick up all three of our plates and carry them to the kitchen, where I quickly rinse them and stack them in the dishwasher.

"What about coffee?" My mom trails me into the kitchen. "Your father and I are going to have dessert."

Of course, she's not going to offer me cake. And if I asked for it, I'll get a lecture about my weight. Sigh. Just another typical dinner with my parents.

"No thanks, Mom. Love you." I kiss her cheek and breeze out of the kitchen. "Bye. See you, love you!" I call out as I beeline for the door.

Alpha's Desire

The Uber pulls in right when I walk out, so I get in and check my phone for texts.

Yeah, I'm hoping to hear from Jared again. Even though that doesn't make sense.

Even though I shouldn't want that.

I shouldn't be excited about seeing him when he drops my car off. I shouldn't want to know more about his mysterious healing abilities.

But he's like an addiction. Now that I've had my first taste, I can't stop thinking about him.

J*ared*

"So when you gonna do it?" Trey asks.

I lower the hood of Angelina's Toyota and use the rag to give it a polish. Tank is handling the large repairs but I couldn't help coming to check out his work. Or maybe I'm just a glutton for punishment—wanting another whiff of Angelina's sweet scent. "Do what?"

Trey rolls his eyes. "Mind wipe the dancer." He leans on the driver's side and I throw the rag at him.

"Quit smudging the window."

"Well, excuse me." He catches the rag in a blur of movement. "Didn't mean to mess up your girlfriend's car."

"She's not my girlfriend." My gut tightens even as I say the words. *Not my girl, won't ever be my girl.* I might have more muscle than brains, but I'm smart enough to know this.

43

Too bad my wolf thinks differently.

I grab my tools and start cleaning up, tossing and banging a bit more than necessary.

"Damn, you've got it bad," Trey observes. "Maybe I should take her to the leech."

"Over my dead body." I straighten and point a finger at the tall shifter. He's my closest friend, but right now, my wolf sees only an opponent. The enemy. Competition.

Trey spreads his hands. "Easy. I'm not going to go near her. But you're only delaying the inevitable."

He's right. If I don't do this, Garrett will kick my ass. And then he'll order Tank or Trey to do it anyway.

"It sucks. She's in college," Trey lowers his voice. "A mindwipe could seriously fuck her up if it's not done right."

I slam down my tools, wanting to kick the cabinet for good measure. "I know. I know."

"Have you—" Trey starts, when a white Camaro rolls into the lot. My friend swears. "Don't tell me we've got customers."

Trey heads to the door and stops in his tracks when three guys unfold from the car. One black haired, one grey, and the third wears an old fashioned hat—a fedora type that gangster would wear—only he's so tall and skinny he looks like a scarecrow. "You called them?"

"I reached out. They wanted to meet." I head to the sink to clean up. "We're going to check out a space to hold the fights."

"Does Garrett know?"

"He knows." My alpha isn't happy, but as more of our pack gets mated off, he sees the benefit of having an outlet for his bachelors to release their aggression. More than just breaking up brawls at Eclipse. My wolf, especially, needs to fight, to bleed on a regular basis.

Alpha's Desire

The way this situation with Angelina has me riled up, I could go twenty rounds with a bruin right now.

Trey prowls alongside me to the parking lot where the three visitors wait. Two of them smoke while the third, the tall one in a fedora, hangs back.

"Parker," I greet the grey-haired one. Despite his hair color, he doesn't look much older than I am. He gives me a nod, expertly averts his gaze—not submissive but not challenging.

The dark-haired one tosses his butt to the ground and regards us without speaking. Declan, the Irishman. I don't remember the third guy's name, but the way he stares over our heads, twitching nervously, he's not going to say much.

My wolf is uneasy as he catches their scent. It's a bit... off. No wonder they're not part of any pack. Healthy shifters don't tolerate messed up ones for long. The way these guys smell, not to mention the tall one's twitching, all but the most controlled, compassionate Alpha would put them down. I don't know exactly what Data-X did to these guys, but from the rumors I've heard, death might be a mercy.

"Glad you could make it. I didn't expect you to have time to meet."

"Chance to expand, we'll make time." Parker's voice is a little raspy. His eyes glow a little—his animal is close. I have no idea what his animal actually is. This doesn't make my wolf happy. But these guys helped out Sam, our pack member and a bartender at Eclipse. And Sam trusts them.

"It's getting too hot for shifter fights in Cali," Declan announces in his subtle brogue.

Trey frowns. "It gets pretty hot here..."

I nudge him in the ribs. "They're not talking about the weather."

45

"The Pit isn't as secure as we'd like," Parker says. "Men have been sniffing around.

"Men?" I look from Declan's grim face to Parker's blank one.

"Human cops." Parker wrinkles his nose. "Coming around asking about illegal fights and gambling. We think someone put them on to us, trying to flush out shifters."

"I thought that trouble was gone." I avoid naming Data-X directly.

Parker grimaces. "Not entirely."

The third guy twitches so hard, his fedora flies off his head. Declan lets out a dog-like whine that cuts off at a sharp shake of Parker's head.

"You'd be welcome to set up fights here," I say, trying to stay nonchalant. These three might be misfits, but when it comes to booking fights and handling bets, they're the best.

"Good," Parker says and excitement surges through me. "I got a lot of animals who want to fight, and nowhere to put them."

"Not to mention the bets," Declan adds.

I nod. "Let's go check out the space." My wolf howls in triumph as we head to our respective rides.

"Damn," Trey says, settling onto his bike next to me. "This is really happening."

"Shifter Fight Club. Just like we always wanted." We exchange grins, but as we roll out mine fades. Tonight we make a decision on the space to host the fights. Tomorrow I have to take Angelina to a leech. He'll wipe her mind, her memory of the accident, along with who knows what else of her brain.

It doesn't seem right that on the eve of realizing my dream, I'm going to ruin her life.

Alpha's Desire

A gent Dune

He unlocks the padlock on the fence and ducks under the plastic police tape he put up around the burned out lab months ago. There's nothing to be found here. He's a damn good agent, he wouldn't have missed anything. But sometimes being on a site gets the wheels turning in a new direction.

At least it gives him something physical to do. And a guy like him fucking needs to be physical. If only high-level agent work was all Jason Bourne style chases and fights. It's not. It's a helluva lot of detective work.

And it's a million times harder when your superiors won't give you all the information to work with. Find the arsonists. Cover up with the locals. Information about the purpose of the lab and the government's interest in it?

Redacted.

Fine. They didn't want to tell him? He'd figure it the fuck out. Just like he did when they left him with no resources but his own wits and a bullseye on his forehead in Afghanistan. And North Korea. And Iraq.

He has a few seconds of footage from the night of the explosions. The rest was obviously redacted. But there's a partially obscured image of a white van. A shot of a couple men. And one face he recognizes from Special Forces. Nash.

The guy he's been trying to find for years.

He figured Nash would pop up at some point on the job. Anyone who disappears that deep is still buried in government secrets. Like him.

So solving this puzzle became more interesting. More personal.

Because Nash is something different. Not human.

And Charlie needs to know what he is.

4

Jared

The next morning, I pull up at Angelina's in her freshly repaired Toyota. Tank was a real bro to me and got it turned around fast. I owe him one, for sure.

I climb out and knock on her door. I texted her, so she's expecting me, but when she comes to the door, she has a breathless, fluttery quality that makes me want to snatch her up into my arms and press her against the door for a kiss.

But I'm not here for kissing. I'm here for something far more distasteful. Something she wouldn't forgive me for, if she remembered it. But, of course, she won't remember.

"Hi." Her lip-glossed smile beams so bright it would melt the fresh coat of paint on her car. I'm almost wounded by it. Like it gets somewhere between the cracks in my chest and fills me too full of her all-good light.

I lean against the doorframe to keep myself from stepping into her personal space. "Hi, yourself."

She steps into mine, placing her hands on my chest and tipping her face up.

Oh fates, I'm not strong enough for this. I lower my head, but don't presume and she gives me a peck on the cheek. I'm both relieved and horrified she didn't go for my lips, because now the need to properly claim her mouth is so strong I have to take a deep breath and count to five. It's like I'm a pup again, trying to keep myself from getting into a brawl.

And my tendency to brawl is exactly one of the reasons I have to keep my mitts off this pretty little human. She's like a flower just bloomed and I'm the weed whacker that would mow her over. I know, I should leave the metaphors to the poets.

I settle for bringing my hand to her face—just briefly. I cup it and stroke my thumb along her cheekbone, my hand large and rough against her soft skin.

Her eyelids flutter, registering surprise and something else I can't read. Hell, I'm surprised, too. Tender caresses aren't usually my thing. I'm more of a hard fuck up against the wall type. Not that I'm not dying to go *there* with her, too.

I force myself to remove my hand and jerk my thumb toward the car. "She's all fixed up, angel. Ready to go."

She beams the thousand watt smile at me again. "Thank you. Um,"--she ducks back through the door and returns with my shirt in her hand—"Here." She thrusts it at me. "All the blood came out."

I take it from her, resisting the urge to bring it to my nose to inhale her scent on it. "You didn't have to do that, but thank you." I hesitate. I'm usually way more smooth with women, but I don't want to do what I'm about to do, so I'm stalling.

Alpha's Desire

"Oh, do you, ah, want to come in?" She steps back as if to let me through.

I shake my head. "No, baby. But can you drive me back to the club? And I just need to make a short stop on the way. Okay?"

"Oh." Her eyes and mouth round. She's so damn expressive, it's a wonder she didn't end up an actress, not a dancer. "Of course! I'm sorry, I—"

"No apologies." I jerk my head toward the car. "Let's go." I smack her ass when she jogs past me with her purse slung on her shoulder. Then I instantly regret it. We're not in the nightclub and she didn't just straddle my shoulder. This is a normal day, in front of her house, and we're not even dating.

Which doesn't mean I don't watch her sexy ass sashay toward the car in front of me. "Sorry," I say. "That was out of line. I won't do it again."

"Oh good, I thought I was going to have to call some other bouncer from Eclipse to tell you hands off."

She's teasing, but the words *other bouncer* make my fingers curl into fists. But when she tosses a smile over her shoulder, I see she's blushing, and it does something twisty to my gut. I want to rush up behind her and catch her around the waist. Press her to her car and spank her until her ass turns the same shade of pink. Bite her neck and wrap my arms around her. And about a half dozen more lurid things.

Damn, this girl never fails to work her magic on me.

She walks around to the driver's side, but I say, "I'll drive, angel."

She turns and purses her lips into a smirk. "You're the kinda guy who always has to be in control, aren't you?"

I shrug. "Yeah." I figure honesty's the best option here.

"And I like to take care of you. But if you really want to drive, I'll back down."

She shakes her head and walks around to the passenger side. "I don't, really." When her smile wobbles, my heart clutches.

"Oh baby." I walk swiftly to her side of the car and fold her into my arms, trying not to crush her against my chest. It feels so right, so necessary to hold her. Different from what I've felt with other females. Have I ever needed to *comfort* another female? "Have you driven since the accident? Are you nervous?"

She accepts my embrace. "A-a little. Not nervous, really. Just—I don't know," she murmurs into my chest. "It scared the crap out of me, hitting you."

I feel like an ass for not thinking she'd be traumatized and then bullying her into letting me drive. She needed to get right back on the horse, and I stole that opportunity from her.

I pull away and hold her arms, stroking her bare upper arms with my thumbs. "You drive, angel. I want you to feel comfortable." I lead her around to the driver's side and hold the door open. "Go on. It will be fine. I'll be right beside you."

I doubt having me right beside her will alleviate any anxiety, but I have to say it—the need to soothe her is so strong. My wolf, tense since the talk with Garrett, relaxes somewhat.

She climbs in and turns the key. A determined expression is on her face and I recognize that inner steel I've always known was inside her. The powerful drive in a human who appears so soft and flexible on the outside. This is the Angelina who conceived and executed the crazy idea

Alpha's Desire

of go-go dancers at Eclipse and wouldn't take no for an answer until Garrett agreed.

Garrett—the toughest, no-nonsense alpha around.

The only sign of nerves I detect is the long inhale she takes before she pulls away from the curb, and then she seems to settle into driving.

"It's fine, right? Just like getting back on the horse?"

Her smile holds relief and the way she slides her eyes over to me gets me hard. "Yes. Thanks. Sorry, I didn't mean to—"

"No apologies. I'm sorry I didn't think of it."

"You're really quite a gentleman, Jared."

The laugh that issues from my throat has a dry scrape to it. "Does that surprise you?" As soon as I ask, I wish I hadn't, because I know the answer. It's the same reason my gut twisted when she said it.

Of course she didn't see a gentleman in me. All she sees is the tattooed meathead that my parents always said would amount to nothing. The kid who never got his temper under control. Who's not good at anything but using his fists.

And obeying his alpha.

I'm the alpha's enforcer. The muscle that backs up Garrett's law. Above that, I'm absolutely nothing.

She gives one of those adorable blushes that gets me hard. "No. It's just, um, really coming into focus. Nevermind. I didn't mean to say that." She flaps her hand and blushes harder.

Damn. The fact I have her flustered thrills the dominant part of me and soothes the part that's banging against the container because I don't get to have her. I'm under her skin —at least for the moment—and I'll take it.

"Where am I taking you?" She pulls the plump flesh of

53

her lower lip between her teeth and I have to adjust my cock in my pants.

"Downtown, to the club. But we need to make a quick stop on the way. Also on Congress Street." It's hard to ignore the sticky sensation of dread in my own veins as I contemplate the errand.

She nods and drives downtown and I direct her to No Return, another nightclub up the street from Eclipse. I called ahead to arrange a meetup with a leech there. He's a nice enough guy. I wouldn't say I trust him, but I don't distrust him either. Wolves don't trust anyone who's not pack, though.

She parks and looks at me expectantly.

"Come in with me for just a second. I want you to meet my friend Fox."

She blinks for a moment.

Fuck.

Either she's picking up my vibe or I'm a shitty liar. "It'll be quick."

But she grabs her purse. "Um, okay."

I'm sure she's wondering why I couldn't just walk from here. It's just a couple blocks to Eclipse—a guy like me shouldn't need a chauffeur.

I walk around the side and catch her hand. She looks up in surprise and I shrug. "I know it's inappropriate, but I'm feeling protective at the moment. Humor me, okay?"

Her laugh is full of surprise and it does something crazy to my body. A flush of warmth floods my limbs.

The club is closed, but I knock at the back door and it opens after a few moments. Fox—ever youthful, never changing—stands there. He's got spiky blond hair and a faint British accent, even though he's lived in the U.S. for over a hundred years.

Alpha's Desire

He extends a cool palm and I shake it, even though my skin crawls. "Jared."

"Fox." I clear my throat. "This is my... friend Angelina." Dammit, if I don't want to say she's my *girl*, not my friend. *Friend* sounds all wrong in a way that makes me want to punch a wall or throw a table.

"Hi." Angelina's still picking up the weird vibe, I'm sure, because her look is attentive. Not quite wary—that would kill me—but watchful. She's trying to figure out what's off here.

Fox extends his hand to take Angelina's and when she meets his gaze, her focus goes soft, her expression blank.

Son of a bitch.

Seeing her under his power makes me want to hurl.

"What am I erasing?" he murmurs, not looking away from her.

White hot anger burns through me. Toward Fox. Toward Garrett, for making me do this. I can scarcely make myself speak, but I manage to snap, "She saw me regenerate."

But then my hand snaps out of its own accord and I cover her eyes.

The moment I do, she starts to struggle—probably frightened. "Hey! What's going on?"

"Nothing. Go wait outside." I release her and put my body between her and Fox.

"What the fuck?" he grits.

I can't find words because I don't know what the hell I'm doing.

I blink and Fox is gone. Fucking vampires! I whirl around just as Angelina screams. Actually, she starts to, but it dies on her lips as Fox takes her under his power again.

"No." My fist swings and connects with the side of Fox's

neck, sending him flying against the wall. If he were mortal, it would've snapped his neck. But he's not.

Angelina screams for real this time and it echoes off the walls of the club.

Fox traces so fast I can't see him before he punches me right in the mouth. With vampire strength. I end up on my ass on the floor, Fox standing over me.

I don't make eye contact. Vampire tricks shouldn't work on shifters, but you never know. I'm not taking any chances. I surge up and lunge for his waist, but he's already traced to the door—the one Angelina opened. He slams it shut on her and she shrieks again.

The terror in her voice makes me see red. I pick up one of the round tables that line the wall and swing it at Fox. He traces away.

"What the fuck is wrong with you?" His voice comes from behind me. He's leaning up against the wall with his arms folded over his chest like he's been there for long time. Fucking tricksy leech. "If she didn't need to be wiped before, she sure as hell does now." He traces again when I hurl the table. It smacks the wall and makes a hole in the plaster.

"You fucking look at her again, and I'll run a stake right through your heart, vampire," I growl.

"Vampire," Angelina whispers on a gasp and shoves the back door open. "Vampires don't exist." She's running before her feet hit the pavement.

Smart girl.

I whirl around, certain Fox will be gone, tracing after her, but he's in the same spot.

"She saw me. She knows."

"I know," I choke. I don't want to start a vampire-shifter war here. Fox was doing me the favor and I just fucked with him, big time, not to mention the damage to the club. I must

Alpha's Desire

look as pole-axed as I feel, because Fox's ancient blue eyes hold compassion.

"You have twenty-four hours to figure your shit out. You know the laws. No loose ends."

I don't stay to argue. Angelina's out there, terrified. I take off after her. "Angelina."

She doesn't stop. I catch up right before she makes it to her car and I catch her around the waist. "Wait, baby."

She slams her heel back into my shin, then stomps down on the top of my foot, cracking the bones. At some point, my little dancer had self-defense training. For some reason, it makes me grin like a maniac to have her attack me.

But I remove my hands from her and hold them up. "Easy, easy. Take it easy, Angelina. I'm sorry."

She goes still, but remains facing the car.

"I know you're scared. I know you're confused. I fucked up. Big time. But I'm not going to hurt you. I promise. And I won't let anyone else hurt you, either."

When she finally turns, tears shimmer in her eyes.

It tears my chest wide open.

Then, without warning, she dives for the door of her car.

I'm the biggest asshole in the world, because I slam my hand down on it to hold it closed. "Don't run. Please don't run from me. The only way I can make this work is if we trust each other."

I don't even know what I'm saying, but I guess on some level, it's true. If Angelina bolts out of here, I will have no choice but to send Fox after her immediately.

And if she doesn't?

That part I don't know. I still should bring her in to Fox. My alpha gave me an order. Fox gave me a deadline. But I'll be damned if I can do it.

A ngelina

V ampires don't exist. Vampires don't exist. Vampires don't exist. Oh my God, do vampires exist?

I'm shaking all over.

If she didn't need to be wiped before, she sure as hell does now.

I'm not sure what just happened in there, but I think Jared brought me here to have my memory wiped. Or my brain wiped. And then he changed his mind. Either way, I'm not sticking around to find out.

There's a *vampire* in there who would probably be perfectly happy to suck me dry, and now I don't trust Jared.

That's the part that hurts. And I don't want to stand here and let him see how badly, either. When he slams his big paw across my car door, I duck under his arm and try to run for it.

Stupid move. He catches me before I've taken two steps. He hooks an arm around my waist and lifts my feet from the ground. I thrash and kick, trying to get my heels high enough to nail him where it will count.

"Angelina. *Angelina.* Oof."

Yep, I kneed him in the nuts.

He reacts, but isn't as disabled as I'd hoped. I go for his eyes, like they taught us in self-defense. My fingernail scrapes the skin of his cheek, but he catches both my wrists and pulls them behind my back. "Okay, *okay.*" And then it's like he's trying not to laugh, which sends my temper

Alpha's Desire

through the roof. "Baby, please stop fighting." I definitely hear laughter in his voice.

"It's not funny," I snarl, kicking with my heels against his shins again.

He jumps back, still holding me by my pinned wrists. "I know it's not. *I know.*" We continue to wrestle—me kicking, him dodging. "You're just so damn adorable and it turns me on when you fight. I'm sorry—I'm sorry. Please, Angelina." He picks me up and sits me on the hood of my car, crowding up between my legs. He still has my wrists pinned, but instead of wrestling, he's going for an embrace. At least, I think he is. He drops his face down into my hair and breathes deeply.

And stays there.

I'm frozen. I don't know what the hell to do.

He nuzzles my neck, the scruff of his five o'clock shadow brushing my cheek. Our breaths mingle in short pants. I swear I can hear both our hearts hammering as one.

He eases his hold on my wrists and slowly pulls away, like he's testing to see if I'll run again.

I draw my hand back and slap his face, as hard as I can.

He doesn't look surprised. It's as if he saw it coming and decided to let it fall.

My eyes water and I slap him a second time.

Again, he lets me.

And he has the grace to look sorry now, instead of laughing.

The tears track down my face. "Tell me what happened in there," I demand, swiping at them with the back of one hand. "You brought me to a v-vampire? Why?"

"Fox has superpowers too. He can wipe someone's memory."

"But why..." Things are so surreal, my mind is whirring. I

59

can practically hear things clicking into place. "The accident. Your superpowers. You don't want me to remember. You brought me to a vampire to erase my memory."

He closes his eyes and leans his forehead against mine. "Yeah."

"What are you, Jared?" My voice cracks. "Not a vampire."

If I'm perfectly honest with myself, I'd realize I'm terrified to hear his answer.

His large hand cups the back of my neck. Not threatening—soothing. His thumb rubs tiny circles on my skin. "Shifter—werewolf."

"Werewolf? That's... that's impossible."

He blinks and his eyes light with an inner fire. Like, seriously, they're glowing.

"No," I half gasp, half moan. "I'm losing my mind."

"No, you're not. You're perfect. I'm the freak."

My mind feels sluggish. "So your superpowers..."

"Speed. Strength. Super healing. And sometimes... I get hairy."

"Hairy?"

"I turn into a wolf."

"Oh my God." We're standing here discussing the impossible—vampires and werewolves—but it all makes sense. I should want to run screaming but, his honesty calms me down.

"But you can't know any of this, Angelina." I hear frustration in his voice. The memory of him hurling a table at the vampire flashes back. The level of violence in there sickened me. But despite the fact that he was the one who brought me there, he'd also been my protector.

I'm still trembling, and it only gets worse with his admission. "Please... just let me go." I mean it when I say it, but the thought of him releasing me, of me getting in my car and

Alpha's Desire

driving away, actually frightens me more. I don't want to be alone right now. Even though he's the one who scared me, there's a solidity to having him here. A certain comfort. And I definitely deserve more explanation.

"I... can't do that, Angelina." His voice is heavy.

"Then what are you going to do with me?" It's barely more than a whisper.

"I don't know." He scoops his forearm under my ass and lifts me so I straddle his waist.

My arms automatically loop around his neck for balance. Even though I want to reject him—reject this, it feels sort of nice. "Take me home." I do my best to keep the wobble out of my voice. To sound demanding, rather than needy. Because despite the trembling, my body has come alive against his, heat building everywhere we're in contact.

"Yeah, baby. I'll take you home." He walks around to the driver's side, but instead of opening the door, he traps my body against the car, his hard cock nesting right between my legs, his lips melding to mine.

I should push him away—punish him for what he's done to me, but my lips have their own idea. I kiss him back, then assert myself by nipping one of his lips.

He laughs against my mouth and goes right back to kissing me.

Damn. Despite my resistance, every twist of his lips, every nudge of his hips fuels me. Power ebbs back into my limbs, builds with the heat in my core.

His hands turn rough, fingers kneading my thighs, squeezing the parts of my ass that are accessible. His tongue sweeps inside my mouth and he consumes me, licking, sucking, nipping, kissing. When he breaks the kiss, I'm panting.

I slap him a third time.

61

There's no downside to it, really. It satisfies me and only amuses him.

He smiles and captures my hand, bringing it to his lips. "I'll take you home, baby, on one condition."

"What's that?" I shove my hair out of my eyes, trying to stop the world from spinning.

"You invite me in."

I don't know why that makes my nose burn again. His recent betrayal still cuts me, I guess.

"Hey." I don't know how he sees my emotions so clearly, but he does. "I'm not making any presumptions here. I'm not asking to come to your bed. I lost your trust and I'm going to have to earn it back. I know that. I just think we need to talk. I owe you an explanation at least."

I blink rapidly and bob my head, not trusting my voice for speech.

Regret washes over Jared's face and he kisses my forehead, then eases me to my feet and settles me in the passenger seat of the car.

When he gets in, he scrubs his face with his hand before starting up my car. I fold my arms across my chest and stare straight ahead. Neither of us speaks for the short ride home.

At my place, he opens the door with my keys and lets us both in.

Why did he want to come in? For a moment, a hundred frightening scenarios run through my head and I take a few steps back.

He holds up his hands, palms out. "I'm not going to hurt you."

"Why are you here, then?" Something about his request doesn't add up.

"I'm here to... monitor you, I guess. I can't have you

Alpha's Desire

calling anyone telling them what happened. I need you to understand what's at stake."

I give a single nod. Okay, that makes sense. I wrap my arms around my waist and perch on the arm of the couch. "So talk."

He sits on the ottoman and waves a hand toward the couch. "Please, sit down."

"Fine." I sit down and he immediately scoots the ottoman forward, until he's sitting right across from me.

"Angelina. I just want to say I'm sorry."

I give a single nod. "Thank you."

"And you should know you were never in any danger. Okay? I took you to get the memory of seeing me heal wiped, that was it."

I purse my lips. "Then why did you stop him?"

Guilt flickers over Jared's face and he rubs his forehead. "It didn't feel right. I didn't like seeing you under his spell." He sounds reluctant to admit it.

Something shifts and rearranges inside my chest.

"I... I'm protective of you, Angelina."

The thing that moved warms.

"I was obeying orders from my alpha, but I couldn't follow through with it, and then I overreacted. But I promise you, no matter how it looked in there, no harm would've come to you. Fox wasn't going to hurt you. I'll never hurt you."

I pinch my lips together because it feels like I'm going to cry again. "Okay," I say on an exhale. "I believe you."

Jared's face transforms, the lines of tension easing, surprise lifting his brows. "You do?"

I nod. "Yeah."

"Come here, baby." I don't move, but he plucks me from the couch and pulls me onto his lap. He buries his face in

63

my hair and kisses my shoulder. "Okay." He sounds relieved. "Good."

"So now what?"

His arms around me tighten and the thread of tension is back. "Now." He sighs. "I don't know. Is there any chance you'd willingly go back to get your memories wiped? All of this?"

I try to lurch off his lap, but he catches me and pulls me back down. "Easy. I'm not going to make you. I'm just exploring possibilities."

"No chance," I say firmly. "No chance in hell."

He chuckles. "Smart woman. And I love your fire, baby."

"Couldn't I just promise never to tell anyone? Take your secret to the grave?"

He's silent for a moment, then he says, "Yeah. I'll need that promise from you, baby."

I swivel on his hard thighs to look him in the eye. "I swear to God. I'll never tell." I cross my heart and hold up three fingers, Girl Scout style.

His lips twitch and he grabs my fingers and pulls them to his lips. His kiss is soft—so much more tender than I imagined him capable of.

"Now you swear to me you won't do it." I hold his gaze.

He hesitates and disappointment runs through me thick and cold. But then he nods. "I promise I won't wipe you, or let anyone else wipe you, unless you consent."

His phone rings and I take the opportunity to jump off his lap. Not because I haven't warmed back up to him. More because I have. This man is dangerously attractive to me.

He curses and stands up. "Hey." He speaks into the phone. "No, not exactly."

I hear a loud male voice on the other end and Jared sends a quick glance my way.

Alpha's Desire

"Is it about me?" I ask.

He holds up his hand, like he's telling me to wait and walks out my front door. I hear him out on the porch but I can't hear what he's saying.

J *ared*

"**W**hat in the fuck do you mean *not exactly*? Were my orders not clear?"

Not surprisingly, Garrett's pissed.

I walk a few paces away from Angelina's place. "I didn't feel right about having that leech in her brain."

"I don't give a shit what felt right to you, an order's an order. This is pack law, and you know it."

"I don't care." I'm so far out of line I could be banished, but I don't give a fuck now. I've already made my choice. I can't—won't—obey my alpha. I'm going to have to face the music now, whatever it is. "Anyone touches her—anyone tries to wipe her—and I'll fucking kill them. That goes for Fox. That even goes for you."

There. I've definitely dug my grave. He can banish me if he wants, I'll take Angelina with me and protect her until the day I die.

Part of me fucking loves that idea, as awful as it is. An excuse to bind Angelina to me.

Garrett goes deadly silent.

My heart thunders in my chest and I have to work to keep from crushing the phone in my fist. If I didn't hear

65

Garrett's sharp inhale on the other side, I'd think he'd already crushed his. He goes through phones faster than I can eat a box of Girl Scout cookies.

"Are you telling me she's your mate?" Garrett's voice is low and laced with danger.

I close my eyes, drawing in a breath, thankful the moon won't be full for another two weeks. I'm barely keeping my wolf in check with the threat to Angelina.

"No," I say at last, even though saying *yes* would solve this problem.

I can't fucking mate Angelina. She's a sweet little human. The mating bite would probably kill her, and definitely scar her delicate neck. Ballerinas don't have hideous scars on their necks. Nor do they take beefy tattooed meatheads for mates—boyfriends—whatever.

Angelina has big aspirations and a bright future. There's no way I could take all that from her. It's not right.

But I also made her a promise. I said I wouldn't let them wipe her.

So where does that leave me?

"What are you fucking telling me, Jared?"

I go for total honesty, because Garrett would see through anything else. "Listen, I don't know. This girl means something to me. I wish it weren't the case, but it is."

Garrett goes silent again. When he speaks, his voice is tense. "I'm gonna give you two weeks. Figure it out. Either mark her and claim her as your own, or wipe her. In the meantime, you stick to her like glue. Make sure she doesn't talk. Understand?"

I shouldn't feel relieved. Two weeks isn't going to solve this fucking mountain of a problem, but I am. It's two weeks I get to spend with Angelina. Two weeks before... fuck.

"Loud and clear."

Alpha's Desire

"Good. And don't think I'm not going to fuck you up when I see you next."

I smile, because, well—I love Garrett. And I don't care if he pounds me into the ground, because I deserve it. "Yeah, I know. Thanks. I still have Fox to deal with. He gave me twenty-four hours."

"She knows about him, too?"

My limbs go heavy. "Yeah."

"I'll talk to him—tell him we have it handled."

"Thanks, bud."

"Jared."

"Yeah?"

"Good luck, my friend."

I give a harsh bark of laughter. "Thanks. I'll need it."

"Yeah, you will."

I'm not even sure what he means, but I remember how crazy he went before he marked his human mate. Trey and I had to hold him back to keep him from attacking her during the full moon.

Does he think I want to mark Angelina?

I haven't had the urge, but then I haven't had sex with her yet. And the fates know she brings up all kinds of terrible desires in me.

Fuck.

My wolf probably does want to claim her. But it's not going to happen. Because

1. I'm a shifter.
2. I'm a fuck up.
3. She's way outta my league. Even if we could get past the mating mark thing, girls like her don't belong with guys like me.

I walk back inside and find Angelina walking out of the bathroom brushing her teeth.

It's such a normal act of domesticity, but it goes straight to my dick, like everything she does. The idea of seeing her like this, as if we're living together, rocks me.

"You want the good news, or the bad news?" I ask.

She bites the toothbrush to speak. "Good news."

I grin like an idiot because she looks so damn cute. "Good news is you've been given a stay of execution." I hold up my hand when her eyes go wide. "It's a figure of speech, that's all. I have time to figure this out."

"Whabs the bab news?" she asks, toothbrush still clenched between her teeth.

"You've got a new shadow. I have to stick with you for a little while. Just until we're sure you won't talk."

I expect her to tell me no fucking way. Maybe slap me again, which shouldn't turn me on so much, but it does. Instead, she blushes right up to the roots of her beautiful red hair. "S-stick with me how? Stay here?"

I nod. "Don't worry, I'll take the couch. I'm not here to force myself on you. Just to..." I stop. Just to what? Decide if she's my mate? Reconcile myself to wiping her? Find out how fucking hard it is to spend the night under the same roof as her without pounding between her legs for every minute of it?

She raises her eyebrows.

"—just to make sure. Like I said."

She backs up toward the bathroom, pinning me with a thoughtful look.

What's going on in that beautiful head of hers?

"Fine," she says before rounding the corner and spitting into the sink. I hear the water running, but I can't stop myself from following her.

Alpha's Desire

I lean against the doorframe. "You know, every time you tell me *fine* with that pouty voice, I want to spank your cute little ass until you squeal?"

Her lips part and she stops drying her hands on the towel, as if I shocked her into stillness. I try to keep myself from looking, but the stiff points of her nipples poke through her thin t-shirt, and I smell the scent of her arousal.

I'd give anything to fuck her now.

It wouldn't be hard to win her over, either. She's already halfway there, just from my crude threat.

But I'm not going to do it.

Garrett didn't assign me to stay here to get in her shorts, no matter how much they fucking turn me on.

And she deserves better than me.

So much better.

"I'll let you off the hook this time," I drawl, giving her what I consider my most charming smirk. "But consider yourself warned." I saunter away, because if I stay a minute longer, she's going to find out first hand just how badly I want to get those shorts off her, but I hear her breathless reply as I walk down the hall.

"I will."

5

Angelina

I don't know how I managed to sleep at all. I dreamed all night about a beefy werewolf coming in my room and pinning me down. Forcing my legs wide and pleasuring me with his mouth and fingers until I scream myself hoarse.

Living with Jared in the house is going to be next to impossible. I hear him rummaging in the kitchen, so I pull a pair of shorts on under my sleep shirt and pad out to the kitchen. I find him looking through my cabinets, appearing disgruntled.

He's even bigger and more impressive in the morning. His muscles stretch his fitted t-shirt and jeans like a work of art. The dancer in me wants to climb all over him like a living jungle gym.

"What are you looking for?" I ask.

He closes a cabinet door and frowns. "Coffee. I was going to make you coffee to start your day. Or don't you drink it?"

I shake my head, trying to tamp down the pleasure at hearing he wants the coffee for *me*, not himself. "Not unless I buy it from Starbucks. I usually make a smoothie in the morning. You want one?"

He appears surprised. "Um, yeah. That'd be nice."

I walk past him to the refrigerator and start taking out ingredients. "What do you usually have for breakfast?" I'm picturing him as a steak and eggs kinda guy, considering he's a wolf.

Speaking of wolf, I thought of a million questions to ask him, but I don't know if he's receptive to answering, considering I'm not supposed to know anything.

"Oh, I'm a can of Red Bull and anything else in sight kinda guy." There's a self-deprecation in his tone that I hate, although I can't put my finger on why it bothers me so much. It's kinda like he's assuming I'm going to judge.

I bustle past him and start throwing stuff into the blender: frozen wild blueberries, organic raspberries, a dash of pure cherry juice, a banana, a couple handfuls of spinach, gelatin for my protein, spirulina, water, and a squeeze of lemon. I blend it up and pour it into two tumblers with lids and straws.

When I hand Jared his, he wears this heavy-lidded gaze, like smoothie making is some kind of erotic artform.

"Thanks." His deep voice sends butterflies fluttering in my belly. He chugs it down in three gulps and wipes his mouth with the back of his hand. "Delicious. Thank you, beautiful."

"I-I'm going to jump in the shower."

"Don't let me slow you down." He lays that charming grin on me, the one that causes girls at the club to flash their boobs and make utter fools of themselves.

Alpha's Desire

I spin around and head for the bathroom, quick, before I join that club.

Of course, the entire time I'm in the shower I'm thinking of him. Imagining what would happen if he decided to barge in. Did I purposely leave the door unlocked?

I fear I did.

But he doesn't come in. Which is a good thing, considering I have classes all day. Still, I'm unbelievably self-conscious as I run from the bathroom to my bedroom in nothing but a towel. Why didn't I bring my clothes into the bathroom with me?

I'm pretty sure I hear Jared chuckle as I shut my door, which makes it all the worse. I shouldn't let him get me flustered in my own home. I throw on my dance clothes and pull a pair of shorts and t-shirt over my tights and leotard. My hair goes up into two buns on the top of my head— antennae style, not the Princess Leia style.

When I come out, Jared's holding up a wall in the front room, looking at his phone. He drags in a long, slow breath when he sees me, eyes devouring me like I'm sex on a stick, not a dorky bunhead who has to dress out for ballet first thing in the morning.

Well, I guess he *is* the big bad wolf.

And that thought shouldn't get me so wet.

"Okay, so I have classes all day—I won't be home until six or so." I raise my eyebrows at him.

He takes my keys from my hand and locks the door after us. "Great. I'll drive."

I stop walking. "Wait... *what*?"

"Did you think I'd just meet you back here at six? No, baby, I'm your shadow. I go where you go." He walks toward my car.

"You-you can't go to classes with me!" I splutter.

73

He stops at the driver's side and leans on the roof of the car. His grin is wicked. "I can, yes."

I arch a brow. "Oh *really*? You're going to take ballet?"

"I'll wait outside."

"So how do you know I won't tell someone during class? This is stupid, Jared. You can't be with me every minute of the day. You don't need to come to school with me."

"I have my orders. I'm to stick to you like glue." He gives my body and up and down sweep. "And that suits me just fine."

The flutters in my belly make it hard to maintain a hard line. I have to admit, there's something appealing about having Jared as an attachment. But it's also utterly ridiculous. I cock a hip. "You can't. You won't fit in. What will I tell people?"

His smile falters and I have the brief impression I've hurt him, although I can't fathom why. "Tell them I'm your bodyguard. Come on, get in. You're going to be late for class."

"You don't even know when my class is!" I protest, but he's right.

"I do, actually. I checked your phone and shared your calendar."

I fish out my phone and stare at it. "And what? Did you bug it, too?"

When he doesn't answer, my jaw drops. "Are you serious?" I'm suddenly scared again. I'm in way over my head with an organization—a *species?*—I don't even understand. I thought I could trust Jared, but now I'm not sure.

"Hey, hey." As usual, he picks up my vibe. "Calm down. What did I promise you?"

I clutch my bag so tight my knuckles turn white. "I don't know," I mutter-snap.

Alpha's Desire

"You're safe with me. I'm not going to let anything happen to you."

"As long as I don't tell." I say it as a statement, not a question.

He nods. "As long as you don't tell."

"And if I do?"

Jared's face clouds, the line of his jaw becomes more defined. "You can't." His tone brooks no opposition. There's no wheedling or calming. He's telling me like it is.

I blow out a shaky breath.

"Are you thinking about telling someone?" There's an edge of danger in his tone, something I haven't heard before. The guy is huge and I've already seen what he's capable of in his short tussle with the vampire. But in this moment, it becomes infinitely clear that he's deadly.

My heart pounds against my ribs.

"Are you?" His tone is sharper than a knife.

"*No!*" I'm both offended and angry. And still scared shitless.

Jared relaxes against the seatback—the one he pushed all the way into the backseat to get in—but a furrow still clouds his brow. "I don't like to smell fear on you, baby." His hands tighten on the wheel, like he's holding on to keep from reaching for me. "I'm sorry I scared you."

My mind swirls with a million unfinished thoughts. The only coherent one that floats to the surface is *he can smell my fear?*

"Sure," he says. I guess I asked it out loud. "And your arousal."

I flush and shoot a glance at him. His lips twitch and I want to punch him. What this man does to me! I don't slap or punch people. Ever.

"I usually park all the way up on 5th street and walk. You can't park on campus." I inform him, to change the subject.

But he turns, pulling right onto campus and stopping in front of the dance building. "You're late. Go on in. I'll park and meet you after your class."

I get out and lean my head in the door. "I have classes here all day. Seriously. Just come back at four."

He shakes his head. "I'll be there after ballet."

I roll my eyes. "Fine," I say before I remember his words last night.

His grin is borrowed straight from the devil, himself. "Now you're in for it."

I slam the door and stomp up the stairs, my face burning red, butt already tingling thinking about his promised spanking.

Jared

There's a special kind of torture for males who dare imagine they're worthy of a ballerina. It's the body-hugging garments they wear that pass for clothing. I'm standing outside the door of Angelina's ballet class peeking through the window and dying.

Literally. I'm dying. My cock is rock hard, especially because now I'm thinking about spanking her and I don't know if I'll make it through the day without letting off some steam.

A group of girls in leotards and tights gather outside the

Alpha's Desire

studio, plopping on the floor and spreading their legs wide to stretch in preparation for the next class. Some of them appear appropriately scandalized to see me here—what I'd expect from the virginal masses of uptight dancers. But some eye me with the bold looks I'm used to getting at the club, gazes traveling over my muscles and tattoos. It's that fascination with the bad boy that makes even good girls make poor decisions.

"Are you waiting for someone?" One of them pipes up.

"Yep."

"Who?"

"Angelina. The redhead." I nod to the window where the dancers are in poses similar to the one of the Romeo and Juliet ballet poster on the wall I'm leaning against.

"Oh yeah. She's great. I love Angelina," one of them gushes, getting even flirtier, even though I just named my female.

"She is," I murmur, watching my girl spin in four consecutive circles on shoes that let her stand right on her toes. Her legs are a mile long and pure muscle. Her body, a work of art. This is a different Angelina than the one I've seen at the club. She's serious and precise. Perfect in every move. And rather unhappy-looking. I sure as hell hope it's not because I'm here.

A door at the front of the studio opens and dancers spill out along with strains of fancy music. Classical or some shit.

"Angelina!" one of the girls near me squeals. "Over here."

Angelina takes one look at me and her lips tighten.

Dammit. I am definitely bringing her down.

She marches over and I half expect her to march right past, but instead she lands right up against my body, face

77

upturned, as if for a kiss. An angry kiss. No—possessive. She's marking me in front of her friends.

Hot alpha female.

Let it never be said I wasted an opportunity. My lips are on hers before she can blink, and it's not a peck, either. I devour her mouth like a starving man, ignoring the twitters of laughter from the gaggle of dancers around us.

When I release Angelina, her lips are swollen, eyes glazed. I wrap my hand around her nape and lean down to murmur in her ear. "You staking your claim, baby?"

She lifts her chin in that adorably stubborn pose I've come to adore. "Maybe." And with that, she sashays off, leaving me to follow after her.

I don't hurry, sauntering behind her, getting my fill of the swing of her ass, the flex of her muscular thighs. She stops and bends over a drinking fountain, even though she's carrying a half-full water bottle. Giving me a show. I arrive behind her and make an approving noise in my throat.

Because I'm fairly certain that's what she wants.

I happen to know her next class isn't for forty minutes, which gives me time to get my hands on her. If I can just get her some place alone. Unfortunately, I'm still attracting stares from every human in the building.

I bump up behind Angelina and wrap one arm around her waist, pulling her back against my body so she can feel my solid erection. "Baby, take me somewhere private and I'll reward you properly for offering up that kiss."

I half expect her to shut me down, but her eyes dart around and then she grabs my hand, pulling me down an empty hallway. She tries a door and finds it locked, then tries another one. It opens.

I follow her in and shove her against the wall beside the door. That way, no one can see us through the window, and I

Alpha's Desire

can stop the door from opening if anyone tries. I have the front of her leotard down in seconds, bra cups peeled off and my mouth over one of her rosy nipples. One hand squeezes her breast while the other rubs between her legs. I go right up her shorts, investigating the outline of her pussy through her leotard and tights.

"Baby, I want to shred these tights with my teeth," I confess.

"No," she pants. "Please don't." She pushes at my chest, and I force myself to draw back. I may be aggressive, but I sure as hell don't force myself on women.

But my little ballerina drops to her knees, head tipped up, gaze on my face.

My nostrils flare and I automatically reach for the outline of my cock in my jeans.

She undoes my button and makes a sexy show of dragging down the zipper. All the while, I'm biting my knuckles to keep from groaning.

She doesn't say a word. Neither of us do. She takes my cock out and wraps her slender fingers around the base.

The minute her lips part, pre-cum leaks out. I'm about two seconds from spending, which isn't like me. I pride myself on stamina. But apparently I have none where this girl is concerned. Especially considering I've been blue-balled for her for days now.

"Fuck, angel," I grit when she licks around the head. "You're going to get off easy, because I'm about two pumps away from coming."

I love the satisfied smile she flashes right before she takes me deep.

Oh fates. My balls tighten up, thighs go rigid. I grasp the back of her head and pump into her mouth like a total jackass. I can't help myself. I need relief so bad I'm going blind.

"Angelina," I choke, trying not to shove all the way down her throat.

She tightens her hold on my cock, and jacks her fist. Her tongue swirls on the underside of my member, lips suction tight.

"Baby—"

I give her control again, and she pumps her mouth in concert with her fist, making it feel like she's taking my full length.

"Fuck. Fuck yes. I'm going to come," I warn her so she can pop off, but she stays on, sucking hard enough to pull the chrome off a bumper. I come in her devastating, hot mouth, my eyes rolling back in my head.

She sucks me clean and stands up while I shove my cock back in my jeans.

"Goddamn." I snag her nape and pull her face up to mine. "Remind me to threaten the welfare of your tights again."

She gives a surprised laugh that lights up her face and I drink it in, still riding the euphoria of my release. "Well, your boner was looking pretty painful."

I grin. "I can't help it. You're more dressed at the nightclub, and you already know how I feel about what you wear there."

She laughs, a husky sound that revives my cock far too soon. It seems I'm going to be permahard for this girl. "You sure it wasn't seeing all the dancers out there?" There's a pointedness to the question and I don't forget her little show of jealousy in the hallway. It's important I set her straight.

"No, baby. Just you." Her tits are still hanging out and I pinch both nipples gently. "But you're welcome to stake a public claim on me, anytime. I sure as hell enjoyed it."

Alpha's Desire

She blushes, but she's still smiling, and I steal a brief kiss.

"Don't think this will get you out of your spanking later, though."

She flushes a deeper red, but leans right up against me. I cup her ass and pull her hips up on mine. "Do werewolves have girlfriends?"

The question is so innocent, but it's loaded.

For both of us.

I ease off my grip on her ass and sag against the wall. "No." It fucking kills me to say it, especially when I see her expression shutter. "Not with humans."

"Oh." She busies herself with putting her tits away and I want to smash my own face in.

"Listen—"

"No, you don't have to say anything." Her voice sounds forced. "I knew you weren't the boyfriend type from the beginning. That's why I was putting on the brakes."

I curl my fingers into my palms to keep from reaching for her. "Yeah, I know. I'm sorry. I'm trying to respect your boundaries. It's just really fucking hard. Humans don't usually tweak me as much as you do."

This earns me eye contact again, which comes as a visceral relief. "I tweak you?"

I drag my lower lip through my teeth. "So fucking much." I adjust my cock, which is already growing again. "But I'll give it rest. Thanks for taking the edge off."

She pinches my nipple through my t-shirt. It's a sassy move, considering I'm the guy who likes to be the aggressor, but I let her do it. "Well, I should get to class."

"Yeah." I open the door for her and let her go through it, but I don't follow. She needs her space, as much as I can give

81

RENEE ROSE & LEE SAVINO

it. I wait until she's almost around the corner before I leave the room.

Dammit.

It feels like I just swallowed a round of lead.

A *gent Dune*

F acial recognition software pulls absolutely nothing on the faces he has from the lab bombing. Including Nash's. It's almost as if they've been buried on purpose. But by whom? His superiors? Or someone on their side? It would take some extremely sophisticated security hacks to be able to fuck with their system, but he's learned never to underestimate anyone. Never underestimate, never make assumptions. You have to stay open to crazy fucking possibilities if you want the real answers.

If he wouldn't have written things off as impossible back when he first saw something unreal about Nash, he might've learned something about his past. What his father was. What happened to him.

So he wasn't going to let the chance slip this time. He'd find the bombers, yeah. But he also was going to uncover whatever fucking secret was being kept at those blown up labs. Whatever Data-X had been up to. Genetic engineering was his guess.

And more than one party wanted it covered up. More than one party has a stake in it.

An incoming alert makes him return his focus to the facial screens.

82

Alpha's Desire

A match.

He read the file. One Parker Jones.

Picked up for questioning related to illegal betting in San Diego.

Subject did not cooperate. Suspected of organizing cage fights and serving as bookie for said fights.

Well, looks like he has a suspect to stake out. He gathers his equipment and already packed bag, checks his weapons and leaves the small government-provided safehouse.

Parker Jones, prepare to give me some fucking answers.

6
———

Angelina

"Turn left here," I direct Jared. He's insisted on driving again, but I'm fine with it because:

A) I get curbside pickup.

B) He stayed out of my way, plus picked up lunch for me, Remy and Talya.

C) All the catty dancers are jealous.

Of course, now everyone thinks he and I are a couple. Too bad werewolves don't date.

"So, what? You can have sex with humans, but we're not good enough for a relationship?"

Dammit.

I was trying to hold that question in. Now I sound like a love-scorned shrew.

The look Jared shoots me is pure misery, which makes it even worse. "No, baby. That's not it."

I wait as he seems to struggle for words. "Wolves are violent. You might call us primitive. Me, especially. When a

wolf mates, it's usually for life. He bites his female to mark her and permanently embed his scent into her skin—to warn other males away. Once wolves are mated, the possessiveness doesn't fade. That's why I say it's usually for life. Even if a couple doesn't get along, a wolf would never let his mate go. He'd follow her to the ends of the Earth. The attraction never fades."

I stare at Jared in shock, trying to decide if he's purposely trying to warn me off. He shrugs. "So yeah. I can't drag you into something like that. You might not even survive the mating bite."

I try to ignore the pleasure tingling through me at the way he's talking as if he's even considered mating me.

I mean, in human terms, we're talking marriage, not dating. But I appreciate the fact that he's not willing to lead me along when there's no chance of a long-term future. I'm also trying to ignore the fact that his description of a wolf's possessiveness turns me on. It shouldn't. It should definitely scare me. I mean, what if the guy was abusive? That would be a legitimate nightmare. But what if he was charming and considerate? Protective to a fault? What if he looked at you like you were the most fascinating creature he'd ever seen? Couldn't keep his hands off you?

I'm not sure I'd be sad about being tied to that situation for the rest of my life.

I mean, hell. If it weren't for the biting part, I might be ready to sign up right now.

Of course there's the not so small issue of my parents never accepting a guy like Jared.

I direct Jared to turn into the parking lot of my grandma's nursing home. I visit her every Monday and Thursday. She's my dad's mom, and Lord knows he doesn't make time

Alpha's Desire

to see her. Just like he never made time for me, growing up. All that man does is work.

But I don't just come out of guilt or obligation. When she's lucid, she's awesome to be around. But sometimes I show up and she's confused, even belligerent. Often she's as cranky as a toddler. I definitely don't want Jared to witness this.

"Where are we?" he asks.

I ignore the question. "You can just drop me off here." I point to the front circular drive.

He frowns.

"Come back in an hour."

He ignores my directive and parks in the lot. When he starts to open his door, I snap, "You're not coming in."

He arches a brow, that hint of a grin around his lips telling me he would love a challenge from me.

I go for pure honesty. "I don't want you to come in. You can wait here, if you want, but..." I abandon all pride and turn on my begging eyes. "Okay?"

He sinks back into the seat and nods.

"I won't take long," I promise, then kick myself, because why should I rush? I didn't ask for an escort.

"Take your time, baby. I'll be here."

"Okay, thanks." I swing my purse over my shoulder and head in, not sure what I'll get today.

J*ared*

I dial Parker's number. He and his friends headed back to San Diego to line up both fighters and attendees for the first Tucson matches. "The warehouse is ours."

"Yeah?"

"Yeah, I rented the whole block of them so we won't have any trouble from neighbors, either. We'll get the cage installed this week."

"Good. We can come down this weekend to take a look."

"What else do you need?"

"Bettors. Lots of them. Start getting the word out. Shifters only, any animal. Call all your connections, my friend. The more attendees, the more money to be had. For us and the fighters."

"I understand. I'll get on it." I know the money will be good, and that part is exciting, but for me, this isn't just about getting rich. My animal craves violence. "When can we schedule the first fight?"

"Let's do it a week from Sunday. That gives me time to line up all the fighters. Are you willing to go in the cage?"

"Does a bear shit in the woods?" I ask. If it were Trey, I'd ask if the pope shit in the woods or if the bear wore a pointy hat, because we like to mix our stupid sayings to crack each other up.

"Good. How about your packmates?"

"I'm sure they'd all be in, but I'll ask around. How many do you need?"

"At least four. We can bill it as California vs. Arizona for the first one. My fighters against yours."

"Perfect. I'll round it up. Thanks, Parker."

"We'll be there this Saturday to touch base," Parker says.

"Sounds good. We'll be ready." I hang up. I have to admit, I feel more than a little dirty organizing cage fights in

Alpha's Desire

Angelina's car. It's like I'm sullying her just by thinking about violent business. Which is exactly why I'm bad for her. I climb out and head into the building.

I know Angelina doesn't want me to go in, and I want to give her space, but I also need to keep an eye on her. Not that I think she's going to tell. Oh hell, who am I kidding? I crave contact with her. I want to know everything about this girl—including who she visits in this nursing home.

A grandparent, presumably. But why doesn't she want me along?

Oh right. Because I'm not the kind of guy you bring home to mama. I knew that all along, and yet remembering it in this moment hits me like a right hook to the jaw.

A sweet-looking older receptionist stops me at the front desk, so I turn on the charm. "I'm just here with Angelina Baker. Do you know which way she went?"

"Oh sure. She's visiting her grandmother in room 115." She smiles and points down the hall.

I smile back and give her a little wave as I head that way. I'm not going to bother Angelina. I'll just wait outside.

When I get to the room labeled *Pearl Baker,* the door is open and an elderly woman—presumably her grandma—is yelling at her. "I'm not taking those pills. They're trying to kill me here! Those pills make me lose my brain power. Haven't you noticed how it's diminished since I moved in?"

Angelina says something soft and placating, and thrusts a spoonful of what looks like applesauce at her grandmother.

"I said no!" The old woman bats the spoon to the floor and splatters Angelina with applesauce.

Even though she's not in danger, I start forward involuntarily.

Must protect. My wolf gets so fucking antsy around her.

89

"Grandma." Angelina jumps up, grabbing a napkin. She sees me in the doorway before I can pull back, so I walk in.

I might as well try to help if I can.

I dial my charm level up to ten and beam it straight at the old woman. "Who's this beautiful lady?" I saunter in the room, hands in my pockets so I don't look threatening.

The old woman glares at me for a moment, but her face clears as she takes me in. Then—I swear to the fates—she beams at me. "Well, hello there, young man."

It doesn't matter what age—I recognize the flirt.

"Hi, Mrs. Baker."

"Jared." Angelina says my name in a grumble.

"Do you know this young man, Angelina?"

"Yes, Grandma. He's a... ah... friend of mine."

"Are you ready to take your pills?" I pick up the tiny plastic cup filled with various colored pills. "I'll get another spoon."

"Well—" the old woman looks from me to Angelina. "I don't like to take them."

"I have a spoon," Angelina chirps. She picks up the pill from the floor and cleans it with a napkin.

I take the spoon and the pill from her and scoop another bite of applesauce. "Here you go, Mrs. Baker." I hold it up to her mouth and give a wink, like I'm offering something secret and fun.

"Oh," she giggles—yes, *giggles*. It's adorable. "Call me Pearl." She takes the bite without another protest and swallows it down. "Sit down with me, young man. How do you know my Angelina? You don't look like one of those *boy dancers*."

"Grandma!"

I sit down beside the old woman and scoot her chair

Alpha's Desire

closer to me. "No, I'm not a dancer. I'm a bouncer. Do you know what that is?"

She actually reaches out and squeezes my biceps. "Oh yes. I'll bet that's how you met my granddaughter, isn't it? Were you protecting her from the nasty boys?"

Angelina stifles a laugh.

"Yes, ma'am. That's my job, but I'd do it even if it wasn't. Your granddaughter is special to me."

Angelina goes still and her grandmother's face blooms into a wrinkled smile. She pats my arm. "That's right. She is. I'm glad you've seen it. You're the first boy she's brought around in a long time, and the only one who's worth his salt."

"Grandma," Angelina admonishes.

I throw her a wink. "Now, tell me something, Pearl. Do you have any more pills to take?"

"No, I—"

"Yes, you do. You have one more, Grandma." Angelina fixes another spoonful of applesauce and tries to feed it to her grandma. When the old woman turns her head away, I take the spoon.

"Come on, Pearl." I infuse a gentle command into my voice.

She obediently opens her mouth.

Angelina gives me an eye roll from behind her shoulder.

"Well, Grandma, we should probably go."

"Not yet! You just got here. Don't we have time for a walk?" The elderly woman sends me a hopeful look.

I unfold my large frame from the chair. "Sure we do. Only if I get to push, though."

Pearl beams. "Big strong man like you—you'd better be the one pushing!" She shoves the table in front of her wheelchair aside.

91

RENEE ROSE & LEE SAVINO

I lift it out of the way and take charge of the chair. "Lead the way, beautiful," I murmur to Angelina.

The old woman catches my words and beams up at me. "Such a charming young man," she says quietly, folding her hands in her lap. "Finally, Angelina's on the right track."

A ngelina

"I 'm sorry, I know you didn't want me in there." Jared steals a glance at me as we walk out.

Jesus—is he actually looking unsure? The cocky tough guy who answers everything with a smirk and confidence? I hate seeing him unsure, except that it's over me, and that makes the gravel under my feet seem to skid and slide.

"Are you kidding? She freaking loved you. I'll bet if you asked her to stand on her head and count to thirty, she would have—just for you. I had no idea Grandma had a thing for muscles." I squeeze his biceps the way my Grandma had.

Touching him was a mistake. The moment my fingers contact his skin, the energy between us sizzles. He loops his arm around me, settling his hand on my hip and tapping my ass.

"You thought she'd hate me." He says it without rancor, but it's not a question, either.

I stop walking. "What? No." Why in the hell would he think that? "That's not why I didn't want you in there. I just —" I break off, struggling to put tangled thoughts into words. "I guess I think of Grandma as kind of personal. No

Alpha's Desire

—" I catch his arm when it drops away from my hip. "I mean in an embarrassing way. She's not always lucid and you heard her—she's homophobic, and racist, and often crotchety and rude. It would be like showing you my dirty underwear."

I jab him with my elbow when I see a wicked smile forming on his lips. "Okay, bad analogy. You probably like girls' panties."

"I sure as hell wouldn't turn down seeing your panties, baby. Not today. Not ever."

I roll my eyes and head to the car. "You're incorrigible."

"And you love me that way." He opens the passenger door for me, then walks around. "Admit it—you have a thing for the bad boy."

"You think you're the bad boy?"

His brows twitch. "Yeah. You don't?"

I don't. Not at all. Sure, he has tattoos, but this isn't the 1980s. Tattoos are the norm these days. No, I don't have one yet, partly because my parents would flip, but I've been planning to get one. As soon as I think of something perfect and decide on a place no one will see it. Like the top of my ass.

"You just held the car door for me. You protect me from creepy guys. You fed my grandma applesauce. No, I'd say you're the hero."

Jared stares at me. His hazel eyes catch the light and glow and I lose my breath for a moment, because I swear I can see the wolf in him. I don't mean he shifted, I just mean... I saw something.

Wolfy.

"Come on. I'm not the guy you'd bring home to meet your mother."

Okay, that's true. For some reason, my stomach knots

imagining it. But that's because my parents are judgemental ladder-climbing high society people who need me to be a certain way to reflect better on them. It has nothing to do with Jared.

I choose not to respond to that line. "To me you're more military hero than bad boy."

Vulnerability flickers over Jared's face before he turns his attention to starting the car and driving.

I don't say anything more because I can tell I've hit a nerve, but I don't know why.

"That's funny." He doesn't look at me. "I was always the good-for-nothing, never-amounts-to-much guy who got into fights."

A chill threads through me, chased by hot anger. "Says who?" I demand. I'm ready to go toe-to-toe with anyone who believes such stupidity.

He shrugs. "My parents. My alpha."

"Garrett?"

"No." He shakes his head. "Garrett's dad. Garrett was a bit of a rebel, too—our leader. We broke off from his dad's pack as worthless teenage wastes and moved here to raise havoc in Tucson."

His words leave a sour taste in my mouth. "You're operating from a pretty outdated viewpoint of yourself, Jared."

Uncertainty flickers on his face again and I lean toward him. "You're the farthest thing from a waste I've ever seen."

A wall falls in place behind his eyes at the word *waste*. "Come on. Garrett may have made something of himself, but I'm nothing but his muscle. A *bouncer* at a nightclub. That's hardly carving a place for myself in the world. Violence is all I've ever been good at."

For some reason, my eyes burn at his declaration. I don't want to believe him—I don't believe him—but the violence

Alpha's Desire

part scares me. He's already made it plain his kind are far more violent than average humans. I realize he's warning me about himself again.

I'd be stupid not to heed the warning.

But even if he is violent—even if he's something I don't understand—I still know the truth.

This man is worthy.

Of so much more than he believes.

"Well—" I clear my throat, trying to reason my way through his beliefs. "There's a place for warriors. If we were in medieval times, you'd be the most revered of all men. The deliverer of justice, protector of honor."

Jared pulls up at my place and turns off the car. He stares at the steering wheel, his expression a turmoil of emotion.

"So you just have to figure out how the warrior fits into modern day times. If it's being the enforcer for your pack and the bouncer at a club, that's not less important than any other role in society. You're still the knight. I mean, you are to me."

Jared throws his door open and gets out without speaking.

Did I offend him? My mind replays what I said.

My door flings wide and Jared reaches in and unbuckles my seat belt. There's dark determination in his face that I can't decipher. He picks me up like a kid out of a car seat, and hooks his forearm under my ass, lifting me to straddle his waist. The moment his lips meld to mine, I understand.

It's not dark determination—it's passion.

He carries me to the front door without breaking the kiss.

Like the princess with the knight, I surrender, arms twined around his neck, lips twisting over his.

Any intellectual objections I might have to Jared are lost

not only to my physical desires—which have been off the charts since our interlude this morning—but now to emotional currents, as well. The intensity coming off Jared in waves is something I'd rather die than interrupt. Because it's all directed at me.

And I'll be damned if I'm going to block it this time. Jared has something to give me. And I want to accept.

He carries me toward the bedroom, but I get self-conscious and break the kiss. "Jared, I should shower—I danced all day."

He veers to the bathroom, taking my mouth again. I'm lowered gently to my feet, and he pulls my t-shirt off over my head. My belly shudders on an inhale as he stares at my bra-clad breasts like a starved man.

And then his mouth is on mine again, his hand tangled up in my hair. He backs me up until my butt hits the bathroom counter and he presses the hard bulge of his cock in the notch between my legs.

I moan against his lips.

Jared breaks away and closes both hands into fists, strain showing in the tightness of his jaw. He cages me between his two fists on the counter, but doesn't touch me.

"Take off your bra, Angelina." His voice is deep and gravelly.

I reach behind me and unhook it, letting the cups fall down as the straps slide off my shoulders.

Jared still doesn't touch me, but his gaze is a laser beam on my breasts, and there's wonder in his expression. "I'm trying to go slow, here, baby." A note of agony creeps into his voice. "Fates know I want to shove those knees wider and pound you until tomorrow."

My pussy clenches at the declaration.

"But you deserve so much better than that."

Alpha's Desire

"Let me get in the shower," I murmur, still intent on cleaning up for him. I changed out of the leo and tights at school, but I still feel grubby from my classes.

His only reply is to slant his lips over mine again, licking into my mouth with his tongue. He eases back, though, pulling my ass off the counter and twists away to turn on the water. He's back a moment later, hands coasting down my sides, cupping my ass.

I yank the button on my shorts open and shimmy out of my panties as he claims my mouth again. It takes all my will-power to pull away, but I do. "I'll be right back," I murmur and back into the shower.

The water is the perfect temperature, but all I can think about it soaping up quickly to get back to Jared. As it turns out, he wasn't waiting.

The shower curtain opens and there he is in all his male glory. And let me tell you—Jared without clothes is breath-taking. He's pure muscle, and a lot of it. Tattoos wind around his shoulders and down his forearms. Golden chest hair curls over enormous pecs. His abs are defined enough to trace, quads thick and powerful. If we'd been coloring a model like him in our anatomy coloring books, I'd remember the curve of every muscle, no matter how small. Because it's clear he uses them all.

And then there's his cock. I saw it this morning, but it's flying full mast now, pointed right at me. In one large paw, he holds a foil packet.

He's on me before I've looked my fill, taking the soap from my hands and rubbing it down my back as he melds his mouth over mine again.

I moan into the kiss, rub my stiff, wet nipples against his chest.

"Angelina." His voice rasps against my neck. The soap

97

drops but he doesn't retrieve it. He reaches the hand cupping my ass between my legs and strokes my swollen pussy.

I've never felt so beautiful, so desirable. My body is on fire for Jared and I want to give back as much as I'm getting. I hike one of my knees up to wrap around his waist, and grind my clit down on the root of his shaft.

His fingers slip between the crack of my ass and I gasp when he zeroes in on my anus with the pad of one finger. Like the first time he touched me there, I squeeze my cheeks closed reflexively. It doesn't stop him, his wet digit slides over my most taboo of holes as if he's confident it will give me pleasure.

And—oh hell—it does. I don't want it to—it's so freaking embarrassing—but yes, I'm rubbing harder over his cock. I've never been this turned on in my life—I'm already halfway over the crest into orgasm, just from his finger between my crack.

But no, it's so much more than that. It's not even the mechanics—it's the energy behind everything Jared brings to this. I sense the gift in it. He's not taking for himself. He's honoring me. My body. With all of him.

I snatch the condom from his fingers and tear it open with my teeth. Jared grips the base of his cock and holds it for me to roll on the rubber. His breath hisses in over his teeth when I make contact and I realize his thighs are shaking as much as mine.

As soon as the condom is on, he pushes me back against the shower wall, pulling my knee up to his hip again. The head of his cock prods my entrance and I mewl with excitement, the need to have him inside me so intense.

"*Yes, Jared,*" I gasp when he rocks his hips and applies a little pressure.

Alpha's Desire

"Does that feel good, baby?" He pushes the wet hair out of my eyes, gazes down with an intensity that rocks me.

My mouth falls open as he parts me, eases inside. "Yes," I manage to answer.

"Good," he murmurs, taking my hips with both hands and tipping me to just the right angle. He drives in deep—so deep I catch my breath as he fills me, and then he's kissing me again, his tongue fucking my mouth with the same rhythm as his long cock.

I can't get enough. I nip his lips, kiss back with all I've got. I need this like I need air to breathe. Water to drink. Dance in my life.

My eyes roll back in my head with every thrust. I'm half gone with delirium—I wouldn't know my own name if you asked me.

Jared's lids droop, his fingers tighten to bruising strength around my hips. The water runs down our bodies, only adding to the intensity of sensations.

Before I come, he turns off the water and throws back the curtain. He pulls my other leg around his waist and carries me out, then grabs a towel and wraps it around my back as he heads to the bedroom.

He lays me on my back on the towel, our bodies still connected intimately. As soon as I'm down, he pistons into me, holding my hips and sinking so deep.

It's on the tip of my tongue to thank him, to beg him, to say a million stupid things, but instead I moan, rolling my head from side to side as he plunges deep and retracts, over and over again.

He brings the pad of his thumb to my clit with one hand, pinches my nipple and pulls with the other.

I arch up, thrusting my breasts toward the ceiling, a hoarse cry issuing from my lips. "J-Jared," I gasp.

"Take it, baby. Take it all."

I let go, flipping backward into a spiral of pleasure, of release. My pussy clamps down on his cock, squeezing and pulsing around his thick length.

I see galaxies, shooting stars, the incredible void of everything and nothing at once. My body knows nothing but pleasure and I succumb to it fully. When my sight returns—or maybe when I open my eyes, I can't be sure—Jared's watching me with that heavy-lidded gaze, rocking slowly in and out.

I realize he hasn't come yet and I scramble up on my elbows. He pulls out and lifts me to my hands and knees, crawling up on the bed behind me.

"Grab the headboard, baby," he directs me softly. There's command, but also so much tenderness in his tone. I've never had a man like him, but it's exactly what I need, what I've always craved. This is the man of the fantasies I didn't even know I had.

I scoot forward to hang on to the headboard.

"That's it. Tell me if it's too much." He thrusts into me again and I instantly understand his concern. In this position he drives even deeper. His hips snap, throwing me forward with force. I have to brace my arms against the headboard to keep from flying into the wall, even though he holds my waist.

It's delicious. Too much and not enough at once. I feel both like a treasured princess and a dirty slut at the same time. I'm flying so flipping high, drunk on Jared, on all the need and desire he's woken in me.

"Fuck, yes. Arch that back for me, baby." He drags a palm down my spine and lays a light slap on the side of my ass.

I arch for him—I'd do anything he asked right now.

Alpha's Desire

Especially when he uses that reverential tone, like I'm the goddess of sex herself.

His breath grows heavy, movements get jerky. It gets too rough—not for my pussy, but for my back and shoulders. Before I have to say something, he shifts, laying his torso over mine and bracing one hand on the headboard next to mine. He brings his other hand to my breast, and pinches my nipple, rolling it between his fingers and tugging.

I moan. He strokes his hand down the plane of my belly and finds my clit again.

I shudder, but he bites my ear. "Not until I tell you, baby."

I quiet, listening.

"Do you understand? You don't come until daddy tells you."

I have no idea why he called himself *daddy*, but it flips some switch in me. It's dirty and hot. My pussy contracts, toes curl, arches lift.

He chuckles, his lips right at my ear. I savor the deep rumble, internalize the notes like it's the music I'm dancing to. He sits back on his heels, pulling my hips with him, so we're both sitting up. I squirm over his cock, missing the thrusting, and he uses his hands at my waist to lift and lower me over it, faster than the Energizer Bunny.

"*Oh my God, oh my God.*" I won't last long. Why did he tell me to wait? I seriously don't know if I can, and yet disobeying him is an impossibility.

I'm lightheaded, every nerve in my body buzzing, buzzing. He's jackhammering into me as I bounce, my small breasts jiggling, my wet hair swinging.

"Fuck, I just can't decide how I want to come in you, baby. Every view is better than the last."

I look over my shoulder at him and he growls. "Yes, *goddammit.* I want to see that pretty face. Turn around."

I spin around and straddle his waist, but he lays me onto my back and sits back up, so my ass lays on his hard thighs, legs wrap around his waist. He curls his hands around the tops of my thighs, wrapping them around to grip my ass and pulls me back and forth over his cock.

"That's it. Look at me, baby. Just like that."

Even if I wasn't too far gone to be self-conscious about being watched while I come undone, his gaze is one hundred percent appreciative. I bask in the hot spotlight of his green stare. He thumbs my clit and fucks me, all the while rumbling—no, growling. But it's more like a purr than a snarl.

He switches his hands, sliding them under my ass and parting my cheeks. When he taps my anus with a finger, I'm lost.

"Now, baby. Come for me." His guttural tone is as urgent as my desire. For the second time, I shatter, my hips snapping up and down, as the release uncoils faster than a whip. The orgasm is even bigger than my last one. I scream, cupping my own breasts, squeezing my nipples like Jared did, pushing and rubbing hard against him.

Jared lets out a roar and rises to his knees. My ankles end up over his shoulders and he fucks me hard, his loins slapping against my ass while he holds the fronts of my thighs. His face contorts, eyes glow more yellow than green.

"Fates, yes, Angelina!" he shouts. His mighty thighs flex, the muscles of his chest and neck bulge and his handsome face contorts. I swear I feel the heat of his cum, even though he's wearing a condom.

A shudder of pleasure runs through me, the aftershock from my orgasm and my pussy squeezes his cock.

Alpha's Desire

Jared groans. "You milking it all out of me, baby?"

"Mmm hmm."

He doesn't move, just watches me with his hooded gaze, his cock still buried deep inside me. After a long moment, he circles an arm around my waist and bends down to kiss my belly.

"Beautiful girl. I don't want it to end." But it does end. He eases out and walks to the bathroom to dispose of the condom. I watch his muscular ass flex as he leaves and sigh.

I don't want this to end, either.

But it has to, doesn't it?

J *ared*

I return to Angelina with another towel. She hasn't moved, her lovely lithe dancer form sprawled on the mattress like a work of art. I guess in her case, her body is her art. Makes her art.

What a spectacular medium.

I should be finished. I just fucked her ever-loving brains out. No—that's not true. I *made love* to Angelina.

It's something I've never done before. I'm a rough lover. Demanding. Dominant. I still feel all those things with her—still want to spank her ass pink and tie her up, but what I just did with her? It was totally fucking different.

And even knowing she didn't want us to be intimate, I couldn't pull back. I needed to make love to her work of art

103

body. I needed to show her without words how much her words meant to me. What she does to me.

And now I can't stop myself from crawling up on the bed and pulling her knees apart. I lower my head and drag my tongue through her folds.

She moans and tries to push my head away. "No more. I can't take any more."

I lick again. "Are you sore, angel?"

"No. Yes. But it's not that. I just—I can't take any more. It's too much."

"Oh baby. You don't get to tell me what's too much. I decide how much pleasure you get. When you get off. How hard. Don't think I didn't notice how much you liked it when I made you wait for your orgasm."

Her pale slender fingers tangle in my hair. Despite her words, she's pulling my mouth closer.

"I know what you need, beautiful." I suck her labia, nip it. I make my tongue flat and stroke over her clit.

Her legs start to thrash on the bed. "Why?" she whines.

"Why what? Why am I going to make you come again?"

"Yeah," she pants.

"Because I need to." It's the goddamn truth. It's like I was born to worship this incredible body of hers.

"Jared," she whimpers, fingers tearing at my hair.

It won't take long to make her come. If I were feeling more dommy, I'd make her suffer longer, but it seems I'm in a generous mood. I spread her wide and rim her asshole, making her shriek and shudder. I lick a long line back and forth between her anus and clit until she's sobbing with need, her inner thighs trembling where they clamp around my ears.

I affix my mouth over her clit and suck.

She screams.

Alpha's Desire

I slide two fingers inside her and find her G-spot on her inner wall. "You may come," I say softly and return my mouth to her clit.

I never said she couldn't, but it's like she was waiting for my command. The second the words leave my mouth, she's clamping down on my fingers. I suck her clit and stroke her G-spot until she finishes.

Her body's shaking, so I wrap her up in the bedspread and spoon her as she comes down from wherever she went orbiting. After a long moment, she says, "I'm starving."

I laugh. "Me too, baby. Should I go get us something? Or can I take you out? Anything you want. You name it."

"Street tacos? On Congress?"

I get up, fully prepared to run the errand, but she gets up, too, pulling on her clothes. I can't deny the small satisfaction of keeping her near me. Of taking her out and buying her food. Providing.

You're still the knight. I mean, you are to me.

No matter what happens between me and Angelina, I'll never forget those words. Not for as long as I live. Hearing that she sees me as a hero not a waste? It rearranged something inside me.

I can't do it now, because I'm still too full of Angelina, but I'm looking forward to reviewing that conversation. Dissecting it. There's something important there—some clue about what's been missing in my life. Angelina may have just brought it into focus.

7

Angelina

The casting list for the faculty show is posted outside the auditorium. All the dance students are gathered there when I arrive, my six foot five shadow ambling behind me.

He took me out to dinner and slept in my bed last night. He's acting like my boyfriend, and it feels too good to tell him to quit.

Even though I know it's going to end.

He knows it, too. He's been quiet—not exactly brooding, but thoughtful. The line between his brows hasn't gone away since dinner last night. I'm a coward, because I haven't had the will to broach the subject of us.

Somehow, I know that tonight he'll be back to sleeping on the couch. And that thought causes an ache right behind my breastbone. Even worse is the thought that at the end of two weeks, he'll leave.

Even now he hangs back, giving me space. Gone are the teasing smirks of yesterday.

I try to push the dilemma from my mind and check the cast list. One ballet dance. One modern. Rehearsals start tomorrow.

I should be grateful. Some dancers nearby are trying not to cry. I note Talya got in the modern dance piece with me. Remy didn't get into anything. She comes up behind me to check and I squeeze her hand.

"Did I get dissed again?"

"I'm sorry."

Remy shrugs, but I know it bothers her. It's one of the reasons I asked her to do the Eclipse thing. No—that's not true. I asked her because I like her and I knew she'd be great. But I also feel like she could shine so much brighter than she does in school. If they would see past the fifteen pounds they told her to lose. Yep, she got the dreaded "fat letter." The one I'm always on pins and needles about getting. It comes with a recommended visit to a campus nutritionist and certain number they want to see by a deadline. Or you're out of the program.

I'm not kidding.

So yeah. I haven't received one yet, but it's always on my mind. This threat looming over me. It's part of why I don't think I fit here. Not that I haven't achieved everything I'm supposed to want to achieve. But it's like this is a life I don't want to live anymore. It's the one my mom wanted. The one my dad thought was practical.

It was never my dream.

I turn around and find Jared still hanging back, but watching me intently, like I'm a puzzle he's trying to decode. I sling my dance bag over my shoulder and walk up to him. Strains of Prokofiev's Romeo and Juliet drift out of a nearby

Alpha's Desire

classroom and I have the sudden giddy urge to dance up to him. But no. As much as I'm already loving having him beside me twenty-four hours a day, I should cut this short. Because seriously—if I get used to this, it will kill me when it's over. I'll probably be begging to have my memories wiped.

I lay a hand on his chest, loving the way his belly dips at the contact. "I have classes again all day, big guy. You really don't have to stay."

His throat works as he swallows, his eyes on my lips. "I do." His voice is rough.

"Jared."

His gaze lifts to my eyes.

"You can trust me with your secret."

He draws in a sharp breath. "I know." The words fly from his mouth, as if he hadn't thought before speaking. "I know," he repeats. His face closes. "I have orders…"

"I'll still be here at three when you pick me up. Nothing's going to happen in the meantime." I lift my pinkie. "Promise."

When the corners of his mouth lift in that familiar grin, my heart picks up speed. He hooks his pinkie in mine, then pulls it to his lips and kisses my fingers. "I'll be waiting out front."

I nod, satisfied. Not because I mind him here, but because I know I need to cut him loose. This is too intense for both of us.

J*ared*

I heave a long section of chain link into place and wait as Trey secures it to the poles we already bolted to the cement floor. After I left Angelina at school, I wasted no time getting ready for the first fight. The fates know I've had enough down time hanging around with Angelina to make my plan.

"Does Garrett know you're not with her right now?" Trey asks, even though he knows the fucking answer.

"Fuck off."

"Thought he told you to stick to her like glue."

"Yeah, he did. And I have. But I trust her. She's not gonna tell. Besides, I have shit to do, or else we won't be ready for this fight. Which is supposed to happen *during* the two weeks I've been shackled to her. You think Garrett wants me to bring her here for it?" My voice is laced with scorn and Trey tosses me a lopsided grin.

"That would be a mistake."

"We both know it's not about me babysitting her."

"Right," Trey agrees. "It's about you figuring out if she's your mate or not."

Hearing it out loud does all kinds of scratchy things to my esophagus. Trey stops moving and looks over at me, trying to read my expression.

"And?" he prompts when I don't spill.

"I don't fucking know!" I shout.

Trey shakes the chain link to make sure it's secure, then hooks both hands thru the links and hangs on it. "I'm thinking you do."

I hurl the pair of wire cutters in my hand at his face, knowing he'll dodge in time. The two of us have been best

Alpha's Desire

friends since childhood. We know each other inside and out. I glare at him, my heart slamming against my ribs.

"I'm not gonna fucking wipe her."

Trey's brows shoot up, which gives me pause. Does that mean *he* thinks Angelina's my mate? Or he thinks I think so?

I give my skull a hard shake, as if it will dislodge the looping thoughts in my head.

Trey walks over and hangs on the fence beside me. I adopt the same pose, staring at a spot on the concrete floor.

"I don't have the urge to mark her," I admit after a long moment of silence.

This is the fact I've been trying to push to the back of my mind since last night. The torment. It should make everything easier, but it doesn't. It only makes it worse.

"I... claimed her last night. No serum on my teeth. No desire to bite."

"Huh." Trey sounds surprised.

I flip around to hang the other way on the fence, facing out.

"Maybe it's different with humans." Trey sounds doubtful.

"It's not. Remember Garrett with Amber?"

"Yeah." Trey flips around, too. "Well, the moon was full then. Maybe that's why he gave you two weeks. Moon'll be full by then."

"Maybe." I'm slightly relieved by Trey's suggestion.

But that means I must *want* Angelina to be my mate. Which is stupid, because I still can't have her. I mean, I won't. I don't want to ruin her. But still, knowing she's my mate would explain why I'm having such a hard time walking away. Cutting her loose and just wiping her.

"You thought I was going to say she's my mate?" I have to

ask. I need to know what signs he saw, other than me being protective of her.

Trey shrugs his shoulders, which makes him do a pull-up of sorts. "Yeah."

"Why?"

"You know why. You're acting crazy. Wrecking your bike. Defying our alpha." He's silent for a moment, and I keep quiet, too. He's the problem-solver between us. I'm the brute force, he directs it. "Was anything different when you fu— claimed her?"

I appreciate his word choice because I would have to beat him senseless for speaking disrespectfully about Angelina.

I hesitate. Trey's the only male in this world I would admit this to. "Yeah. It was different. The opposite of what I thought it would be, actually. I didn't go agro on her at all. In fact, I was..." I give an embarrassed laugh and kick the chain link with my heel. "Fucking tender. It was the first time in my life I made love instead of fucked. Never thought I'd say that, either."

Trey's silent but this time it kills me not interrupting his thoughts. I just hung myself out there, and it feels fucking exposed. "Maybe," Trey says slowly, "Your wolf calms down around her. You're more violent than most. If you got *more* amped up around her—a fragile human—you could kill her."

"I *know.*" I start doing backward pull-ups on the fence to work out the violence growing in me, fueled by frustration. "That's why I don't want her to be my mate. I could never claim her."

"You're not listening. What if your wolf knows better? He calms your aggression when you're around her. He's keeping

Alpha's Desire

you in check, including the desire to rip her shoulder open to leave your scent."

"Then why did I try to break Fox's neck for wiping her? I knew I was wrong doing it, but I couldn't stop myself."

"Duh, dumbshit. The wolf always protects his mate."

I'm relieved at Trey's goading me by calling me dumbshit. I'm on him in a second, getting a solid punch in before he dodges and kicks my ass. I tackle and take him to the ground, wrestling until I have his head in a chokehold.

Trey slaps the floor and I release him. Both of us stand up grinning. "Asshole," he mutters without any rancor.

"So how do I figure out for sure?"

Trey clomps around to setup the last section of fence to make the cage. "Wait until the full moon."

"And if I still don't want to mark her?"

Trey slaps the fencing in place. "Dude. Don't be an idiot."

"What?"

"You already want to mark her. And you've already made some decision about why you can't. Why don't you just let that decision go? Just until the deadline. Things might become clear."

"I hate you."

It's a mark of our friendship that Trey's face lights up with a surprised grin and not hurt. "Why?"

"Smart fucking asshole."

He looks far too pleased with himself as he hooks the fencing to the pole. "You gonna help me here, or do I have to put you in this ring and show you a thing or two about fighting?"

I laugh, because we both know I'll win every fight I enter in that cage. "I'm helping, I'm helping."

113

For the first time since I claimed Angelina last night, the heaviness lifts from my chest.

I have two weeks. No need to come to any conclusions until then.

A ngelina

Jared's waiting for me outside the dance building and I can't deny the pleasure that blooms in my chest at seeing him waiting for me. I remember in high school the popular, more socially well-rounded girls—girls who didn't have ballet five nights a week—got picked up by older boyfriends from school. It seemed so exciting and romantic. Something I'd never have.

In college I've had boyfriends and I've even had a couple hookups, but never the formal dating. I haven't had the guy who wants to drive and take me out to dinner and pay. I didn't even know I wanted that.

Turns out I find it pretty hot.

Or maybe it's just because it's Jared.

I've changed into my shorts and he gives me that look when I get in the car—the one that says he'd like to eat me alive.

Instantly, my whole body lights up, as if my very cells are vibrating and heating just being close to him. The memory of sex last night—the best sex of my life—almost makes me blush.

"How'd it go, baby?"

I shrug. I definitely don't want to talk about school right

Alpha's Desire

now. Or anything real life. I'd rather know everything there is to know about werewolves. Too bad he won't tell me.

He rocks his large hand over the steering wheel. "I always love watching you dance, angel. From the first time you got up on those boxes at the club I was hooked on you."

Now I do blush. Because it's *Jared*. Admitting he's had a thing for *me*.

"And I loved watching you yesterday in that ballet class."

I sense a *but* coming, and I stiffen, as if he's my mother getting ready to offer constructive criticism.

Like usual, he's too damn in tune with me. He glances over, a startled wrinkle between his brow.

"Is there a *but*?" I ask. Might as well make it easy for him.

The way he turns his focus back to the road and rolls his grip on the steering wheel tells me I'm right.

What could it be? I'm not as skinny as the rest of the bunheads? Too uptight?

"There was no joy. When I see you dance at the club, you're alive. Shining. What I saw yesterday? Made me want to throat punch your professor for sucking the life out of you."

The sound that comes out of my mouth is a half-laugh, half-sob. How is it possible that in five minutes Jared saw what my mom couldn't see in eighteen years? What I couldn't bring myself to admit out loud for the past four? What my dad would never even understand?

He pulls up in front of my house and reaches for my hand. "I'm sorry, I didn't mean—"

"No." I pull my buns out of my hair. "I'm upset because you're right. And it's the center hub my life spins around. This thing that doesn't work for me."

I stare at him, hopelessness rising up and drowning me.

115

He narrows his eye. "So I do get to go and throat punch your professors?"

I let out a watery laugh. "If only that would fix this." I push open the car door, suddenly way too constricted inside.

He follows me out and opens my front door. "Fix what?" His voice is sharp, like he's determined to fix my life any way he can.

I shake my hair down, walking away.

"Hey." He catches me around the waist and pulls my body back against his. "You don't get to turn your back on me when you're upset. Not for a goddamn second." His voice is a growl in my ear, the rough stubble of his face scraping my cheek.

Everything I've been bottling in that's been straining to get out as my graduation approaches jostles up into my throat.

"I hate it!" I admit. "I don't fit the mold and I can't make myself *want* to fit it anymore."

Jared drops me and spins me around. His green eyes bore into me. "So don't."

The laugh-sob comes up again.

"Who are you doing this for? Your teachers? Your old self? It's okay to change your mind. It's okay to veer from the path you set for yourself."

A tear leaks out of my eye. "See that's the thing. I don't even think I set this path. I think my mom did."

Jared's lip curls but he doesn't say anything.

"I think she wanted to be a ballerina but her parents couldn't afford lessons, so she's living vicariously through me. I don't even know if I ever liked dance, or if she just told me I did."

Alpha's Desire

Jared shakes his head slowly. "You love it on Saturday nights."

"That's not really dance," I mutter.

"The hell it's not." He gets right up in my face, but it doesn't scare me.

Instead, I square off against him. "What do you know about dance?"

He blinks and swallows. Backs off. Shoves his hands in his pocket.

Have I hurt his feelings? Crap.

"You're right. I don't know dance. But I know you. Whatever it is you do on Saturday nights, you love."

I step into him, my need to soothe him apparently as strong as his for me. My hands hit his chest and the sizzle of contact runs through me. "That's about... the joy of creation. It's my baby. I dreamed it up. I staged it. I got Garrett to agree to it."

He covers my hands with his. "Yeah?" It's a prompt. He wants me to go on.

I draw in a breath, following the thread. "It's the only place in my life I got to be in charge. To execute *my* vision. Do you know what I mean?"

He nods and pulls one hand from my chest. "Come on, let's go for a walk."

"Why?" I ask, but follow his lead out the door.

"When I need to work through stuff running always helps me." He leads me at a brisk pace. It's beautiful out. I love spring in Tucson, when the air is warm and everything starts to bloom. The sweet smell of citrus blossoms perfume the air. Pink penstemon are making their bell-flower appearance just in time for Easter.

I have to admit, walking feels good. Like I can leave the

117

shit pile of my situation behind. "So what other visions do you have?"

I'm unbelievably grateful for the question. It would be so easy to start complaining about my controlling parents right now. Or how every day that draws closer to graduation I feel more and more stuck.

"Well, honestly? I'd love to have my own dance company."

There. I said it out loud. The angels of dance didn't even strike me down.

"Mmm hmm. What would your dance company be like?"

I have to take long strides to keep up with Jared, which is freeing. "It wouldn't be a ballet company. I guess more contemporary, but I see it as more of a hybrid. Like one part performance art, three parts dance—but any kind of dance —ballet, modern, hip hop."

"Uh huh. Is that what you do at the club?"

"Yes, but what we do there is just the tip of the iceberg. I have this idea for a totally interactive show. Something that entertains an audience and doesn't just cater to the old fogies who want to be high-brow and say they went to see the Nutcracker. Something anyone and everyone would like. All ages. All backgrounds."

"Wow."

I steal a glance at Jared to gauge his reaction. I can't believe I've actually expressed the ideas out loud, but now that I have, my excitement rolls behind them like a giant bulldozer. There's no keeping it back. I've been stewing on these ideas since high school, for God's sake.

Jared smiles. "That sounds incredible, baby. What would it take to make it happen?"

Alpha's Desire

And then everything goes flat. That familiar choking heaviness returns.

"Whatever you just thought about, you'd better kick it the fuck out of your head," Jared growls, surprising a laugh out of me.

"I thought about what I'm *supposed* to be doing when I graduate."

"Which is?"

"My dad's willing to invest in my career, but only to help me open a dance studio. For kids. Which is cool and all. I like teaching okay, but..."

"That isn't your dream."

I have a little more room to breathe just with him saying the words. "Right."

"So the plan is open a ballet studio, teach what you learned from your uptight professors, and be a good little ballerina?"

That laugh-sob is becoming my new go-to reaction. "Pretty much. The thing is—I don't even consider myself a ballerina. If I were a serious ballerina, I'd be at least fifteen pounds lighter and I would've been apprenticed to a professional company by the time I was fourteen. My mom wanted this for me, but not badly enough to ship me off to New York or San Francisco.

"It's probably not too late for a performing career in modern, but it still would involve me going to New York City. The 'ents don't like that."

"Do you want that?"

For some reason, I have the sense Jared's holding his breath.

I consider it. The idea excites me, but it might only be because I want anything different than what I have now. Would I create my company there? It's doubtful. I'd prob-

ably get swallowed whole by all the desperate dancers clawing to succeed. Get caught up in waiting tables and going to auditions. Struggling to please a new master. Stuffing this inner voice of mine back down again.

"No. Not really. I still wouldn't be doing what I want to do—choreographing. Creating."

"Okay, so back to my question. What do you need to execute your vision?" There's a determination in Jared's eyes, like he's going to make this happen for me. I shouldn't get excited, but I can't help it. It's the first encouragement I've had, and I'm going to take it and run with it.

"I picture it in a warehouse. Some place we could transform for different shows. I'm picturing silks and trapezes or hoops rigged from the ceiling, dances in water tanks—crazy stuff! The audience would be led through the space—almost like a haunted house. There would be a new performance around every corner. They'd stop and watch and then their host would bring them to the next spot. Maybe six minutes for each piece—everything perfectly timed and coordinated."

"I can get you a warehouse."

I stop and stare at him. "What?"

He rolls his tongue under his lower lip, pushing it out. "I have a warehouse space you can use."

"Are you serious?"

"Yeah. What else do you need?"

I swallow. "Um, I'm not sure. I'd have to trick it out. I don't really have money for that, and my dad would never invest in something that's not a solid business venture, like a ballet studio."

"Why isn't this a solid business—nevermind. Forget your dad. He isn't your only resource. Tell me what you need and we'll figure it out." We've circled around a few

Alpha's Desire

blocks by now and are back in front of my place. "Want to do another loop?" he asks.

I grimace at my flip flops, which weren't the best choice for walking. "No, not now. But thanks. You were right, walking helped." We head up the steps to my place. "So you're a runner?"

He unlocks the door and lets me in. "Er, no. I mean yes, but four-legged," he says with the sexy grin that makes my knees go weak.

I stop and face him, tipping my face up with my best puppy eyes. "I want to see. Show me your wolf? Please?"

His arms loop around my waist and he palms my ass, yanking my core up against his jeans, where his very impressive erection bulges. I see indecision dance over his expression. "I can't, baby," he says on an exhale.

I try to hide my disappointment. Try to remember why we can't do this. We aren't a couple. We never can be. We're forbidden to each other.

Romeo and fucking Juliet.

I think I'll make a dance about it when I have my show. Throw myself off a balcony in a dive that makes the audience gasp before the bungee around my ankle picks up the slack.

Oh my God, I can't believe I'm actually thinking like I'm really going to have the performance.

"So I want a list of what you need in the warehouse. The setup—everything."

"Jared—" I take a step back, out of the circle of his arms. We're not even dating. Not a couple. I can hardly ask him to let me use his warehouse for my show. Not when his existence may be wiped from my mind in less than two weeks. "I appreciate your offer, but I can't accept. I need to do this on my own."

8

Jared

I open my mouth to argue but she lifts her chin at that stubborn angle I find so adorable.

Fuck.

My fingers curl up with frustration, but punching a wall isn't going to help. Angelina's pulled back, cutting me off. As she should.

I'm not part of her future. It's wrong of me to try to insinuate myself into it. But I'll be damned if I'm going to let her give up on her dream. To wither away and die under the expectations of prescribed perfection.

She kicks off her flip flops and heads into the kitchen.

I follow, unable to stay out of her business. She takes out lettuce and tomatoes, puts them in a bowl.

It may be exactly what she wants to eat right now, but the sight of it makes my wolf growl. She thinks she weighs too much to be a ballerina. She's been starving herself to fit into some mold that I want to fucking destroy right now.

"Is that what you want to eat?" I ask, sounding grouchier than I mean to.

She whirls and puts her hands on her hips, one leg jutting out. "I can't eat street tacos and beer with you every night, wolfie." She slaps the sides of her hips. "Wouldn't want to get a fat letter from the faculty."

A real snarl comes out of my throat. I prowl closer. "Do you think you need to lose weight?" There's danger in my tone, but she doesn't recognize it. Or if she does, she's ignoring it because she's shutting me down.

"Five or ten pounds lighter would be ideal."

I cage her against the counter. "No baby, you're perfect." Too perfect for me. Way outta my league. I grit my teeth. Fuck those dance professors. I better not ever meet them, because there's no telling what my wolf would do to the people who made my girl cry.

I wish she could be my girl forever so I could protect her from the world. Maybe after we split, I'll keep an eye on her. Have my wolf check on her. 'Cause that's not fucking pathetic.

But no, this girl doesn't need protection. She just needs to get out from under the weight of other people's expectation. To start living for herself.

"Fuck ideal. Do *you* think you need to lose weight?"

She's holding her breath. Neither of us moves. My body is up against hers, but barely touching.

"No." She sounds relieved when she says it. "If I did, I would've already lost it. I don't want to look like a toothpick."

"That's my girl." I lower my lips to her forehead and press them to her smooth skin.

"I'll make the salad—or I'll go buy us some fucking steak, if you want it."

Alpha's Desire

She laughs, the puff of air hitting my throat.

"I want you to make the list of what you need for the show. Not for me. For you. It will help you get clear on exactly what you need."

"Oh, well—"

I step out of her way. "I mean right now, Angelina. Sketch it out. It's important to take action on your dreams. Take this one small step right now."

"Fine," she says in that sassy way that gets me harder than stone.

Does she remember what I promised to do the next time she said it? But hell, I shouldn't, not when—

She sneaks a guilty look, like she's checking to see if I noticed.

Hunger hits me. My cock punches out, straining against my jeans.

Angelina laughs and darts past me.

Foolish, foolish girl.

Does she have any idea what happens when you goad a wolf into the chase? I catch her and swoop her up over my shoulder in about two seconds flat.

Her giggle tells me she wants this and fuck if that doesn't release the dam on my self-control. I smack her upturned ass and jog into the bedroom. I drop her onto her feet and turn her to face the bed. I'm not ready to start spanking yet, though. I wrap one arm around her waist and cup her mons, rubbing the seam of her shorts into her slit.

She writhes, pushing back against me, her breath ragged.

I slow my movements. "You know what's going to happen now?"

"You're going to spank me?" She sounds breathless.

"That's right, baby." I unbutton her miniscule shorts and

let them drop to the floor. Her tank top is easy to peel off. "Take off your bra and panties." I like taking her clothes off, but I also enjoy making her bare herself for me. That way I know I'm not bulldozing her.

She looks over her shoulder at me—a redheaded coquette—and it's all I can do to keep from shoving her over the bed, spreading her wide and pounding into that sweet pussy until she's hoarse.

But no. I get to spank her first. A pleasure I will relish until the day I die.

"Panties off." I make my voice firm. Or maybe that's my need bleeding into my tone. Either way, she jumps to obey, hooking her thumbs in the waistband and slipping them down her legs.

I work to control my breath. The scent of her arousal fills the room and my hands have already found her bare skin, gripping her hips with authority. "Bend over, baby."

She rests her hands on the bed.

"All the way over. And baby? When I'm disciplining you, answer me with respect."

I know she has no clue what I'm talking about. I'm not even into BDSM, except that wolves are over the top dominant. But I'm dying to hear the words from her lips. "Say, *yes, daddy.*"

She lays her torso on the bed. "Yes, daddy." Her voice wobbles, but I'm ninety-nine percent sure it's with need, judging by her scent.

I give her the lightest of slaps. I don't want to scare her—not now, not ever.

She moans and waggles her ass.

I spank her again. "That's for keeping me hard every minute of the day. Every goddamn time I'm in your presence." Another slap, a little harder.

126

Alpha's Desire

She catches her breath.

I change things up, let my fingers go where they've been dying to be—between those shapely thighs of hers. They glide along her slit—which is dripping wet. The evidence of her excitement nearly makes me come.

I spank her several more times, sharp and crisp. My hand leaves pink stains on her porcelain skin.

And then I'm lost. I place a hand on her lower back to hold her steady and spank away, craving the punitive contact, the stinging blows, the way she jerks and gasps with each smack.

"Spread your legs, beautiful." My voice sounds like I have rocks in my throat.

She obeys, widening her stance to one only a dancer could pull off.

"Fucking perfection." I bring my hand up smartly between her legs and slap her pussy.

She shrieks, but doesn't move.

I drop my face to her level and wrap a fist in her hair, turning her to me. I need to see in her eyes that she's okay with this level of intensity.

She's bitten her lip, but her eyes are glazed with pure lust.

I kiss her, sucking the blood from her plump flesh. She kisses back, her tongue sweeping into my mouth.

I bite back a curse. "I'm not done spanking you yet, angel."

I return to my position behind her and spank her some more, giving her ass a rosy glow. "If you were mine, I'd be spanking this ass every night, baby. Every fucking position. Over my lap. On your hands and knees. Bent over the couch. Tied to the bed." I slap between her legs, aiming for her clit. "Yeah, tied to the bed, legs spread wide. I'd save that posi-

tion for when you're really naughty. Maybe use my belt a little to make you scream."

I slap her juicy pussy again, several times.

"Wh-why?" she pants.

My chuckle is dark. "Because this ass just begs for it, baby. And to pay you back for keeping my goddamn balls tied up and in your back pocket."

She laughs, a husky sound that makes my erection punch out painfully. I unbutton the denim and slide the zipper down to free my length. I give my cock a hard squeeze.

"Don't worry, baby. I'd make sure you liked it. Or I'd make it up to you afterward if I was too rough."

I aim a few hard slaps to the place where ass meets thigh. "I have a feeling that would be often."

She wiggles her ass and tries to sneak a hand down between her legs.

"Uh uh." I catch her wrist. "No relief for you, baby. Not yet. Not until you've been thoroughly punished."

I snag a condom from my back pocket and tear open the foil, roll the rubber over my throbbing dick. I have to give it a couple quick yanks, because I'm dying here. I know my girl is, too, though, and I'm going to give it to her good. I drag the head of my cock through her juices. A hot shiver runs through my body, straight to the base of my spine. My belly shudders in.

Angelina moans encouragingly. I push into her, my eyes flipping back into my head at the contact of her sweet sheath around my swollen member.

"You want my cock, angel?"

"Yes, please. I mean, yes, daddy."

Fuck. The word *daddy* makes me shove hard into her, all the way.

Alpha's Desire

She gasps, her pussy clenching around my length.

"You like that, don't you?" I arc in and out slowly, closing my eyes to shove down my mounting desire.

"Yesssss."

I pull out. "Sorry, baby. That's not where you're taking my cock tonight."

Her breath stutters, but she doesn't offer up any complaint. My girl's nervous—I get that—but she's game.

I run my palm over her blushing ass, loving the sight of my handprints there. "I'll make it good for you, angel." I reach down and hook my pinkie through hers where it lies on the mattress. "Promise." I rub her ass some more. "Now don't move from this position. I'm going to go get some oil. If you move, I'm going to spank you again when I get back before I take your tight little virgin ass. Understand?"

"Yes, daddy."

I groan. To reward her—no, who am I kidding? It's for me, too—I take a deep plunge into her pussy, rolling my hips once I'm inside. A couple more deep thrusts and I pull out, holding the condom in place while I kick off my pants and stalk to the kitchen. I find a jar of coconut oil in one of the cabinets and scoop some into a bowl.

When I come back, I find Angelina in the exact position I left her—she hasn't moved a muscle.

"Good girl," I purr as I scoop some of the coconut oil and rub it liberally around her anus.

She shivers and shifts on her feet, but doesn't tighten or move from her position.

"I'll bet you have the tightest ass in the history of all asses," I murmur, working one well-lubed finger into her back hole. "All those twirly turns and deep bends."

Her husky laugh surrounds me. "Pirouettes and pliés.

Yeah, my pelvic floor is probably made of steel. Does that mean it will hurt mo—"

"No way. It's not going to hurt, angel. I would never hurt you. At least not in a way you don't love." I slap her ass again.

Fates, I love the sound of my hand smacking her fuck-tastic ass.

She moans into the covers.

I work a second finger into her ass and massage around the tight ring of muscles, working her open, preparing the way for my cock.

I lube up my member and press the head right up against her entrance, holding her cheeks wide. "Take a deep breath, baby."

She holds it instead.

I laugh. "Deeper."

She laughs, too. "Deeper, right. Okay." She draws in a breath.

"Now blow it out slowly and relax." I apply gentle pressure as she exhales, but I'm not going anywhere. "Push back at me, angel. Like you're trying to push me out, not let me in. That's it." Her sphincter muscles open and I gradually work the head of my cock through. I reach around under her hips and rub her clit as I inch in, giving her the pleasure she needs to let go.

And then I'm in. I don't move, except to stroke her pussy as she gets used to the intrusion.

"Good girl. You took my whole cock, baby. Right in that tight little dancer's ass. How does it feel?"

She's panting. "Go slow."

I lean over and trail my lips between her shoulder blades. "I will, baby. Does it feel good?"

"Sort of. Yes. Yes, daddy."

Alpha's Desire

Oh fates. It's all I can do not to rock back and slam in deep, but I hold back, sweat gathering at my forehead, my thighs shaking with the effort.

Need her, need her, need her.

I ease back a little, then seat my cock again, paying attention to her reaction.

A wanton moan.

I repeat the action.

"Jared." The slight alarm that tinges her voice tells me she's getting close to orgasm.

I pump into her ass, slow and steady, smooth predictable strokes.

Her breath grows shorter, a little moan coloring each exhale. "Need. Jared. I need—"

"I know what you need, baby." I grip her hips and fuck harder, making my strokes shorter.

She lets out the cutest uh-uh-uhs and my world starts to spin. My vision changes, mouth grows wet with saliva. Without thinking, I let my fingers dig into her hips to hold her still for my onslaught.

"Is this what you needed?"

"Yes!" she gasps. "Yes, *please.*"

"Take it, Angelina. Take my big cock in your tight little ass. Take everything I have to give you." I finger fuck her pussy, three fingers sliding in and out, the heel of my hand grinding over her clit.

She screams and clenches hard around my cock, wrenching my orgasm from me. I lose all control, pounding into her as the most intense release of my life plows through me like a fucking hurricane.

When I open my eyes, I'm draped over Angelina, fingers still buried in her pussy, cock still in her ass. Our breath moving in perfect synchronicity.

RENEE ROSE & LEE SAVINO

I rock into her, undulate my fingers to finish us off, laying a thousand kisses along her neck, her ear, her cheek, her back. I'm humbled. Grateful.

In love.

Fuck.

I'm totally, hopelessly in love with this girl.

The one I can't have.

9

———

Jared

The crew from San Diego is even twitchier than usual. Parker bounces on the balls of his feet, his focus pinging around the warehouse. Laurie's stutter is worse. Declan has a wild aggression pouring off him.

"So full disclosure—" Parker sucks his lower lip into his mouth. "We're totally shut down for the moment in San Diego. I got picked up on gambling charges, but they couldn't make it stick."

"It was a catch and release," Declan declares with a reckless grin. "Shakin' us down to see who's involved."

Trey and I shoot a glance at each other. "So they busted up a fight?" Trey asks.

"Not exactly," Parker explains. "Two humans show up like they're going to slide right in. They didn't make it through the doors, of course. The bears took it upon themselves to teach the fellas a lesson, so they flashed their badges.

"The place cleared out in minutes, and I was left to talk to them. They brought me in, but I knew they had nothing on me."

"Yeah, but now they have your identity in their system." Trey frowns.

Parker shakes his head. "We have false identities Sam tells us are 'airtight.' It probably was just local cops. If the feds involved with Data-X traced it back, I'd already be dead."

"M-m-m-maybe," Laurie says, flapping his long slender fingers. "Maybe not. We don't know. Better to lie low in Tucson for a spell."

I nod, slowly. "Sure. We can put you up here. No problem. You helped Sam. I'm sure our alpha will provide pack protection."

"Th-th-thank you." Parker bobs his head.

"I wonder if Kylie can scrub that police record," Trey muses to me.

I nod. "Will you ask her?"

He pulls out his phone and starts texting.

"You'll have to meet our alpha, Garrett," I say. "I'll text him to arrange it."

A thread of unease runs through me. Am I bringing danger to the pack by starting this shifter fight club? I sure as hell hope not.

But it fits right in—my violence always makes me a danger to the people in my life.

You just have to figure out how the warrior fits into modern day times. You're still the knight.

Angelina believes I'm the fucking knight. But is this the way I serve in modern times? Somehow a fight club and illegal gambling doesn't quite seem like something Angelina could tell her parents about.

Alpha's Desire

And goddamn if I don't still harbor some tiny hope I can make this work with her. But I'll never be able to if I can't figure out a way to be her knight.

A gent Dune

He pulls his ball cap lower over his brow and shuffles past the warehouse. His dingy old t-shirt reeks of cheap alcohol. A large styrofoam cup of watered down liquor in his hand completes the derelict image. He's been casing the place for a few hours. The warehouse is like any other in an industrial area near the railroad tracks south of Downtown Tucson.

This is where he followed Parker and the other two from his screen captures.

He couldn't get close enough to hear their conversation inside, but it was easy enough to guess what was going on. They're setting up cage fights in a new city. So all he has to do is keep an eye on them and slip into the next fight.

Because he has a feeling whatever he sees going on in that cage is going to make things a helluva lot clearer.

10

Angelina

I fit a pair of hoops through my earlobes and rub my lip glossed lips together, looking in the mirror. Jared's already at the club working—he's eased off sticking with me every second of the day, but it's Saturday night and I'll be down there to dance in an hour.

My limbs are loose, my butt still tingles and I'm sore in several key places from the spanking and sex Jared gave me before he left.

He said if he didn't, he wouldn't be able to stand watching me dance up on the box tonight. That he'd tear the heads off all the guys who looked at me and the spanking I'd get after would be way worse.

It's so wrong that I want to tempt that fate. Because every minute I'm with Jared brings the sharp pain of knowing we can't be together, even though we're perfect for each other. With him, everything is easy. He gets me. Makes me laugh

with his teasing, knows when to be serious. Understands what makes me tick—more than I do, I sometimes think.

And sex with him?

Better than dancing.

The first time I had sex was the summer after I graduated from high school. I told my boyfriend at the time it was almost as good as dancing. Needless to say, he was totally offended.

But the sex with Jared goes way beyond anything I've done with or to my body. It's more artistic than a quadruple pirouette. More satisfying than the best choreographed piece. He lays me bare. Not just my body, but my very being —who am I at the core—and then he honors me. Pleasures me. Gives so much while he takes it all.

I sketched out my ideas for the warehouse, as he demanded. And I even made a list of dancers I'd like to ask to participate. I couldn't quite bring myself to ask them, though. Because where would we rehearse? When? We're all busy with the faculty's stupid dances.

We've also carefully avoided the topic of our relationship. Like we both have this unspoken agreement to just enjoy this time while we have it.

But I know when he walks away, when the two weeks are up and he cuts me loose, I'm going to be begging to have my memories erased.

Because I won't be able to live with the pain of what I've lost. What I can't keep.

I grab my purse and hook it over my shoulder before I step out the door. My body's already tingling with the excitement of seeing its master again.

When I leave to pick up Talya and Remy I can scarcely believe it's only been one week since the crash. My whole world has changed. *I've* changed.

Alpha's Desire

I pull up in front of Remy's first and she comes out—all aglow with excitement. And she hasn't even hooked up with a hot dominant werewolf who insinuates himself into the very fabric of her being.

But she's like me, I guess. More excited by this dancing than what we have at school.

"How's it going, girl?" she sings as she slides into the front passenger seat. "Ready to rock it?"

"You know it." I take off before she's buckled her belt. "Remy, do you have more fun with this dancing than school?"

"Hell, yes!" She doesn't even hesitate.

"Why, do you think?"

"Oh my God, so many reasons." She starts ticking off on her fingers. "I get to insert my own creativity in the process, we have a live and appreciative audience who aren't all over eighty, I get to dance with my best friends, there's no one breathing down my neck telling me I'm doing it wrong, there's no one standing in the wings dying to stab me in the back to take my place... shall I go on?" She casts a look at me. "Why? What are you thinking?"

I shrug, deciding whether to hold back the words that have already tumbled to the tip of my tongue. "What would you think about doing a full length show? Like something super out there but totally entertaining? One part Cirque du Soleil, one part Blue Man Group, one part... I don't know, what we do at Eclipse?"

"Hell, yeah!" Again, there's no hesitation. I pull up in front of Talya's house and when she gets in, Remy says, "Angelina's going to choreograph a full length show for us. Total performance art badass shit."

"Well, wait. I'm just thinking about it," I splutter.

Talya leans forward from the back seat. "Do it! I'm totally in. One hundred percent."

The twitters of excitement that I've flirted with ever since I first voiced my dream out loud to Jared flare up, flapping their wings so fast I lose my breath. "You are? Both of you?"

"Are you kidding?" Remy laughs. "I'd drop out of school and follow you anywhere to do this work. In a heartbeat. If you said we're going to take this show on a tour of the country in a VW bus, I'd organize the bake sale to fund it." She grins. "I've been dying for you to do more work like this."

"Me too." Talya smacks my shoulder. "I can't wait! When do we start?"

"Um, well, I have to find us a space to rehearse in. And to perform. I want it to be an ongoing show—not just a weekend or two, but every weekend. Something that goes on the list of Things To Do in Tucson. Something we could make real money from—paid performances."

"Okay, then I will have to worry about someone standing in the wings to take my place," Remy says, but there's a laugh in her voice. "That would be freaking amazing. My parents would die—they've always said I'll never make any money as a dancer."

"Same," Talya says.

"Same," I agree. "Let's prove them wrong."

J*ared*

Alpha's Desire

I scent the moment Angelina enters the club. You might say that's impossible in a club filled with over one hundred moving, sweating bodies, but it's true.

My wolf instincts kick into high gear and I whirl around, turn predator the moment I catch sight of her.

Oh fates, she's wearing those short shorts. And a fucking halter top. The kind that ties right between her breasts and leaves nothing to the imagination.

Which can only mean one thing—she wants me to spank her again.

Heat coils in my belly, streaks down my spine. I stalk through the club.

She's not a wolf, but her instincts are still good. She turns in my direction and we lock eyes. Her hair is in goddamn pigtails tonight, beautiful auburn fountains where she usually wears the cinnabons.

The second I get to her, I reach my hands under her armpits. She somehow intuits exactly what I'm going to do, because she springs up, her lithe little dancer's body attaching itself to mine, muscular legs wrapping around my waist.

"Hi ladies." I wink at her friends. "I'm going to borrow your girl for just a few minutes."

One of them waggles her brows while the other gives us the wiggly finger wave. "Have fun!"

I carry her right back to the storeroom. The place where this all started. I'm praying it doesn't remind her of how we left things after I got her off. Because I only want to make my girl hot right now.

The door doesn't lock, but I carry her back behind the stacks of boxes, where no one will see us, even if they come in. "Baby, what are you wearing?" I growl.

She grins up at me, pure impish pleasure on her beautiful face.

My hands coast all over her ass, around the curves, between her legs, under the shorts. "You're going to have my handprints all over this ass for all to see. Is that what you wanted, baby?" I nip her shoulder, flick her earlobe with my tongue.

She gives one of those sweet blushes. "I didn't think about that part."

"Oh you didn't?" I rub firmly between her thighs, make her dampness soak through her satin panties. "But you knew you'd get spanked, right?"

She lifts her face to mine, her breath warm on my face. "Oh, I knew." Damn that husky tone makes me want to throw her over a couple boxes and pound into her until she screams.

A little more finesse, buddy.

"You're making it hard for me, baby. I really want to mark you so every fucker out there knows you belong to me." I'm palming her ass with both hands, kneading the firm flesh with a hard, possessive grip.

A moment of insecurity flashes in her eyes and I curse our fucking situation. If she were a wolf, she'd already be marked. Permanently.

"But I don't want to embarrass you, either." I yank her up over the bulge in my pants and let her slide back down to her feet slowly. "So maybe I'll settle for a good, hard fuck. And a few spanks where they can't see them."

"Mmm."

"Jesus, Angelina, do you have any idea what you do to me?"

"Um…"

Alpha's Desire

"Do you?" I growl, spinning her around. I open her shorts and shove them, with her panties, down her legs.

"Y-yes?"

"You do?" I pull her hands behind her back and pin them with one hand. Putting my foot up on a box of wine, I fold her torso over my knee and smack her ass. "Let's see..." I lay three hard smacks right in the middle of her cheeks. "They won't see here." Three more.

She lets out a cute little gasp and moans.

I stroke between her legs. Juicy wet. Pure heaven. Need slams through me even harder, but I push it back.

"They won't see here." I slap her pussy.

"Oh God, Jared. Please."

Oh God, Angelina. And shifters don't even worship the god with a capital G. But hearing her beg me in that needy tone does something crazy to my insides. I have a finger wedged inside her before I even decide to do it. She struggles against my hold on her wrists, grinding her hips back into me to take my digit deeper.

I pull my finger out and slap her pussy again. "No, I said a hard fuck. That's what this naughty pussy deserves. Tempting me all over again when I just fucked her raw a few hours ago."

I slap her ass a few more times, then pick her up and sit her on top of a stack of boxes, waist height. Eyes glazed, she spreads her knees wide for me.

"That's right," I growl, freeing my erection from my jeans. "Spread those milky white thighs wider. Show me where I'm going to pound."

She reaches down and spreads her pussy wide with her fingers and I nearly cum all over my hand.

"Fuck, Angelina. How in the hell do you think I'm going to keep my sanity tonight? Knowing this sweet little pussy's

hiding right there, under those shorts?" I fumble to get a condom on.

She rubs herself and whimpers.

I grab her wrist. "Uh uh. *Mine.*" I line up with her entrance and ease in. "Mine, mine, mine, mine." I slap my loins into the cradle of her legs, getting deep inside her.

She's tippy on the boxes, and she grabs my forearms to keep from falling back.

I growl and shove another stack of boxes behind the one she's on, lay her back. "How's that baby?"

"P-perfect." Her teeth chatter with my thrusts, because I can't stop giving it to her hard, marking her in the only safe way I can.

"Squeeze those nipples. Pinch them hard. This is punishment, baby. Daddy's going to make it hurt before I make it better."

She laughs, throaty and sweet. "Too late. It's already good... so good."

I can't help but smile back, because she's so damn adorable. Sweat gathers at my brow and my muscles strain, but I don't ever want it to stop. "Guess I'll have to fuck your ass again when we get home," I threaten.

She orgasms, her pussy tightening and releasing around my cock.

I thrust deeper. Harder. Faster. "Yeah, you're definitely taking it in the ass later. I never said you could come."

Her eyes roll back in her head, mouth opens in a silent scream. I clench my teeth, balls tightening up. I close my lips around my own roar and bury myself deep inside her. I lean forward and attack one of her breasts, pulling it out of her halter top and bra, sucking, squeezing, kissing.

Biting.

She arches up into my mouth with a mewl.

Alpha's Desire

"Fuck, I want to take your ass right now." I reach under her ass and find her back pucker with the pad of my middle finger.

Her pussy squeezes again, milking the last drops of cum from my johnson.

The storeroom door opens and I pull her down, quickly, hiding our bodies behind the boxes.

She laughs silently as we yank our clothing back in place. I fall on her mouth, kissing away her lip gloss and squeezing her ass. I can't get enough of this girl—even fresh off an orgasm.

"Fates, I think I will have to give you the belt tonight. I'm going to be harder than marble all night watching you."

She looks up and blinks. "Do your eyes change color?" She sucks in a quick breath. "I thought I saw that once before. Is that your wolf?"

I go perfectly still, staring down at her. "Are they yellow?"

She nods.

My hands on her tighten. Does this mean—? Could she be my mate? Is my wolf coming to the surface to mark her?

She rises to her tiptoes, balancing easily as she bats those long lashes. "I want to see your wolf." It's an excited whisper. Not a request, but not an assumption, either. She watches me with hopeful expectation.

How in the fuck can I say no?

I crush my lips against hers.

"Is that a yes?" she asks breathlessly when we break apart.

"Tomorrow," I promise. "I'll take you up to Mt. Lemmon."

"Yes!" She bounces on her feet and pulls me down for another kiss. "Thank you. I can't wait!"

145

Things have shifted. There's a weight to my commitment. Not a heaviness, just a significance. I've agreed to show her my wolf.

Because she's my mate?

Is it wrong that I'm starting to hope so?

Yes, definitely. Because I still can't keep her. But fuck if I don't want to.

A *ngelina*

J ared isn't in the bed when I wake up. He had to stay late at Eclipse for pack business and I was asleep when he came to my place. But I am sure he came in last night. I remember him climbing into bed beside me and curving his large body around mine.

Pure heaven.

All these little moments are ones I haven't had with past boyfriends—not that I've ever really taken a serious boyfriend. I mean, I've dated a little. But I've never stuck with a guy for more than a few months, and while they may have spent a night at my place on weekends, it was never like *this*.

I've never felt more wrapped up in a relationship than I do with Jared.

The one guy I can't have a relationship with.

I hear the sound of a motorcycle outside and I scramble out of the bed and look out my window.

There he is. Unbelievably hot in a tight black t-shirt, tattoos snaking down his forearms, a new motorcycle

Alpha's Desire

between his powerful thighs. At least it looks like a new motorcycle.

He parks it in my driveway and picks up a helmet that's hanging from the back seat.

I go running for the door and fling it open.

"Hey, baby. You're up." He looks so genuinely happy to see me.

I don't know why that surprises me. Maybe because I grew up feeling like a nuisance to my dad and before Jared I picked indifferent men who couldn't really give me their full attention.

Now I've picked one who gives me more attention than I've dreamed of, but I can't have him.

Same story, different twist. Unavailable.

He sets the helmet on the table by the front door and comes at me, his hands reaching for my waist, tugging up the little pink cami I slept in.

I giggle and catch his hands. "Did you get a new bike?"

His eyes gleam with hunger. "I did." He ignores my attempts to stop him and tugs the cami off over my head.

I turn to run—only because I love when he catches me —and he does.

"Baby, you come to the door in nothing but a few scraps of fabric, you'd better know I'm going to be putting my hands all over you."

I giggle. "I know." That certainty is part of the massive appeal to Jared. I'm desired. Every minute of the day.

He kisses my neck, backing me down the hall.

"Is the helmet for me?"

"Mmm hmm." He nips my ear.

"For the trip to Mt. Lemmon?"

"Yes. Unless you're scared."

"I'm not scared," I say quickly. The fantasy of riding on

147

the back of Jared's bike has been with me since I first started dancing at Eclipse. And knowing he will show me his wolf at the end of the ride completes it.

"Good." He pushes me into the bathroom. "Were you going to shower before we go?"

"Um..." I'm only confused because his hands are all over me, his tongue in my ear.

"I'll help you." He shoves my panties down my thighs until they drop to the floor.

I loop my arms around his neck. "That sounds like a plan."

Angelina

The hour long ride up Mt. Lemmon is spectacular. I'm a little wind-worn by the time we get there, but I loved every second of it. Jared drives the bike like it's an extension of his body, control and power humming beneath us.

He pulls up at a cabin nestled in the woods and turns off the bike.

"What is this place?" I step off the bike and try to find my footing on my wobbly legs.

"It's a cabin owned by one of our kind. Not exactly a pack member, but a friend of the pack. Real wealthy guy. I asked for permission to use it today, and he agreed." Jared pulls a saddle bag from the motorcycle and carries it up the door, where he punches a code into a keypad.

Alpha's Desire

"Cool." I follow him in, taking in the rustic, yet very well-appointed cabin.

He unloads the saddlebag, which is filled with food from a deli—fresh cut up fruit, fried chicken, potato salad, and a sack of brownies. "Hungry?"

I eye the food. "Um. I probably shouldn't."

He lifts a brow. "What the fuck does that mean?"

His tone stings, and I turn my head to hide a flush.

In a flash I'm in his arms, my cheek pressed against his chest. "Baby, that came out wrong. Are you telling me you're hungry but don't think you should eat? Because that's not gonna slide with me."

I nuzzle into him, loving this protective streak he has for me. "I'll eat," I concede quickly. "I definitely don't want to go up against an angry wolf."

He chuckles and strokes the back of my head. "I didn't mean to scare you, angel. Did I?"

"You hurt my feelings a little. I don't like to get yelled at. But it's all good. I appreciate what you're doing for me."

He drops a kiss on the top of my head. "I won't yell again." He sits in a chair at the table and pulls me into his lap, then proceeds to hand feed me until he's satisfied I've eaten enough. Only then does he eat what's left.

"Okay, angel. You ready to meet my wolf?"

I jump up from his lap. "Yes!"

He stands and peels off his t-shirt. "It's bigger than a normal wolf. Don't be afraid, okay? I won't hurt you."

"I'm not afraid." Excitement wings through my chest. It's like I have some secret belief that seeing his wolf will close the gaps between us. The differences keeping us apart.

He kicks off his boots, then unbuttons his jeans and shucks them. His boxers and socks come off last, and then he's naked. With the world's biggest boner.

Again.

It seems this man never gets tired of me.

"I'll probably need to run. If I leave through the doggy door, just make yourself at home here, okay? I'll come back when I get my animal under control."

I don't understand what he's talking about, but I nod, anyway.

Jared gives a curt nod and then his eyes turn gold. He drops to all fours, a giant white and silver wolf. So beautiful I want to weep.

Maybe I do weep.

I definitely drop to my knees and throw my arms around his furry neck. He whines and licks my face while I stroke him all over. Beautiful, soft fur. Massive animal.

I'm in total awe of him.

"Jared," I breathe.

He shudders and bolts, running straight for the doggy door in the kitchen. And then he's gone.

I fling open the door, not to follow, just to watch. He covers ground swiftly, his massive paws leaping across the soft forest floor.

"Have fun," I murmur, leaning my hip against the doorway.

Incredible, gorgeous wolf.

Seeing him sets off a longing I can't describe. It's a tug in my belly. A deep need or desire that I don't even understand.

Do I want to be a wolf too?

No, that's not it.

I want *him*.

I want to keep him.

Forever.

Tears spear my eyes.

Alpha's Desire

Why can't this work?

J*ared*

Angelina seems subdued after she sees my wolf. Maybe she finally understands how inhuman I am. How we can't be together. That thought shouldn't make me feel so fucking desperate, but it does.

She presses her body right up against my back on the ride down the mountain, like she can't get close enough, and yet there's a flavor of melancholy to her.

Is this goodbye?

Fuck.

I fear it is.

I take her back to her place and we walk in, slowly. "So what do you have going for the evening?"

I saw her time blocked off on her phone, but it didn't say what for. It was a recurring Sunday night date, whatever it is.

"Oh, um, not much," she says. "Are you hanging around?"

I slow to a stop at the weird strain in her voice.

Did she just *lie* to me?

When she looks at me, guilt washes over her expression.

I stunned at how badly it hurts. Unbelievably. Like a monster truck just rolled across my chest.

"I usually have dinner with my parents on Sundays."

There's the truth. But the pain doesn't ease. It amplifies.

Because Angelina's voicing what I've always known but somehow tricked myself into believing wasn't true.

I'm not good enough.

Not for Angelina's parents, who want what's best for her. Hooking up with me may be fine for a two week fling, but I'm not the guy she brings home.

Ever.

I shove my hands in my pockets. "Yeah, I got it. That's cool." My voice sounds strangled. The urge to hit something is huge.

Or to shift and run.

"Yeah, I have pack business to take care of. I'll catch you later." I head for the door. I literally can't stand another minute in her place because I'm suffocated by loss.

Which is stupid, because she was never mine to lose.

But this is a good thing. Because I'd just started wondering if she's really my mate and whether I can figure out how to make this work.

The answer is no.

Which I knew from the start.

So walk away. And even though it kills me, I'll have to break my word and get her wiped. Maybe I can get her to agree to it. That needs to be my one and only strategy.

Stop fucking her.

Convince her to let go of these memories.

Our memories.

"Jared."

I stop at the door and look back, arranging my face into what I hope is a pleasant expression.

"Yeah?"

"It would just be awkward with my parents—"

I wave my hand. "Oh, I know. That's why I'll stay out of your hair. Catch you later."

Alpha's Desire

I walk out, leaving my bludgeoned heart flopping around on her living room floor.

But there's nothing that can be done. I did this to myself. And to her.

I have no one to blame but myself.

11

Angelina

Jared isn't at my place when I get home. Nor does he show up before I go to bed. My stomach is in knots.

I'm pretty sure I offended him.

I was trying to keep him from my parents for his own sake—because they can be rude, arrogant, judgemental assholes. I don't want them to judge him.

And I know they would.

They'd take one look at the beefy arms covered with tattoos and write him off as a Hell's Angel or something stupid like that.

They would never look beneath the surface to see the amazing man he is. The caring, considerate, thoughtful, *charming* guy who only seems to want to support me. And fuck my brains out.

And I would hate—absolutely die—if they were rude to him.

So it was for his protection that I didn't want to invite him over to meet them.

But I keep remembering what he said after we visited my grandma.

You thought she'd hate me.

He already believes this about my family. And in my parents' case, it would be true. But *God*, I don't want him to feel like I think he's *less than*. Just because my parents are stuck up foothills assholes doesn't mean they're better.

I stand at my window looking out. As if he's going to pull up on that sexy motorcycle any minute.

Even though I know he's not.

How do I explain this to him without making it worse? *Yes, I thought my parents would hate you, but I'm not hiding you from them, I'm hiding them from you.*

Not sure he'd believe that.

And dammit—I shouldn't have lied when he asked where I was going. It only made it seem so much worse. I should've tried to be super upfront, right from the beginning. *Hey, my parents are jerks and I'd be embarrassed for you to meet them, so do you mind if I don't introduce you?*

Damn. I don't know. Should I try to text him? Try to explain? Or will I just make this rift deeper?

Wow, we really are Romeo and Juliet. My parents and his pack are keeping us apart.

I rub my eyes, nauseated.

Of course, to make matters even darker, dinner was the absolute worst ever. Or maybe I'm just noticing more now that I've had Jared fluffing me up for a week. It seemed like all I heard from my parents was what and who they wanted me to be.

My mom went on about my weight and how I'm looking a little doughy. My dad wouldn't stop about the cocktail

Alpha's Desire

party next Sunday and how he needs me to be there to meet the bigwig Jackson King.

It's the most ludicrous thing I've ever heard. Who needs their daughter to stand around and look pretty to close a business deal? In what reality did he cook up this role for me?

And yet I feel the chains of bondage from them as if I am the maiden locked up in the castle, ready to be sold by her father to increase his land shares. Maybe in other lifetimes I was. Maybe we'll keep repeating this interaction until I finally stand up to them and tell them I'm not their puppet.

But the thought literally throws me into quicksand. They're my parents. I'm their only child. They've supported me—financially, maybe not emotionally—for my entire life. They still pay my tuition and room and board. I teach classes for my spending money. Is it fair or right for me to dig my feet in?

What's the big deal about one stupid charity cocktail party anyway?

Except the thought of putting on a dress and attending their party next week feels akin to cheating on Jared. Seeing my parents again without mentioning Jared feels like a betrayal.

Even though he and I aren't even supposed to be a couple, I'm locked in tight with him. And I don't want him believing he's anything less than a freaking hero to me.

I square my shoulders and turn away from the window.

I'm going to introduce him to my parents. I don't give a shit what they think. I'll warn him that they're assholes and that I'm embarrassed of how they might treat him, but I'll stick by his side. Jared is too amazing to be bothered by them. It's my behavior that bothered him, and I can fix that.

I pick up my phone and text him. *I miss you. I wish I'd brought you to my parents'. Are you coming over?*

He texts back immediately. *It's all for the best, baby. Get some rest. I'll see you soon.*

Well, shit. There's a note of distance in his text that sets alarm bells clanging in my head.

But maybe I'm reading too much into it.

Texts can be weird that way.

I sure as hell hope that's all it is.

J*ared*

Is it totally backwards that even as I contemplate letting Angelina go, I'm trying to make myself worthy of her?

I sit across the desk from our pack attorney—who is also Garrett's mate—with my knee bouncing up and down. It's been over twenty-four hours since I've seen Angelina and the hole in my heart is getting larger.

I have to take some action, do something to try to make my life respectable.

"Listen, I was thinking about those kids—all the foster kids you help. Maybe the older ones?"

"Yes?" Amber wears polite pleasant expectation on her face. She's classy, this one, even though she's a product of the foster system herself.

"Well, do you think they'd like a boxing gym? A place to work out their aggression—if they have any? I was thinking

Alpha's Desire

maybe I could, ah, coach them or something. Teach them how to box."

I'm unprepared for the way Amber's face lights up. "Jared, that's an amazing idea! You'd be perfect for coaching troubled teens. Would you really do that?"

I've cast the die, there's no backing out now. Not when Amber has that full-force ahead look on her. I clear my throat. "Well, maybe we could try it out? See how it works? I rented this warehouse for, uh—" I stop, not wanting to involve Amber in anything illegal.

"I know about your fight club," she breezes, like it doesn't bother her a bit. "And yes, this would be the perfect way to make a legit business organization around fighting. I think it's the most brilliant idea I've ever heard."

I grin. "I don't know if I'd go that far."

"Yes, truly. Have you talked to Garrett?"

I shake my head. "I wanted to ask you first. I know Garrett's gonna be in on anything you green light." I wink.

She laughs. "Clever wolf. Okay, I will make some calls. Maybe you could start with a one-time workshop to gauge interest—both on your part and theirs. You know, just see how it goes. And if everyone likes it, we can set up something more permanent. But you'll have to get everything legal and above-board—liability insurance, fingerprinting, CPR training."

"I'll work on that this week. Anything else?"

"Are you going to buy mats and make it look like a real gym?"

"Yeah. Definitely." A gym/dance studio/performance space. With cage fighting in the back. There's something about having a full row of warehouses to work with that makes it seem like anything and everything is possible.

Even winning Angelina.

159

I head over to Home Depot to pick up the plywood and foam core necessary to spring the floor in the dance studio, warehouse, and the gym. I'm going to trick out the space in every way possible, because my future is tied up in this. I don't know what it will look like, but I have to take steps to get there.

A *ngelina*

Three days. That's how long I go without seeing Jared. He sent texts—friendly ones. Asked how my day was. Wanted to know if I'd moved forward on planning my big show. Told me to give my professors hell and kept promising to see me soon.

But it's been three days and anxiety builds in me like I'm going to blow. I hate this unsettled feeling—not knowing what's happening with us. Not that I ever knew, but at least he was at my place, in my space, crowding all my doubts with his large presence.

I change out of my leggings and tank top and pull on a sundress before I step outside of the dance building. And then my heart skips a beat.

There he is. On his motorcycle at the curb.

My heart double-pounds and a smile stretches across my face. It's all I can do not to run straight over.

He dismounts and pulls me into him, his mouth on mine like nothing happened.

I should shove him away and demand we talk. Hash through our relationship and what's going to happen. But

Alpha's Desire

that sounds terrible. And his lips over mine are so much better than terrible. They're divine.

Like coming home.

So yeah, talking can wait. I just want to be with Jared for now.

"I missed you," I say honestly when we break apart.

"Baby, I fucked my hand so hard I got blisters missing you." A shocked laugh spills from my lips and Jared shrugs. "You oughta know."

"Then why'd you stay away?" Damn. I really don't want to have this conversation because I'm terrified of his answer.

His face clouds and he presses his lips together. "I'm trying to figure my shit out." His voice is gruff.

I wrap my arms around him and squeeze hard, as if I can somehow make him stay in my life forever.

He tips up my chin. "You okay?"

"Yeah." I sound breathless. *Now that you're here.* I look at the bike. "Are you going to take me for a ride?"

He smiles and picks up the helmet. "A short one. Because you're not dressed appropriately." His eyes trail to my bare legs, lips kicking up like he loves what he sees. "I'll take you to your car."

I'm dying to ask, "And then?" To beg him to come back to my house, but I don't want to come off as crazy needy here. I climb on the back of the bike and wrap my arms around his solid waist. He eases us into motion and I lean my face against his back, breathe in his scent.

The trip to the car is short—far too short. I climb off and fiddle with my dance bag. "Now what?"

Jared shoves a hand through his short hair. "Now..."

"You should probably come to my place so I can take care of that, er, problem of yours," I say, eyeing his bulging cock.

He lets out a strained laugh. "Fuck, baby." He looks around, like the answer is written on one of the trees.

I moisten my lips with my tongue, making sure he sees the motion.

He groans and gives his cock a squeeze through his jeans. "I never could resist you. I swear to the fates—even if I'd had you wiped, I'd be right back here again making new memories."

Something flutters in my chest. *New memories. Yes. Please.*

He captures the back of my head and melds his mouth over mine again. The kiss is possessive, dominating. "You go home and take your shower, little girl. I'll pick up some food and meet you there. What sounds good?"

"You."

His eyes change to yellow, right there in the street and he lets out an inhuman growl. He shoves me up against the car, his movements rough. He pushes his knee between my thighs, spreading my legs. "You keep talking like that, you're going to get yourself fucked up against this car in broad daylight."

I'm helpless with need. I love dominant but gentlemanly Jared, but this side of him? This out of control growly thing? I'm lost. I grind down on his leg, rub my breasts against his chest.

"Seriously," he splutters, one hand wrapping in my hair and pulling it taut. His other hand strokes down my hip. "If I touch your skin, it's all over."

Somehow, some sense of appropriateness takes over and I catch his hand before it reaches my bare thigh. "I'll be ready for you," I promise, my voice not sounding remotely familiar, it's so husky.

He pulls my hair harder and drags his open mouth down the column of my neck. "You'd better be."

Alpha's Desire

Fireworks go off in my lower belly, and in my head. I crave this aggressive side of Jared more than ever. He bites my neck—hard enough to leave a mark, but I don't whimper.

Dancers don't register pain the same as most people because it's always mixed with pleasure. Dancing in toe shoes until your feet are bloody comes with the satisfaction of accomplishment.

Maybe that's why I love it so much when Jared spanks me. Maybe the aggression he warned me about won't be an issue.

Somehow I extricate myself from his grip, slither down into the driver's seat of my car. He leans against the vehicle, peering in the window like he's not sure he's going to let me drive away. And considering the way he picked up his huge motorcycle like it weighed nothing after the car accident— he probably could stop it with one hand. Instead he thumps the ceiling, still peering in at me as I slowly pull away.

I wriggle in my seat, my pussy hot and damp, already more than desperate for him.

The little voice of reason in my head screams, *what are you doing?* Every time I have sex with Jared, it makes our impending separation worse.

But I can't make myself care. I went three days without seeing him and my body is now desperate for the satisfaction only he can deliver. I'm desperate to give him satisfaction.

And I guess if I'm totally honest, I'd admit there's some chirpy optimist in me who still hopes maybe we can make this work.

I'm out of the car as soon as I pull up, dashing for the door. I take the world's fastest shower, but then I can't figure

163

out what to do with myself. Put my clothes back on? Stay in the towel?

Turns out I don't have to wait to find out, because Jared barges in my house a moment later, his boots sounding in long, heavy strides down the tiled hallway.

I peek out of the bedroom, wet hair dripping, towel cinched up under my armpits.

Jared growls. Yes, a real growl. Like wolf-sounding growl. His eyes glow yellow.

My pussy clenches, belly flutters.

Maybe because I'm a little nervous about his dominance, I take charge. I square off to face him when he comes in my bedroom. "Show me your cock."

His surprised grin changes his eyes back to green for a moment, but the moment he takes his cock out and fists it, they glow yellow.

I lift my arms and let my towel drop.

He reaches for me, but I dance out of the way.

"Nuh uh. I'm going to take care of you first." I drop to my knees on the towel and slide his jeans and boxers down his legs. He kicks off his boots and steps out of the tangle of clothing. I close my hand around where he still grips the base of his cock, and guide the head to my mouth.

"Angelina," he chokes. "I can't—I don't—"

I ignore him and take the tip between my lips, licking a bead of pre-cum from his slit.

He catches the back of my head and wraps his fist in my hair again, shoving me forward on his cock. I'm pretty sure he was going to tell me that he couldn't hold back, because there's no gentleness to his touch. He holds me immobile and thrusts deep in my throat, then backs out and shoves again. My eyes water but I'm beyond excited at his desperation for me.

Alpha's Desire

I massage his ball sac, try to wrench his grip on his cock free so I can fist him instead. He seems to gather himself and stops thrusting, removing his hand and standing there, panting.

I look up at him, watching his reaction as I slowly take him deep.

Another snarl.

"What are you doing to me, baby?" His teeth are clenched together, fist still tight in my hair. "I can't take much more of this."

I suck harder, bob my head over him faster. "I'm gonna come down your throat, baby." He starts to thrust again, taking over, imprisoning my head for his jerky movements. "You don't want that, do you?"

I make a sound and nod my head and he roars, coming. His hot salty seed spurts into the back of my throat and I swallow and swallow until it's all down.

Jared doesn't lose any of his intensity, though. He pulls out of my mouth and picks me up, tossing me on my back on the bed. He dives between my thighs, licking into me with hot, strokes. He bites and sucks and flicks, devouring me with a hunger I didn't know was possible. "I'm gonna fuck you," he rumbles, shoving his fingers inside me. He pumps them up to the knuckles.

I arch up off the bed.

He finds my g-spot and that quickly, I'm orgasming. He hardly waits for me to finish.

"I can't stop now. I'm going to fuck you all night, baby. You won't be able to walk straight tomorrow."

I don't offer any protest. Yeah, I'm a little daunted by that promise, but my desire, my excitement greatly outweighs any fear.

"Fuck me," I challenge.

He lifts his head and stares me down with those beautiful golden eyes. "I won't be gentle." It's a warning I didn't need. He's already half animal—his voice deep and rough, the fervor behind his touch seeming more instinctive than meditated.

"Fuck me," I repeat.

He flips me over onto my belly and grips my hair again, tugging my head up and causing me to arch backward. "I'm gonna fuck you from behind because I love this ass of yours."

Sadly, he doesn't stop to slap it. But then I forget that fleeting disappointment because he puts on a condom and shoves into me. I don't know how his cock is already hard again, but it is. The simultaneous sting of my scalp and deep pleasure of being filled by him bring me to a heightened sensitivity. I moan for more.

Jared rides me, using my hair for leverage until he grows tired of the position and releases my wet locks. He twists my hips to the side, lifting one knee to fuck deeper, harder, holding me by my nape and thigh to thrust deeper.

It's all a blur of sensation, of pleasure. I have no control of the situation, so I surrender, allow him to use my body however he chooses. And he definitely keeps choosing. He pushes me to my back and falls on my breasts like a starved man while he continues to pound me with his cock. Then I'm on my hands and knees, his fingers digging into my hips as he slaps his balls against my clit. He reaches around and rubs that magic place and I come again, bucking against him. He pulls my torso up against his chest and squeezes my breasts roughly, biting my neck.

Then we're off the bed. He bends my torso down on the mattress. "Spread your legs wide."

Wide is easy for a dancer. I take the widest second posi-

Alpha's Desire

tion in *relevé*—which is the fancy French way of saying on the balls of my feet—and arch my ass back at him.

He snarls his appreciation, spanking me in a swift flurry of slaps. He spanks my ass, the backs of my thighs, my pussy. Even the inner thighs receive his delicious brand of torture.

"If you weren't so goddamn wet, I could hold back," he growls. "But how can I when you love taking it as much as I love giving?"

"More," is all I can choke.

"I can't restrain myself enough to take your ass gently. But you want that, don't you?"

I guess I do. It's intense—so intense—but the pleasure is out of this world.

He slaps between my legs. "I'll have to spank this pussy until you come. Do you think you can come again just from having your pussy slapped?" He shoves a digit in my channel then pulls it out and circles my anus with it.

"I-I don't know," I gasp.

"I think you can, baby. You're going to do it for me." He spanks me faster, only between the legs, still massaging around my anus. He spanks much lighter there than when he slaps my ass, but now he applies a little more force.

"Ow," I whimper.

He doesn't stop, just keeps on with the steady, firm smacks. "You're going to come and then I'm going to fuck your sore little pussy until I come again. And that will teach you to tempt a wolf this close to the full moon."

His words make me come. Just hearing about his wolf thrills me beyond belief. My pussy clenches and squeezes on nothing, and I don't care how sore he's made my core, I definitely want him in me again.

He lifts me onto my knees on the bed, pushing my torso flat against the mattress. He spanks me again, but I'm not

registering anything as pain anymore—it's all pleasure. It's all hot, tingly fabulous contact. He peppers the back of my legs and my ass with sharp slaps, punishes my inner thighs again. Then he pins my hands behind my back and pushes into me.

I love the feeling of being his captive. He pulls my elbows to ram in deeper, punishes me with his thick cock. He drives in harder, faster, his loins making a slapping sound against my stinging ass.

I start babbling, pleading. I need to come, but more importantly, I need him to come. I want him to reach his satisfaction with me.

"Fuck yes. I love it when you beg, baby," he growls. "Who paints your ass red and makes you needy for his cock?"

"You do. Jared! Jared, *please*."

"I can't get enough." He fucks me so hard it rattles my teeth.

"Please!"

An unearthly growl rips through the room and Jared comes. I clench around him in the most mind-blowing orgasm of my life.

He continues to fuck me in hard thrusts, roaring the whole time.

And then we're somehow down on our bellies, his body draped over mine, his breath hot in my ear. He nips and licks and bites my neck, still rocking his cock into me, but gentle now.

"Are you okay?" he murmurs.

I can't answer for a moment, I'm too out of breath, too replete. In a flash, he pulls out and flips me onto my back. His eyes are back to green and his gaze is worried.

"I'm okay," I manage. "I'm great."

Alpha's Desire

His brows slam down and he backs off me, rolling my hips to one side and another. "I bruised you."

I smile. "I don't care."

But anguish washes over his face and he shoves his hand through his hair. "I care."

I reach up and grab his t-shirt, pull him down for a kiss. "Stop being stupid. I loved your aggression."

His brows lift and he sucks in breath. "You did?"

"Yeah."

He pulls up one of my knees and angles his cock back to my entrance. I wince when he sinks in because—yeah. I've already taken a lot.

He sees the wince and immediately pulls out. "Shit, baby. I have to get out of here." He starts shoving his legs in his boxers.

I sit up, pulling the covers over me as if they'll shield me from his abandonment.

"I meant it when I said I'd fuck you all night. I mean I really can't stop. And I'm afraid something bad will happen next time. Worse than bruises." He yanks on his jeans and zips them. "Believe me, I want to stay. But there's no way I can. I care about you too much to risk your life this way."

He stops to kiss me. I expect a quick peck—I think that's what he went in for, but suddenly he's claiming my mouth with the same aggression he claimed my body, tongue plunging between my lips, hand rough on the back of my head.

He curses when he pulls away. "I gotta go." There's an urgency in his tone, like he's a ticking time bomb about to explode. "Really."

"Okay." I can't hide my disappointment. My sadness.

He sees it and regret swims in his expression, but then

he's gone, leaving without another glance, his motorcycle roaring to life outside.

I can't stop the tears from falling down my cheeks.

Of course he's gone. I knew that's how this would end all along.

J ared

"D ammit!" I pull the drill out of the plywood and pluck out the broken bit. It's the fourth one I've broken from leaning on the drill too hard. I worked all night and straight through the day today working on Angelina's warehouse. I set up a studio in the back, complete with a sprung hardwood floor, mirrors, and barres. She can teach dance there if she wants to do classes, or use it as her rehearsal space. The main section of this warehouse is her performance space. That's where Trey and I are working now. I'm finishing up the stage.

Anything to keep myself from rushing back to Angelina's place and marking her. Trey was right—the full moon brought on the urge.

She's definitely my mate.

Which makes this warehouse transformation all the more important. The warehouse and my own transformation.

I try to see myself through her parents' eyes. Would they view me any different if I was coaching disadvantaged

Alpha's Desire

youth? Or would they still just see a guy covered in tattoos who uses his fists for a living?

One who lets their daughter ride on the back of his motorcycle in a sundress?

Fates, I'm an asshole. I put her in danger on my bike and last night she was in danger with me. But I'm going to prove to her, and her parents, that I'm worthy.

And then maybe I can keep her without marking her. I could just disappear during the full moon. Keep my distance for her safety.

The moon is full in two days. Parker scheduled the first fight for tomorrow night, which gives the wolf participants —my pack—an advantage. If we're fighting other kinds of shifters, that is.

"Hey Jared, like this?" Trey's up on a ladder hanging the rigging for the aerial dance Angelina envisions.

"Yeah, looks good. Hang three of them like that."

Next I'm going to build wooden flats—like room dividers on locking wheels, so she can move them around to create the space any way she wants it. I ordered a ton of black stage curtains, too, which can also be setup on movable tracks.

I don't know anything about art, but as I shape what Angelina sketched, I grow more and more excited. She really has an incredible vision here.

"So you just going to keep working in here until you collapse?" Trey asks when he comes down from the ladder. "Have you even eaten anything since yesterday?"

"Nah. I'm not hungry."

"You're trying to stay busy to keep from marking her. Is that what this is about?"

I wipe the sawdust off my hands. "Yeah."

"If you figured out she's your mate, why aren't you over

there figuring out how to claim her without too much damage?"

I pick up another board and put it in place. Trey holds it for me while I drill a screw through. "I can't just claim her. Not without her permission. Not until I've proven—" I wipe the sweat dripping into my eyes and hang my head, feeling the weariness for the first time. "That's why I'm here. To set things up so I have something to offer her."

"Ah."

I can't stand the sympathy I hear in that single syllable.

"Do you really think that's necessary? I mean, I think she likes you for you already."

I shake my head and drill another screw in. "You don't get it. Her parents have plans for her. She needs someone respectable. Someone she can introduce without cringing."

"If you're just doing this boxing thing with the kids for her, then—"

"I'm not," I cut in. "I want to do it. It's the one thing I know how to do, right? So wouldn't it be good if I used it to help people instead of hurt them?"

Trey stares at me for a long moment. "Yeah. But only if that's what you want. Not if you're doing it to impress a girl."

"I'm not." I'm actually certain of this. Angelina inspired me, and yes, I am trying to prove something to her parents, but the idea is my own. And it's one that excites me.

"'Kay. I'm gonna take a break and get something to eat." He waits a beat to see if I'll offer to quit, too, but I don't. "See you later."

"Yep. Later."

I'm relieved when he's gone, even though I appreciated his help. For some reason, this journey feels personal— something I have to do on my own.

I pull out my phone and text Angelina. I texted her last

Alpha's Desire

night once my head was clear to apologize for running out on her. Her only answer was *thank you*, which pretty much ripped my chest open.

That means I hurt her when I left. And she hasn't forgiven me.

I texted again this morning to say I still needed to stay away, but I hoped she had a great day.

She just sent back a heart emoji. That's it.

So I hope this text will show her I'm really thinking about her.

I want to show you my warehouse space. It might give you ideas for your show. I'm working on it today, but can you come by tomorrow afternoon? 874 S. Ryndall.

She responds immediately. *I have rehearsal but I'll come afterward.*

I smile like a fool at my phone. *Great. Can't wait.*

Me neither.

And just like that, I'm transformed from haunted to happy.

This plan is good. It's going to work.

A*ngelina*

O*h for fuck's sake.*
It figures that the first time Jared wants to see me this week is the evening my parents decide to drop by and take me to dinner.

I'm sitting at the downtown restaurant, eating my salad without dressing, my stomach in a knot.

Everything about this feels wrong.

I should be over at the warehouse with Jared. I texted him but haven't received a response. When I tried to call, it went straight to voicemail, like his phone was off or the battery dead or something.

Halfway through the meal, the cause of my anxiety finally clicks. What can I say? I'm most blind when it comes to family dynamics. I'm betraying Jared again. Choosing my parents over him. Showing him that he's less important than they are.

Me shutting him out for dinner was the first rift between us. The full moon is a far more minor one, and one I can understand. One that's actually quite flattering when I think about it.

I set down my fork and clear my throat. "So, I'm dating someone."

Okay, that doesn't ease the tension in my midriff, it only makes it tighter, but I'm not going to stop now. I'm tired of hiding who I really am from the people who raised me. Who ought to know me best.

My dad shows no expression at all. My mom raises her eyebrows. Somehow, I sense judgement from them even though I haven't even told them who I'm dating. Or maybe I'm just imagining it all. Projecting my fears onto the situation. That must be it.

"His name is Jared. He works at the club where I dance."

There. The scorn I expected is on both their faces.

"Doing what?" My dad asks.

"He's a bouncer." I fight the urge to explain more. Why does Jared's job require justification. It's a perfectly decent, legitimate job. No, it doesn't require a college degree, but who cares?

My dad rolls his eyes.

Alpha's Desire

"Well, everyone needs a little fling," my mom trills.

I lift my chin. "No, I really like him, and..." My mouth goes dry. "I'd like you to meet him." Oh God, did I really say it? Yes, I did. And there's no going back.

"Well, I don't think that's necessary." My mom's already decided he's not worth meeting.

Fuck her.

"Yes. I want you to meet him. After dinner. We'll drop by his warehouse."

This catches my dad's attention. Real estate is something he's always interested in. "He has a warehouse?"

I shrug. "I guess so. You know, the owner of Eclipse owns half the real estate downtown. I wouldn't be surprised if Jared's invested as well. He always seems to have plenty of money."

My dad exchanges a skeptical look with my mom.

I shove my half-finished salad away from me and signal to the waiter. "We're ready for our check."

It's funny how such a tiny act of independence feels like rebellion. We all have roles. Mine is to be the dutiful daughter. I don't call for the check, because I never pay. That's my dad's role.

Well, I have my payout from Saturday night dancing. I pull out the bills and toss them on the table. "Dinner's on me."

My parents gape at me.

Yep. Things are changing. Get used to it.

I get in my parent's car and plug the address Jared gave me into my phone. My dad acts impatient and put out the whole time, but he drives there anyway.

The parking lot of the row of warehouses is packed with cars and motorcycles. I double-check the address, but it's the right one. At least, the address he gave me is one side of the

175

warehouse. It's the other side that's drawing the crowd. A garage door stands open and bodies throng around the open entrance.

I knock on the door of the address he gave me, but no one answers. People are staring at us like we're wearing neon *you don't belong* signs. And I guess we don't. Because the crowd appears tough. Very tough.

Are all these guys shifters?

I'm not familiar enough with his motorcycle to know if one of these is his, so I decide to just peek in.

Two burley men move to block me.

"I-I'm just here to see Jared. Do you know if he's around?"

One of the guys leans forward and takes a deep whiff of me.

"Angelina," my dad says sharply.

The guy who sniffed me throws an arm out between me and my parents. "You can go in. They stay out here. Your boy's inside, but he's busy at the moment."

Shouts and cheers erupt from inside, like there's some kind of show going on. I push through the crowd.

There's a large cage set up in the middle of the warehouse and the rough crowd gathers all around, hanging on the chain links, shouting jeers and taunts at the people in the cage.

I can't figure out what's going on, but something makes me push forward. I've come this far, I need to see Jared. They said he was here.

I hear the sound of thuds and my stomach knots up even tighter. What's going on in that cage? I push my way through the crowd.

"Where in the fuck do you think you're going, red?" A giant, chip-toothed man hauls me up off my feet.

Alpha's Desire

I shriek and smack his arm at the same time I hear a roar. From my higher vantage point, I can now see into the cage.

Jared's in it, shirt off, sweat glistening over his muscled, inked chest. He's fighting someone, his bare knuckles smashing into the guy's face with a bone-crunching sound.

I gasp, sickness lurching in my belly.

At the same moment, Jared turns and zeroes his gaze on me, as if he's sensed my presence. His opponent takes that opportunity to throw a punch at his face, breaking his nose. Blood splatters onto the concrete floor.

The guy holding me starts to carry me away from the fight, and I struggle to get free.

Jared roars—a full-on, werewolf sound—and chaos erupts all around me.

J *ared*

B lood streams in my eyes as I blunder toward the cage door. A hand lands on me and I snap around, driving my fist into my opponent's face. He drops. The crowd hollers louder, faces pressing against the chain links. Beyond them, a flash of red hair—Angelina. She's in a shifter's arms, her small hands pushing at the tattooed brute. He laughs and lifts her easily, ignoring her angry cry.

A roar surges from my body.

My opponent staggers up and weaves toward me and I kick him so hard in the gut, his body flies to hit the opposite

wall of the cage. I hit my side of the cage, razor claws shooting from my fingers. I don't think. I grab the links and pull, parting the metal. A few more tugs and I'm free. "Angelina!"

Shocked faces rise around me and fall away as I tear across the space, hard on the shifter's heels. They're halfway to the door before I catch up.

I slam into the thug, tearing at his flesh. He drops Angelina and I dart in front of her, roaring in challenge.

"What the fuck?" the wolf shouts, blood dripping from his torn shirt. A wolf I know—club name Bruiser. From Garrett's dad's pack. "Fuck, man, I was getting her out of there for you! She's not safe here."

I don't give a fuck. He laid his hands on my girl. He's gonna bleed.

"Mine," my wolf roars.

"Jared, wait, stop." Trey pushes through the crowd.

"Jared?" A soft cry from the floor. Angelina's eyes flash wide, horror reflecting off the blue. Oh fuck—she's looking at me like I'm a monster.

Sirens fill the air.

"Cops are here! It's a raid!" someone screams, and shifters stampede for the exits.

"Fuck," Trey explodes.

"Angelina—I'm sorry—" I grab her. Gotta get her out. Gotta get her safe. I propel her to the door. We burst outside —the fresh air pelting me. I blink stupidly, disgusting beast, covered in blood.

"Oh my God, you're hurt," Angelina's hands flutter over my flesh. Her nails are so shapely and perfect, her blue eyes wide with fear. She's so beautiful, and I'm such a beast.

I grab my shirt and wipe my eyes, not that it does much

Alpha's Desire

good. Angelina's pale face looks so fragile. She's streaked with blood. My blood. The blood of a beast.

"Government agent. Everybody freeze!" a guy yells behind us.

My blood turns cold.

How in the fuck did a government agent get *inside* the warehouse? No human should've gotten in.

"Jared?" Angelina chokes out. She's looking at me like I'm a criminal. Can this get any fucking worse?

How much did she see? Did she see the fight? How I lost control? I don't want her to witness this. Not any of it.

"Get out of here, baby. It will be okay." I start to touch her and stop. I'll just cover her with more gore. My stink spreads all over her. She shouldn't be here. What the fuck is she doing here?

Why the fuck did I ever think she could be with a guy like me?

Mine, my wolf howls. He ripped through a steel cage to get at her. Proof that he's laid claim to her. Proof that I'm too much of a monster to ever deserve her.

The government agent has his eyes on me, pushing through the crowd, but I'm not waiting around. I duck outside, after Angelina. I have to make sure she's safe.

Lights flash all around. The sirens blare, cops shouting on megaphones.

"Everyone cooperate," Trey shouts. "This is a misunderstanding." He has enough Alpha dominance in his voice that the spectators obey. Thank God. This could turn into a massacre.

I look around at my worst nightmare. Armed officers charging at shifters, guns out. Some tattooed thugs fall to their knees, hands on their heads. The cops swiftly

surround and question them. A few lucky shifters make it to their motorcycles and roar away.

"Angelina," a woman screams. She comes flying over.

"Oh my God," a guy in a golf shirt follows, revulsion scrawled across his face. "What is going on? Angelina, get away from him!"

"Get out of here, angel," I say. "Just go."

"No," her bottom lip puffs out. "You're hurt. Again. I'm going to make sure you're okay."

"The cops are here. Angelina, don't be a fool—" the man lays his hands on her and I grab the front of his collared shirt.

"Don't fucking touch her." My wolf is off his leash. My eyes must be glowing like Kryptonite right now.

Golf shirt guy's face goes white.

"Jared, stop," Angelina stops. "Let him go. Dad—it's okay—just—"

"Dad?" I reel, taking in the older couple. Sure enough, the woman is petite and lovely like her daughter, and there are glints of red in Golf Shirt Guy's hair.

Fuck. Fuck. Fuck. My girl brought her parents to meet me —right in the middle of a police raid on my cage fight.

I remove my hands from the guy so fast he staggers. His wife catches him. She's crying, mascara running down her face.

"Angelina—" I start when an officer runs up shouting.

"That's the one!" the government agent yells.

"Get on the ground! Get on the ground!" The cop waves his gun. I see red again—if he's not careful, he'll shoot Angelina.

"All right," I shout, stepping between her and the crazy cop, hands on my head for good measure. "Calm down, we're cooperating."

Alpha's Desire

"Get on the ground," he screams again. I fall to my knees. He grabs me and I let him slam me into the pavement.

"Stop," Angelina cries. "He's cooperating—he's bleeding. Can't you see he's hurt?"

"Angelina, get away from him," her father shouts.

A boot hits my side. I grunt but stay down. The cop kneels on my neck to cuff me, grinding my cheek into the gravel. I look up at my beautiful girl.

"Angelina," I breathe her name through cracked lips. "It's okay. I'm okay. Please leave."

"But you're hurt," she says. Her parents reach for her and she shakes them off. "I'm not leaving."

"Just go, baby. Go."

Face stricken, she mouths my name at me as her parents drag her away. Peering past the cop's boots, I watch her climb into a gleaming Mercedes. A howl tears from a chasm deep within me as the car squeals out of the lot, carrying my mate away.

A*gent Dune*

"S*o was this guy taking bets?" the local cop asks him dubiously. When the police showed up at the warehouse, he had no choice but to flash a badge and take claim of the scene. He sure as hell didn't want them in there fucking everything up.

He still hadn't found out who the fuck placed the 911 call

they were responding to, although his money was on the redhead's dad.

And the redhead seemed to be linked to this guy.

The one he wanted to question.

He'd purposely allowed the rest of the major players to escape. Parker and the other two bookies slipped out the back when the chaos began. They were more useful to him free. He'd learn more about their kind with surveillance.

So he'd let the cops grab this guy, the one who'd been fighting in the cage. The one making a big fuss outside the building. And now he'd insisted on questioning him. In private.

Because after seeing Jared Johnson fight, he knew he was the same as Nash. Altered. Enhanced, somehow.

He gazes through the two way mirror at the bloodied, tattooed hulk cuffed to the table

"I'm not sure we can hold him on any charges that will stick," one of the cops says. "We'll probably have to let him go."

"Not before I question him."

"Alone? You sure about this, Agent?"

"Quite sure."

Dune shrugs out of his jacket, folding it and laying it over a chair. He's a big man, not as big as the fighter waiting to be questioned, but powerfully built and ripped in a way that shows an obsession with strength training, beyond the basic fitness requirements.

"It's your show," one of the cops murmurs.

"Remember that," he warns. Checking his gun, Agent Dune saunters in.

Jared watches him, alert. Wary. Not guilty, like a criminal. No, he behaves more like an agent would. Ready for

Alpha's Desire

trouble from any side. Suspicious. He's much more than a dumb guy with big muscles. He's a warrior.

Like Dune.

He took a seat across from Jared and fixed him with a steady gaze.

Jared stared back. He didn't get nervous the way most guys do under questioning, and Dune had questioned a lot of guys. He knew and used torture methods taught to him by the government meant to make any guy talk.

He didn't plan to use many of them today. Not in a local police station with cameras everywhere. But if the cops had to fuck with his investigation, he sure as hell was going to question this guy.

"I saw you fight," Dune says at last.

Jared doesn't answer. Doesn't look away.

"Saw you tear open a steel cage with your bare hands."

He still doesn't answer.

"What kind of... man... has that kind of strength?"

Jared purses his lips but still doesn't answer.

"Someone who's not just a man. Someone who's been enhanced. That's what I think."

Jared shakes his head. "I don't know what you're talking about."

"You know anything about two labs being blown up in southern California?"

A momentary tick before he hides it. Yes, he knows something. Dune's instincts weren't off.

"What do you know?"

Jared shakes his head. "Have no idea."

Dune slams his fist down on the table. *"Bullshit."*

Jared doesn't jump. He doesn't even stiffen, which tells Dune the guy isn't the slightest bit threatened by him.

183

Because he wouldn't be if he'd been altered by Data-X, would he?

"What'd they do to you? In that lab? Did they make you into a monster?"

A slight wrinkle appears on Jared's forehead before it smooths out. Which means something in Dune's questioning is off. So the guy didn't come from those labs. He must've come from another one.

He lunges for Jared, gripping his hair and yanking his head back. "I know you have superhuman strength." He hopes to piss the guy off enough to see him change the way he'd seen Nash change.

He slams Jared's head down on the desk and yanks it back up. His nose re-breaks and blood streams out, but Jared squeezes his eyes shut so he can't tell if they changed color.

"Open your goddamn eyes," he growls.

"Fuck off."

He pushes his thumb into the other man's eye and prods a lid open. The iris seems to be yellow, but the other man draws his head back for a head butt and Dune has to dodge it, so he's not sure.

Then the man stands, pulling the chain on his handcuffs taut. "You don't know what I am, do you?"

There's an odd triumph in the other man's face that makes the back of his neck prickle with warning.

"You don't know what *you* are," he says in a low voice, the corners of his mouth curving.

The door bursts open and a small blonde in a suit and heels stomps in, flanked by two cops. The cops seem oddly protective of her, even though if she's an attorney—and he'd bet she is—she can't be on their side.

Alpha's Desire

"Step away from my client, Agent Dune." Her voice is ice cold. "Did you break his nose?"

"He came in with a broken nose."

The pretty attorney shakes her head. "That looks like a fresh break to me."

So Blondie must know what he is, or she wouldn't know how fast the guy heals. Good to know.

"You have no right to hold my client here. No charges have been filed and he hasn't broken any laws. I demand he be released, immediately."

Dune shrugs even though he was just getting somewhere with Jared Johnson. Making ripples with the locals would only cause more hassle. Better to cut him loose and set up surveillance.

Later, in a moment of total honesty, he'd admit to himself he was unnerved by what the man had said. How had he known?

A*ngelina*

S hock careens through me as we drive away from the warehouse. Both my parents are yelling at me at once, but I have no idea what they're saying.

What in the hell just happened?

Jared was fighting in a cage?

My dad drives straight to my parents' house. I think there was some discussion about taking me there instead of home, but I can't remember—I was too busy replaying the surreal scenes back at the warehouse.

185

Why did they take Jared away in cuffs? Did he do something wrong? He's not a criminal. He can't be.

Can he?

I realize I don't know enough about Jared and how he gets his money. How does he have enough to rent that huge warehouse on a bouncer's income? Does he have some other, less legal source of funds?

But I quickly reject the idea. No. Not Jared. He's too honorable.

"Go and take a shower," my mother orders as soon as we're inside. "You're *disgusting*."

I look down at my clothes, but there's nothing on me. Oh wait—one splatter of blood. I do as she orders, only because I can't really think for myself at this moment and a shower might help.

Unfortunately, it's the worst choice ever, because all I can think about is that incredible shower with Jared. The one where he worshipped my body and made me feel like a goddess. The one where he gave me something significant. Something I don't think he's shared with anyone else.

Or is that just my fantasy talking?

I don't really know what's real and what's not anymore. Werewolves? Vampires? Fighting in a cage?

It all seems so impossible. I step out of the shower and dry off. In my childhood bedroom, I throw on an old pair of sweats and tank top and crawl into my bed.

Being here, in my old room, makes me feel so small. Was it just yesterday I felt like anything was possible?

Now I'm suffocating under my parent's roof like a teenager again.

I don't know how long I lie there. An hour or two. And then I hear the sound of a motorcycle.

Alpha's Desire

I run for the balcony off my bedroom and throw open the door.

"Jared!"

He's off the bike and running toward the balcony in a flash. "Angelina—are you all right? Were you hurt at all?"

My chest tightens. He just got a boot in the ribs and taken away to the police station in handcuffs, and he's asking if *I'm* all right?"

I lean over the rail, trying to get a closer look at him. His shirt's covered in blood, but he appears fine. Well, of course he does—I've seen first hand how fast he heals. "Are you all right? What happened with the police, Jared?"

He shakes his head. "It was just a misunderstanding. Everything's fine—no charges filed."

I swallow. "What was that fight?" My throat is tight and pressure builds behind my eyes.

Regret washes over Jared's expression. "Let me come up there, baby. I need to see you up close. Talk face to face."

I give a wobbly nod and start to head for the door to let him in, but he's already scaling the rain spout, then spider-walking sideways along the top of a downstairs window casing to reach the balcony.

And that's when all hell breaks loose.

My dad bursts outside as Jared swings on leg over the rail. He's pointing a gun—yes, a gun. I didn't even know he owned a gun!

"Turn around, and go right back down the way you came," my dad growls. "I've already called the police. I doubt you want a second trip to the station tonight."

"Dad, stop. This is crazy. Jared's just trying to talk—"

"*Leave.* Now."

"Listen, Mr. Baker—"

RENEE ROSE & LEE SAVINO

My dad takes a menacing step forward and I fly between them. "This is crazy. Dad, you need to leave."

"Mr. Baker, I'm—"

"The hell I'm going to leave," my dad roars. "This is *my* house. *My* property he's trespassing on." He leans around me to level the gun at Jared again. "Get out of here. Don't ever contact my daughter again. If you do, I will make your life a living hell. Understand?"

"That's enough!" I shout, turning to face my dad head on. "You don't get to make those decisions for me."

"The hell I don't. My daughter will *not* run around with a member of a motorcycle gang who gets in fights for the fun of it. You are so far beneath her, it's laughable. Go back to the rock you crawled out from."

Something in Jared changes. Like an icy wind blew through and froze him solid.

"Dad!" I shriek and literally put my hands on his chest and shove. "Get. Out. Actually, move out of my way. I'm leaving with Jared."

"No." Jared's voice is hollow. "No, stay, Angelina. I'll go." He drops to hang from the balcony, then lets go and falls softly to his feet on the grass below.

"No." I fight past my dad and dash for the stairs. I fly outside in my bare feet just as Jared's starting up his motorcycle. "Wait!" I yell.

He turns his head in my direction but doesn't look at me. His focus is a million miles away. He's receded into a shell of his normal self.

"Jared, wait. I'm really sorry about that. I don't know why my dad's acting so crazy. It's just been a weird night."

"No," he cuts me off. "Your dad is right. This isn't going to work." He revs the gas and shifts the motorcycle into gear.

188

Alpha's Desire

"Wait." I grab his forearm. If I could just get him to look at me.

To come back to me.

But he's gone. Not physically, yet. But emotionally. The Jared I know isn't there.

"Jared, please. Can we talk? I don't even understand what's happening here."

He turns and his expression is hard. "Yes, you do. You and I weren't meant to be, angel." His use of the endearment without any of the usual feeling flays me. "We knew it from the start and we were fighting fate. It's better if we cut ourselves free now, before things get even harder."

He looks at me for one moment longer while I struggle to speak, and then he guns the motorcycle and shoots off, down the street.

"Jared!" I scream at his back, but he doesn't turn. Doesn't respond. Just drives away, his broad back getting small until he disappears around a bend.

I drop to my knees. "No."

"Angelina, Angelina, come *in.*" My mom's scandalized voice reaches me, but I don't move. "What's the matter with you? Get up, honey. This is ridiculous." She hauls on my arm until I blink away the tears enough to stand up and get myself inside. Back to my stupid frilly bedroom, where I collapse on the bed and cry myself to sleep.

12

I'm the hollow man.

What was that stupid T. S. Eliot poem they made us read in high school? I can't believe I remember it. I seriously can't. I remember very little from high school, but for some reason, that poem is what surfaces now.

Because I'm a lovesick fool, I look it up on my phone.

This is the way the world ends. Not with a bang, but a whimper.

Yeah, that pretty much sums it up. No wonder that poem surfaced. It's the same depressing bullshit I'm feeling right now.

It's been five days since I drove away from Angelina's parents' house. Five sleepless nights. One hundred twenty hours logged in the warehouse, making everything goddamn perfect for Angelina.

Is it ironic that I still need to help her even though she won't remember me? Won't know why I'm doing it?

That I loved—no, *love,* present tense—her?

Because Garrett's sent the order to have her wiped. He was patient at first—gave me a few days to make certain I

wasn't going to change my mind. I refused to talk about what happened between us with any of them—even Trey. All I said was that it was for the best.

This is the way things have to be. Angelina's dad was right. I have nothing to offer their beautiful rising star. I would only drag her down.

A nightclub bouncer who uses his fists more than his brains? I'm nothing compared to her.

So yesterday Garrett came over to the warehouse and picked up a paint roller and a can of paint and helped me paint the entire set black. Then he told me it had to be done and asked how I wanted it taken care of.

Trey was there and offered to take care of it, which was a relief. Because he's the only guy I trust and there's no way I can handle that shit. I guess I'm a fucking coward.

I didn't ask when it was going to go down. I really don't want to know. So long as it's done by the next time I see her. Because I only want to see happiness on that girl's face. If I see any more pain, I'm going to tear the roof off this fucking row of warehouses.

I still don't know how I'll present the warehouse to her. Maybe just chat her up at the club and mention I stumbled on a great performance space and I think she should check it out.

And that thought feels about as good as getting hit by train. Or a car. No, I'd get hit by Angelina's car again in a heartbeat. I'd groundhog that day over and over again because it was the night I finally got to kiss her. To touch her. To make her scream in pleasure.

She's still my mate. Even if I can't have her. I will watch over her and protect her until the day I die. Even if it means watching her take some human asshole for a husband. I'll be goddamn happy for her as long as she's happy.

Alpha's Desire

And I'll do whatever I can to make sure her dreams are fulfilled.

Even if that means sacrificing my own chance at happiness. My own future with a mate and pups.

I don't care.

As long as Angelina doesn't get hurt.

Angelina

I drive home from rehearsal and park my car in front of my place.

I don't know how I've managed to get up in the morning. To get myself to school. I'm like the walking dead. I can't eat. Don't sleep. I pick up my phone and stare at it, hoping to see something from Jared, but it never comes.

I tried him a few times at first. I apologized for my dad's behavior. Told him I didn't feel the same way and I really needed to see him. But he didn't text back.

So I guess I know where I stand with him. We're done.

And that thought makes me throw up. I get out of the car and retch, but nothing comes up.

Ugh. Between not being able to eat and throwing up every time I realize it's over with Jared, I've already lost five pounds.

That should make my mom happy.

But no. I'm done with my mom. Done with my dad. I wouldn't say this is exactly their fault, because I'm adult enough to own my part in it. If I didn't let my parents run my

193

life, Jared would've known their disapproval wouldn't sway me from our relationship.

But I did let them run my life.

I let them choose my career. My appearance. My college. Even my friends, to some extent—at least in high school. But no more. They're not choosing my boyfriends.

They don't get any say on who I date. Who I sleep with. Who I marry. If I want to marry a drug-dealing gangster with gold teeth, they'll have to deal or lose their relationship with me. If I choose to marry a woman, they'll deal. If I choose anything at all that offends them, that's their damn problem.

And I'm not going there for Sunday dinners anymore, either.

It's time for me to live my life for me.

I enter my house, cringing at all the memories that crowd me the moment I walk in. Jared, chasing me down the hall. Holding me on his lap on the couch. Bringing home takeout. Jared laughing. Listening. Paying so much attention to me.

A knock sounds at the door and for one half-second, I imagine it might be him. My heart leaps and soars before I remember it can't be him. He's cut me loose.

I peek through the pinhole. It's Jared's friend Trey, another bouncer at the club. The guy with thoughtful eyes and a pierced lip.

I open the door, not surprised to see him. I figured one of their pack would be coming by sooner or later. "Hey."

Trey appears uncomfortable. "Hey."

"You here to wipe my mind?" I see a flicker of relief in his expression, but he quickly takes on a sincere look.

"Not your mind. Just a few memories."

Alpha's Desire

"No, take them all. I don't want to remember Jared even exists." I can't keep the bitterness from my voice.

Jared gave up on us. He abandoned me. I'm not sure I'll ever forgive him for that. Good thing I won't have to.

Surprise flickers over Trey's face and a trace of something else. Anger? "Yeah?"

I shrug, grinding my teeth to keep down the swell of emotion threatening to flood through me. I don't want to cry in front of Trey. I just need this all to be over. "Yeah."

Trey won't let it drop. He's definitely gone cold now. He steps aside and waves me out of the house, but as he trails me to the Range Rover parked in front, he says, "You're mad at him, huh?"

My nose burns, eyes prick. "I don't want to talk about it." I can't keep the tears out of my voice.

He stops and leans against the car, studying me. "Did you break it off with him or him with you?"

A tear falls and I curse and wipe it back. "None of your business." If Jared didn't tell him, I'm sure as hell not going to.

His jaw tightens. "Actually, it is kind of my business. Jared's my best friend. He's been killing himself for the past two weeks trying to make himself worthy of you, but I guess it wasn't enough."

The accusation stings. So much more than I would've thought possible. It's like a freaking javelin's gone through my chest.

Tears spill from both my eyes, tracking down my cheeks. "That's not true."

"Do you know about the gym?"

I shake my head, biting my lip to keep Trey from seeing it wobble.

"He's started coaching underprivileged kids in boxing.

Says he wants to use his talents to give back to the world. Something about being a modern day warrior or knight."

My heart lurches, tightens with overwhelming tenderness. Teaching boxing to underprivileged kids? He's a freakin' saint. Talk about heroes. But I never needed that from him. He was already a hero. "That's so amazing. But I never asked him to change for me." I need Trey to know that.

Trey's face remains stony. "Have you seen the other warehouse?"

I shake my head and mop the tears with my hands.

He opens the door for me. "Get in. I'm going to show you first. You ought to know what you're giving up before you wipe him out of your existence."

My temper flares. "*I'm* not wiping *him*." I poke his chest with my finger, even though I know he could crush me with flick of his hand. "*He's* the one who gave up on us. I guess I didn't mean as much to him as he meant to me."

Trey's expression dissolves into sympathy. "Come on." His voice is more gentle now. "I really have to show you something."

I get in the vehicle and fish a tissue out of my purse to blow my nose.

Trey drives us to the same warehouse where I saw the fight. Sure enough, in the daylight, I can see a freshly painted sign on the warehouse on one end—Boxing Gym. The warehouse in the middle is where I saw the fight.

But Trey leads me to the warehouse on the other end. He unlocks the door and I step into... a dance studio?

It is—a perfect dance studio, complete with mirrors and a hardwood floor. Barres on the freshly painted walls.

"Wh-what is this?" I whisper.

Alpha's Desire

Trey doesn't answer. He just beckons me through the door at the end, which leads to another space.

My mouth drops, fresh tears blur my vision. It's my performance space. Exactly the way I sketched it. No—better. The stage is up against one wall, and ropes and silks hang from the ceiling for aerial dance. An entire row of black movable flats are lined up against another wall, waiting to shape the space into smaller quadrants.

Someone comes in the door at the other end and freezes.

Oh God. It's Jared. He looks terrible--haggard and pale. Just seeing him makes a fresh gash across my chest.

"Angelina?" he clears his throat. Looks at Trey quizzically.

He doesn't know whether I've already been wiped. That he would let that happen to me comes as a fresh betrayal and I march right over to him and slap his face. Just like I did the first time he tried to wipe me.

"Angelina."

"How dare you give up on us, you asshole! You care about me. You did all this—" I throw my arms wide and take another sweep of the incredible space—"for me. But then you're just going to send me off with your buddy to forget about you? How could you? I loved you, Jared. I. Love. You. Even if you wiped my mind a thousand times, I'll still love you. My heart knows who it belongs to. So if you're so fucking stupid you want to give up just because my parents are close-minded assholes, then you're not the hero I thought you were. You're—" I splutter off because truly, even as angry as I am, I'm incapable of insulting him. Nothing fits. He's my everything.

And then I see something that makes my world spin and dumps me on my head.

Jared's blinking back tears.

197

My Jared. The strongest man in the history of the world. Crying. Over me.

I throw myself at him, legs around his waist, clinging like a burr. "Please don't let me go," I plead, my face wet against his neck.

He drops to his knees. *"Never."* His voice is fierce. "I'll never fucking let you go. I'm sorry—I'm an idiot. My head got wedged. I thought I was doing you a favor. I never want to hurt you, baby. Not ever."

I pull away and slap him again. Not hard, because he's too close to get a good swing. It falls like a love-slap. A tenderness between us. "You did hurt me."

"I know. I'm sorry. I'm so fucking sorry."

I press my forehead up against his, roll our heads together. "You'd better be." I'm still crying, but it's turning into the laughing kind of tears now.

"Baby, you have to know what this means. If I mark you, you're mine for life. Do you understand? And you become part of the pack—sworn to secrecy under penalty of death."

I nod, happiness bubbling up like a fountain of goodness. "Yours for life sounds perfect."

"Are you sure? You're pretty young to make that—"

I smack him again, definitely a love slap this time. "Don't you go questioning my life choices too."

He laughs. "I love you."

"Ditto."

"Come on." He stands up, still holding me wrapped around him. "I need to make you mine right now. Before my chest explodes."

"Sounds good to me."

I look around, but Trey has tactfully disappeared. I owe him a huge thank you for bringing me here instead of to the

Alpha's Desire

vampire. I mean huge. Like, I should name our first child after him.

"Will we have shifter babies?" I ask as Jared carries me outside to his car.

He laughs, bouncing me higher on his hip.

"Depends. Some halflings can shift, some can't. Some females do if they get pregnant with a shifter—the baby's DNA tips the scales."

"I hope we have baby werewolves."

"It doesn't matter to me," he promises. "I will love them either way."

"You'd better." I bite his ear.

Angelina

I'm shaking by the time we get back to my place—not out of fear. Out of desire. Excitement.

Jared's going to mark me.

I don't even care if it hurts.

He peels off his shirt the second he walks in my door, then kicks off his boots. I shriek when he throws me over his shoulder and carries me down the hall to my bedroom. He eases me to my feet and pulls my shirt over my head.

"All your clothes off. Now." He uses a bossy tone that's new. I've heard commanding with a teasing flavor but never this. Now his deep rumble carries dark promise.

Shivers thrill through me as I strip off my clothes and stand naked before him.

His eyes change to yellow. Beautiful, beautiful wolf.

Slowly, he unbuckles his belt, keeping his gaze locked on me.

A hint of fear surfaces, but it only increases my arousal. Is he going to whip me like he promised he'd do if I ever made him jealous?

Oh God. I hope so.

He pulls his belt from the loops and doubles it, slapping it lightly into his palm. I jump a little.

"Go get me your tights. Four pair."

Four pair of tights? What could—oh. I'm pretty sure I know what he's going to do with them and the flutters of excitement launch. I fumble with my dresser drawer and pull out a bunch of tights.

He takes them and lifts his chin toward the bed. "On your tummy. Spread eagle."

Oh God, yes.

I scramble up on the bed and spread my arms and legs wide. Using the tights, he ties my wrists to the headboard, my ankles to the footboard. Then he shoves a pillow up under my hips to raise my ass.

All this time he hasn't touched me and my every nerve is on edge, my senses heightened. I'm dying for his touch, desperate for it.

"Jared?"

There. He strokes between my legs. A shiver races up and down my spine.

"You're awful wet for a little girl who's about to get spanked."

My pussy clenches. *Yes, please.*

"I need to spank you, do you know why, sweet angel?"

"Why?" My voice wobbles.

"To get your ass all warm and ready for your marking."

Alpha's Desire

I lift my head, slightly confused. "You're going to mark my ass?"

"Yep. I've spent many hours trying to figure out where and how to mark a human. I can't hit a vein and I don't want to leave a scar others would see. And I know how much skin you show when you perform. That doesn't leave me many options. It came down to breasts or ass. You know I'm an ass man. I love this juicy ass." He squeezes my cheek roughly and I roll my hips.

"So I'm going to warm that perfect ass with my belt. Then I'm going to fuck you long and hard. You're going to wait to orgasm until I give you permission. Understand?"

"Yes, daddy."

He growls his approval. "If it's too much, baby, just say stop. I'll never take you somewhere you don't want to go. Okay?"

I wiggle my butt. "Stop talking and start spanking."

"Mouthy." He winds the buckle end of the belt around his fist until the length shortens to about a foot and a half. "Just for that, I'm going to whip your pussy, too."

I shriek and try to move my legs together, but I can't. He's tied them wide open. I pull and tug on all my bonds, loving feeling captured by him. At his disposal.

He slaps my ass lightly with the leather—more like a kiss than a real stroke. He continues, his strokes gradually getting harder, delivering a sting that makes me clench my cheeks and jump.

It's still not pain—just delicious sensation. He starts to pick up speed, slapping the underside of my buttocks, the backs of my legs. I hump the pillow, growing frenzied with need.

"This ass belongs to me now," he says. "I hope you understand that. I'm the guy who gets to spank it. Fuck it.

Spank it again. I'm the guy who's going to punish you, night after night, just for having an ass this juicy."

I moan.

"I'm the only guy who's going to make you scream. Who gets the pleasure of watching you reach orgasm. Over and over again, if I decide."

I rub my bare breasts over the bedspread, grind my clit down into the pillow. I need relief. Now. "Please, Jared," I whimper.

"Not until I say, baby." The warning is firm and I love when he plays stern with me.

He stops to shuck his jeans and boxers. I'm certain he's going to claim me now, but instead he straddles my waist, facing my ass. He palms my cheeks roughly and spreads them wide. "There's that tight little hole that makes me crazy. I'm not going to take you there tonight, baby, but you're going to get that ass fucked often. Every time I see those hips swaying. Those thighs that just beg me to part them and bury my tongue in your sweet spot." He rubs said sweet spot and I buck beneath him. "But I believe I promised you a pussy whipping."

"Oh," I moan, not sure how I feel about a real pussy whipping. With a belt.

But of course Jared knows how to do it. He taps the flat of the leather between my legs, then swings lightly.

It's delicious.

"More."

"Greedy girl." He whips me again. And again.

I moan and wiggle, rolling my hips, trying to get satisfaction. He stops and rubs my slit with his fingers. "I'll bet you're hungry for my cock."

"Yes, daddy."

"Good girl. I love it when you call me daddy." He

Alpha's Desire

changes position and I hear the snap of the foil packet telling me he's putting on a condom. Then he's there, between my legs. Right where I've needed him since the moment we got to my place.

He teases me, rubbing the head in my juices but not entering.

"Please."

He groans and eases in. "Baby, I'm not gonna be gentle. I've been trying to reconcile myself with never getting to claim you again, and now that I have you under me—" He withdraws and slams in. If I weren't tied snugly to the bed, I would've gone flying forward.

It's a wonderful sensation of support—like my bonds are in place to make this more pleasurable for me, rather than to keep me captive.

Jared plants his fists beside me on the bed and pummels my ass with his loins. Every stroke evokes more satisfaction than the next until I'm a moaning, desperate woman. Harder, faster he pumps. My natural juices make me so slick that he glides in with ease even though it's rough and demanding.

I claw the bedspread, certain I can't wait another second.

Jared plunges deep and roars. "Now, angel!"

My body responds before my brain has even processed the command. As my pussy squeezes his cock in quick pulses, pleasure radiates through my entire body. Jared pulls out before I'm ready, but then his fingers replace his cock and his teeth sink into the meat of my left buttcheek.

I bite the bedspread to keep from crying out. I won't lie —it stings. But the finger-fucking and my finishing orgasm gives it a sexual edge that makes it register as erotic titillation rather than pain.

He unclamps his hold on me and eases off, licking the wounds.

My pussy clenches around his fingers with the last of my orgasm.

Jared kisses up my back to my neck. "Are you okay, baby?"

"Yes. Totally." I don't want him to worry. "Am I yours now?"

"You're mine." There's a pride in his voice that makes my head swim with happy delirium. He works to untie the knots on my tights and free me and then I'm cradled in his lap, a cool washcloth held against my wounds.

His eyes are a clear green—the yellow completely gone and his gaze is sharp and alert, traveling over my face, watching me.

My head swims. It's not an unpleasant sensation—more like I had too much too drink. "I feel a little funny," I confess.

He strokes my cheek with the backs of his fingers. "There's a coating on my teeth—the serum I embed in your skin—it drugs you a bit. It should wear off soon." His brow furrows.

"It's okay. I like it. But it makes me horny. Is it safe to have sex again?"

*J*ared

Alpha's Desire

My girl needs my tongue between her legs all night long. By morning, the wounds are closed enough that I let her ride my dick with her on top, my hands on her hips to help.

She can't get enough.

Even after her third orgasm since waking up, she has the glazed eyes of a nympho. I would call Trey to ask if this is normal when a human gets claimed, but I figure this is a problem I can handle on my own.

You know, it's a tough job, but one I'm willing to take on. It *is* my duty and all. Hell, yeah.

She ends up divulging that she keeps a couple vibrators, so I tie her to the bed and stuff both holes full.

"Do *not* orgasm until I give you permission, little girl."

Her frantic gaze follows me, but she nods. "I'm going to keep you like this. Let it build. Maybe if we wait, and your orgasm is strong enough, it will satisfy you for more than a minute."

She whines and tugs at her bonds.

I tug both her nipples, pinch and roll them, watching her expression. It's only pleasure. Only desire.

"Please, Jared. I'm ready now. Let me ride you again."

I give a firm shake of my head. "You can beg me, baby. I love it when you beg. But I'm not going to relent. You need this tension to build."

I lean over and suck her breasts, stroking every inch of her body until she thrashes and cries. "Please, please, please, please, Jared. I need you. I need you so much. I need you now. You have to let me. I need to come. Please, Jared."

My cock is harder than stone, but I have to pick another position where she's on top. I untie her and remove the vibrators, then let her straddle my waist, sitting up on the

205

edge of the bed. She lowers herself onto my sheathed cock with a hoarse groan.

Beautiful girl.

There's no warm-up. She pumps her hips like her life depends on it.

"That's it, angel. Take what you need to take—"

"May I?" she croaks.

"Almost." I put a hand at her lower back and help her take me deeper on each in-stroke. My own orgasm is right at the surface, too, my thighs flexing, balls tight.

"Jared," she pants. I think she's going to beg again, but she says, "I love you. You're mine forever, too. Mine, mine, mine."

I roar and come, almost forgetting to give her permission. "Come, angel!" I shout and she does, in a silent but cataclysmic release, her entire body shuddering with the explosion.

Afterward, she falls into my arms, limp and trembling. And then she's asleep. My girl finally got enough and can rest. I settle her into her bed and curve my body protectively around her.

"Sleep, angel," I murmur, kissing her hair.

13
———

Jared

I squeeze Angelina's hand as we walk up the drive to her parents' house for their cocktail party. Angelina didn't want to go at all. I think she wanted to punish her parents for not accepting me, but I insisted she go.

She insisted on bringing me. I guess it's her *fuck you* to her parents. But I put on a button down shirt and a pair of khakis and did my best to look respectable. Angelina's my girl. I'm going to have to figure out how to get along with her parents. Because I'm not going to have my girl go through her life with discomfort and tension over her choice of partners.

She pushes the door open without knocking and we go in. The place is huge and nicely appointed. Very foothills. Pretty sure I can smell a pool out back. Angelina tugs me toward the kitchen where there's a bartender standing behind the breakfast counter, ready to serve.

"Beer?" I ask doubtfully, not sure what to expect. Maybe they only drink champagne at these soirees.

The bartender rattles off some choices and I pick an India pale ale.

"Angelina!" Her mom spots us. Angelina told her parents she was bringing me, so I don't see signs of shock, but her mom's face is tight.

I step forward and hold out my hand. "Jared Johnson."

Her mom looks flustered for a moment, then shakes my palm, blushing. "Delia. Nice to meet you." She turns to Angelina and says in a low voice, "I think he just arrived."

Angelina presses her lips together and steps into my side. I loop an arm around her protectively.

I don't know who *he* is, or why it should make Angelina tense, but I'm sure as hell going to find out.

The front door opens and Delia bolts for it. Her husband also jogs in that direction. A broad-shouldered man ushers a beautiful brunette in and I have to turn away to keep from laughing.

It seems the guest of honor is Jackson King.

Richest wolf in the country. Good friend of the pack.

Angelina looks up at me quizzically and I lead her to the foyer. Her father has arrived and pumps Jackson's hand. It seems like he's purposely positioned himself to block me. I suppose he thinks I'm going to embarrass him. Maybe start a brawl. I can't really blame the guy.

Jackson's mate Kylie peeks around the side of Delia. "Jared!"

I grin and fold her in my arms, laughing my ass off as Angelina's parents stop their ass-kissing and stare.

Jackson comes in next for a man hug, complete with back thump.

"Jackson and Kylie, this is my girl, Angelina Baker.

Alpha's Desire

Angel, remember the cabin I took you to on Mt. Lemmon? Jackson was the friend who was kind enough to let us use it."

I ignore her parents' gapes, but Angelina doesn't. She shoots them a *did you hear that?* look.

Jackson's nostrils flare and I know he's scenting me on Angelina, realizing I've marked her. "Well chosen," he murmurs to us both as he shakes Angelina's hand. Angelina beams, tucking herself up against my side.

"Well, uh... you two know each other?" Angelina's dad can't make sense of it. He stares from one of us to the next.

"Sure."

"How?" Leave it to him to come right out and ask.

I hesitate, but Kylie says sweetly, "Jackson's part of Jared's fight club."

I choke on my beer and Angelina has to cover her grin.

Even Jackson, who is the most stoic of wolves has to clear his throat. "Yes." He's known for monosyllabic answers, so I figure the one word is the highest endorsement I'll get from him. Still, it's enough.

Angelina's dad cocks his head. "No... not really?"

"Yes," Jackson, Kylie and I answer in unison.

"Speaking of which—we want to talk to you about the trouble you had over there. See if there's anything we can do to help," Kylie says meaningfully. She and Jackson are both infosecurity geniuses, but Kylie is probably the best hacker in the world. She's been helping to unravel the weird shit that our pack member Sam uncovered with Data-X before he blew up their labs. I think she helped Parker, Declan, and Laurie with new IDs.

Garrett would've filled her and Jackson in on the shake-down I received from the mysterious government agent last week, but they probably want to hear it straight from me.

I nod. "Sure. Thanks, I appreciate that."

"Well, how about if I get you a drink and we can talk shop a bit?" Angelina's dad attempts.

"Later," Jackson says. "I'm going to catch up with Jared first."

Jackson's always blunt. He doesn't sugarcoat anything. It's hard to say if this is just him or if he's purposely dissing Angelina's dad, but I'm going with dissing because it makes me chuckle.

Jackson lifts his chin in the direction of the door that leads to the patio.

"I'll get your drinks," Angelina offers, making her mother beam with pride.

A few minutes later, the four of us are settled on patio furniture looking over the pool. I launch right into it. "The agent was a wolf. Or at least part wolf. I couldn't figure out how he got into the warehouse until I smelled him. I don't know if he's another experiment subject like Parker's gang. He doesn't even seem to know about the shifter part, so I'm guessing he's never met his animal. He asked about the explosions. Tried to hurt me to get my eyes to change color."

Angelina stares at me with wide concerned eyes and I realize there's so much she still doesn't know. I reach for her and pull her onto my lap. "I'm sorry, you don't know about any of this yet, baby. There's a very long pack backstory that I'll fill you in on when we get home, okay? Just know most of it doesn't involve me."

"Okay." She leans into me, the soft waves of her hair brushing my face, her vanilla scent growing straight to my dick. I gotta get my girl alone soon. Enough business talk.

"I ran his information—had to hack a lot of databases to get it. He's a ghost. There's hardly anything on him," Kylie reports. "I can share with you what I have."

Alpha's Desire

I shrug. "Yeah. He might be trouble. I don't think I'm a particular target except that I was the one who let his abilities show during that fight. If this was about breaking laws, they would've picked up Parker and the other bookies."

"Agreed," Jackson says. "What does Garrett want to do?"

"Nothing for now. He's not even shutting down the fights. If anything, he figures it could draw this guy out. And next time, we'll be the ones taking *Dune* somewhere for questioning."

Jackson nods.

"And now for the *important* news." Kylie turns to Angelina, eyes sparkling. "Congratulations on your new wolfmate."

Angelina smiles. "Thanks."

"I'm a cat, Jackson's a lone wolf. I take it this is your parents' place?"

"Yes." She blushes. "My parents have been trying to get a meeting with Jackson for ages and they don't approve of Jared, so you just flipped everything on its head when you said Jackson was in his fight club."

Kylie winks. "I kinda figured it was something like that. I have instincts for these things."

"Thank you."

Kylie's face softens. "Of course. I'm happy for you both."

Angelina's dad saunters over, so I seize the opportunity and stand up. "We'll leave you to talk business," I say and tug Angelina around the corner of the house.

"What are you doing?" she giggles when I press her up against the adobe brick and run my hands up inside the skirt of her sundress.

"Claiming you," I growl. "Right in your father's garden." I drag my palms up her firm thighs until I hit panty.

She lifts her mouth to mine, yielding so beautifully, like

211

she always does. She trusts me, despite the brewing pack trouble, despite the way I left her last time we were at this house. She loves me. Needs me as much as I need and love her.

I rub my knuckle over her clit and she gasps against my lips. "Tell me you want me to fuck you right here, up against this wall." I slip a finger under the gusset of her panties and stroke her dewy slit.

"I want you to fuck me," she breathes.

"Where?"

"Right here."

Fuck. I can't resist. I chase a condom out of my pocket and unzip my pants, sheathing my member for her.

She lifts one thigh and wraps it around my waist, taking my cock in her hand. When she guides it to her entrance, I shudder with anticipation, a flash of white hot need zinging at the base of my spine.

I sink slowly into her, and she wraps her other leg around my waist. I move my arms behind her back to protect her from banging against the brick because then I'm lost. I thrust mindlessly, my hard cock scything in and out of her sweet channel.

She bounces over my dick, rising up and down in my arms. She's breathing in quick, desperate gasps. When she starts to cry out, I cover her mouth with my own, swallowing her screams.

"I need to come, I need to come, I need to come," she breathes against my ear when I release her lips.

I want it to last forever, but for Angelina's sake I make it quick. A few more thrusts and fireworks go off. I shove deep and come. "Now, baby," I growl.

She comes silently, but judging by the squeezing of her

Alpha's Desire

thighs, her pussy around my cock, her arms tight around my neck, she came hard.

We catch our breaths together, but I'm reluctant to put her down. To pull out.

"I love my new wolfmate," she croons, biting my ear.

"I'm so fucking proud to be your male," I tell her. "You have no idea."

She kisses my neck. "I think I do. You've always treated me like a princess."

"Because that's what you deserve, baby." I lean my forehead against hers. "I love you."

"Mmm. I love you more."

I have to stop and breathe because my chest feels too full. There's too much joy bouncing around, making my heart swell to an uncomfortable size.

EPILOGUE

SIX MONTHS LATER

Jared

I'm in a suit. Yes, you heard that right. An actual, fucking suit. I'm standing outside the warehouse like a goddamn maître d'. Angelina is somewhere inside right now, flitting all over the place like a mad woman, answering the million questions being fired at her by her company dancers and the pack members I hired to help make her debut run smoothly.

She can invest in real theater tech staff in the future, once we've fine tuned the production and know exactly what she needs. Or we can keep it just pack, which Angelina seems to love. Probably because they treat her like a goddamn princess, or they know I'll smash their faces in.

Trey arrives in Angelina's car. I sent him on a last minute run to the store to get more refreshments for the post-performance reception, because, well, Angelina didn't realize how much pack guys eat.

"You gotta see this." Trey smacks my belly with a folded newspaper.

I unfold the *Daily Star* to the Tempo section on top—the arts / events weekend section. There, on the cover, is my girl. She's flying on a rope in a dramatic split, one leg on the rope, the other pointed straight to the floor. The headline reads, *Local Dance Troupe Debuts AngelWolf, A Must-See Production.*

Trey points at the byline. "That was the reporter Angelina hoped was coming last night." Angelina's company had done a live dress rehearsal performance last night for Amber's foster family group. Angelina had asked us a million times if we'd seen a reporter at the show, but neither of us could say for sure.

I grin like a fool as I read the copy.

Choreographer Angelina Baker takes dance to new heights in her dramatic production AngelWolf. The interactive production combines contemporary dance, performance art, and circus tricks for a thrilling show that will please all ages.

According to the program, the recent University of Arizona graduate put together the performance based on a vision she had of "bringing dance to the masses."

The quality and creativity of the show rivals the calibre of big-budget performance audiences might find in Las Vegas or New York City, yet Baker created the show on a shoestring budget, largely with volunteer labor.

"My hope is to establish this show as an ongoing performance so I can provide employment to the talented dancers and performers right here in Tucson," Baker said in an interview prior to the show.

The article goes on to describe some of the performances of the show, naming favorites and praising performers.

Alpha's Desire

"Thanks, man. I can't wait for Angelina to see this." I beam at Trey as if it's my performance receiving the accolades. "I'm going to run and bring it to her before the show. Will you hang here at the door?"

Trey nods and I jog through the performance space. If I weren't a wolf, it would be difficult to find her in the maze we've created out of moveable walls, but I follow her scent and find her standing outside the dressing room, in a group hug / huddle with her dancers.

I clear my throat and they jump apart, giggling. "I want you all to know, the Arizona Daily Star thought you were a big hit last night." I wave the paper.

The dancers grab for it and huddle around it, but Angelina throws herself at me, wrapping her long legs around my waist and her arms around my neck. She kisses my ear. "Thank you," she breathes.

I shake my head. "Don't thank me. This is all you, baby. Your dream. Your vision. Your brilliance."

"You made it happen." Her voice is clogged.

"No, I just helped it get started. You did all the rest."

She kisses my ear. "I love you."

I lower her to the ground. "Baby, I have something for you." I shove my hand in my pocket. "I was going to wait until after the show, but suddenly it feels like I should give it to you now." My throat goes dry.

She looks up at me with her big, trusting gaze. "Is it a present?" She bounces on the balls of her slippered feet.

"Yep." I pull the little ring box out and crack it open. "You're already mine, according to shifter law. But I thought you might want something to show the parents. You know, so they understand I'm serious about being your man."

Her eyes widen at the emerald cut pink diamond set in gold.

217

"I, uh, got it because it reminded me of your ballet slippers. I mean your tights." Oh fates. I should've just kept my mouth shut. Who buys an engagement ring to match ballet tights? I'm a fucking idiot.

But she laughs, tears welling in her eyes. "I absolutely love it!"

My heart starts beating again. "You do?"

She slips it on her finger. "It fits perfectly. Can I start wearing it?"

My throat closes up and all I can do is nod. "I understand if you don't want to. I don't want it to give you blisters when you're on the ropes or anything."

She slips it on her ring finger and stretches out her hand to admire. I catch her fingers and bring them to my mouth.

"Hey you two lovebirds!" Trey calls down the hallway. "Channel four and nine are here and *want to know where they can set up their cameras.*"

Angelina and I give each other matching *holy shit* looks. "I'll take care of it." I squeeze her hand. "Good luck. I mean *merde.*" I love knowing the inside term dancers use to wish each other a good show. I love knowing everything about Angelina's life.

"Thank you!" she calls over her shoulder as we split, departing swiftly in opposite directions.

The parking lot outside has transformed. Tank, one of my packmates, and his mate Foxfire have jumped in to help direct the parking, because cars are streaming in from all directions. The lot is full, as is the street in front of the warehouse.

Television crews are unpacking their cameras from vans, double parked behind our vehicles.

Jackson, Kylie, Kylie's cat shifter grandmother, and their

Alpha's Desire

toddler arrive with other pack friends Sam and Layne. Jackson greets Angelina's parents in the parking lot. I stand a little taller as they approach, as if it might help me measure up to her parents, but they're all smiles tonight.

"Did you see the article in the paper?" her dad says to me, like we're old buddies. We've definitely been trying to get along over these past few months. I've joined their family's Sunday dinners. Once I fanagled them an invitation to a barbecue at Jackson King's place last month, I seemed to have proven my worth. Especially because afterward, Jackson agreed to invest heavily in Angelina's dad's company.

I smile and nod. "Yes, what Angelina's doing here is going to be a real money maker." I speak in the terms that matter to him. "And prove her creative worth to the world, as well." That part is for her mother.

They both beam.

"Come on in, I saved you a front row position for the first performance. I lead them in with the others, allowing them to skip the growing line of ticket buyers.

"We're going to sell out," Trey murmurs to me.

I love that he said *we*. I'm in total gratitude for all the support the pack has given this show. Garrett closed Eclipse for the night so all the staff and patrons would come here tonight instead. He's opening it later for a post-performance party—invite only.

"Your girl is blowing it out of the water," Garrett says with a huge grin as he walks by. Once I marked Angelina, he accepted her into the pack, no questions asked. Even though she's a human.

I'm truly humbled by the support of my alpha and longtime friend.

Hell, I'm humbled by the glory of every day spent as Angelina's mate. It just gets better and better.

A*ngelina*

I stand on the stage for a standing ovation, a bouquet of white roses tucked into my elbow, trying not to cry. Over to the right, I spy my college professors. I can't believe they came! One of them's even smiling at me.

But the truth? I don't even care what they think. I wouldn't have cared if they hated it, or even if my parents hated it—which I know they didn't because they were the first to stand up.

All that matters to me is that I fulfilled my vision. Something I wanted to create—for me. For my friends.

And I did it all with the support of the most wonderful wolf in the universe.

All the rest? Gravy.

And there's a lot to brag about. We performed to a full house. Tickets sold out through next weekend. Television coverage, newspaper reviews. Opening night already covered the majority of our expenses, other than what Jared put into this, which he refuses to allow me to repay.

I take a bow and turn on the mic. "Thank you all so much for coming to our debut performance. We hope you enjoyed the show."

The cheering picks up again. Whistles, hollers. Those are from the shifters.

"We're honored to have our friends, family, and former

Alpha's Desire

teachers here to support us. I'm especially honored to have the support of one special person in my life who helped make this happen." My voice wobbles, but I push forward. I need to say this in public, in front of God and everyone. I will never, ever be ashamed of Jared and I don't want him to ever believe such a thing again.

"The man who gave me this ring tonight and asked me to make it official." I hold up my hand and the huge ring winks in the spotlights.

My mother's mouth drops open.

My friends and Jared's pack start cheering and the rest of the audience claps politely.

"Jared, will you come up here?" I blink into the lights, not sure where he is, but then I see his big form moving through the crowd. He climbs the stairs to the stage and walks forward, his cocky swagger firmly in place, the way it was the day I met him. I grab his lapel. "This man let us use his warehouse, and he transformed this space for the show. He's encouraged me every step of the way, and he's always cheering us on. Thank you."

Jared hooks an arm around my waist and pulls me up against him for a kiss.

The audience whoops and cheers and I laugh when he holds me a moment too long.

Jared grabs the mic. "If you liked the show, tell your friends! These dancers are going to make it a permanent thing."

I lean over to speak again. "Thanks for coming. Good night!"

Right on cue, the house lights come up, everyone's talking. Bodies start moving.

I don't notice any of it, because Jared's gone back to our kiss, melding his mouth over mine, licking into my lips.

"I love you, baby," he murmurs when he finally lets me up for air. He leans his forehead against mine. "You're a goddamn inspiration."

"And you're a hero," I tell him, looping my arms around his neck, offering up my lips for more kissing. Because, yeah. I just got engaged.

To the wolf of my dreams.

WANT MORE? ENJOY THIS EXCERPT FROM ALPHA'S WAR

Alpha's War - Chapter 1

Cold light. Grey light. The howls rise in my ears.

The concrete walls never change, but at night, they close in. My lion can see in the dark but that doesn't mean night doesn't affect me. I always know when it falls.

And those howls.

I don't know whether they're real, or imagined. I've killed so many. Their screams are my penance. Awake or dreaming, it's all the same. My life is the nightmare that never ends.

Someone, somewhere is singing.

"When Irish eyes are smiling..."

Barred sunlight trickles over my face. I'm in bed, not a cot. The walls are no longer concrete but dingy white. And paper thin. I hear voices murmuring in the living room, along with the Irish caterwauling. The sound washes over me and my knotted muscles relax.

My vision, tinged red, clears as my lion retreats. I'm in a bedroom, not a cell with guards outside the door waiting to

Want More? Enjoy this Excerpt from Alpha's War

burst in. But my animal is ready to fight. He always is. Years of abuse have permanently broken him.

Sweat soaks the sheets under me. Another bad night, filled with dreams of being locked in a cell. Or flashbacks. But sometimes, the dreams feel more real.

I pull myself out of bed and make it with military precision, like I have every damn day since week one of bootcamp. "You can take the man out of the army, but not the army out of the man," my drill instructor told us. He was right. But sometimes I wonder if I'll ever be able to take the killer out of my lion.

As soon as I open my bedroom door, the singing stops.

"Nash?" a head pops into the hall.

"What are you doing here?" I glare at the shifter, a young face with a shock of prematurely grey hair.

Parker shrugs and steps back so I can enter the living room. "Got kicked out of my last place. They saw my animal running around and told me *no pets*. And you have an extra room."

I have nothing to say to this, so I turn to the other two interlopers lounging on the battered couch. Two men, one with black hair and a bottle of rotgut in his hands, the other taller than all of us and too thin. The tall one wears glasses and blinks constantly. The black haired one is grinning.

"I told you not to come here," I growl to the room at large.

"You've got the biggest place." Parker hides a smile. For a moment I consider wiping it off his face, then wiping the floor with him. But no. He's my manager. If I kill him, who will schedule my fights? Bleeding an opponent on a regular basis is the only thing keeping my animal alive.

"Hey." I point to the black-haired man, who's opening a

Want More? Enjoy this Excerpt from Alpha's War

bottle with an illegible handwritten label. "What the fuck is that stuff? Stinks like paint remover."

"This? Just a wee bit o' hair of the dog. Had a good night last night drinkin' and such. This will perk me up right quick." The Irish accent penetrates and my brain throws up a name. *Declan.* Shifter—animal unknown. He smells a bit like a wolf, a bit like... something else. A shifter mix, a product of the experiments in the underground labs of Data-X. The Irishman is one of the few that survived. I'd call him lucky, but he's not. The lucky ones died.

"Ya want some?" Declan offers the bottle. My lion surges to the fore. I beat him back down. As tempting as it is to get drunk before noon, I didn't break out of the prison lab to waste my days.

"No. Drink it outside. Or better yet, use it to kill the grass in the driveway."

"Right ya are, sir." The black-haired man throws off a mock salute. "You're the alpha."

I'm not your alpha," I call as I head to the kitchen. Breakfast. Food. Normalcy. Go through the motions, even if normal is a foreign country I'll never visit again.

"You're the king of the beasts, aren't ya now? If you're in a pack, you'll be at the lead."

"We're not a pack." I open the fridge and grab the first thing that looks good—a carton of milk. I tip it up and drink straight out of the carton, ignoring Parker leaning in the door.

"Ready for the big fight?"

I grunt.

"Another grizzly shifter. This one from Saskatchewan or some Godforsaken place. I swear all they do in the lumber yards is fight."

"Good." Less chance my lion will kill them.

Want More? Enjoy this Excerpt from Alpha's War

"Betting's pretty evenly split," Parker muses. "The bruins are the only ones who can take you."

A plastic container filled with some sort of homemade biscuits sits on my counter. I tap it. "What's this?"

"Scones. Laurie made them." As soon as he says it I smell the feathery scent of the owl shifter along with the sharp sugary tang of the baked good. I open the container and take two.

My pocket vibrates and pull out my phone. A text from an unknown number.

Layne and I are driving over. We have intel for you.

I type back, *I'll be at the Pit.* And because I can't stop myself. *What intel?*

Kylie got a hit on a woman living alone in Temecula. Going to confirm now, but we think it's Denali.

Denali.

Red. Black. *The cell door opens, I stand at ready. The guards come in, weapons trained on me. I expect them.*

I don't expect her. The scent of cinnamon fills the air. Cinnamon... and arousal.

"Nash? Nash?"

The memory goes dark, and ebbs away, leaving Parker's worried face. Behind him, Declan and Laurie stand at the door, staring at me.

The world tints red for a second. My lion trying to take hold.

"I gotta go." Two steps to the door, and I reverse, grabbing another scone and holding it up for the tall man to see. "Thanks. These are good."

The owl shifter blinks at me from behind his Coke-bottle glasses.

I leave out the back door.

226

Want More? Enjoy this Excerpt from Alpha's War

This time of day, the Pit is mostly deserted, which is a good thing, My lion is riled up enough at the lingering smell of shifters. I let him out and prowl around the grounds. We're far enough in a run down industrial district that no one will see a lion pacing the perimeter of a dingy warehouse. No one comes back here but shifters, and the shifters who come here will recognize me. This is my territory. My kingdom. I let my mad lion mark his territory, slinking along the chain link fence that surrounds the parking lot, then I shift and head inside for a drink, trying not to think of how pathetic I've become.

A few minutes later, a sandy-haired man steps inside, sniffing the air. At the bar, I raise my glass in invitation. He nods and steps back, allowing his companion to enter before him. A striking, young woman with long dark hair approaches. She stares right at me. I meet her gaze in mild challenge. She's a new shifter, and dominant. My lion normally wouldn't tolerate her boldness, but right now he doesn't see her as a threat. This is a meeting of allies, and he knows he's about to get what he wants.

Sam sits. Without a word, he lays his phone on the bar, screen up. There's a picture of a woman leaving a house, her face half shuttered behind the screened door.

My chest tightens. *Denali.* The room blurs, turning red.

Sam puts a finger on the screen and swipes to show me the rest. Denali headed down the drive, entering a car. Long legs in cutoff shorts, a plain white tee showcasing lean taut arms. "My contact took them this morning. Confirmed the address of the house. She seems to be living there." Sam slides a piece of paper to me, but I can't tear my eyes away

Want More? Enjoy this Excerpt from Alpha's War

from the picture. In every photo, there's a serious expression on her face—not quite sad. Distant.

"Is this her?" Layne asks.

"Yes." I find my voice. "It's her." *Denali. Mine,* my lion roars, shaking the bars of his cage. He wants to come out and go on the hunt. Find Denali, make his claim. *Mine.*

Red clouds my vision. I blink and everything goes black.

I raise my head, realizing I've been silent for a few minutes. The air is thick with tension. Layne's eyes are shifter bright.

"Sorry it took so long," Sam says. The hair on his arms stands on end, but his voice is calm. He might not be the biggest shifter, but he's a cool head under pressure. Unlike the rest of them. "I thought for sure we had her last time."

I nodded. "She moves around a lot."

"She seems to have settled. The landlord of this place says she moved in six months ago. Longest she's been in one place." Sam flicks the paper bearing the address. "But we better move fast. Layne and I can—"

"No." I pocket the paper. "Just me. Alone."

"With all due respect." Sam eases off the barstool a second after me. He doesn't try to get in my way but he steps too close. Red explodes behind my eyes. Darkness dances at the corners, then takes over.

A second later, I come to. My hands are fisted in Sam's shirt. I've slammed him against the bar. His hands go up, spread in surrender, but my lion doesn't care. My canines ache as they grow, a growl blasting from my throat.

A second later pain explodes in my back.

"I wouldn't if I were you." A purr in my ear, soft and sibilant. The claws in my skin flex and tighten, ten points of agony, needle sharp. "Be a good kitty and let him go."

Want More? Enjoy this Excerpt from Alpha's War

Wrenching hold of my lion, I release Sam's shirt, and snarl as the claws bite deeper.

"Layne," Sam murmurs. A half purr, half growl and the weight leaves my back abruptly. I stretch, ignoring the shriek of pain along my spine, and turn slowly. The little woman faces me, staring straight at me with almond-shaped cat eyes.

"Most wouldn't provoke the King of the Beasts in his territory."

She says nothing. Sam slips to her side and she takes his hand without breaking her gaze. *Then don't threaten my mate,* she seems to say. My lion grudgingly approves.

"Maybe it's best if you do go alone." Sam tugs Layne to the door.

As soon as they step outside, I cover my face with a hand. My forehead is clammy with effort from keep my lion on a chain. He's violent, lashing out at friend and foe. Desperate. I'm dying, and there's only one cure.

Denali.

The paper in my pocket nudges my palm. I crumple it, and fight the rising red tide that threatens my vision. It hurts, but I push it back.

"Well, boss? You gonna get her?" Parker stands in front of me.

"I can't," I force the words out, ignoring my lion's howl of loss.

"Ya must," Declan says at my side. "Your lion can't hold on any longer."

"I know." I close my eyes. I was supposed to find Denali, go to her. Apologize. Make sure she's safe.

It's too late. My lion is out of control, and I need to find someone to kill him. To kill me.

"If someone was able to kill you, they would've by now,"

Want More? Enjoy this Excerpt from Alpha's War

Parker points out and I realize I spoke aloud. "You fight every night—and win. The biggest baddest shifters, the half deranged—anyone who will step into the ring. Sometimes two at a time."

"Ya can't stop fighting," Declan murmurs. "Not that I'm complaining. Business is good. Bets are up. The cops stopped sniffing around, and the Shifter Fight Club only made us more famous." He swirls his drink. "The Pit. Home of the King of the Beasts."

I snarl. I'm tempted to walk out, to drive to Denali's house and tell her everything. She might forgive me, once she gets over the shock.

But I can't. Between the dreams, and my lion's insanity, I've built a cage stronger than any Data-X used to hold me.

Later that night, I head into the ring. The crowd cheers, but all I hear are screams. How many did I kill as a soldier? They're here, ghost like faces turned vicious, ready to drag me to death.

My vision goes red, then black.

Next thing I know, I'm in the ring and Parker signals the start of the match. The bruin turns and his profile reminds me of one of the Data-X guards. A sadistic fuck who liked to strap down small shifters and pump them full of juice until they smoked. *Snack-sized,* he said.

Red. Black. The bruin falls, his face a bloody mask. The bouncers enter, drag him out. Another fighter takes his place. Young. Cocky. Like the prisoners when they entered, thinking they were part of an experiment. A master race.

"We'll find the best for you Nash," the doctor said. Light

Want More? Enjoy this Excerpt from Alpha's War

hair like Sam's. I don't remember his name. "You'll breed the Master Race."

Red. Black. Another fighter in the ring. Two this time. They rush me together and their fists fall. Pain washes me clean.

I'm back strapped onto the chair, sides bruised. Mouth parched, body smoking. "Not so strong now?" the guard asks. Raises the stick.

I roar and two startled faces blur in front of me. I reach through the red haze, grab both by the scruff of their necks and slam their skulls together. Two in one.

The crowd screams. My head rings. Declan stands in front of me, offering water.

"How many?"

"One more." He sounds worried. "But you don't need the fight. We can—"

"No." I lumber to my feet as a mean-looking fighter lumbers into the ring. My lion won't be deprived his prey.

"We need to stop it," Declan says to Parker, who nods. "I've never seen him like this."

Parker turns and raises his megaphone. "That's all for tonight, folks—"

The crowd boos. They want blood. I'll give it to them.

I rise to my feet and plod to the center of the ring, the crowd's cries washing over my bruised flesh. "Nash. Nash." They chant. "King of the Beasts."

My opponent turns with a mean smile. I grin back, and let loose my lion.

Red. Black. Black. Black.

"Nash, stop, stop!" Grey head flashes in front of me. Parker, shouting, mouth open and wild. "You won. He's down. Stop before you kill him." The air is heavy with the scent of blood. My lion approves.

Want More? Enjoy this Excerpt from Alpha's War

"You won," Parker repeats. I try to take a step and stagger under the weight of several bouncers. Panic rises and I thrash to throw them off. No use. The prison guards have shock sticks.

"Let him go," Parker cries and the men release me, jumping back. But I run, claws out. I'm blind, blood streaming into my eyes. I reach the fence. It's not electric. Someone turned the power off. This is my chance.

"Nash—" Declan is on the other side of the fence.

I raise my hands—now tipped with black claws—and swipe through the metal.

My claws tear and I howl but don't stop until there's a hole big enough for a lion to rush through.

Then I run. My lion is out, people are screaming, scrambling out of my way. Red claws at my eyes, black lurking in the corners, threatening. One final burst of speed and I'm outside. Falling to all fours, I let the darkness consume me.

I wake in the car, my mouth full of blood. I cough on the tang and almost spatter the wrinkled piece of paper lying on the dash. Denali's address. The lion found it and put it there.

"All right. All right."

Every inch of my body screams. My hands are swollen, bloody. Over the past few months, the shifter healing works slower, and that can only mean one thing: I'm dying. It's only a matter of time. It's only a question of how many I take with me.

I can't risk Denali. But the next time I black out, my lion might take me to her door. There's no telling what he'd do.

Want More? Enjoy this Excerpt from Alpha's War

He's made it clear, if I let him die, he'll take everyone he can down with him.

I put the car in gear and drive, not sure if I'm a dying man headed for the gallows, or a cure.

The address leads me to a little house in Temecula. I pull up and idle a moment. My hand shakes as I park. Excitement? Or the last stages of madness?

It's a mistake to come here. I know this as soon as I step onto the little porch, and her scent hits me. Blackness curls from the edges of my vision, pulling me under.

The guards have guns on her. My lion surges to the fore, angry. It's been so long since he's killed. But when the woman stumbles forward, I catch her. My arms close around her body. She's tall, her head coming just under my chin, soft hair a cloud in my face. The cinnamon scent hits me again, until I taste it.

"Another one for you, Nash." The guard's voice is harsh, mocking. They see what I do with the women they bring me. There are cameras in the corners of the room. They watch.

My grip tightens on the woman's body, she turns her face to hide it in my chest.

"You know what to do. Get to it. Or else." The threat hangs in the air.

The door scrapes as they leave.

I don't want to move. I could hold her like this for the night, and never feel wanting. But desire's there too, bubbling up, the first hint of warmth after a long winter.

"Hey," she says. Shy, but not embarrassed. I sense anger in

233

Want More? Enjoy this Excerpt from Alpha's War

her, rising, matching mine. Frustration. A spirit uncowed. Brave. Naked and defenseless, but not afraid.

Filling my lungs with her delicious scent, I tip her face up to mine. "What's your name?"

"Denali." I whisper. Inside, my lion waits, patient on this hunt. I follow the cinnamon scent on the air to the screened door.

And I see her. Long, lean limbs, flawless dark skin. She's barefoot at her kitchen counter, weight on one hip, pert ass encased in cutoff shorts. Her elegant neck curves as she looks down at what she's doing.

Unable to stop myself, I push the door open and enter silently. I'm back in the jungle, a soldier, a predator stalking my prey.

Her head turns slightly.

Her name is on my lips when she turns. Her eyes flare with an amber light.

"Nash?" she chokes out.

I walk toward her. Her head rears back on her lovely neck, chest fluttering.

"It's all right, Denali." I stop and lift my hands. "I'm not here to hurt you."

A tremor runs through her. Once, twice, and the spiced scent rises between us.

Mine. My lion snarls. *My mate.*

"Denali, I—" my voice cracks but it's too late. She whirls and runs out the back door.

Alpha's War ~ Coming May 8th

Want More? Enjoy this Excerpt from Alpha's War

Nash

I've survived suicide missions in war zones. Shifter prison labs. The worst torture imaginable.

Nothing knocked me off my feet... until the beautiful lioness they threw in my cage. We shared one night before our captors ripped us apart.

Now I'm free, and my lion is going insane. He'll destroy me from the inside out if I don't find my mate.

I don't know who she is. I don't know where she lives. But I'll die if I don't find her, and make her mine.

I'm coming for you, Denali.

Denali

They took me from my home, they killed my pride, they locked me up and forced me to breed. They took everything from me and still I survived.

But one night with a lion shifter destroyed me. Nash took the one thing my captors couldn't touch—my heart.

Somehow I escaped, and live in fear that Nash and the rest will come for me. It's killing my lioness, but I've got to hide. I've got to protect the one thing I have left to lose: our cub.

WANT FREE BOOKS?

Sign up for Renee Rose's newsletter and receive a free copy of *Theirs to Protect, Owned by the Marine, Theirs to Punish, The Alpha's Punishment, Disobedience at the Dressmaker's* and *Her Billionaire Boss*. In addition to the free stories, you will also get special pricing, exclusive previews and news of new releases.

Go to www.leesavino.com to sign up for Lee Savino's awesomesauce mailing list and get a FREE Berserker book —too hot to publish anywhere else!

BONUS SHORT STORY

Have you read this Bad Boy Alpha Bonus Story?

LOVE IN THE ELEVATOR
(Bonus Scene from *Alpha's Temptation*)

By Renee Rose
© Renee Rose Romance

Jackson

I haven't seen Kylie since I got to work and my wolf is getting cranky.

Usually, once a wolf has claimed his mate, the itchiness to always be near her eases. Or at least I thought it would. But it hasn't with Kylie. Probably because she's carrying my pup. Or kitten. We'll see. I'd be happy with either.

Because I'm possessive as fuck, I prefer to drive into work with Kylie. I like knowing which superhero t-shirt she's wearing, whether she put on Converse or heels. I like

Bonus Short Story

prolonging the time we're together before we have to be apart. But I had an early meeting this morning, and with the pregnancy, she needs more rest, so I let her sleep in. Now, I drum my fingers on my desk as my executive team reports on the monthly earnings.

A message box pops up on my screen and my wolf is instantly mollified.

BATGIRL4U: Today is our two month anniversary.

All it takes is seeing her moniker and my cock lengthens.

KINGI: Oh yeah? From the day we met?
   BATGIRL4U: The day you groped me in the elevator.
   KINGI: I know how and where I want to celebrate
   BATGIRL4U: How?

I hesitate, knowing she's not going to like my answer. I didn't actually grope her in the elevator. She was interviewing with my company and a power outage stranded us in the elevator together. She's claustrophobic and had a panic attack. I wrapped my arms around her to press her sternum and activate her calming reflex. That was before she ran her mouth about me. Before I knew she was the hacker who'd nearly taken down my multi-billion dollar company.

KINGI: Nailing you in the elevator
   BATGIRL4U: Hell, no

I expect that reply. My lips quirk, the thrill of punishing her already making my hips shift to accommodate my growing cock.

240

Bonus Short Story

KING1: Do you get to tell me no?
BATGIRL4U: ...Yes?
KING1: My office, 10 minutes.

Returning my focus to my team, I clear my throat, cutting off the CFO, who is going on about quarterly earnings. "All right, let's wrap this meeting up. Send the reports to me via email."

They're used to me. I'm always abrupt, usually an asshole, although having Kylie has softened me. I watch them file out and loosen my tie.

Kylie walks in and my heart stutters. She's wearing the same outfit she wore the day we met. Tight t-shirt with the Batgirl symbol in hot pink glitter across her perfect tits under her slender black jacket. Short, fitted skirt, no hose, high heels.

"Lose the jacket," I command.

Her hips sway as she saunters forward. She knows the power she has over me, even though she lets me call the shots. Gaze locked on mine, she slips the jacket off and tosses it over the back of a chair.

I stand and stride to meet her, hunger for her gnawing at me, even though I claimed her last night. And on our lunch hour yesterday. And that morning. Still, it's been twelve hours and my wolf is restless to smell her, taste her, watch her come unglued.

I grasp the hem of her t-shirt and yank it up above her glorious breasts, shove the fabric between her lips. "Hold this," I command and she bites down. I groan when I see my favorite red lace bra, the one she wore the first time I undressed her. I shove the cups down to take in her hardened nipples. She's not showing yet, but her breasts have grown, swelling more each day. I measure their weight in my

Bonus Short Story

hands. I want to suck them rosy, but this is punishment, so I force myself to be content with pinching each nipple.

"Bad girl," I murmur in her ear as I circle around behind. I smell the sweet honey of her arousal, sense the tremble in her legs. She loves punishment as much as I love giving it.

I propel her forward until she's up against the full-length windows that give my office a view of the Catalina mountains. The glass is mirrored, so I can see out, but no one can see in. "Hands on the glass, kitten. Spread your legs." I nudge her high heels apart.

She widens her stance as far as her tight skirt allows. I press my body against her back and reach around to cup her breasts. "Are you allowed to tell me no, baby?" I slide a hand down the front of her until my palm meets the skin of her thigh, then I reverse direction and coast up the inside of her thigh, rucking up her skirt as I go. My fingers reach the apex of her thighs and I cup her mons, pressing the heel of my hand against her clit.

"Jackson," she moans, dropping the t-shirt from her teeth. I let it go.

"Are you, baby?"

"N-no," she says hoarsely, head thrown back on my shoulder.

"Who calls the shots, kitten?" I slip my middle finger inside her panties and stroke along her dewy slit. "Hmm?"

"You do." Her inner thighs tense and shiver as I tap-tap-tap my finger over her clit.

I penetrate her, pushing my digit into her sopping heat, loving the way her responsive little body convulses at the sensation.

"If I want you in an elevator, I get you in an elevator. Don't I?"

242

Bonus Short Story

She stiffens slightly. I know this is a challenge for her. It's not that I want to torture her—I love this female more than I ever believed possible. But I want to help her overcome her past trauma. With the right measure of lust and the trust between us, I think I can get her to lose her phobia of elevators. I've already had her in a shower stall and that's a much smaller space.

"Jackson—"

I pull my finger out and slap her pussy. "You will yield, baby. You can do it now or you can do it after your punishment, but I'm going to get my way." I bite her ear. "Now, which is it going to be?"

I'm hoping she chooses after punishment, not only for the pleasure it will bring both of us, but because I think it will be easier to get her to let go in the elevator if she's already drunk with lust.

When she doesn't answer, I spank her pussy again. I use one hand to pull her panties to the side and the other to deliver light slaps on her bare sex, right over her clit.

"Punishment it is."

~.~

Kylie

It's a good thing my palms are flattened against the window, because I need them to hold me up. As Jackson spanks my pussy, lust storms through me like a hurricane, making me sway on my high heels. I'd take them off, but I know Jackson will never allow it. He loves the heels. Often orders me to strip out of everything but the heels.

Bonus Short Story

Jackson would never let me fall, though. He must realize my predicament, because he circles my waist with one strong arm and brings his lips to my ear. "I bought something for you, kitten."

"What is it?"

"Don't move."

He eases his body away from mine and we both groan. I feel the loss every time our bodies separate. From his desk drawer he produces a gadget or device—a bulbous metal... "Is that butt plug?"

Holy buttstuff, batman.

I don't know why I'm surprised. It's just that Jackson's dominance comes from being an alpha wolf, not from following the trappings of a BDSM fetish. He smacked my ass the very first time he got me out of my clothes and has never stopped since. Still, I appreciate his investment in keeping things fresh.

Even if I'm not so sure how I feel about having a stainless steel plug shoved up my ass.

He uncaps a tube of lubricant and squeezes a dollop onto his finger. "This will help you remember who's in charge when we're in the elevator." He rubs the lube between his thumb and forefinger. His hungry green eyes have changed to pale blue; his wolf is riled up for me.

Damn. He's still on the elevator idea. Not that I thought he'd drop it. Jackson King didn't build SeCure into a multi-billion dollar company by taking no for an answer. But I'm way more into wearing my interview outfit to celebrate our two-month anniversary than re-creating an elevator stall-out.

He walks around behind me and tugs my panties down. My skirt is still rucked up around my waist, legs splayed wide. Pregnancy has done nothing to dampen my ever-

Bonus Short Story

present desire to be claimed by my mate at all hours of the day.

Jackson wedges the lubed tip of the plug between my ass cheeks and nudges my back entrance. He's punished me with his cock there before and I admit, I loved it. There's something so taboo, so wrong in all the right ways. It requires my complete surrender, not that any sex with Jackson doesn't, especially during the full moon. He's always rough, always demanding. He can't help himself, which, in turn, makes me feel powerful. Desirable.

Still, I resist the cool metal intrusion, squeeze my cheeks to prevent its entry. Jackson slips a hand into the front of my panties and twiddles my clit. The rush of pleasure loosens my muscles and I inadvertently relax. He breaches my tight entrance. I mewl and pant, working to drop my resistance. The plug stretches me, fills me. I groan, my pussy dripping.

"That's it, kitten." His hot breath feathers across my ear. "Almost there." The plug seats, but my relief is short-lived. The fullness, the stimulation on my anus have me squirming for satisfaction.

I shift on my feet, pressing my mons into his hand.

He tsks and removes his fingers, leaves me trembling against the window, waiting.

"I prefer to spank you bare-skinned with my hand." He walks to the end of the wall-length window and unhooks the plastic tilt wand from the blinds. "There's nothing more satisfying than your ass under my hand."

I struggle to think of a snarky comeback, but the buzzing in my clit is too distracting.

"But I'd hate for my secretary to hear. So I'll have to use something quieter." He slaps the tilt wand into his palm.

I eye it doubtfully. It looks mean, even with my newly activated shifter DNA, which makes any pain or marks

Bonus Short Story

disappear in a matter of hours, if not minutes. Apparently, my pussy doesn't object, because my arousal drips onto my thighs. Jackson's nostrils flare and I know he smells it.

A low growl rumbles in his throat. "Push that ass out, kitten."

Tingles race over my skin, my breath rises and falls quickly as I hollow my lower back and present my plugged ass to him.

The wand whips through the air and lands across the middle of my buttocks. A line of fire streaks across my flesh and I yelp. "Fuck!" My hands fly to cover my ass and I whirl around to face Jackson.

He smothers my planned protest with a hard kiss, stamping his lips over mine, coaxing his tongue into my mouth. He keeps kissing me until I whimper and soften against him, arms looping around his neck. When, at last, he pulls away, he closes his teeth around my lower lip and pulls it out before he releases it with a pop.

"That fucking *hurt*," I complain.

He cups my ass, rubbing and massaging away the pain. "Ready for the elevator?"

I lift my chin. "No elevator."

The hands on my ass roam lower, slide between my legs and stroke my wet pussy. "This pussy, baby,"—he demands another kiss—"belongs to me. *And I need it in the elevator.*" He kisses me again, more gently, lips stroking mine, nibbling lightly. "You know you're safe with me. If you get scared, I'll take care of you. You're mine, baby. I'll always protect you."

A shiver of something much deeper than lust runs through me and tears prick my eyes. I drop my cheek to his chest and press my body against his to recover my breath.

246

Bonus Short Story

He continues his steady torment, stroking my throbbing clit while nudging the butt plug with his arm.

"Okay," I whisper. "Let's go."

Jackson's grin is one hundred percent wolf. He puts my clothing back in place and cradles my neck, tipping my head to the side to drag his mouth up the column of my neck in a slow, open-mouthed kiss. "I'll make it good for you, kitten. I promise."

I wrap his tie in my fist and tug his mouth down to mine. "You'd better."

~.~

Jackson

I straighten my tie and usher Kylie out of my office.

"Oh Mr. King?" My secretary, Vanessa, tries to get my attention.

"I'll be back in five," I say. Or twenty. Depends on how long it takes to get my beautiful mate off in a tight space.

I haven't officially acknowledged my relationship with Kylie at work, because it's none of their goddamn business, but Kylie pulls the alpha female with Vanessa every time she tries to overstep, so my secretary must know by now we're an item.

I should probably buy Kylie some kind of diamond ring to mark her in the human fashion as mine. Make sure no humans who can't smell my scent on her think she's fair game.

Kylie stiffens as the doors to the elevator swish open, but I place my hand on her lower back and guide her gently

Bonus Short Story

forward. As far as I know, she hasn't been in the elevator since the day she interviewed. She always takes the stairs.

I hit the "R" for rooftop. My office is on the top floor, but the elevator goes up one more level, and heading in that direction insures we'll be alone.

"What is R?" she asks. The elevator doors close and her swallow gives away her nerves.

"Rooftop." The elevator ascends. "You're okay, baby." I spin her around and press my body against the back of hers, pushing her up against the wall.

She's breathing quickly, but judging from her scent, it's more fear than arousal.

The elevator stops and the doors slide open, letting the Tucson sunlight stream into the compartment. I push my thumb over the "door open" button and hold it in. "There, baby. The doors are open. You can breathe fresh air. But you're still in the elevator. And I'm still going to nail you against this wall."

Her body melts against mine, breathing slows.

"That's it, kitten."

The elevator makes an angry beep to let me know I'm holding the button too long. I ignore it.

"Now, I need you to peel that skirt of yours up to your waist."

She removes her hands from the wall and tugs up the hem of her black skirt.

I use my free hand to yank her panties down in back. My own pants give me a bit more trouble opening one-handed.

Kylie rotates and slithers into a wide-kneed crouch at my feet, reaching to unbutton my trousers. It's quite possibly the hottest thing I've ever seen and I reach for her head, forgetting about the elevator button. The doors snick closed and I

Bonus Short Story

lunge to catch the button again, just before the elevator car starts to plunge back down.

Kylie's gold-flecked eyes are on me and her gaze doesn't waver as she releases my cock and licks around the head.

I curse, threading my fingers through her hair, urging her to take me into that sexy mouth of hers. I love when she turns the tables on me. I'm supposed to be the one seducing her, but I see the glory of power and control shining in her eyes, and there's nothing I'd do to change it.

"Fuck, Kylie. Take me deep."

She does. She slides her full lips down the length of my cock, tongue massaging the underside. Then she clamps down and sucks hard as she pulls back.

I shudder, my thighs tightening. I use my fist in her hair to pull her head off. "Up," I command, my voice so deep I hardly recognize it. "I need to be in you, baby." I help her up. Her panties are still up in front, so I say, "Lose the panties."

She does the stripper-perfect squat again to get them off and I nearly jizz all over her face. The minute she stands up, I tug her thigh up to my waist and line the head of my dick up to her slick entrance. One thrust is all it takes to sink into her wet heat.

I pin her back against the wall to get leverage and do my best to dial it back, which results in slow, hard thrusts that send her higher and higher on the wall.

She lifts the other leg up and wraps them both around my waist. I hook my forearm under her ass and pull her hips forward on the perfect angle to go deep.

Her mouth opens in a silent scream, eyes roll back in her head.

"Next time you need to come up to my office," I manage to say through gritted teeth, "you take the elevator." I slam in harder and harder, making her take every solid inch of me.

Bonus Short Story

"And you think about this, baby. Think about who fucked you in this elevator." I pump faster, with shorter strokes. "Remember that I'll never let anything bad happen to you again. Understand?"

"Y-yes, sir," she pants, then strangles on a scream.

I claim her mouth, swallowing her cries as her pussy clenches and contracts around my length. The second she squeezes, I come, her muscles milking my cock, wringing me out the way she does every fucking time.

The elevator buzzes again, a loud warning.

Still holding my beautiful mate, I stoop to snag her panties from the elevator floor and step out into the sunlight.

"Marry me." It's not a question, it's a demand.

Kylie's still in another world, her eyes glassy, lips swollen from my kiss. "I already have."

"I want you the human way, too. Mrs. Jackson King. Ring, marriage certificate, all that."

Her body is soft and relaxed against mine. She rests her head on my shoulder. "Yes," she whispers.

"Yes, what?"

She laughs the husky, throaty sound that drives me wild. "Yes, sir."

To read Jackson and Kylie's full story, check out *Alpha's Temptation*.

To get all the bonus scenes, including when Sam met Jackson, be sure to sign up for either Renee or Lee's newsletters!

OTHER BOOKS IN THE BOY ALPHAS SERIES

Alpha's Temptation

MINE TO PROTECT. MINE TO PUNISH. *MINE.*

I'm a lone wolf, and I like it that way. Banished from my birth pack after a bloodbath, I never wanted a mate.

Then I meet Kylie. *My temptation.* We're trapped in an elevator together, and her panic almost makes her pass out in my arms. She's strong, but broken. And she's hiding something.

My wolf wants to claim her. But she's human, and her delicate flesh won't survive a wolf's mark.

I'm too dangerous. I should stay away. But when I discover she's the hacker who nearly took down my company, I demand she submit to my punishment. And she will.

Kylie belongs to me.

Publisher's Note: *Alpha's Temptation* is a stand-alone book in the *Bad Boy Alphas* series. HEA guaranteed, no cheating. This book contains a hot, demanding alpha wolf with a penchant for protecting and dominating his female. If such material offends you, do not buy this book.

Other books in the Boy Alphas Series

Alpha's Danger

"YOU BROKE THE RULES, LITTLE HUMAN. I OWN YOU NOW."

I am an alpha wolf, one of the youngest in the States. I can pick any she-wolf in the pack for a mate. So why am I sniffing around the sexy human attorney next door? The minute I catch Amber's sweet scent, my wolf wants to claim her.

Hanging around is a bad idea, but I don't play by the rules. Amber acts all prim and proper, but she has a secret, too. She may not want her psychic abilities, but they're a gift.

I should let her go, but the way she fights me only makes me want her more. When she learns what I am, there's no escape for her. She's in my world, whether she likes it or not. I need her to use her gifts to help recover my missing sister —and I won't take no for an answer.

She's mine now.

Alpha's Prize (Bad Boy Alphas, Book 3)

MY CAPTIVE. MY MATE. MY PRIZE.

I didn't order the capture of the beautiful American she-wolf. I didn't buy her from the traffickers. I didn't even plan to claim her. But no male shifter could have withstood the test of a full moon and a locked room with Sedona, naked and shackled to the bed.

I lost control, not only claiming her, but also marking her, and leaving her pregnant with my wolfpup. I won't keep her prisoner, as much as I'd like to. I allow her to escape to the safety of her brother's pack.

But once marked, no she-wolf is ever really free. I will follow her to the ends of the Earth, if I must.

Sedona belongs to me.

Other books in the Boy Alphas Series

Alpha's Challenge (Bad Boy Alphas, Book 4)

How to Date a Werewolf:

#1 Never call him 'Good Doggie.'

I've got a problem. A big, hairy problem. An enforcer from the Werewolves Motorcycle Club broke into my house. He thinks I know the Werewolves' secret, and the pack sent him to guard me.

#2 During a full moon, be ready to get freaky

By the time he decides I'm no threat, it's too late. His wolf has claimed me for his mate.

Too bad we can't stand each other...

 # 3 Bad girls get eaten in the bedroom

...until instincts take over. Things get wild. Naked under the full moon, this wolfman has me howling for more.

 # 4 Break ups are hairy

Not even a visit from the mob, my abusive ex, my crazy mother and a road trip across the state in a hippie VW bus can shake him.

#5 Beware the mating bite

Because there's no running from a wolf when he decides you're his mate.

Alpha's Obsession (Bad Boy Alpha's Book 5)

A werewolf, an owl shifter, and a scientist walk into a bar...

Sam

Other books in the Boy Alphas Series

I was born in a lab, fostered out to humans, then tortured in a cage. Fate allowed me to escape, and I know why.

To balance the scales of justice. Right the misdeeds of the harvesters.

Nothing matters but taking down the man who made me what I am: A monster driven by revenge, whatever the cost.

Then I meet Layne. She thinks I'm a hero.

But she doesn't understand—If I don't follow this darkness to its end, it will consume me.

Layne

I've spent my life in the lab, researching the cure for the disease that killed my mom. No late nights out, no dates, definitely no boyfriend.

Then Sam breaks into my lab, steals my research, and kidnaps me. He's damaged. Crazy. And definitely not human.

He and his friends are on a mission to stop the company that's been torturing shifters, and now I'm a part of it.

Sam promises to protect me. And when he touches me, I feel reborn. But he's hellbent on revenge. He won't give it up.

Not even for me.

Alpha's Desire (Book 6)

She's the one girl this player can't have. A human.

I'm dying to claim the redhead who lights up the club every Saturday night.

I want to pull her into the storeroom and make her scream, but it wouldn't be right.

She's too pure. Too fresh. Too passionate.

254

Other books in the Boy Alphas Series

Too *human.*

When she learns my secret, my alpha orders me to wipe her memories.

But I won't do it.

Still, I'm not mate material--I can't mark her and bring her into the pack.

What in the hell am I going to do with her?

Publisher's Note: *Alpha's Desire* is a stand-alone book in the *Bad Boy Alphas* series. HEA guaranteed, no cheating. This book contains a hot, demanding alpha wolf with a penchant for protecting and dominating his female. If such material offends you, do not buy this book.

ABOUT RENEE ROSE

USA TODAY BESTSELLING AUTHOR RENEE ROSE is a naughty wordsmith who writes kinky romance novels. Named Eroticon USA's Next Top Erotic Author in 2013, she has also won *Spunky and Sassy's* Favorite Sci-Fi and Anthology Author, *The Romance Reviews* Best Historical Romance, and *Spanking Romance Reviews'* Best Historical, Best Erotic, Best Ageplay and favorite author. She's hit #1 on Amazon in the Erotic Paranormal, Western and Sci-fi categories. She also pens BDSM stories under the name Darling Adams.

Please follow her on:
   Bookbub | Goodreads | Instagram

Renee loves to connect with readers!
www.reneeroseromance.com
reneeroseauthor@gmail.com

CHECK OUT RENEE'S ZANDIAN MASTERS SERIES!

HIS HUMAN SLAVE - EXCERPT

CHAPTER ONE

Zandian Breeding season.

That was the last consideration in his mind before liberating his planet from the Finn.

Breeding season.

Zander sat at the round platform, looking at the faces of the elders he respected most, the ones who had risked their lives to save him when the Finn invaded Zandia and wiped out the rest of their species solar cycles before.

"You can't be serious."

"Dead serious," Daneth, the only Zandian physician left in the galaxy said, tapping his wrist band. "You are the best male representative of the Zandian species, the only one left of the royal bloodline, and, more importantly, the only one young enough to produce healthy offspring. If you go to battle without first procreating, our species will die with us."

Check out Renee's Zandian Masters Series!

He gestured around the room at the other members of his parents' generation.

He leaned back in his chair and closed his eyes in exasperation. "And exactly which female do you think I will produce these offspring with? Last I heard, there is no Zandian female under the age of sixty left alive."

"You will have to cross-breed. I purchased a program and entered your genetic makeup. It uses all the known gene files in the galaxy predicts the best possible mate for breeding.

He raised his eyebrows. "So have you already run this program?"

Daneth nodded.

He looked around the table, his gaze resting on Seke, his arms master and war strategist. "Did you know about this?"

Seke nodded once.

"And you approve? This is foolish—my time should be spent training with the new battleships we bought and recruiting an army, not—" he spluttered to a stop.

"The continuation of the species is paramount. What is the point of winning back Zandia if there's no Zandians left to populate it?"

He sighed, blowing out his breath. "All right, I'll bite. Who is she? What species?"

Daneth projected an image from his wrist band. The image of a slight, tawny-haired young female appeared. "Human. Lamira Taniaka. She's an Ocretion slave working in agrifarming."

A human breeder. A slave.

Veck.

Zander didn't have time for this excrement. "There's been a miscalculation." He waved his hand at the hologram.

"No, no mistake. I ran the program several times. This

260

Check out Renee's Zandian Masters Series!

female bested every other candidate by at least a thousand metapoints. This female will produce the most suitable offspring for you."

"Impossible. Not a human. No." Humans were the lowest of the social strata on Ocretia, the planet where his palatial pod had been granted airspace.

"I realize it seems an unlikely match, my lord, but there must be some reason her genes mix best with yours. The program is flawless."

"I thought you might suggest someone worthy of formal mating—an arranged marriage with royalty of another species. Not a breeder. Not a *pet*." Humans were not mates, they were slaves to the Ocretions. An inferior species. He hadn't had much to do with them, but from what he understood, they were weak, fragile. Their lifespan was short, they did not recover from injuries quickly. They spread disease and died quickly. They lacked honor and fortitude. They lied.

Zandians—his species—never lied.

"I was not seeking a lifemate for you, I found the best female for producing your offspring. If you wish to find a mate, I will search the databases for the female most compatible to your personality and lifestyle preferences after you have bred. But this is the one you must breed. And now, during the traditional Zandian breeding season."

He closed his eyes and shook his head. The breeding season didn't matter. For one thing, they weren't on Zandia —weren't affected by her moons, or her atmosphere. For another, he wouldn't be breeding with a Zandian female coming into cycle.

But Daneth was like a sharkhound on a hunt—he wouldn't stop until the stated goal had been reached. He'd been his father's physician and had served on Zander's

Check out Renee's Zandian Masters Series!

council as a trusted advisor since the day they'd evacuated Zandia during the Finn's takeover. He'd been only fourteen sun-cycles then. He'd spent the last fifteen sun-cycles working every day on his plan to retake his planet. He'd settled in Ocretia where he'd amassed a small fortune through business and trade, making connections and preparing resources, training for war.

"I will take care of everything. I will purchase her and bring her here until you impregnate her. Once it's done, you can send her away. I'm certain you'll be satisfied with the results. The program is never wrong."

"She's human. And a slave. You know I don't believe in keeping slaves."

"So set her free when she's served you." Lium, his tactical engineer spoke.

"A slave will have to be imprisoned. Guarded. Disciplined."

"She's beautiful. Would it be such a hardship to have this woman chained in your bedroom?" This from Erick, his trade and business advisor.

Beautiful? He looked again at the holograph. The female looked filthy, with dirt covering her hands and cheeks, her unkempt hair pulled back and secured at her nape. But upon closer inspection, it seemed Erick was right. She was pretty—for a human. Her tangled hair was an unusual copper color and wide-set green eyes blinked at the imager that had captured her likeness. A smattering of light freckles dusted her golden skin. She wore drab shapeless work garments, but when Daneth hit a command to remove the clothing and predict the shape of her naked body, it appeared to be in perfect proportion—round, firm breasts, wide hips, long, muscular legs. His horns and cock stiffened in unison.

262

Check out Renee's Zandian Masters Series!

Veck.

He hadn't had that reaction to a female of another species before. He'd only grown hard looking at old holograms of naked or scantily clad Zandian females from the archives.

For the love of Zandia.

He didn't want a human. He wanted the impossible— one of his own species, or if not, then a female of a species that was superior to his own, not inferior.

"Why do you suppose her genes are best? What else do you know about her?"

"Well, there's this." Daneth flashed up a holograph of a human man, dressed in combat gear, a lightray gun in his hand, blood dripping from his forehead. "He was her father, a rebel warrior who fought in the last human uprising before her birth. He may have even led it."

"Hmm." He made a noncommittal sound. His species were warriors, why would he need the human genome for that? "What about her mother?"

"Not much to be found. She's still alive—they're together now, working on Earth-based plant and food growth production. Keeping their heads down, is my guess. The data about her father isn't in the Ocretion database file. My program gene-matched to give me that information. I'm surprised the Ocretions don't do more gene study."

"I'll probably split her in two the first time I use her. Humans aren't not built for Zandian cocks."

"The program can't be wrong."

He sighed. "Is she even for sale?"

"No, but you are a highly-esteemed royalty and unofficial ambassador from Zandia. I'm sure she can be purchased for the right price." Daneth referred to his position on the United Galaxies. Since the Finns were not recognized by the

263

Check out Renee's Zandian Masters Series!

UG due to their genocidal practices, Zander served as the Zandian ambassador. Not that it did much good. No one on the UG was willing to put their resources behind him to overthrow the Finns.

He made a grumbling sound in his throat. "Fine. But don't spend too much. Our resources are needed for recruiting soldiers."

"Your offspring are top priority. Even over the war plans," Seke said. The male didn't speak often, and when he did, it always had a definitive ring to it, as if his word was the last and only word.

"As you wish. I'll breed her. But if she doesn't survive the first coupling, her death is on all of you."

Daneth chuckled. "Humans aren't that weak."

~.~

Lamira crouched beside the row of tomato plants and flicked a bug off the leaf before anyone saw it. The Ocretion foremen always wanted to spray the plants with their chemicals at the first sign of any bugs, even though it had been proven to harm the plants.

Her stomach rumbled. The tomatoes looked so juicy. She longed to just pluck one and pop it into her mouth, but she'd never get away with it. She'd be publicly flogged or worse—shocked. The fresh Earth-based fruits and vegetables they cultivated were only for Ocretions. Human slaves had to live on packaged food that wasn't fit for a dog.

Still, her life was far better than it might be in another sector, as her mother always reminded her. They lived in

Check out Renee's Zandian Masters Series!

their own tent and had little contact with their owners after work hours.

It might be worse. She could be a sex slave like the sister she'd never met, her body used and abused by men every day. After the Ocretions took her sister, her father had led a human uprising, which had resulted in his death. Her mother, pregnant with Lamira, had been picked up by slave smugglers and sold to the agrifarm. Her mother had been careful to hide her beauty and taught her to do the same, keeping mud on her face and hair and wearing clothes that were too big. They hunched when they walked, ducked their heads when addressed, and kept their eyes lowered. Only in their own ragged tent did they relax.

"You, there—Lamira." A guard called her name.

She hunched her shoulders and looked up.

"The director wants to see you."

Her heart thudded in her chest. What had she done? She was careful, always careful. By the age of seven her mother had taught her to distinguish what was real—what others knew—and what was claircognizance. She'd learned to keep her mouth shut for fear she'd slip up and say something she knew about someone without having been told. Had she made a mistake? If she had, it would mean certain death. Humans with special traits—anything abnormal or special—were exterminated. The Ocretions wanted a population they could easily control.

She dropped the bushel of tomatoes and walked up to the main building, showing the barcode on her wrist to the scanner to gain admittance. She'd never been in the administration building before. An unimpressive concrete slab, it felt as cold and dreary inside as it looked from the outside. One of the guards jerked his head. "Director's office is that way."

265

Check out Renee's Zandian Masters Series!

The gray concrete floors chilled her dirty bare feet. The director was a fat, pasty Ocretion female with ears that stuck straight out to the sides and cheeks as paunchy as her belly. Beside her sat a male of a species she didn't recognize.

"Lamira." The director said her name, but didn't follow with any instructions.

She stood there, not sure what to do. She tried for a curtsy.

The humanoid male stood up and circled her. He appeared middle-aged and stood a head taller than a human, but unlike the doughy Ocretions, he was all lean muscle. Two small horns or antennae protruded from his head. "She's in good health?"

The director shrugged, looking bored. "I wouldn't know."

The male lifted her hair to peer under her ponytail. He lifted her arms and palpated her armpits. His skin was purplish-peach, a nice hue—an almost human color. His interest in her seemed clinical, not sexual, more like a doctor or scientist.

"What is this about?" she asked.

The male raised an eyebrow, as if surprised she'd spoken.

The director touched the fingertips of her four-fingered hands together. "They are not house-trained, the humans we keep here. They're mainly used for outdoor agricultural work."

House-trained. What in the stars did that mean?

He cupped her breasts and squeezed them.

She jerked back in shock.

"Stand still, human," the director barked, picking up her shock-stick and sauntering over.

Lamira froze and held her breath. She hated the shock-

266

Check out Renee's Zandian Masters Series!

stick more than any other punishment. She'd heard if you get shocked enough, permanent paralysis or even death may result. In her case, she feared she might say something she shouldn't while coming out of the daze from it.

"I'll take her. We'll require a full examination to ensure her good health, of course, but if everything seems in order, I will pay for her."

The director folded her arms across her chest. "Well, we weren't planning to sell her. I understand Prince Zander has a lot of influence with the United Galaxies, but—"

"Two hundred steins."

Her breath caught. Surely they weren't negotiating for *her*—for her life? What about her mother? Her plants? She couldn't leave.

"Three hundred fifty."

Her head swam and she swayed on her feet. No. This couldn't be happening. Her claircognizance should have warned her about this, but it never worked in her favor— just told her meaningless things about other people. A true curse.

"Done." The male punched something into his wristband and a beep sounded on the director's hand held communication device.

The director looked down at it and smiled. "When do you want her?"

The male gripped her upper arm. "I'll take her now." He bowed. "It was nice doing business with you."

She swung around to meet him, terror screaming in her chest. "I can't—wait—"

The male ignored her, pressing a device to the back of her neck.

She felt a sting before everything went black.

267

Check out Renee's Zandian Masters Series!

HIS HUMAN SLAVE (Book One)

COLLARED AND CAGED, HIS HUMAN SLAVE AWAITS HER TRAINING.

Zander, the alien warrior prince intent on recovering his planet, needs a mate. While he would never choose a human of his own accord, his physician's gene-matching program selected Lamira's DNA as the best possible match with his own. Now he must teach the beautiful slave to yield to his will, accept his discipline and learn to serve him as her one true master.

Lamira has hidden her claircognizance from the Ocretions, as aberrant traits in human slaves are punished by death. When she's bought by a Zandian prince for breeding and kept by his side at all times, she finds it increasingly harder to hide. His humiliating punishments and dominance awake a powerful lust in her, which he tracks with a monitoring device on her arousal rate. But when she begins to care for the huge, demanding alien, she must choose between preserving her own life and revealing her secret to save his.

OTHER TITLES BY RENEE ROSE

Paranormal

Bad Boy Alphas Series

Alpha's Desire

Alpha's Obsession

Alpha's Challenge

Alpha's Prize

Alpha's Danger

Alpha's Temptation

Love in the Elevator (Bonus story to Alpha's Temptation)

Alpha Doms Series

The Alpha's Hunger

The Alpha's Promise

The Alpha's Punishment

Other Paranormals

His Captive Mortal

Deathless Love

Deathless Discipline

The Winter Storm: An Ever After Chronicle

Sci-Fi

Zandian Masters Series

His Human Slave

His Human Prisoner

Training His Human

His Human Rebel

His Human Vessel

His Mate and Master

Zandian Pet

Their Zandian Mate

His Human Possession

Zandian Brides (Reverse Harem)

Night of the Zandians

Bought by the Zandians (coming soon)

The Hand of Vengeance

Her Alien Masters

Dark Mafia Romance

The Russian

The Don's Daughter

Mob Mistress

The Bossman

Contemporary

Black Light: Roulette Redux

Her Royal Master

The Russian

Black Light: Valentine Roulette

Theirs to Protect

Scoring with Santa

Owned by the Marine

Theirs to Punish

Punishing Portia

The Professor's Girl

Safe in his Arms

Saved

The Elusive "O"

Regency

The Darlington Incident

Humbled

The Reddington Scandal

The Westerfield Affair

Pleasing the Colonel

Western

His Little Lapis

The Devil of Whiskey Row

The Outlaw's Bride

Medieval

Mercenary

Medieval Discipline

Lords and Ladies

The Knight's Prisoner

Betrothed

Held for Ransom

The Knight's Seduction

The Conquered Brides (5 book box set)

Renaissance

Renaissance Discipline

Ageplay

Stepbrother's Rules

Her Hollywood Daddy

His Little Lapis

Black Light: Valentine's Roulette (Broken)

BDSM under the name Darling Adams

Medical Play

Yes, Doctor

Master/Slave

Punishing Portia

ABOUT LEE SAVINO

Lee Savino is a USA today bestselling author, mom and choco-holic.

Warning: Do not read her Berserker series, or you will be addicted to the huge, dominant warriors who will stop at nothing to claim their mates.

I repeat: Do. Not. Read. The Berserker Saga. Particularly not the thrilling excerpt below.

Download a free book from www.leesavino.com (don't read that, either. Too much hot sexy lovin').

EXCERPT: SOLD TO THE BERSERKERS BY LEE SAVINO

Sold to the Berserkers

A ménage shifter romance

By Lee Savino

CHAPTER ONE

The day my stepfather sold me to the Berserkers, I woke at dawn with him leering over me. "Get up." He made to kick me and I scrambled out of my sleep stupor to my feet.

"I need your help with a delivery."

I nodded and glanced at my sleeping mother and siblings. I didn't trust my stepfather around my three younger sisters, but if I was gone with him all day, they'd be safe. I'd taken to carrying a dirk myself. I did not dare kill him; we needed him for food and shelter, but if he attacked me again, I would fight.

My mother's second husband hated me, ever since the last time he'd tried to take me and I had fought back. My mother was gone to market, and when he tried to grab me,

something in me snapped. I would not let him touch me again. I fought, kicking and scratching, and finally grabbing an iron pot and scalding him with heated water.

He bellowed and looked as if he wanted to hurt me, but kept his distance. When my mother returned he pretended like nothing was wrong, but his eyes followed me with hatred and cunning.

Out loud he called me ugly and mocking the scar that marred my neck since a wild dog attacked me when I was young. I ignored this and kept my distance. I'd heard the taunts about my hideous face since the wounds had healed into scars, a mass of silver tissue at my neck.

That morning, I wrapped a scarf over my hair and scarred neck and followed my stepfather, carrying his wares down the old road. At first I thought we were headed to the great market, but when we reached the fork in the road and he went an unfamiliar way, I hesitated. Something wasn't right.

"This way, cur." He'd taken to calling me "dog". He'd taunted me, saying the only sounds I could make were grunts like a beast, so I might as well be one. He was right. The attack had taken my voice by damaging my throat.

If I followed him into the forest and he tried to kill me, I wouldn't even be able to cry out.

"There's a rich man who asked for his wares delivered to his door." He marched on without a backward glance and I followed.

I had lived all my life in the kingdom of Alba, but when my father died and my mother remarried, we moved to my stepfather's village in the highlands, at the foot of the great, forbidding mountains. There were stories of evil that lived in the dark crevices of the heights, but I'd never believed them.

Alpha's Desire

I knew enough monsters living in plain sight.

The longer we walked, the lower the sun sank in the sky, the more I knew my stepfather was trying to trick me, that there was no rich man waiting for these wares.

When the path curved, and my stepfather stepped out from behind a boulder to surprise me, I was half ready, but before I could reach for my dirk he struck me so hard I fell.

I woke tied to a tree.

The light was lower, heralding dusk. I struggled silently, frantic gasps escaping from my scarred throat. My stepfather stepped into view and I felt a second of relief at a familiar face, before remembering the evil this man had wrought on my body. Whatever he was planning, it would bode ill for me, and my younger sisters. If I didn't survive, they would eventually share the same fate as mine.

"You're awake," he said. "Just in time for the sale."

I strained but my bonds held fast. As my stepfather approached, I realized that the scarf that I wrapped around my neck to hide my scars had fallen, exposing them. Out of habit, I twitched my head to the side, tucking my bad side towards my shoulder.

My stepfather smirked.

"So ugly," he sneered. "I could never find a husband for you, but I found someone to take you. A group of warriors passing through who saw you, and want to slake their lust on your body. Who knows, if you please them, they may let you live. But I doubt you'll survive these men. They're foreigners, mercenaries, come to fight for the king. Berserkers. If you're lucky your death will be swift when they tear you apart."

I'd heard the tales of berserker warriors, fearsome warriors of old. Ageless, timeless, they'd sailed over the seas to the land, plundering, killing, taking slaves, they fought

for our kings, and their own. Nothing could stand in their path when they went into a killing rage.

I fought to keep my fear off my face. Berserker's were a myth, so my stepfather had probably sold me to a band of passing soldiers who would take their pleasure from my flesh before leaving me for dead, or selling me on.

"I could've sold you long ago, if I stripped you bare and put a bag over you head to hide those scars."

His hands pawed at me, and I shied away from his disgusting breath. He slapped me, then tore at my braid, letting my hair spill over my face and shoulders.

Bound as I was, I still could glare at him. I could do nothing to stop the sale, but I hoped my fierce expression told him I'd fight to the death if he tried to force himself on me.

His hand started to wander down towards my breast when a shadow moved on the edge of the clearing. It caught my eye and I startled. My stepfather stepped back as the warriors poured from the trees.

My first thought was that they were not men, but beasts. They prowled forward, dark shapes almost one with the shadows. A few wore animal pelts and held back, lurking on the edge of the woods. Two came forward, wearing the garb of warriors, bristling with weapons. One had dark hair, and the other long, dirty blond with a beard to match.

Their eyes glowed with a terrifying light.

As they approached, the smell of raw meat and blood wafted over us, and my stomach twisted. I was glad my stepfather hadn't fed me all day, or I would've emptied my guts on the ground.

My stepfather's face and tone took on the wheedling expression I'd seen when he was selling in the market.

Alpha's Desire

"Good evening, sirs," he cringed before the largest, the blond with hair streaming down his chest.

They were perfectly silent, but the blond approached, fixing me with strange golden eyes.

Their faces were fair enough, but their hulking forms and the quick, light way they moved made me catch my breath. I had never seen such massive men. Beside them, my stepfather looked like an ugly dwarf.

"This is the one you wanted," my stepfather continued. "She's healthy and strong. She will be a good slave for you."

My body would've shaken with terror, if I were not bound so tightly.

A dark haired warrior stepped up beside the blond and the two exchanged a look.

"You asked for the one with scars." My stepfather took my hair and jerked my head back, exposing the horrible, silvery mass. I shut my eyes, tears squeezing out at the sudden pain and humiliation.

The next thing I knew, my stepfather's grip loosened. A grunt, and I opened my eyes to see the dark haired warrior standing at my side. My stepfather sprawled on the ground as if he'd been pushed.

The blond leader prodded a boot into my stepfather's side.

"Get up," the blond said, in a voice that was more a growl than a human sound. It curdled my blood. My stepfather scrambled to his feet.

The black haired man cut away the last of my bonds, and I sagged forward. I would've fallen but he caught me easily and set me on my feet, keeping his arms around me. I was not the smallest woman, but he was a giant. Muscles bulged in his arms and chest, but he held me carefully. I

stared at him, taking in his raven dark hair and strange gold eyes.

He tucked me closer to his muscled body.

Meanwhile, my stepfather whined. "I just wanted to show you the scars—"

Again that frightening growl from the blond. "You don't touch what is ours."

"I don't want to touch her." My stepfather spat.

Despite myself, I cowered against the man who held me. A stranger I had never met, he was still a safer haven than my stepfather.

"I only wish to make sure you are satisfied, milords. Do you want to sample her?" my stepfather asked in an evil tone. He wanted to see me torn apart.

A growl rumbled under my ear and I lifted my head. Who were these men, these great warriors who had bought and paid for me? The arms around my body were strong and solid, inescapable, but the gold eyes looking down at me were kind. The warrior ran his thumb across the pad of my lips, and his fingers were gentle for such a large, violent looking warrior. Under the scent of blood, he smelled of snow and sharp cold, a clean scent.

He pressed his face against my head, breathing in a deep breath.

The blond was looking at us.

"It's her," the black haired man growled, his voice so guttural. "This is the one."

One of his hands came to cover the side of my face and throat, holding my face to his chest in a protective gesture.

I closed my eyes, relaxing in the solid warmth of the warrior's body.

A clink of gold, and the deed was done. I'd been sold.

280

Alpha's Desire

Almost immediately, the warrior started pulling me away.

I fought my rising panic, wishing that my stepfather's was not the last familiar face I saw.

"Goodbye, Brenna," my stepfather smirked as the warriors streamed past him, following their blond leader into the forest.

"Wait," the blond stopped. Immediately the warriors grabbed my stepfather. "Her name is Brenna?"

"Yes. But you bought her. Call her what you like."

The dark haired warrior tugged me on. I half followed, half staggered along beside him. My nails bit into my palms so I could keep myself from panicking. Fighting the giant beside me wasn't an option. Neither was trying to outrun him.

The blond joined us, and the two warriors pulled me into the dark grove. Terrible thoughts poured into my mind. I belonged to these men, and now they would rape me, sate themselves with my body, then cut my throat and leave me for the wolves.

My eyes filled with tears, both angry and frightened.

They stopped as one and drew me between them. I shut my eyes in defiance, and the tears leaked out.

As I healed from the attack, I could make some noises, horrible, animal things, but they were so ugly, I stopped making any sounds at all. Sometimes, when alone, I'd sink into the river, open my mouth and try to scream. But no sound came out anymore. My throat had forgotten my voice.

Now the only sound in the grove was my harsh breathing.

I sensed the warriors on either side of me, their massive

shapes towering over my fragile body. I was much smaller than them, tiny and petite beside their massive forms.

Right now I tried to remember to breathe and submit to these men. One blow and they could kill me.

My heart beat so hard it was painful. I was ready to die.

But when they touched me they were gentle. A hand brushed back my hair, then stroked my jaw. One steadied me from behind as the other cupped my head and turned my head this way and that. The one behind me gathered my hair behind me. I held my breath as the two massive warriors handled me.

I realized the smell of blood had fallen away, replaced by another scent, an animal musk that was much more pleasant.

A finger ran over my neck, near the scar and I sucked in a breath. The hands dropped away.

Their faces dipped close to mine, and I felt their breath on my skin as if they took deep scents of my hair.

"So good," one of them groaned.

I didn't understand. I was afraid of them taking me but I didn't know why they weren't.

"It's working," one murmured to the other. "The witch was right."

As they dipped their heads and scented me, my heart beat faster in response to their proximity. Something stirred deep inside me. Desire. A few minutes alone with these men and I'd been more intimate with them than any other.

As one they bent their heads to mine, nuzzling close to my neck a tingling spread over my skin.

I felt it then, unbidden, a stirring in my loins. Ever since I had come into womanhood, my desires were strong. Every month I fought the pull to find a man and join with him. I was hideous and destined to be an outcast and alone. But

Alpha's Desire

each full moon my body came alive, beset by waves of roiling lust until I felt desperate enough to grab the nearest man and beg him to give me sons.

The heat poured over me until I heard a gasp—one of the warriors jerked back and stepped away.

"She's ready," one growled. Instead of frightening, the sound excited me.

What was happening?

"Not here, brother," the blond rasped.

Without answering, the dark-haired one pulled me on.

For a while we walked, pushing through the forest and forded a stream. The heat in me faded as I followed, weak with hunger and fear, eventually stumbling on exhaustion numbed feet.

The dark-haired warrior stopped, and I flinched, expecting him to bully me into continuing on.

Instead, he guided me to face him. Again his hands came to me, stroking back my hair. I winced when I realized what he was doing: looking at my scar.

Involuntarily my head jerked and he let my chin go, offering me water instead. He held the skin while I drank, and when I'd had my fill he offered me dried meat, feeding me from his hand. I stared into the strange golden eyes, unable to keep the questions off my face: Who are you? What are you going to do with me?

When I was done, he lay a hand on his chest and uttered a guttural sound I didn't understand. He repeated it twice, then lay his hand on my chest.

"Brenna." I could barely make out my name, but I nodded.

A shadow of a smile curved his full lips. Shrugging off the gray pelt he wore, he wrapped it around my shoulders before pulling me back into the circle of his strong arms.

My heart beat faster. The pelt's warmth seeped into my tired body, and the big man held me steady. I still felt frightened, but waited obediently in the dark haired warrior's embrace. I dared not struggle.

The brush around us rippled and the warriors surrounded us. I shrank towards my black-haired captor, but he held me fast, turning me so I faced the warrior who seemed to be their leader.

The blond was so huge, my neck had to tip back to see him. He moved forward and I couldn't help trembling so hard I would've fallen if the dark haired warrior let me go. Every instinct in me screamed that this was a wild man, a beast a dangerous monster and I needed to run.

He reached out and I flinched.

His hand halted.

He swallowed, as if trying to remember how to use his voice.

"Brenna." My name was no more than a soft growl. "We mean you no harm."

I studied him. As big as the warriors were, the blond was one of the largest. He walked lightly, muscles bulging. Long locks of blond hair brushed his broad shoulders. His face was rawboned and half covered in a beard, the defining feature his great gold eyebrows over those amazing eyes.

When his gaze caught mine, his eyes glowed.

His hands touched my face, a thumb stroking my lips. He tilted it to and fro. He pushed my hair away from my neck. I shut my eyes, knowing what he saw, the white weals and gnarled tissue, healed into a disfiguring scar that had taken my voice, and nearly taken my life.

I barely remembered the attack: a large dark shape rushing at me from the shadows, then pain. Lots of pain. My

Alpha's Desire

mother told me I lay near death for days. No one thought I would survive, but I did.

Some believed it would be better if I hadn't. Even though I healed from the attack, the scars marked my face and my life. The boys used to chase me down the street, throwing things. I grew up learning to blend into the shadows. To move silently so I wouldn't draw attention to myself. Later, when my mother married my stepfather, I learned to cower and hide.

Her body is pretty enough, my stepfather had said. *Just put a bag over her head so you can stand it.*

Now my new owner tipped my head this way and that, studying the scar. He nodded, looking satisfied. "The mark of the wolf," he rasped.

A ripple went around the assembled men, and the other warriors pressed closer. The black haired man held me still, hefty arms around my body.

I wished I could ask what the blond warrior meant.

The men surrounded me, staring at my hideous scars.

My blond captor released my jaw and I ducked my head down again in shame. His large, rough hands caught my head again, and raised it, but this time he cupped my face.

I shut my eyes. I couldn't even cry out. This man now owned me. I'd resigned myself to living life with a disfigured face, unwanted and unloved, but I'd never thought I'd become a slave.

"Brenna," The command came in that rasping growl. "Look at me."

Somehow I obeyed and met the leader's steady gaze. Something in that golden glow mesmerized me, and I felt calmer.

"Do not be afraid." His throat worked for a moment, as if

he was trying to remember how to speak. "Is it true you cannot speak?"

I nodded.

"Can you read or write?"

I shook my head. This was the strangest conversation I'd had in my nineteen years.

He looked frustrated, exchanging glances with the warrior who held me.

A voice spoke at my ear, still rough and guttural, but a bit more clearly than before. "We would like to find a way to talk to ye." The speaker turned me to face him, and I flinched as he brought his hand up, but he only examined the scars as the blond had.

By the time he was done, all warriors but the blond had melted away. Dark hair touched my cheek and I winced, realizing there was a bruise on my face from when my step-father struck me.

The blond crowded closer, a sound rumbling in his great chest, not unlike a growl.

"Brenna," he said. "We will not hurt you. I swear it. No one will ever hurt you again."

The dark haired one took a few locks of my hair in his hand, gripping them lightly and raising them to his face. He breathed in my scent, then looked at me with glowing eyes and said in a clear voice.

"Ye belong to us now."

Sold to the Berserkers

When Brenna's father sells her to a band of passing warriors, her only thought is to survive. She doesn't expect

Alpha's Desire

to be claimed by the two fearsome warriors who lead the Berserker clan.

Kept in captivity, she is coddled and cared for, treated more like a savior than a slave. Can captivity lead to love? And when she discovers the truth behind the myth of the fearsome warriors, can she accept her place as the Berserkers' true mate?

Author's Note: *Sold to the Berserkers is a standalone, short, MFM ménage romance starring two huge, dominant warriors who make it all about the woman. Read the whole best-selling Berserker saga to see what readers are raving about...*

THE BERSERKER SAGA

Sold to the Berserkers

Mated to the Berserkers

Bred by the Berserkers (FREE novella only available at www.leesavino.com)

Taken by the Berserkers

Given to the Berserkers

Claimed by the Berserkers

Rescued by the Berserker - *free on all sites, including Wattpad*

Captured by the Berserkers

Kidnapped by the Berserkers

Bonded to the Berserkers

Berserker Babies

Night of the Berserkers

ALSO BY LEE SAVINO

Exiled To the Prison Planet

Draekon Mate

Draekon Fire

Draekon Heart

Draekon Abduction

Draekon Destiny

Draekon Rescue

Printed in Great Britain
by Amazon

69392280R00173